PRINCE CHARMING OF HARLEY STREET

BY
ANNE FRASER

THE HEART DOCTOR AND THE BABY

BY
LYNNE MARSHALL

D0711704

MILLS & BOON

This month, Mills & Boon® Medical™ Romance
are treating you to a double helping of

TALL, DARK
AND DELICIOUS DOCS!

Cool and controlled in a medical crisis, but blazingly
passionate under their professional exteriors, these
desirable doctors are every woman's dream come true!

Be captivated by the Hon Dr Jonathan Cavendish's
charm and integrity in

PRINCE CHARMING OF HARLEY STREET
by Anne Fraser

Fall for the delectable Dr Jon Becker
as he discovers the joy of unexpected love in

THE HEART DOCTOR AND THE BABY
by Lynne Marshall

PRINCE CHARMING OF HARLEY STREET

BY
ANNE FRASER

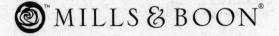

All the characters in this book have no existence outside the imagination
of the author, and have no relation whatsoever to anyone bearing the
same name or names. They are not even distantly inspired by any
individual known or unknown to the author, and all the incidents are
pure invention.

First published in Great Britain 2010
Harlequin Mills & Boon Limited,
Eton House, 18-24 Paradise Road, Richmond, Surrey TW9 1SR

© Anne Fraser 2010

ISBN: 978 0 263 87909 4

Harlequin Mills & Boon policy is to use papers that are natural,
renewable and recyclable products and made from wood grown in
sustainable forests. The logging and manufacturing process conform
to the legal environmental regulations of the country of origin.

Printed and bound in Spain
by Litografia Rosés, S.A., Barcelona

Anne Fraser was born in Scotland, but brought up in South Africa. After she left school she returned to the birthplace of her parents, the remote Western Islands of Scotland. She left there to train as a nurse, before going on to university to study English Literature. After the birth of her first child she and her doctor husband travelled the world, working in rural Africa, Australia and Northern Canada. Anne still works in the health sector. To relax, she enjoys spending time with her family, reading, walking and travelling.

Recent titles by the same author:

For Stewart—
Thanks for the idea and, as always,
your help and support.

CHAPTER ONE

ROSE whistled under her breath as she glanced around the reception area in the doctor's surgery. It was nothing like anything she had seen before. Instead of the usual hard plastic chairs, dog-eared magazines and dusty flower arrangements, there were deep leather armchairs, piles of glossy magazines and elaborate—she would even go as far to say ostentatious—flower arrangements. She sneezed as the pollen from the heavily scented lilies drifted up her nostrils. They were going to have to go. Otherwise she would spend her days behind the burled oak desk that was her station with a streaming nose.

Grabbing a tissue from the heavily disguised box on her table, she blew her nose loudly and pulled the list Mrs Smythe Jones, the receptionist—no, sorry, make that personal assistant—had left for her.

The writing was neat but cramped and Rose had to peer at the closely written words to decipher them.

It was Dr Cavendish's schedule for the week, and it didn't look very onerous. Apart from seeing patients three mornings a week, there were two afternoons blocked off for home visits. That was it. Nothing else, unless he had a hospital commitment that wasn't noted on the schedule. It seemed that Dr Cavendish must be winding down, possibly getting close to retirement. A vision of an elderly man with silver hair, an aristocratic nose and possibly a pince-nez popped into Rose's head.

Apart from the schedule Mrs Smythe Jones had also helpfully detailed Dr Cavendish's likes and dislikes. Apparently these included a cup of coffee from the cafetière—not instant—black, no sugar, served in a china cup and saucer which Rose would find in the cupboard above the sink in the kitchen in the back, and a biscuit, plain digestive, in the cupboard to the left of the one holding the cups. Patients were also to be offered tea— loose tea only, served in a teapot—on a tray, bottom-right cupboard, coffee, or bottled water, sparkling or still, from the fridge.

Looking at the schedule, it seemed that the first patient, an L. S. Hilton, wasn't due to arrive until 9.30. Plenty of time for Rose to have a good look around in advance. The cleaner, who had let Rose in a few minutes earlier, had disappeared, although she could hear the sound of a vacuum cleaner coming from somewhere further back.

There appeared to be two consulting rooms. Each of them bigger than most sitting rooms Rose had ever been in and almost identical to each other. There was the usual examination couch and screen, a sink, a desk and two armchairs, as well as a two-seater sofa in the corner by the window. There were landscapes on the wall, traditional in one of the rooms but modern brightly painted ones in the other, slightly out of sync with the antique furnishings of the room.

Rose stepped across to study the pictures more closely. Whoever had painted them had a sure eye and a love of colour. Like the pictures in the other room, these were also landscapes, but that's where the similarity stopped. Unlike the sedate country images next door, these were painted in sure, bold brushstrokes and depicted wild, stormy scenes which spoke to Rose of passion and loss. Whoever had picked them for the wall was someone with unconventional taste.

A polite cough behind her made her whirl around. Standing by the door was a man in his late twenties dressed formally in a suit and tie with black shoes polished to within an inch of their lives. He had light brown hair that was worn slightly too long and fell across his forehead. His face was narrow, his nose straight, and startling green eyes were framed by dark brows. But it was his mouth that caught Rose's attention. It was wide and turned up at the corners as if this was a mouth that was used to laughing.

'I'm sorry,' she apologised. 'You must be here to see the doctor. I didn't hear you come in.' For the life of her she couldn't remember the name of the first patient, only that it reminded her of a famous hotel chain.

'And you are?' The words were softly spoken with just the merest hint of bemusement.

'I'm Rose Taylor, the temporary receptionist.' She stepped back towards the door but the man stayed where he was, blocking her path.

'Where's Tiggy?' he asked. 'I mean Mrs Smythe Jones.'

'Mrs Smythe Jones is on leave. Now, if you wouldn't mind taking a seat in the waiting room, I'll just get your notes out.'

'Take a seat? In the waiting room? My notes.' The smile widened. 'I see. I don't suppose there's any chance of a cup of coffee while I'm waiting?'

'Of course,' Rose replied smoothly. 'I'll just pop the kettle on.'

When she came back from the kitchen, carrying a tray and trying not to feel too much like a waitress, he was sitting in her chair, leaning back with his arms behind his neck and his long legs propped on her desk.

'Excuse me, sir,' she said as politely as she could manage through gritted teeth. 'I think we agreed you'd take a seat in the waiting room.' He was beginning to annoy her. The way he was behaving as if he owned the place. However, on her first day she didn't want to cause a fuss. She needed this job. It paid well, extremely well paid, in fact, and the hours were flexible enough to give her time to help look after Dad. Perhaps this was the way all Harley Street patients behaved. How was she to know? Nevertheless, it was unacceptably rude of him to put her in this position. What if Dr Cavendish walked in to find she had allowed a patient to take over her desk? She couldn't imagine him being best pleased.

The man jumped to his feet and took the tray from her hands. 'Please let me,' he said, laying the tray down on the desk. He looked at the single cup and saucer and raised an enquiring eyebrow. 'What about you? Aren't you joining me?'

Rose forced a polite smile. 'No, thanks.' She slid behind her desk before he could reclaim her chair. 'Now, what did you say your name was?'

'Jonathan.' He stretched out a hand. 'Jonathan Cavendish.'

'You're related to Dr Cavendish?'

The smile grew wider. 'I *am* Dr Cavendish.'

Rose was aware her mouth had fallen open. She quickly closed it.

'But you're young,' she protested, feeling her cheeks grow warm. What an imbecilic thing to say.

He looked puzzled. 'Twenty-seven, since you ask. How old are you?' He leaned towards her and lazy eyes swept over her. 'No, don't tell me. Twenty-five?'

'Twenty-six, actually,' Rose conceded reluctantly. He was laughing at her, making her flustered. And she didn't do flustered. 'My name's Rose Taylor. The agency sent me over. To fill in until your usual receptionist returns.'

'Where did you say Mrs Smythe Jones was? I'm sure she didn't say anything about going on holiday.'

'I don't think it was a holiday.' Didn't this man know anything about the woman who worked for him? 'She had an emergency to do with her sister apparently. She called the agency on Friday, to ask for a temp.'

Jonathan frowned. 'I knew her sister hadn't been well. I was away this weekend, skiing. Couldn't get a signal on my phone—you know how it is.' He pulled his mobile out of his pocket. 'Still no message. I'll phone her later, after I've seen my patients.' He snapped the phone shut.

'Okay, so now we've that sorted, let's move on. Who's the first patient?'

Rose was still reeling from the discovery that this man was the doctor. Where was the elderly silver-haired man of her imagination? She was rapidly trying to process this new information. But it wasn't making any kind of sense.

As if he'd read her mind, Jonathan said, 'There is another Dr Cavendish, my uncle. But he retired last year. I took over the practice from him.'

Still confused, Rose studied the list in front of her. 'You have three patients this morning.' Only three! And each of them had been given half-hour slots. Half-hour slots! In the practice where she normally worked, the patients were lucky to get ten minutes with the overworked and harassed medical team. Either Dr Cavendish wasn't very good and no one wanted to come and see him, or he didn't like to work too hard. But it was none of her business how he ran his practice. 'And then you have a couple of home visits this afternoon. That's all Mrs Smythe Jones has marked down for you, unless there's another list somewhere?' Come to think of it, perhaps that was the answer?

She glanced around the desk. No, apart from this ornate leather-bound appointment book there was nothing else with information on it. Her eyes came to rest on the computer. That was it. There must be a computerised patient list. She stopped herself from smacking her head at her stupidity. Of course there would be a full list on the computer! The patients Mrs Smythe Jones had marked down in her neat hand must be additions.

Rose smiled apologetically at Jonathan, who was waiting patiently for a response, and booted up the hard drive. There had to be a password here somewhere.

'Oh, I'm sorry,' she apologised as the computer hummed into life. 'That must be the add-on list. As soon as I can get into the clinic on the computer, I'll be able to tell you who else is down for your clinic.'

The half-smile was back. 'You won't find anything on there. Mrs Smythe Jones doesn't believe in computers, I'm afraid. She uses it for letters, but that's it. The list you have in front of you is it.' He stood and straightened his already immaculately tied tie. 'Three patients sounds about right.' He held out his hand for the book. 'When the first patient arrives, just press this buzzer here.' He leaned back over the desk and Rose caught the scent of expensive aftershave. He straightened and pointed to a set of oak filing cabinets. 'Notes are in there. Now, if you'll excuse me. Vicki, my nurse, should be in shortly—she'll keep you right.' Without waiting for a reply, he retreated into the consulting room and closed the door behind him.

The first patient wasn't due to arrive for another half an hour. The cleaner came in and picked up the tray from the desk.

'His Lordship in, then? I'm Gladys by the way,' she said.

It was getting more confusing by the minute. His Lordship? Who the hell was she referring to? Did she mean Jonathan? In which case, it wasn't a very respectable way to speak about her boss.

Gladys chuckled. 'You haven't a clue what I'm talking about, dearie. Do you? His Lordship? Jonathan? The Honourable Jonathan Cavendish?'

Oh, my word. She was working for aristocracy.

Speechless, Rose could only indicate the closed door of the consulting room with a tip of her head.

'That's me, then, luvvie,' Gladys was shrugging into her coat. 'I'll get myself away home. Nurse will be in in a minute. I'll see you tomorrow. Ta-ra.'

Rose sat at the desk, completely stupefied. When a harassed staff member from the agency had rung her late on Friday afternoon, she'd been only too glad to get a job for the next few weeks. She hadn't stopped to ask about the practice, and even if she had wanted to, the voice on the other end of the line had made it clear she was in a rush.

'It's a minimum of four weeks, more likely five. Harley Street. Please say you can do it. They're new clients and we really want to keep them on our books. It involves the usual medical secretary work, plus manning the reception with possibly a bit of chaperoning thrown in. It'll be a piece of cake for someone with your experience.'

It had sounded right up Rose's street. Ever since Dad had had a stroke she'd known she would have to put her job in Edinburgh on hold and go and help her mother. Her parents hadn't wanted her to come home to London, but to Rose there had been no choice. Happily the practice she worked for as a practice nurse had been sympathetic and agreed to give her five weeks' leave, more if she needed it. The next few weeks would give her time to assess the situation at home and decide whether she should return to London permanently.

Harley Street was a couple of tube journeys away from her parents' house and meant an hour's commute at either end of the day, but it was a job and Rose had snatched the opportunity with both hands. Now she was wondering if she'd done the right thing. Then again, she hadn't much choice. There weren't that many temping jobs and she needed the money. Whatever reservations she might have about her new boss, the job was perfect.

She sighed and helped herself to another chocolate in the bowl on the desk. She let the rich flavours roll around her mouth. Delicious.

The door opened and an older woman with neatly coiffed hair and a small dog tucked under her arm swept into the room. Rose glanced at her sheet. Could this be L. S. Hilton?

'Such a naughty boy,' Mrs Hilton clucked. 'Snapping at that poor man's ankles. If you do that again, Mummy will get really angry with you.' Before Rose could react, she thrust the dog into Rose's arms. He was wearing a little coat that covered his legs and a scarlet ribbon in the hair on his head. 'Could you find him some chocolates? He always gets grumpy when his blood sugar gets low.' Then she peered at Rose over her spectacles. 'Oh, I don't think we've met, dear. Where is Tiggy?' She glanced around the room as if she might find her hiding somewhere.

'She's had to go away for a bit,' Rose said. The dog looked up at her with a distinctly unimpressed air. Rose was worried that he'd take a snap at her and she looked him firmly in the eye. She was used to dogs. Her parents had always had one when she had been growing up. You had to show them who was boss straight away. The dog whimpered and relaxed in her arms. She looked over to the desk for the chocolates. Her cheeks burned as she realised that she'd scoffed the lot. She should have known better than to leave the bowl in a place where her fingers could wander of their own accord. To her huge relief, Mrs Hilton didn't seem to notice the now empty bowl.

'Mr Chips likes you,' Mrs Hilton said approvingly. 'He doesn't usually take to strangers. And certainly not when he's grumpy.'

'If you could just take a seat, Mrs Hilton, I'll let the doctor know you're here. Then I'll see what I can find for Mr Chips. Can I get you something? A cup of tea, coffee?'

Mrs Hilton sat down on one of the chairs and picked up a magazine. 'No, thank you. Too much caffeine isn't good for my arthritis and…' she eyed Rose severely '…don't you know it's terribly bad for the skin? Like chocolates.' Her eyes flickered to the empty bowl and Rose felt her cheeks grow warmer. 'Although it seems you have good skin. Good girl. Most girls don't think about their skin until they reach my age and by then it's far too late to do anything about it. At least—' her eyes twinkled '—without the expertise of a good surgeon.'

Rose couldn't work out whether she was annoyed or flattered by Mrs Hilton's personal comments. But the gleam in older woman's eye made her go with the latter. She meant no harm.

Rose buzzed through to Jonathan to let him know Mrs Hilton had arrived.

'It's Lady Hilton,' he corrected mildly. 'I'll come out.'

The door opened almost before Rose had time to replace the handset. Jonathan paused in the door way and his mouth twitched as he noticed Rose trying to juggle Mr Chips with one arm while she searched for Mrs Hilton's notes with the other.

'Sophia,' he said, striding towards the older woman. 'How lovely to see you.'

Lady Hilton raised her face to his and Jonathan kissed her on both cheeks.

'You know I would have come to the house to see you? It would have saved you a journey into town,' he said.

'I had to come in anyway. I needed to do some shopping. And I wanted to talk to you about Giles—away from the house. He doesn't know I've been feeling poorly. And…' she looked at Jonathan sternly '…he's not to know.'

'Sophia, everything that you tell me is always in complete confidence,' Jonathan said firmly. He placed an arm under her elbow and without appearing to add any pressure, eased her to her feet. Despite the look of resolve on the older woman's face, Rose could tell the movement caused her some discomfort. Probably arthritis. Or something like it.

'Do you mind awfully keeping Mr Chips while I'm in with the doctor? He gets so restless if I don't pay him my full attention,' Lady Hilton asked Rose.

It wasn't really a question. Dog-sitting hadn't been in the job description. But, hey, it wasn't as if she was overrun with work, and he seemed to have gone to sleep in her arms.

Rose smiled. 'Don't worry. He'll be fine with me. If he wakes up and starts looking for you, I'll bring him in.'

While Rose waited for the next patient to arrive, she looked around for something to do. She liked to keep busy. Not that she could do much with a dog asleep in her arms. Spotting her discarded cardigan hanging on the back of the chair, she used one hand to form it into a little bed on the floor under her desk. She placed the sleeping dog on top. He looked at her with one eye, then gave a contented sigh and settled back down to sleep. Okay, what next? Perhaps she should ask Jonathan whether he would mind if she brought in some textbooks and did some revision in between patients? She couldn't see why he'd object. Unless she had more to occupy her, she'd go mad with boredom.

Her glance fell on the pile of magazines Lady Hilton had picked up in the short time she'd been in the waiting room. They were a mix of high-fashion glossies and society-gossip magazines, the type Rose never ever looked through—or at least never bought. She had to admit taking a sneaky look once or twice when she was at the hair-dressers, but that wasn't the same as buying them. Other people's lives didn't really interest her, not unless they were doing something remarkable, like climbing Everest or walking unaccompanied to the South Pole. Now, those were people with intriguing lives, not folk who were famous, well, because they were married to a footballer or had a rich father.

Casually she flicked through the first magazine she picked up, curious despite herself. She came to a few pages near the middle, which had photographs of celebrities out on the town. Suddenly she stopped. Staring out at her, his arm around the waist of a woman with long wavy red hair, a figure to die for and a dress that would have cost Rose a year's salary, was Jonathan. He was dressed in a dinner jacket and a white shirt and appeared relaxed and at ease. Rose peered closer. Although he was smiling, there was something in his eyes that suggested he wasn't best pleased to be photographed. The caption underneath read 'The Honourable Jonathan Cavendish and his girlfriend, actress Jessamine Goldsmith, at the premiere of her film *One Night In Heaven*.'

Rose was having a hard time getting her head around it. He was an honourable, the son of a lord, his girlfriend was a movie star. And he was her boss. A GP. She felt her lips curl in disapproval. That wasn't the kind of doctor she approved of. People should go into medicine to help others, not to finance some gad-about lifestyle. However, it was nothing to do with her. She was here to do a job and as long as her new boss didn't actually go around killing his patients with his incompetence, who was she to judge?

The door swished open and she dropped the magazine as if it were a hot potato.

A woman with short curly hair and a look of panic rushed into the room. She ran past Rose without saying anything, heading straight for the staff bathroom. Once again, Rose was bemused. It was beginning to feel as if she had walked in to a madhouse. Who on earth was that? She hadn't rung the doorbell so she must have a key. And she knew exactly where the staff bathroom was. Could this be the missing Nurse Vicki?

A few minutes later, the woman reappeared. Although she still looked pale, some colour had returned to her cheeks.

'I'm so sorry,' she said collapsing into a chair. 'You must be the temp covering for Tiggy. She phoned me on Saturday to let me know she was going to be away and there would be a temp filling in.' She took a shuddering breath. 'You must think me incredibly rude, rushing in like that without so much as a good morning.'

Rose crossed to the woman's side. 'Are you all right?'

'Not really.' She grimaced before holding out a hand to Rose. 'I'm Victoria, my friends call me Vicki. I've just been terribly sick. Thank God I made it here in time. It would have been too embarrassing throwing up in public.'

'Should you be at work?' Rose said. 'Couldn't you have taken the day off?'

'I would have. If I hadn't known Tiggy was off. Or if I'd known I was going to feel this bad. I felt okay until I got off the tube, then I just started to feel worse and worse.'

'Dr Cavendish is in with a patient. Should I call him?' Vicki did look awful. There was no way she should stay at work. Rose watched in alarm as the colour drained from the nurse's cheeks again.

'Oh, no, sorry.' Vicki clamped a hand across her mouth and bolted for the bathroom.

While she waited for Vicki to re-emerge, Rose switched the kettle on again and finding some peppermint tea set about making a pot. She hoped the drink would help settle Vicki's stomach. There was no way she could be allowed to return home until she stopped feeling ill.

'You must wonder what kind of place you've walked into.' Vicki's voice came from behind her. 'The nurse more ill than the patients. And I see Lady Hilton has brought Mr

Chips in again. I do hope he won't relieve himself in the plant pot again. Oh, is that tea? Could I have some?'

'I think you should try a couple of sips. Why don't you sit down? You look as if you could collapse at any minute.'

Vicki sat on one of the chairs at the kitchen table. 'Jonathan is not going to be happy about this,' she confided. 'The last time I was off the full eight months. He had to find someone to replace me, and she didn't turn out to be great.'

Realisation was beginning to dawn on Rose.

'You're pregnant?'

Vicki nodded. 'Oh, I'd better not do that again,' she moaned. 'Any movement just makes it worse.'

'And you had hyperemesis with the last pregnancy.'

'Hey, you're pretty switched on. Have you had it? Is that how you know?' She was too polite to say so, but Rose guessed she was wondering how a medical secretary would know about the condition an unfortunate few women suffered in pregnancy.

'I'm a trained nurse. Poor you. How badly did you have it last time?'

'Bad enough to put me in hospital, I'm afraid. And to keep me off work for most of my pregnancy.' She took a tentative sip of her tea. 'I'm dreading having to tell Jonathan.'

'He doesn't know you're pregnant?'

'I wasn't going to tell him just yet. I'm only eight weeks. And I hoped that I would be better this time around.'

'I'm sure he'll understand.'

'He's a real softy. Of course he'll understand. I just hate letting him down. The patients like to see me. They're used to me. Most of the older ones hate change. My obstetrician tells me it might get better by around twelve weeks, but I'm not holding my breath.'

The sound of a door opening alerted Rose to the fact that Jonathan's consultation with Lady Hilton had ended.

'I'll be back in a moment,' she reassured Vicki. 'Just you stay there until I get back.'

She scooped up Mr Chips from his nest in her cardigan and carried him over to Lady Hilton. The movement roused the dog from his nap and he reached up, attempting to lick Rose's face. She just managed to avert the doggy kiss by passing Mr Chips over to his owner.

'Has my baby been a good boy, then?' Lady Hilton cuddled her dog as if it had been days rather than minutes since they'd been together. But as she buried her face in her pet's fur, Rose noticed tears in the corner of her eyes.

'I'll come to the house to see you and Giles later this week,' Jonathan said. 'In the meantime, we'll try this new prescription. See if that makes a difference.' He patted her arm. 'The next few weeks are going to be rough,' he said. 'Call me any time. I mean it.'

He looked around. 'Rose, have you seen Vicki? She's usually in by now.'

'In the kitchen, having a cup of tea. I'm afraid she's not feeling very well.'

A look of concern swept across Jonathan's face. 'I'll go and check up on her. I'll see you soon, Sophia. Take care.' He kissed the woman on the cheek again and Rose showed her out.

Rose retreated behind her desk, giving Vicki the chance to tell Jonathan her news. She ran through the condition in her mind. Although hyperemesis was hugely debilitating, it was rarely life threatening. However, being constantly sick would prevent Vicki from working and might well require another stay in hospital.

Jonathan appeared with his arm around Vicki's shoulder. 'I'm going to take Vicki home,' he said. 'Do you think you could hold the fort until I come back? I'll be about an hour.'

'Your next patient is due in about ten minutes,' Rose reminded him. 'Lord Bletchley?'

'I can manage, Jonathan,' Vicki said weakly. 'I'll take a taxi. You stay and see your patient. You know what Lord Wretchley—I mean, Lord Bletchley's like. He'll go through the roof if he's kept waiting.'

'He'll just have to,' Jonathan replied, looking determined. 'I don't want you to go in a taxi. Not when you might throw up again. You know what some of these drivers are like. They might well kick you out.'

'Couldn't I take your car and drive Vicki home?' Rose offered. 'My insurance allows me to drive any car. That way you could see Lord Bletchley on time. It does mean there wouldn't be anyone to cover reception, but seeing as it's only the one patient we're expecting, that shouldn't be too much of a problem. You can man the desk, whereas I'm not too sure he'd like to be seen by me.'

Jonathan smiled and Rose's heart gave a little blip. No man should have a smile like that, she thought. It just wasn't fair on women.

'Despite what anyone may have told you, I'm perfectly capable of answering the door.' He dug in his pocket. 'If you're sure you don't mind? My car's parked outside. Vicki knows which one it is.' He tossed a set of keys to Rose. 'It has satellite navigation so you should be able to find your way to Vicki's house and back okay.'

Ignoring Vicki's protests that really she could manage by herself, Rose retrieved a sick bowl from the treatment room and ushered her out the door.

'Okay, which one is his?'

Vicki pointed at a low-slung sports car. Rose felt the colour drain from her face. Although she knew relatively little about cars, she knew enough to know that the car must have cost at least as much as her parents' house. For a second, she was tempted to go back inside and tell Jonathan she had changed her mind. But one look at Vicki told her that she needed to be at home and in bed as soon as possible. If she put a scratch on the car, Little Lord Fauntleroy would just have to live with it.

Thankfully, Vicki knew how to work the sat nav and soon Rose was threading her way through the London traffic.

'You don't have to hold the steering-wheel as if it's a wild animal about to attack you,' Vicki said with a smile.

She was right. A child on a three-wheeler would move faster. Rose forced herself to relax her grip. Now if only she could unclench her teeth, perhaps she could talk as well as drive.

But it seemed as if Vicki no more capable of chatting than she was. The nurse leaned back against her seat and closed her eyes. Rose followed the instructions of the disembodied voice from the computer and by some miracle managed to find her way to Vicki's house without any disasters. Now all she had to do was make it back in one piece.

'Is there anyone at home to look after you?' she asked Vicki as they drew up in front of a small Victorian terrace.

'My husband,' Vicki replied. 'He's a police officer. He's on night duty so he'll be sleeping like the dead, but I'm sure he won't mind me waking him if I need anything. Our daughter is in nursery school.'

'I'll just see you safely in,' Rose said, and before Vicki

could protest, she was out of the car and around the other side, helping her out.

Vicki smiled at her. 'Are you always this capable?' she said.

Rose smiled back. 'I can't help it. I was always the Guide who finished her badges long before anyone else did. The one who got the campfire going even when it was raining. It's social occasions that get to me. Doing is better than talking, if you know what I mean? Although I'm getting better at that. Needs must. In my other life I'm a nurse.'

Vicki frowned. 'Why are you covering for Tiggy as the receptionist? Oops, I mean personal assistant. That's how Tiggy prefers to be referred to. She's a sweetheart, but she thinks it's important everyone knows their place. Titles are important to her. And not just work ones either.'

'The job I was offered was as receptionist. I used to work as a medical secretary before I did my nurse training. I was happy to do either since I just wanted something short term.'

Vicki pulled a bunch of keys from her bag and opened her front door. 'I can manage from here,' she said. 'I'm sorry that you've had all this dumped on you on your first day. I hope we haven't scared you off. Johnny will need help. Would you be a sweetheart and phone the nursing agency and find out about a replacement for me?'

'Don't worry, I'll sort it out. You get to bed and I'll see you whenever you come back to work.'

Vicki grimaced. 'God knows when that'll be. Jonathan made me promise not to come back until I've stopped being sick. If it follows the same pattern as last time, it could be months.'

'I'll speak to him about finding someone to cover for

you as soon as I get back to the office.' Rose made her voice stern. 'Now, inside and off you go to bed.'

By the time Rose, with an enormous sigh of relief, returned to the surgery, it seemed as if Lord Bletchley had been and gone. Jonathan was back at her desk with his feet up, flicking through the magazine Rose had skimmed through earlier. He was scowling.

'Bloody paparazzi,' he muttered. 'Can never get their facts right.' He flung the magazine aside and got to his feet. 'How is Vicki?'

'She was going to go straight to bed. Her husband's on night duty, so he'll keep an eye on her.'

Jonathan pulled his hand through his thick dark hair. 'I can't see her being back for at least a month. If then. Would you mind getting onto the nursing agencies? You'll find the number of the one we use regularly in the diary. Ask if there's anyone who could cover on a day-to-day basis for the next four weeks at a minimum.'

An idea was beginning to form in Rose's head, but she liked to think things through before she spoke. Jonathan looked at his watch. 'I'll be in my room if you need me. I've a couple of phone calls to make.'

Could she? Should she? Rose rolled the idea around in her head. It would be the perfect solution. She was a trained nurse and there really wasn't that much to keep her busy at the desk. Mrs Smythe Jones had told her that she hoped to be back in a week or two. Rose could combine both roles for a short time. She'd much prefer to be kept busy. And if they needed someone to man the desk while she was in with a patient, she thought she had a solution to that too.

The ringing of the door interrupted her musings. She pressed the door release and watched bemused as a teenage boy with a resentful expression was almost dragged inside by an irate-looking woman.

'Come on, Richard,' the woman was saying. 'We might as well see the doctor now we're here.'

The boy looked at Rose through long hair that almost covered his face and Rose bit down the stab of sympathy that swept over her. He had the worst case of acne she had seen outside a textbook. His face was covered with angry raised bumps and he looked utterly miserable. Underneath the bad skin, Rose could see that he could be a good-looking boy, if it weren't for the surly expression and terrible acne. It brought back memories of her own teenage years, when she had felt as self-conscious with her height as this boy clearly did with his skin.

She smiled at the boy, knowing how embarrassed he would be feeling.

'You must be Richard Pearson,' she said. 'If you want to take a seat with your mother, I'll let the doctor know you're here.'

All Rose got in reply was a grunt. Nevertheless he sat down, dipping his head so his hair covered his face.

His mother looked at him with a mixture of frustration and love. 'I apologise for my son's rudeness,' she said. 'He didn't want to come.' She turned her back to her son, leaned across the desk and continued, her voice lowered to a whisper, 'I'm at my wits' end. He's refusing to go to school now. He just sits in his room, playing on his computer. I've tried other doctors. Dr Cavendish is my last hope. I heard from a friend that he helped her daughter.' She glanced behind her again. Richard was engrossed with his mobile; either playing a game or texting.

'I'm sure Dr Cavendish will do everything he can. I'll

just let him know you're here.' Rose certainly hoped he could help. Nothing so far had given her any confidence in his medical ability. Oh, he was certainly charming. The way he had been with Lady Hilton had made that evident, but no amount of charm was going to help this poor unhappy boy. At the very least surely he would refer him to a dermatologist?

She buzzed through. 'I have Richard Pearson to see you,' she said.

'I'll be right out.' He really did have a lovely voice. Deep with just a hint of a Scottish accent.

As before, he was out of his room almost before she had a chance to put the phone down. He went over to the boy and held out his hand. 'I'm Dr Cavendish. But you can call me Jonathan, if you like. Why don't you come into my room and we can have a chat?'

Richard reluctantly got to his feet, and scowled at his mother.

Something in his expression must have caught Jonathan's attention. 'Why don't you stay here, Mrs Pearson?' he said, his voice as smooth as silk. 'And have a cup of tea while I talk to your son on his own for a bit. Then if you have any questions, I'll be happy to answer them.'

'I'd like to come in with my son,' Mrs Pearson said stubbornly.

Richard looked at his feet and shuffled them uncomfortably.

'Richard? What would you like? I see from your notes that you're seventeen so I'm happy to see you on your own. However, if you'd prefer your mother to come in with you, that's perfectly all right too.'

'On my own,' Richard mumbled with an apologetic

look at his mother. 'I'll be okay, Mum. As the doctor says, I'm almost eighteen.'

Mrs Pearson seemed unconvinced. Rose touched her gently on the elbow.

'Why don't I get us both a cup of tea?'

Mrs Pearson watched Jonathan lead her son away, but then let Rose guide her over to one of the armchairs and sit her down.

'I don't really want any tea,' she said. 'I just want to get my son helped. This time last year he was popular and outgoing, and he seemed so happy. But ever since the problem with his skin, he's become so withdrawn and miserable. I keep telling him that it'll get better in time, but he says he doesn't care. It's now that matters.' She drew a shaky breath. 'I'm so scared he'll do something silly.'

Rose sat down next to the distraught mother. 'There are medicines that can help. It's often just a case of finding the right one. As soon as he knows we can improve his skin, he'll be happier. It's too cruel that he's been hit with this just at a time when his hormones are already all over the place.'

'I hope you're right.' The woman sniffed and then looked at Rose, puzzled. 'I guess you pick up all sorts of information working in a doctor's practice.'

'I guess you do.' Rose smiled. There was no point in telling her that she had spent the last four years studying nursing, and dermatology had been one of the last modules before she'd qualified. And as for understanding teenage angst, it hadn't been that long since she'd been through it herself. She remembered only too well how awful it felt to be the odd one out. Somehow at that age you could never accept that others had the same feelings of inadequacy and that they were just better at hiding it. Not that she could imagine Dr Jonathan Cavendish going through anything like it. She doubted that he'd had a moment's uncertainty about his looks in his life.

She chatted with Richard's mother until almost half an hour had passed. Eventually, Richard emerged with Jonathan. To her relief the teenager seemed much happier. He almost managed a smile for his mother.

'So take the tablets for a week and come back and see me. If things haven't improved substantially, we'll think of what to do next. One way or another, we'll get on top of this.'

Richard's mother looked uncomfortable for a moment. Rose guessed instantly that she might be worrying about the cost of the consultation and medication.

'Oh, and by the way, the follow-up consultations are included in the price of this appointment. I've also given Richard a letter to take to his GP, who'll be happy to give him the prescription on the NHS. I hope that's okay.'

There was no disguising Mrs Pearson's relief. Rose warmed to Jonathan. He had done that so gracefully she doubted Mrs Pearson or her son suspected for a moment that he was lying about the cost of the consultations. It was all there in the brochure she had read that morning. Thankfully, Mrs Smythe Jones had said on her detailed list that she'd catch up with the billing on her return. So many of their patients had different arrangements for payment that it would be far too complicated for a temp to work out who was to be billed what and when.

As soon as mother and son had left, Rose turned to Jonathan.

'What did you prescribe?'

He looked at her baffled. 'Amoxicillin. Why do you want to know?'

Rose felt her cheeks grow warm. She hadn't decided whether to tell him she was a nurse, but now it seemed as if she had no choice.

'I'm a trained nurse,' she admitted finally. 'A practice nurse, and I not too long ago completed a course on dermatology, so I kind of wondered what you thought you could do for him. I know topical retinoids can help when antibiotics don't.'

His frown deepened. 'A nurse? Why are you working as a…?' He stopped in mid-sentence.

Rose had to smile at his obvious discomfort. 'I'm on leave from my job for a few weeks for personal reasons. I was a medical secretary until five years ago, so I'm also qualified to do this job. When I was working as a medical secretary, I realised as I typed up the notes for the doctors that what I was reading really fascinated me and I wanted to know more.'

Oops. What was she doing? There was something in the way he was looking at her with those steady curious green eyes that was making her babble. And she was usually so reticent when it came to talking about herself.

He did look genuinely interested, although Rose had the strong suspicion that was just part of his practised charm. In which case, why on earth was she telling him? But she could hardly stop now. 'Anyway, my boss encouraged me to study for my A levels in my spare time and then apply to university, and they accepted me.' Try as she would, she couldn't quite prevent the note of pride creeping into her voice. She was the first person in her family who had gone to university and her parents had almost burst with pride.

'So why are you here?' He sounded puzzled. 'Why didn't you take a nursing job? God knows, this city is desperate for trained nurses.' His eyes were casually moving up and down her body, as if he were a cat and she the cream. She should have been annoyed, but she knew it couldn't be because he found her attractive. Not this man. Suddenly she regretted wearing her old interview suit and primly buttoned-up blouse. Nevertheless, there was something deliciously unexpected about the way it made her feel. For a second she almost forgot the question.

'Rose?' he prompted.

Now see what she had started. This was where she should tell him about her home situation and despite his interested gaze she wasn't sure he would really want to know.

'Go on,' he encouraged. 'I'd really like to know,' he said as if reading her mind. He leaned against the filing cabinets and folded his arms, his eyes never straying from her face.

'Let's just say family circumstances and leave it at that?' She kept her voice light, but returned his stare directly. It really was none of his business. He was her boss but that didn't give him the right to give her the third degree. Okay, so it wasn't exactly the third degree, but it was more than she wanted to tell him.

He was still studying her intently and she could see the same thought processes going through his head as had gone through hers earlier. She was a nurse. He needed a nurse, and quickly.

'Did you have any luck with the agency? About a replacement for Vicki?' he asked.

'I haven't called yet,' she admitted. 'I was thinking…' She took a deep breath. What if he hated her suggestion? For all she knew, practices like this wanted their nurses to have the right kind of accent. The right kind of image.

Although there was nothing wrong with the way she spoke, her voice didn't have the plummy ring to it that Vicki's voice did.

'That since you're a nurse, you could fill in for her? Exactly what I was thinking. But what about the office? I'm not sure you could do both jobs.'

Rose hid a smile. She could easily manage both jobs if it were a simple case of workload, but he was right. There did need to be someone at the desk if she was in with a patient.

'I know just the person for the office,' she said. 'She's young, but keen. She's at a bit of a loose end while she's looking for a permanent job. I know she'll be glad to work any hours needed, but she also won't mind if you need to let her go at any time.'

'Cool. Can I leave you to sort it out? Tiggy always manages that side of things. I'm afraid I'm useless at anything except the medical side.' He glanced at his watch. 'Lunchtime! Where do you fancy eating?'

Rose gaped at him. There was no way she wanted to go to lunch with him. Not today, possibly never. She was having way too odd a reaction to him, and she wanted some time to examine what was happening. It had always worked in the past. Thinking about something logically made it easier to deal with. Besides, she had brought her own snack. She really couldn't afford to eat out.

'I brought a packed lunch,' she said primly. 'I'm quite happy to have it at my desk.'

His lips twitched, but he didn't try to persuade her. He was probably relieved she had said no. No doubt it was his impeccable manners that had prompted his offer in the first place and no doubt he would have been mortified had she said yes. Somehow she guessed that the hired help going out with the boss wasn't the way things were done in this part of London.

Jonathan ran down the stairs of his London consulting rooms and into the frosty spring air. He couldn't help smiling when he thought of the temp. She was a lot better looking than Mrs Smythe Jones, that was for sure. Although he had a soft spot for the elderly receptionist, who had been there since he'd been in short trousers, he was looking forward to the next few weeks. Rose Taylor intrigued him. The baggy cardigan she was wearing couldn't quite disguise a figure that would make most of his female acquaintances weep into their champagne. Luckily he was a connoisseur of women though; anyone else would have failed to see that she was a stunner under that shapeless cardigan and old-fashioned glasses. And he'd liked the way she had dealt with his patients. Solicitous but not overbearing. He couldn't help but notice the way they responded to her. Even Lady Hilton, who usually was as narky as the dog she insisted carrying everywhere, had been like putty in her hands. She was the most intriguing woman he had met since—well, for a long time. The unusual mix of prickly personality, which reminded him of a teacher he'd had at school, and hidden sex appeal. How could a woman be sexy and sexless at the same time? He whistled as he made his way to the restaurant. It was going to be interesting having Rose Taylor around.

CHAPTER TWO

ROSE waited until the door had closed behind Jonathan before she let out her breath. She collapsed in the chair. He was gorgeous—and that smile! Did he have any idea what it did to women? Of course he did. Rose's experience of men was limited but even she recognised a man who was used to being admired. She had never met anyone like him. After all, how could she have? Those weren't the circles she moved in. But good looking though he was, she was not sure whether she approved of him. She much preferred men who had a sense of purpose, men who had some ambition, and taking over the family practice in order to have an easy life was as far off ambition as she could imagine. Not that she'd had many boyfriends. Three at the last count and none of them could be called exciting. But at least they were reliable. Reliable and safe. Somehow she knew safe wasn't a word that could be applied to Jonathan Cavendish.

And it was just as well she preferred sensible men, she thought ruefully. The chances of Jonathan Cavendish being interested in her were less than zero. All she had to do was look at that flame-haired bombshell in the picture with him. She was so perfect—there was no way she would be found absent-mindedly munching her way through a bowl of chocolates.

She glanced around the surgery. Enough of that sort of thinking. What now? He had left her his Dictaphone with his notes about the patients he had seen, so she could type them up and have them ready for him to sign on his return. And as for the rest of the afternoon? There were three home visits marked down in the book. What was she supposed to do while he was away? She swallowed a sigh. It was going to be a long day.

As she'd expected, it only took her thirty minutes to type up the letters on the computer. The note paper was as grand as the rest of the consulting rooms.

Just as she was preparing to eat her lunch, there was a frantic knocking on the door. She opened it to find a woman about her age with a young child of about two in her arms.

'Please,' she gasped. 'Is there a doctor around? My daughter's having difficulty breathing. I don't know what happened—one minute she was okay then she started wheezing. My mobile's battery's flat or else I would have called an ambulance. Then I looked up and saw the doctor's name on the door. Please help me.'

Rose could see that the young mother wasn't far off hysteria. The little girl was having difficulty breathing but at least her lips were pink and the muscles in her neck weren't standing out with each breath. The little girl was clutching a teddy bear as if her life depended on it.

She gripped the woman's shoulder. 'I know it's diffi-cult,' she said, 'but you have to calm down. Your little girl will get more distressed if she sees you panicking. Now what's her name?'

'Sally,' the woman replied after taking a couple of deep breaths. 'I'm Margaret.'

'Could she have choked on anything? Inhaled something? A button? A peanut? Anything?'

'Not as far as I know.'

'Sally, I'm just going to look inside your mouth. Okay?' Rose said calmly. The little girl looked at her with frightened eyes. Rose gently checked inside her mouth. There was nothing obvious blocking the little girl's throat. If there had been, her breathing would have been much noisier. It was still an emergency, but not one that was immediately life threatening.

'Okay, Margaret, come with me,' Rose said, taking the little girl from her mother's arms and walking briskly to the treatment room.

'I was just having a coffee in the café round the corner and she was fine then.' Margaret had calmed down a little, although anxiety and fear were still evident in her eyes.

'Has this happened before?' Rose asked. 'Any history of asthma or allergies?' There were two obvious possibilities as far as Rose could tell. Either Sally was having an asthma attack, in which case she needed a nebuliser, or she was having a severe allergic reaction, in which case she needed adrenaline. But which one was it?

'Could you open your mouth as wide as you can, Sally? I'm just going to shine a torch down your throat. It won't hurt at all, I promise.'

The little girl did as she was told. Rose shone the torch. As far as she could see, there was no swelling of the throat.

'Is it possible she's eaten a peanut? Or some other food she's not had before?'

The mother shook her head. 'She was in her high chair. All she had was the juice I gave her.'

In the background Rose heard the slamming of the door and then a voice calling her name. A wave of relief washed over her. It was Jonathan. At least now she'd have help.

'In the treatment room,' she called out. 'Could you come, please?'

He appeared at the door of the room and took the situation in at a glance. He crouched next to the chair where Rose had plonked Sally back on her mother's lap.

He touched the little girl lightly on the cheek. 'Hello, there,' he said softly. 'What's all this, then? You're having difficulty breathing?'

While he was talking to the girl, Rose had located a nebuliser and some liquid salbutamol. As he started to listen to the little girl's chest she held the vial up to him and he nodded approvingly towards her.

'Margaret, do you know how much Sally weighs?' Rose asked. 'It'll help us work out how much medicine to give her.'

'I'm not sure, maybe about twelve kilograms. I haven't weighed her recently. There's been no need.'

Now that Margaret knew her daughter was getting the help she needed, some of the terror had left her voice.

'It's okay. We can make an estimate.'

Rose reached for a pulse oximeter. 'I'm just going to put this on your toe,' she said to Sally. 'It won't hurt either. It's just a little toy I have to help me. Okay?' Rose turned to Margaret. 'It'll monitor Sally's blood oxygen levels. Tell us how much oxygen she's taking in.'

The child was still having problems with her breathing, but now that her mother had calmed down, some of the panic had subsided and her breathing was becoming easier. Nevertheless, she still needed treatment.

'I think your daughter is having an asthma attack,' Jonathan said, taking the nebuliser from Rose. 'I'm just going to put this over your mouth, Sally, and I want you to take slow, deep breaths.'

The little girl shook her head from side to side, the panic beginning to return.

Frantically Rose looked around then she had an idea. She lifted the teddy from the little girl's arms and placed a second nebuliser over the toy bear's mouth. Rose crouched by Sally's side and, placing her hands on either side of the little face, forced her to look into her eyes.

'Watch me, Sally. We're going to play a game. Every time I take a breath, like this, Teddy's going to take a breath. You copy us, okay?

It seemed to work. Her eyes fixed on Rose and the teddy bear, Sally copied every breath Rose took. Jonathan watched carefully not saying anything. Slowly, Sally's breathing returned to normal and after a while Jonathan removed the mask from the little girl's face.

'Your breathing should be all right now, Sally.' He turned to her mother.

'This is the first time it's happened? Never before?'

Margaret shook her head.

'It probably didn't seem that way to you but I think that some of the problem was that Sally was getting quite panicky when she felt her breathing was tight. We could tell from looking at her breathing that she was still managing to take plenty of air into her lungs—her oxygen reading was ninety-eight per cent, which is pretty good, even when she was at her most distressed. Even so, it was a very scary experience for you both,' Jonathan explained.

Sally's mother looked weak with relief. The little girl hid her head in her mother's neck and closed her eyes. Rose knew that sleep would be the best thing for the child now.

'We had been to the park to feed the ducks with a friend. Sally was sleepy so she went for a nap in my friend's arms. When she woke up she needed to go to the bathroom, so I took the chance to have a coffee. She had been coughing in the park a little, but I didn't think anything of it. It was only when we were in the coffee shop that she seemed to have difficulty getting her breath. I thought she'd be better in the fresh air but she kept on getting worse. Then I saw the name on the door. I hoped there would be someone who could help.'

She looked at Jonathan and Rose, her eyes glistening. 'Thank you, both. I don't know what I would have done if you hadn't helped me.'

'I think it's Rose who deserves most of the thanks,' Jonathan said, straightening. He looked at her as if she puzzled him—as if she were a crossword and he was missing several clues.

'You should see your own doctor as soon as you can. I suspect Sally is going to need regular medication for a while,' he told Margaret.

Rose was turning over what Sally's mother had said.

'Do you have pets, Margaret?'

'No, we don't. Sally's dad is allergic to animal fur.'

'What about this friend? The one you met in the park?'

'Linda? Oh, yes. She has about five cats. She loves them and is always rescuing another one.'

Rose caught Jonathan's eye and knew he was thinking the same thing she was.

'I think we might have found the culprit. It's possible your daughter is allergic to cat fur. Perhaps there were cat hairs clinging to your friend and when Sally fell asleep in her arms she inhaled some of the allergens. Anyway, it's only a possibility, but one worth thinking about and mentioning to your GP when you see him,' he said.

Margaret refused a cup of tea, but accepted Rose's offer to call her a taxi. Ten minutes later she was climbing into the cab, her sleeping child in her arms, still thanking Jonathan and Rose effusively.

When they had left, Rose turned to Jonathan. 'I hope you're all right with me bringing them in. I realise it wasn't anything to do with your practice and if I had messed up, you could have been held liable.'

Jonathan looked at her his expression serious. 'And if I told you that it was unforgivable, that you have never to help a passer-by again, what would you say?'

'I would say that you need to find another temp,' Rose replied hotly, before she noticed that corners of his mouth had lifted in a smile. 'You're kidding, right?' she said, embarrassed she had jumped to the wrong conclusion so quickly.

'Of course I'm kidding,' he said. 'I wouldn't dream of employing someone who would think of rules before they acted. That wouldn't be right and…' his smile grew wider and Rose felt the strangest feeling in the pit of her stomach "…so boring.'

He levered himself away from the wall against which he'd been leaning. 'I think you've had enough excitement for the day. Why don't you do the letters from this morning and then get away home?'

'Letters are done, just waiting for your signature,' Rose replied. What on earth did he think she'd being doing while he'd been out to lunch? She glanced at her watch. 'It's only two o'clock. I can't possibly leave this early.'

He looked thoughtful.

'How would you like to come on a home visit with me, then? From what I saw back there, the way you dealt with Margaret and Sally, you'd be perfect to step in for Vicki. What do you say? It'll mean more money, of course.'

The nervous flutter in the pit of her stomach spread upwards. The look in his eyes was a heady mixture—sexy, naughty, mischievous. Rose had never felt so flustered in her life, but she was damned if she was going to let him see the effect he was having on her. She held out her hand. 'You have a deal. And if you're happy for me to find someone for the office, I can do that too. I'll write down a name and number so you can check my references.'

He raised his eyebrows at her before shaking her hand. 'Somehow I get the feeling they're going to be first class.'

Rose tried to ignore the warmth that was spreading through her body.

'Is it usual for you to take the office staff on a home visit?' she asked.

'Not really. But the visit I have down for the afternoon isn't the easiest.'

For the first time since she'd met him, he looked uncomfortable. 'It's to Jessamine Goldsmith's house.' She was the actress, the one who had been with him in the photograph in the magazine. His girlfriend.

'And let's just say that it would make me feel much more comfortable having you there.'

'Isn't she your girlfriend?' What on earth was Jonathan

thinking? It was completely against the rules for a doctor to date a patient.

He narrowed his eyes at her. 'What makes you say that?'

Involuntarily, Rose's eyes slid to the magazine.

Jonathan's eyes followed hers. He looked none too pleased when he realised what she'd seen.

'Let's clear one thing up,' he said. 'Never ever believe what you see in these magazines. Jessamine Goldsmith is *not* my girlfriend and never has been. She's a patient who just happens to move in the same social circles as I do.'

'In which case…' Rose raised an eyebrow while hiding a smile '…what are we waiting for?'

As he manoeuvred the car through the thick London traffic, he flicked a switch and the rich sounds of Debussy filled the car. It was a composer Rose loved. She sat back in her seat, aware of the scent of expensive aftershave mingling with the smell of leather. It was so much better being in this car without having to drive. All she had to do now was relax.

'How come we're going to see Miss Goldsmith at home? Is she really unwell?'

Jonathan flicked her a smile.

'Jessamine's almost certainly fine, believe me. She simply prefers to have me see her at her house. A lot of the patients do. They find it less stressful.' Again there was the smile. 'Naturally, if they need to come to the consulting rooms for tests, then they do. Or if they're shopping nearby. Some, however, prefer me to come to them. It's much more discreet. Take Jessamine, for example, the press follow her everywhere, as they do many of my patients. Any visit to the doctor is viewed with curiosity and speculation. As you can imagine, most people prefer not to have that kind of conjecture in the public domain.'

'But aren't they equally curious about a visit from the doctor?'

At this point they had left the traffic behind and were driving through one of the more exclusive parts of London. Jonathan pulled up outside a house that could have been a hotel it was so large. The Victorian façade was the grandest she had ever seen. Two tall pillars framed a massive front door.

Jonathan turned off the ignition. 'Except that they can never be sure whether I'm visiting as a doctor or as a friend. Most of my patients belong to the same social circle as I do. You can't imagine how many off-the-record consultations I do at a party or at Ascot.'

All this was more and more confusing. Rose frowned.

'That can't be good. Surely there needs to be some distinction between the doctor and the patient?'

He jumped out of the car. 'Nope. It works just fine, believe me.'

The door was opened, before they had a chance to knock, by a man dressed in a formal suit.

'Good afternoon, sir,' he said. 'And miss. Miss Goldsmith is waiting for you in the drawing room. She said I was to show you straight in.'

Rose wanted to giggle. It was like being caught in a time warp. But if Jonathan found it amusing, he gave no indication of it. Instead, he stepped back to allow Rose to go through the door in front of him.

She stepped into a hall, so enormous her parents' whole house could have easily fitted into it—possibly twice. The floor was marble, paintings hung on the wall, and sculptures and large vases holding extravagant flower arrangements were placed around the space. To one side was a fire-place and a small sofa.

'I know my way, thank you, Robert,' Jonathan said, and taking Rose by the elbow steered her across the hall and up a flight of stairs that wouldn't have looked out of place in the foyer of the grandest cruise ship. Everywhere Rose looked there were ornate statues and gilt ornaments. Although someone had lavished a fortune on the interior, it wasn't to her taste. Rose much preferred a minimalist, uncluttered look.

Inside another equally impressive room, almost hidden in the depths of a sofa, was a woman with fine features and a mass of red hair. As soon as she saw Jonathan, she jumped to her feet and came towards him, arms outstretched.

'I've been waiting all day for you to come.' She pouted, holding up her face to be kissed.

'I do have other patients, Jess,' Jonathan said, bending and kissing her on the cheek. 'I've brought someone with me. This is Rose Taylor, my…er…nurse for the next few weeks.'

Rose stood trying not to shuffle her feet like some sort of servant from the Middle Ages. She smiled and held out her hand. 'I'm pleased to meet you, Ms Goldsmith.'

Jessamine studied her for a second, her glance no doubt taking in the cheap suit Rose wore. Whatever she saw seemed to reassure her and she smiled, the famous smile Rose knew from the times she had seen her in the movies. It lit up her face, turning her from a petulant teenager into a woman of remarkable beauty.

Jessamine ignored Rose's outstretched hand and dropped two air kisses on either side of Rose's cheeks.

'Would you like something to drink? Champagne perhaps? Tea?'

'Tea would be lovely,' Jonathan said firmly. 'Now, Jessamine, what can I do for you?'

'It's my stomach,' she said. 'It hurts like crazy.'

'Why don't you lie down while I take a look?' Jonathan suggested.

'Perhaps Rose wouldn't mind going downstairs to organise the tea while you're examining me?' There was no mistaking the glint in Jessamine's eye.

'Sorry, Jess, I need Rose here.' He sent Rose a look that implied that if she even thought about leaving him alone, she would have him to answer to. 'In case I need to take blood. Now, don't be difficult, let's have a look. Have you been eating properly? You know we spoke about this before. Your tummy hurts because you're hungry. You have to have more than five hundred calories a day.'

'That's all very well for you to say.' Jessamine pouted again. 'You know how the camera adds pounds and I have an audition tomorrow.'

Jessamine lay down on the sofa and lifted her T shirt, revealing her stomach. It was, as Rose had suspected, as flat as a pancake. But Jonathan was right, she was too thin. Rose could almost count each individual rib poking through the skin. When Jonathan made Jessamine sit up, so he could listen to her breathing from her back, it was the same, each vertebrae sticking out like a railway track.

'Your chest is fine and so is your heart. Rose, could you take Jessamine's blood pressure, please?'

It took Rose about two seconds to wrap the cuff around the too-thin arms. The blood pressure was slightly on the low side, but nothing particularly concerning. Despite her thinness, Jessamine was, on the surface, in good physical condition. While Rose was taking her blood pressure,

Jessamine was talking to Jonathan. She was speaking too fast, her eyes bright and feverish.

'I hope you haven't forgotten about the Wakeleys' yacht party next weekend, Johnny? All the crowd is going. I know you and Felicity aren't together any more, but you mustn't stay at home and mope. You must come too, Rose,' she added as an afterthought.

Rose knew it was only politeness that had made Jessamine invite her.

'I'm sure Rose would love to come,' Jonathan said before Rose could decline. 'In fact, I'll bring her myself.'

The response was obviously not what Jessamine had been hoping for. She narrowed her cat's eyes at Rose, and then with another dismissive glance seemed to remember that Rose offered no competition.

Rose opened her mouth to protest. She might be working for Jonathan, but that didn't give him the right to accept invitations on her behalf. Besides, she had her own plans. She would be going down to the pub, her old local, to meet up with friends she hadn't seen for months. Nevertheless, she felt slightly wistful. When was the last time she'd been to a party? And when would she ever have a chance to go to one like the one Jessamine was talking about? Never was the answer. But there was no point in even thinking about it: she'd be completely out of her depth. She caught Jonathan's eye. He was looking at her, willing her not to contradict him, so she wouldn't. She could always send her apologies with him on the night.

Eventually, after Jonathan had taken some blood and given Jessamine a lecture about eating properly and had received a promise in return that everyone in the room knew was empty, he made their excuses.

'We'll see you a week on Sunday, Jess,' he said. 'And I'll come back and see you before then. I don't think there's anything to worry about at the moment, but I'm going to keep an eye on you. But you have to eat more regularly. If you don't, you will continue to suffer from indigestion. But that's not the only thing. You're harming your body by starving yourself.' He frowned down at her. 'Is it really worth putting your health at risk, Jess?'

'Please don't tell me off, Johnny. I promise I'll be good. I just have to audition for this next film and then I'll put a few pounds back on, I promise.'

She held up two fingers in a salute Rose knew well. 'Brownies' honour.' She slid a pointed glance at Rose. Her look was mocking and challenging at the same time. She had taken a dislike to Rose, that much was obvious, and Rose had no idea why.

Outside, Jonathan held open the door of his car. 'Can I drop you off at home?' he asked.

Rose shook her head. 'I think there's a tube station not far from here. I need to pick up a few things on my way home so, thanks, but no thanks.'

'Then I'll drop you off at the station. Hop in. We can have a chat about Jessamine on the way.'

Rose did as he suggested. 'You seemed pretty sure it was indigestion,' she said.

'I am. Given her lifestyle, it's the likely diagnosis. But I'm not ruling out other possibilities just yet either. I want to check her blood count—do a full blood screen, just to be on the safe side.'

Although it probably was just indigestion, Rose had been worried that Jonathan didn't seem to be taking the

symptoms seriously enough. There was something about
the casual way the consultations were held, the familiarity
with the patients, that disturbed her. Jonathan's manner
was so easygoing, her earlier doubts were resurfacing. Did
he really know what he was doing? However nothing in the
thorough way he examined the patients or his detailed notes
suggested otherwise. Perhaps it was simply that this world
was so different from anything she had ever encountered.

'You think it could be more than indigestion?' she asked.

'Let's just say I'm not going to take any chances.'

Rose was relieved by his reply. Apart from the ethical
considerations of working with a less than thorough doctor,
it had become important to her that Jonathan had a
modicum of respect for the profession in which he was
practising.

Suddenly he grinned at her and her heart gave a disconcerting lurch.

'How was your first day, then?'

'Not really what I'm used to,' Rose admitted. 'But
interesting.'

She wasn't lying. But the most intriguing thing about
the whole day was this man sitting beside her. She studied
him surreptitiously from under her eyelashes. She had
never met anyone like him before. How could she have?
Her upbringing had been as different from his as it was
possible to be. Her father and mother had worked hard just
to keep their heads above water. Treats had been few and
far between, but if material possessions had been in short
supply, Rose had always felt treasured and loved.

She had always been studious, but she had never really
been ambitious. After leaving school, without sitting A
levels, she had done a secretarial course and had taken a

job as a medical secretary with an out-of-town practice. It was there that she had realised that she wanted to do more with her life. The patients and their illnesses had fascinated her and she'd found herself becoming immersed in their lives. Soon the patients had been stopping by her desk on a regular basis to tell her the latest on their families, sharing their hopes and fears with her. One of the doctors had noticed how easily the patients spoke to her and how quickly she picked up the medical terminology and had suggested medicine or nursing as a possible career. She had taken her A levels at evening class and followed up her excellent results with four years studying for her nursing degree at Edinburgh University. The circle of friends she had formed there had shared her interests—walks, music, theatre and opera. University had introduced her to things she had never been exposed to before and she had lapped it up. After graduating, she had easily found a job she loved in Edinburgh, within walking distance of her flat.

It had been a warm, comfortable, if unexciting life. One she had cherished. Why, then, was she beginning to wonder if something had been missing?

CHAPTER THREE

'I'M HOME,' Rose called out, heaving a sigh of relief as she dropped her bags of shopping at the front door. The tube had been packed as usual, bodies pressed up against each other as the train had rattled and swayed. She had stopped off at the supermarket for something for tonight's dinner and had then had to complete the second half of her journey home. The walk from the station only took ten minutes but, laden as she was, combined with heels that, although sensible by most women's standards, were still an inch higher than Rose was used to, had felt every painful step of the walk home.

Her mother came out to greet her.

'How was it, love?' She reached for one of the shopping bags. 'Why don't you go in and see your dad while I put this away? Then you can tell us all about it over a nice cup of tea.'

'How is he, Mum? What sort of day has he had?'

'Not too bad. He ate his breakfast and his lunch, then we did the exercises the physio showed us. He's a bit tired now. I'll help him to bed once we've had supper.'

Rose found her father in his usual chair by the window. Her heart squeezed as she took in his useless arm and downturned mouth. The stroke had left one side of his body pretty much paralysed, as well as impairing his speech. Her father had been a vigorous man who had enjoyed going to football matches and playing cricket and golf, and now he was reduced to sitting by the window, watching the world go by. Rose knew how much he loathed needing help. If he would barely accept it from his wife, he hated taking it from his daughter. There had been a small improvement since he'd been discharged from hospital and Rose prayed with the proper treatment he'd continue to make progress.

'Hey, Daddy. How's it going? Seen any suspicious characters out there today?' She dropped a kiss on the top of his head and he gave her his lopsided smile.

'Hello, sweetheart,' he said. Although the words were indistinct, Rose knew that was what he was trying to say.

She sat down beside him and took his hand in hers. 'You have no idea what sort of day I've had, Dad.' She told him about the chocolates, Mr Chips, the visit to Jessamine's house, embellishing her stories to amuse him. Not that they needed much embellishment. She rubbed her stocking feet as she spoke, knowing she'd need a plaster or two before she could wear the shoes again.

'What's he like, then, this doctor you're working for?' Her mother appeared in the doorway, tea towel in hand. She had only very reluctantly agreed to Rose coming home to help look after her father. They had been so proud of her, the first in their family ever to get a university degree, and had wanted her to carry on building her career. In their minds, Rose knew they had her as Hospital Matron within a year or two. Rose had tried to tell them hospital matrons didn't exist any more, but they chose not to believe her.

Of course Rose had had to come home. She'd had to see

her father for herself and she'd known the first weeks following her father's discharge would be tough, so she'd applied for, and been granted, five weeks' special leave. After that? She shrugged inwardly. She'd have to see. Her mother wasn't getting any younger.

'Dr Cavendish?' Rose paused. How could she describe him? 'Well, he's young. Not much older than I am. About six foot and kind of lean. Apparently he's the son of a lord.'

'Well, I never. The son of a lord! What's he doing working as a doctor, then?'

'Apparently the practice belonged to his uncle who was doctor for the Queen's household. The uncle's retired now and Jonathan has taken over.'

'Is he poor, then? That he has to work for a living?' Rose's mother crossed over and plumped the cushions behind her husband's back. 'I know not all of the aristocracy is well off.'

'I don't think so, Mum. He drives a Lotus, although I suppose that could belong to the business. I don't really know much more about him. I can't say I've ever heard of his family.'

She closed her eyes and immediately an image of smiling green eyes and a mischievous grin flickered in front of her. How could she even begin to explain someone like Jonathan Cavendish to her parents when she could hardly explain her reaction to him to herself?

'Let's just say that I think the next few weeks are going to be interesting. Instead of acting as receptionist and medical secretary, it seems as if I'm to be nurse and chaperone.' Rose filled her parents in about Vicki before continuing, 'He has patients all over the country, and in Europe, and he's asked me if I can travel with him.' She looked at her mother. 'It does mean I won't be around to help as much as I'd like.' She paused. 'Maybe I should tell him I can't do it. Come to think of it, I must be crazy.'

Her father reached out and patted her on the arm. 'Do it,' he said. 'I want you to. It would make me feel better knowing that I'm not holding you back.'

Rose hugged her father, feeling his too-thin frame under her arms. Where had the strong muscular father of her teens disappeared to? He had always been there for her, now she wanted to be there for him and her mother. But he hated being dependent. And she had to make sure she didn't make him feel worse.

'By the way, Miss Fairweather phoned.' Rose's mother mentioned the name of the neurosurgeon Rose had seen after her father's stroke. 'She wants you to call her at the hospital. She wouldn't say any more. There's nothing wrong, is there, love?'

Rose felt a shiver of alarm but pushed it away. Her father's GP had recommended she see the specialist after discovering her father's stroke had been caused by an aneurysm. He'd told Rose that the condition often ran in families and to be on the safe side she should have herself checked out. Miss Fairweather had agreed and advised Rose to have an MRI. That had been on Friday and she had refused to let herself think about it over the weekend. She had been positive that there was nothing to worry about. After all, it wasn't as if she had any symptoms. No headaches, tingling sensations. Nothing. She dismissed the uneasy feeling that was creeping up her spine. No doubt the consultant just wanted to let her know that her results were all normal.

'I'm sure she just wants to let me know everything's okay, Mum. Don't worry. I'll give her a ring now.'

But when Miss Fairweather asked Rose to make an appointment to see her as soon as possible, Rose knew it wasn't okay. Had her results been fine, the neurosurgeon would have said so over the phone. Rose replaced the receiver, having made an appointment at the end of the week. She returned to the sitting room and her mother looked at her, alarm written all over her face.

'Not bad news, love?' she asked, the colour draining from her face.

There was no point in worrying her parents until she knew what Miss Fairweather had to say.

'No, Mum. Everything's fine,' Rose lied.

The following days at Jonathan's practice settled into a pattern. Patients would come to see Jonathan in the morning, then in the afternoon he would go out on visits, leaving Rose to type up notes if she wasn't needed. Some of the patients Rose recognised from the newspapers or TV, some she didn't recognise, but felt she should. Jonathan treated them all with the same easy grace and familiarity. Some afternoons she'd accompany him on his house visits, each home almost more spectacular than the last. Whenever Rose found herself thinking about her upcoming appointment with Miss Fairweather, she would push the thought away. There was no point in worrying until she knew what the neurosurgeon had to tell her.

But at home, in the privacy of her bedroom, she spent her evenings searching the net for information about aneurysms. None of it gave her much cause for optimism.

When Jonathan turned up for work in the morning, he'd sometimes look tired, as if he'd spent most of the night clubbing, although he never appeared hungover. And sure enough, there were photographs of him in the tabloid press, outside clubs and restaurants, with one glamorous woman after another on his arm. If it gave Rose a strangely uncomfortable feeling to see him with different women, she would dismiss the thought with a shake of her head. It was none of her business what he chose to do in his own time.

Once there was a photograph of him playing polo and she discovered that at least two of his free afternoons were given over to the sport. In the picture, he was swiping at an object with a long stick. Dressed in a white shirt and light-coloured trousers, his hair flopping over his eyes as he concentrated on his task, he looked like someone out of a regency romance. No wonder women seemed to find him irresistible.

She had managed to get in touch with Jenny, who had been delighted at the offer of some short-term work.

'I'm going mad having nothing to do,' Jenny had confided in Rose. 'I've sent out hundreds of applications but no luck yet. A bit of actual work experience can do me no harm. Especially if Dr Cavendish likes what I do and is prepared to put a word in for me.'

Rose had met Jenny the day she had gone to sign on with the agency. She was nineteen, having just finished her secretarial course, and full of boundless enthusiasm.

'Could you just tone down the hair?' Rose asked, remembering the spiky haircut. 'And perhaps remove the piercings, especially the ones from your nose and lip? Somehow I don't think it would be appropriate for the practice.' Even if quite a few of the patients had tattoos and piercings themselves.

'No problem,' Jenny said. 'I promise you you won't recognise me when you see me next.'

And true to her word, Jenny had turned up with hair neatly slicked into a bob, piercings removed and wearing a skirt that, while short, was just on the right side of decent.

She had regarded the consulting rooms with undisguised glee.

'This is a bit of all right,' she said. 'Now, where is this Honourable Dr Cavendish? And what do I call him? My Lord? Sir?'

Rose laughed. 'I think Dr Cavendish is just fine. Come on, I'll take you in to meet him.'

Happily, Jonathan seemed to take to Jenny. And the young girl, being smart and quick on the uptake, was soon ensconced behind the desk.

'He's a bit of all right,' Jenny confided. 'If he wasn't so old I could go for him myself.'

Rose laughed. 'He's hardly old. Twenty-seven.'

Jenny sent her a look that suggested that anyone over twenty-five was middle-aged in her opinion. Then she scrutinised Rose. 'But he's the right age for you.'

Rose smiled uncomfortably. 'I don't think I'm his type. Or he mine, for that matter,' she added quickly.

Jenny was still studying her critically. 'You know if you lost the glasses, maybe got some contacts, got a more modern hairstyle and some decent clothes, you'd be quite pretty.'

Rose couldn't make up her mind whether she was insulted or flattered. Get some new clothes and haircut indeed. Jenny watched too many films. Whatever, she knew Jenny didn't mean to be offensive.

'I appreciate your…' she searched for the right word '…opinion. But I'm happy the way I am. I like my clothes—they're comfortable. And I don't fancy poking my fingers into my eyes every morning and evening.

Besides…' she glanced behind her just in case Jonathan was within earshot '…I'm not looking for a boyfriend. And if I were, Dr Cavendish wouldn't be him.'

'But…' Jenny started to protest.

'No buts.' Rose cut her off. 'Whatever thoughts are in that head of yours, get rid of them. I'm here to do a job. That's it.'

But after Jenny had returned to her work, she thought about what she had said. It was true she wasn't looking for a boyfriend, and even if she were, Jonathan wasn't for her, or she for him. Although he made her pulse race uncomfortably, she doubted whether he took anything in life seriously. And even if he were her type or she his, she had far more important things on her mind than the dishy Jonathan Cavendish.

One morning, towards the end of the week, a well-known footballer came to the surgery, accompanied by his wife. Rose vaguely remembered reading about their wedding in a magazine she had picked up on the train. The footballer was even better looking in real life, his wife petite next to his six-foot frame. Whereas he was dressed simply in a pair of jeans and T-shirt, his wife was dolled up to the nines.

While Jenny organised drinks for them Jonathan called Rose into his consulting room.

'Mark and Colette came to see me a couple of weeks ago as they are thinking of starting a family,' he said. 'The last time they were here I arranged for them to have some tests. I have the results back. And I'm afraid it's not going to be the best news they ever heard. IVF is the only way forward for them unless they adopt. I'm going to arrange for them to have further investigations at the London Fertility Clinic, but in the meantime I think it would be helpful if you could sit in while I chat to them. If they agree.'

Rose nodded. She often sat in with the doctors in her surgery when they were giving unwelcome news. That way she could be there if the patients telephoned later, looking for clarification. A large number of patients were unable to take in everything they were told when they first heard that there was a problem.

The couple were happy to have Rose present. From their smiling faces, Rose knew they weren't expecting bad news. At least until something in Jonathan's face alerted Colette

'What is it, Jonathan? Something's wrong. I can tell from the way you're looking at me.' Colette's voice shook and Mark took her hand firmly in hers.

Jonathan pulled his seat around to the side of the table where Colette was sitting. His green eyes were full of sympathy.

'The initial bloods I took from Colette the last time she came to see me suggest that her ovaries are working normally. That's good. Although I think you should have the test repeated at the London Fertility Clinic. They will probably also suggest an ovarian scan, just to confirm the results of the blood test.'

'So there isn't a problem, then. We should just keep trying. We don't need to be referred.'

'There doesn't seem to be a problem with Colette.' Jonathan kept his voice steady. 'Although that's not a helpful way of looking at it. As if it's a problem belonging to one of the partners. Whenever couples are having difficulty conceiving, we like to think of it as a couple thing.'

'Come on, Jonathan. Stop beating around the bush. We come to you because we know we'll get straight answers.' Mark said.

'The difficulty is on your side, I'm afraid,' Jonathan

said sympathetically. 'The semen sample you gave last week had very few motile sperm. The clinic will want to repeat the test again, but it would seem that you are unlikely to conceive without ICSI. That's an IVF procedure where Colette goes through IVF treatment to stimulate her production of eggs then her eggs are injected with one of your sperm. It's very successful. If…' He stressed the last word while looking Mark directly in the eye. 'If they can find sperm that's healthy enough to do the procedure.'

Mark looked as if he'd been poleaxed. 'Are you kidding? But I'm healthy. You won't find anyone fitter this side of London.'

'I'm sorry, Mark. As I say, you'll need to have more tests, but I'm pretty sure. That's why it's a good thing you came to see me sooner rather than later. The quality of your sperm is only likely to deteriorate the longer we wait.'

The shock on the couple's faces tore at Rose's heart. She could see Colette making a determined effort to pull herself together.

'I don't mind, darling,' Colette said. 'I don't care about having IVF as long as we can have a baby. Jonathan's not saying we can't have children and that's all that matters.'

But Mark was still looking dumbfounded. Suddenly he got to his feet and lurched out of the room. Jonathan looked at Rose, and reading the unspoken question in his eyes she nodded. 'I'll stay with Colette.'

Jonathan followed Mark, leaving the two women alone.

'Jonathan can't be right,' Colette said after a moment. 'It's not possible. Mark won't accept it. We always assumed that if there was a problem it was me.'

Rose pulled a chair closer to where Colette sat and took her small hand. Her heart went out to the woman sitting next to her. In the last few days she too had had to face the real possibility that she might never have children. If she did have an aneurysm there would never be any children. Not even with IVF. A pregnancy would be too dangerous. Rose would never be able to carry a child. As her throat tightened, she pushed the thought away. She needed to focus on her patient.

'He'll come to terms with it in time, I'm sure. It's been a shock. And it sounds, from what Jonathan's being saying, that a child is not out of the question. It might just take a little help, that's all.'

'We didn't seriously think there was a problem, you know. We just came to see Jonathan because we wanted to make sure we were doing everything right for the baby from the moment it was conceived. You know, folic acid, vitamins. All that stuff. But when he heard we'd been trying for almost a year already, he suggested doing the tests—just to be on the safe side.'

'The procedure Jonathan's talking about isn't too awful, you know. And if you have a healthy baby at the end of it, what does it matter if you've needed a little help on the way?'

Colette still looked doubtful. 'We always assumed we were going to have a family. At least three. Maybe four.' She smiled wanly. 'I think he wanted to start his own five-a-side football team.' Her voice cracked. 'The thing is, I don't know if he'll agree to IVF at all. I think he might take it as a slight to his masculinity—you know how some men are. What will we do then?'

'You'll need to give him time, Colette. Once he understands exactly what's involved, I'm sure he'll come round.'

'You don't know that!' Colette protested hotly. 'You don't have any idea how we're feeling. To think one day that you have everything happiness, wealth, fame, only to have your dreams stripped away the next.'

A wall of pain slammed into Rose.

Colette had no idea that she understood only too well.

Eventually Jonathan and Mark returned. 'We just walked around Regent's Park for a bit,' Jonathan told Colette. 'Mark's had time to think it over, and he's agreed that the best thing to do is have you both seen at the fertility clinic. You just tell me when it suits you and I'll fix up an appointment. Then I'll see you back here and we can take it from there. Okay?'

The couple just nodded. Rose knew it would take them a little time to get their heads around what Jonathan told them and her heart went out to them. As Colette had said, what did wealth and fame matter if you couldn't have what your heart truly desired?

Jonathan was unusually sombre after the couple had left.

'They'll be okay, won't they?' Rose asked.

He pulled a hand through his thick, dark hair. 'I hope so. They've had a shock. They're a lovely couple. Despite Mark's fame, and despite his reputation for being a little wild on and off the field, he's down-to-earth, kind. So is she. If ever a couple would make great parents, it would be them. And as I told them, ICSI has a very high success rate. Even higher than getting pregnant naturally. As long as the embryologists can find any motile sperm.'

Jonathan gave his head a little shake as if to banish whatever thoughts were troubling him. He picked up tickets Mark had left on the desk when he'd first arrived.

'You fancy going to a football match?' he asked. 'Mark left some tickets for the Arsenal game next Saturday. I would go, but I already have tickets for the one-day International at Lords. I like football, but next to cricket…' He grinned. 'No competition, I'm afraid.'

'No, thanks,' she said regretfully, thinking of her father. 'Although you have no idea how much I'd like to accept. My Dad and I used to go all the time before I left home. He hates missing all the matches. He's been an Arsenal fan all his life.'

'Then give the tickets to him,' Jonathan said, thrusting them in her direction. 'They're for a box. He'll get a grand view.'

Rose wished she could accept on behalf of her father. It would be just the tonic he needed to lift his spirits. But getting him up and down flights of steps was more than she and her mother could manage.

'I wish he could go,' she said softly.

'So take him,' Jonathan persisted.

Rose turned away so Jonathan wouldn't see the tears that sprang to her eyes. 'He had a stroke about two weeks ago. He lost the use of his left side. He doesn't go out much any more. He hates the indignity of being seen out in public, and even if he didn't, until I get a new car that can take his wheelchair, he's pretty much trapped at home.'

Jonathan took a long look at her. Then he grinned and his eyes glittered. Rose's stomach flipped. 'You probably don't know this, but my family motto is *Where there's a will there's a way*. Actually, it's not, it's something far grander, but it means the same thing.'

Before Rose could ask him what he meant, his next patient arrived and Jonathan led him into his room.

'I'm so sorry,' Miss Fairweather told Rose. 'I really wish I was giving you better news.'

The room swayed as a wave of nausea hit Rose. She had known that there was a good chance the news would be bad, but she hadn't allowed herself to believe it. Now her worst fears were being realised. She did have an aneurysm.

Gathering her courage, she sat up straight in the hard backed chair and looked the young consultant in the eye.

'Okay, so what are my options?'

'You have two choices. You do nothing, and decide to live with the aneurysm.'

'Which would mean what exactly? Please, Doctor, don't mince your words. I need to know exactly what I'm facing.'

Miss Fairweather leaned forward. 'It is possible that you could live the rest of your life without the aneurysm bursting, but if it does, and there is no way of predicting how likely that would be, you could have a stroke and depending on the severity, you could be left with a number of physical problems—loss of speech, the use of your legs, or…'

'Or I could drop down dead,' Rose finished for her. 'Suddenly and without warning. Mmm, doesn't sound like much of a choice to me. What are my other options?'

'You can have an operation to remove it. Unfortunately there are a number of risks associated with the procedure too.'

'Such as?' Rose gripped her hands together to stop them shaking. Her mind flicked to her parents. They'd be devastated. She was their only child and knowing her father he would blame himself for passing on the genetic condition to his much-loved daughter. The same thing that had caused his stroke. How long had he been living with the time bomb inside his head? How long had she? She pushed the thoughts of her parents away. There would be time enough later to think about them. Once she had all the facts. Once she knew what she was going to do.

'Death, stroke. The complications of surgery aren't too different from the results should your aneurysm burst, I'm afraid. The problem is where your aneurysm is. The location makes the surgery riskier than usual.'

'Not a great choice, then.' Rose smiled wryly at the consultant. She *had* asked for her to be straight with her.

'On the other hand, if we manage to remove it through surgery, there is a good chance you could live to a ripe old age, have children, do everything you hoped for before this.'

'And if I don't? What then?' Rose knew the answer, but she wanted to hear it from Miss Fairweather. Maybe she had misunderstood what she had read about the condition on the internet.

'I'm sorry. You wouldn't be able to risk having children. It would put too great a strain on the blood vessels inside your brain. Otherwise, the risks are as I outlined earlier. But you don't have to decide straight away. You should go away and discuss it with your parents and boyfriend. Have a think. Make sure you understand the risks of both options. However, I wouldn't leave it too long. If you do decide to have the operation, the sooner you have it the better.'

Ten minutes later, Rose was outside the hospital. Although summer was supposed to be on its way, the wind still had a wintry feel to it. Wrapping her coat tightly around her, Rose stumbled to a bench and finally let the tears that had been clogging her throat for the last half an hour fall. She could die. Maybe tomorrow, maybe in ten years, maybe twenty. Miss Fairweather admitted that there was no way of telling. How could she live the rest of her life not knowing if every minute was going to be her last? On the other hand, if she had the operation Miss Fairweather had suggested, she could still die. Or be left paralysed, in a wheelchair—or worse. That prospect didn't have much going for it either. In fact, the thought was even worse than death. At least that would come quickly. The thought of a slow death, having to be looked after by her elderly parents, was infinitely worse. Being dependent on anyone didn't bear thinking about.

She blew her nose loudly. Behind her she could hear the sound of a baby crying. She had never imagined that she might not be able to have children one day. Never hold a child in her arms. Maybe never again go for a walk in the rain, watch an evening sky change colour as night approached. Never learn how to ski, or speak Spanish. All the things she had told herself she had plenty of time for. Perhaps it was just as well that she had never met anyone she cared enough about to marry. What should she tell her parents? Nothing. Not yet. They had enough on their plates right now with Dad's stroke without having to worry about her.

So there would be no more tears. No self-pity. She would do as Miss Fairweather had suggested. She would think long and hard about what to do. In the meantime she'd treat every minute of her life as if it were her last. No more hiding away. No more not doing something because it was too expensive, or scary, or any of the hundred reasons she had given herself in the past. From now on, she would say yes to every experience life had to offer. From now on, she would make the most of every second she had left.

During the long nights that followed her appointment with Miss Fairweather, Rose tossed and turned, trying to decide what to do. In the end, she decided she couldn't have the operation. What if it went wrong? And she ended up like her father, or worse? How would her mother cope with two invalids? Besides, if her father hadn't had a stroke, she would never have known about the ticking time bomb inside her head. She would have carried on living her life the way she was doing now.

In the small dark lonely hours of the night, she had tried to draw up a list of things she wanted to do before…well, before it was too late, but had given up on the list when she'd come to number fifty and scored it through. Instead, she promised herself she would try and live each day as best she could, taking any opportunities that came her way. She still couldn't get her head around the fact she could die any time. She felt so healthy and life had never seemed so painfully precious and filled with promise.

CHAPTER FOUR

JONATHAN habitually asked her if she wanted to go to lunch with him, but she always refused. The first sunny lunchtime, she asked him if it would be okay if she took a little longer than her usual half-hour.

'I'd like to take my lunch to the park,' she said. 'It's such a beautiful day and I could really do with some exercise. Jenny will be fine on her own for an hour.'

'Good idea,' he said. 'I'll come with you. There's a deli on the way, I could pick up something to eat from there. It will make a change from the stodge they serve up in my club. God, it reminds me of school dinners.'

Rose was taken aback, but she could hardly refuse. 'You can share mine, if you like. My mother always insists on making my lunch and she puts enough in to feed an army. I think she worries I don't eat enough.' Rose laughed. 'I eat like a horse, I just don't seem to put on any weight.'

Jonathan's eyes slid over her and she felt her cheeks flush under his gaze. She pulled her cardigan around her. What on earth had possessed her to say that? And as far as offering to share her lunch, she had the distinct impression Jonathan wasn't used to having egg and cress sandwiches or whatever her mother had packed for her. Didn't people like him have caviar or some other such stuff for snacks?

'Come on, then, if you're sure you've enough. We'll pick up a couple of coffees on the way.'

As they walked Rose felt inexplicably tongue-tied. It was different when they were working. Somehow, without patients to discuss, it was different.

After picking up their coffees they found a bench looking over a small lake. The good weather had brought out mothers and children, or was it their nannies? There were also a number of people strolling or jogging. Rose handed Jonathan a sandwich and lifted her face to the sun.

'Have you lived in London long?' he asked between mouthfuls.

'I was brought up here. My parents have lived in the same house all my life. I went away to university. Edinburgh, actually. I have an aunt who lives there so I was able to stay with her. It helped keep the cost down. What about you?'

'I boarded at Gordonstoun. I was almost six when my father sent me there. I studied medicine at Cambridge.'

Rose had heard of Gordonstoun. She knew it was a famous and very expensive school in the north of Scotland where many of the rich sent their children. She had also heard that the regime was very tough.

'Isn't that where Prince Charles went?'

'Yes. But long before my time.'

'How awful to be sent away to school when you were so young. Weren't you terribly homesick?'

Jonathan turned to her, looking surprised. He really did have the most amazing eyes, Rose thought. Dark green, and ringed with an even darker shade. He had the kind of eyes that made her feel he could see right into her soul.

'You know, I never really thought about it. It was just something that happened. I suppose the first few years were hard. I missed my home. But all the other boys were in the same situation. And there were the holidays—at least, some of the holidays. My father was away a lot, so I stayed with schoolfriends most of the time.' His eyes darkened and he looked away into the distance as if he found the memory unpleasant.

'I don't think I could ever send my child away. Especially at that age,' Rose said thoughtfully. 'But I guess your parents must have had their reasons. Would you send your child?'

Jonathan's eyes narrowed. If it were possible, he looked even bleaker. Rose could have kicked herself. She had no right to question the way he had been brought up.

'My child? You know, I can't say I've ever thought about it. Children have never really figured in my plans for the future. Somehow I don't ever see myself having them. They require commitment. And I'm not that kind of guy.' He grinned. 'Life is too full of possibilities to settle on one.'

Rose eyed him speculatively. Maybe when he met the right woman he would feel differently. Then again, maybe not. Somehow she couldn't see Jonathan giving up the lifestyle he enjoyed for the restrictions a domestic life would inevitably bring.

'I don't think my mother would have sent me if it had been up to her. She died when I was five, and my father sent me away soon after the funeral,' he continued after a moment.

Rose was shocked. How could a father send away a child who had just lost his mother? And not just down the road, but several hundred miles. An image of Jonathan as a little boy wearing long shorts and a peaked cap, standing alone outside the school while his father drove away, flashed through her mind and her heart twisted with sympathy for the little boy he'd been. What kind of man was his father if he could do that to his son? Rose thought if she ever met him, she would dislike him intensely. No wonder Jonathan seemed to have little faith in the joy children could bring. It was ironic: Jonathan didn't want children, although he almost certainly could have them; and she wanted them, desperately, yet couldn't have them. If she had been able to have children, she would never send them away. She would have kept them close to her, making the most of every precious moment with them. A wave of sadness washed over her. She forced her thoughts away. Thinking like that was pointless.

'I'm so sorry, Jonathan. I can't imagine what it was like for you. To lose your mother when you were so young and then be sent to boarding school.'

'Don't we all do things because we have to? I know duty is considered an old-fashioned concept, but you must believe in it too. You came back here to look after your father. You must have had a life in Edinburgh.'

Rose forced a smile. 'Of course. But as you say, sometimes we have to do what is right rather than what we want. My parents needed me.' She shrugged. 'So I came. My life in Edinburgh can wait.' *If* she had a life to live.

'No boyfriend?'

'No one serious.' She wanted to change the subject. It was far better for her to keep her mind off her future—and the possibility she might not have one.

'Why did you decide on medicine?' she asked him, genuinely interested. From what she had gathered, Jonathan's family was rich enough for there to be no need for him to work at all.

Jonathan smiled ruefully. 'As I told you, my uncle was a doctor. He was apothecary to the Queen. He used to talk to me all the time about cases he had came across when he was still working in a hospital. I loved listening to him and I can hardly remember a time when I didn't want to be a doctor. I needed to do *something* with my life. My father hoped I'd take over the family business, but it wasn't for me.'

'But Harley Street.' Try as she would, Rose couldn't quite keep the disapproval from her voice.

'My uncle built up the practice. People liked coming to see the man who looks after the Queen's health. You can't get a better recommendation than that. I was going to set up a practice somewhere else, but then he became ill and wasn't able to carry on. Back to duty, I guess.' He took a gulp of his coffee. 'I couldn't let him down.'

'You don't miss real medicine, then?'

He looked at her, amusement making his eyes glint.

'You know, even the rich and famous get ill. In the end, birth and wealth don't prevent you from experiencing health problems. Like Mark, for example.'

Yes, she should know how arbitrary illness could be. Despite the warmth of the sun, she shivered.

He looked at his watch. 'Speaking of which, I have to visit Lord Hilton this afternoon. You remember his wife coming in to see me on your first day? She has arthritis and he has terminal cancer. He really should be in hospital, but he refuses point blank. Says he has no intention of dying anywhere except the home he's lived in all his life.' Jonathan studied Rose thoughtfully. 'How would you feel about coming too? If I remember correctly, she took a shine to you.'

'Poor Lady Hilton. I had no idea. Yes, of course I'll come. If you need me.'

What Rose didn't know and what Jonathan neglected to tell her was that Lord and Lady Hilton lived a hundred miles from London and that they were sending their private helicopter to bring Jonathan to their country home. The helipad was a ten-minute drive from the surgery.

Rose had never been in a helicopter before, let alone one that had leather seats as wide as armchairs in the back.

'You didn't tell me we were flying to our visit,' she accused Jonathan when he pulled up at the helipad on the Thames.

His eyebrows quirked in the way she was beginning to know well. 'You didn't ask. About fifty per cent of my patients live outside London. In fact, they sometimes fly me out to see them when they're on holiday. Wherever that might be.'

'They don't see someone locally? Surely that would be better?'

Jonathan gave her a half-smile. 'I see you have a lot to learn, Rose Taylor. Most of my patients are so rich that is doesn't occur to them not to fly their doctor out. In the same way that they'd fly out their hairdresser or stylist. They like to see the same physician.' He shrugged. 'And I don't mind going. I've known some of my patients most of my life.'

It was a different world. One where Rose didn't know the rules. But it was a job. As long as she got paid and as long as Jonathan's patients didn't suffer, who was she to judge? And, she had to admit, it was exciting to be part of it, even for a short time. She sucked in a breath as she remembered the promise she had made to herself. *Live every day to the full*. At least working with Jonathan was bringing new experiences and every minute was exciting. How much of the excitement was down to new experiences and how much was due to being in the company of the man sitting next to her, she didn't want to think about.

Jonathan gave her a radio set to wear, partly to drown out the noise of the engine and partly so they could hear each other speak. Below her the river Thames cut its way through London. She could see Buckingham Palace and the Tower of London as well as the pods of the London Eye revolving slowly.

'Have you been in it yet?' Jonathan asked, pointing to London's newest tourist attraction. 'Sorry, silly question. Of course you have.'

'As a matter of fact, no. I haven't had the time. I'd love to some time.' One more thing to add to her steadily growing list. 'Have you?'

'Once or twice.' He grinned. 'One of my friends is having a party there in a few weeks' time. You should come.' It was another invitation, but Rose knew that Jonathan was just issuing them out of politeness. If she accepted, he'd probably be dismayed.

Soon they were leaving London behind and passing over the countryside. A short time later they flew over a house bigger than most hotels Rose had stayed in and were touching down in what was the back garden, but which anywhere else would have been a park.

'Oh, my word,' Rose said as she stepped out of the helicopter. 'The last time I saw a house like this it was in a film. How many people live here?'

'Just Lord and Lady Hilton. His sons live in London. They come up when they can.'

A man dressed in the traditional garb of a butler walked towards them. Rose smiled. It was just like being on a movie set.

'Good afternoon, sir, miss,' the butler said. 'Lord and Lady Hilton are expecting you.' He turned to Rose. 'What name should I say?'

'This is Miss Taylor, Goodall. She's a nurse at the practice. Lady Hilton and Miss Taylor have already met.'

'Lord Hilton is in his bedroom. Lady Hilton said she'd like a word before you go in to see him, if that's all right?' Goodall said.

Jonathan chatted to the butler as they walked the few hundred yards to the front door. From the snippets of conversation Rose caught, it seemed they knew each other well. Following behind, Rose took in the formal garden with its neatly trimmed hedges and flower beds. Dotted throughout were nude sculptures, some modern, some more classic. It must have taken an army of gardeners, Rose reckoned, to keep it looking so perfect.

Inside, the hall was twice as large as the one in the town house belonging to Jessamine. There was a grand central staircase in the middle of a polished marble floor. Someone had lit a fire in the huge fireplace that dominated one side of the hall and with the large bowls of brightly coloured flowers it had a cheerful air. Despite the grandeur, Rose knew immediately she was in someone's much-loved home.

Goodall showed them into a room which, while as grand as the hall, had been decorated in thoughtful, homely fashion. Large squashy couches with brightly coloured cushions and a rug that had seen better days added a splash of colour to the otherwise muted room. Light was flooding in from the floor-to-ceiling windows overlooking the front garden, but a fire burned brightly in this room too. After the coolness outside, it was almost suffocating.

Mr Chips jumped down from an armchair and pattered

across to them, his tail wagging. Rose bent to pat him, and in return received ecstatic doggy kisses on her hand. In an armchair next to the window was Sophia Hilton. Her silver hair was perfectly coiffed but despite the heat in the room her face was pale. Rose was sure there were more lines around her eyes and mouth than there had been when they'd first met. She was dressed in thick stockings and a tweed skirt and the hand she held out to Jonathan had the slightest tremble. Rose knew immediately that this was a woman who was under enormous strain, but desperately trying not to show it.

Jonathan bent down and kissed the older woman on each cheek.

'Sophia, how are you? And Lord Hilton?'

'Jonathan, dear boy. How good of you to come and see us. And Miss Taylor, an unexpected pleasure to see you again too. Jonathan told me you're filling in for Vicki until she's well enough to return.' Her mouth trembled slightly. 'Giles isn't good, I'm afraid.'

Jonathan pulled up a chair next to Lady Hilton and Rose sat on the sofa opposite. 'Tell me what's been happening,' he said gently.

'He's fading. He hardly eats at all now. He says he has no appetite. He gets up for an hour or two but that's all he can manage.' She dropped her voice to a whisper. 'We're losing him, I'm afraid.'

'You're both still sure you don't want to try another bout of chemotherapy? I could have him in hospital by this afternoon.'

Lady Hilton shook her head regretfully. 'He won't hear of it, I'm afraid, and I have told him I'll respect his wishes. That's why I don't want you to try and persuade him. He's too weak to put up a fight, so he made me promise to speak to you before you saw him.'

'The chemotherapy might help.'

'Will it prolong his life?'

Jonathan looked her directly in the eye. 'I'm not going to lie to you. It might give him a little more time, ease his symptoms, but, no, the outcome will be the same.'

'And the chemotherapy will make him feel even worse in the short term, won't it?'

'He didn't react to it very well before. So, yes, I'm guessing he'll feel even more rotten than he does right now.'

'Then nothing's changed since we last had this conversation. Except it's getting closer.'

'Have you thought any more about bringing in nurses to help? I thought Rose here might be able to convince you. She worked in general practice before she joined us in London.'

Rose leaned forward. 'If it's okay with you, I'd like to see your husband and have a chat with him before I advise you. But Dr Cavendish is right, there are lots of options that would allow you to keep him at home but help you keep him comfortable at the same time.'

'Of course.' Lady Hilton stood. 'I'll take you both upstairs.'

Rose and Jonathan found their patient sitting in a chair by the window with a rug over his knee. A book lay by his side, and a still full cup of tea sat ignored on the table next to him. His eyes were closed and his face had the grey gauntness that Rose had seen too often before. She knew immediately that Lord Hilton didn't have much longer.

His wife touched him gently on the shoulder.

'Darling, it's Jonathan and his nurse come to see how you are.'

Eyes flickered open and as they focused on his wife, a

look of such love that Rose had rarely seen filled the pale blue eyes. Her heart contracted.

'Jonathan, my dear boy. How are you? And your family?' The voice was weak but clear.

'Father is always asking after you.' As he spoke, Jonathan placed his fingers on the old man's wrist.

'Any word of getting married yet? Isn't it time?'

Jonathan laughed. 'No. Can't find a woman who is crazy enough to have me.'

'What about this girl here?' For a moment Rose squirmed. He couldn't be alluding to her as a possible wife? The poor man must be confused.

'This girl, as you put it, is my nurse. Victoria's pregnant. Unfortunately she's being very sick again so has to take time off. Rose is filling in for the time being.'

Rose stepped closer so that she could be seen. 'Dr Cavendish thought I might be able to help make you more comfortable—or at least suggest some things that could help.'

Rose watched carefully as Jonathan finished his examination. While he was doing that she was assessing how Lord Hilton moved and how much pain he seemed to be in.

'Why don't we have a little chat while Jonathan talks to your husband?' Rose said to Lady Hilton. 'You can tell me what help you have at the moment.'

Once they were back in the sitting room, Rose broached the subject of nursing care.

'I don't want strangers looking after him,' Lady Hilton protested.

'What about a night nurse at least?' Rose suggested gently. 'Someone to sit with him through the night so you can get a good sleep?'

'There's Goodall,' Lady Hilton said firmly. 'He'll attend

to Giles if he needs anything at night. He also helps him shave and wash. He's been with him for thirty years and knows his ways.'

Rose had to admit that having someone to help who Lord Hilton knew well would be far less stressful than bringing in new faces at this stage.

'I know Dr Cavendish—Jonathan—is likely to suggest a morphine pump. That way the pain can be controlled. Will you consider it? You'll need to have a nurse call at least every second day to check on it, but that shouldn't be too intrusive.'

Lady Hilton blinked furiously. 'Why did Victoria have to be unwell now of all times? Oh, don't mind me, I'm just being selfish. Of course, it's important that she looks after herself now that she's pregnant. But Giles knows her. He would have been happy to have Goodall fetch her from town every day.'

'I'm sure there will be equally good nurses locally that would be happy to come to the house.'

'That would mean interviewing people. It would be terribly time-consuming. I don't want anything to interfere with the time we have left. I know there's not much time.' Her eyes locked onto Rose's and she could see the spark of hope there. But just as quickly it was replaced with resignation. 'You don't have to pretend otherwise, my dear. I know it and Giles knows it.' She paused for a moment. 'Couldn't you come? He's met you and he seems to have taken to you. And Jonathan wouldn't have brought you here if he didn't think highly of you. We could arrange for you to be collected and brought back every day. Please say you'll agree.'

Although Rose felt for the older woman's distress, she

knew what she was suggesting would be impossible. Just as she was trying to find the words to let her down, Jonathan walked back into the room.

'He's sleeping now. Goodall and I helped him back into bed. I think he should have something more regular for the pain, however. I can come and see him whenever you want, but analgesia as and when he wants it would be better.'

'Miss Taylor was just suggesting the very same thing. But she tells me a nurse will have to come in regularly to check the pump. I asked her whether she could come. What do you think, Johnny? Could she?'

Jonathan looked at Rose. 'I'm afraid I need her in London,' he said.

The old lady looked so woebegone that Rose couldn't help herself. With Jenny manning the desk, she could come and help the Hiltons. It would keep her busy. She had too much time to brood as it was.

'What about if I came after my shift? Would that work?'

Jonathan frowned. 'Would you excuse us for just a moment?' he said, and taking Rose by the elbow steered her out of earshot.

'I know you want to help, but don't you have your own situation to think about? It'll be too much.' For a second Rose thought that somehow he had found out about her condition, even though she knew it was impossible. 'Coming here and putting in a full day's work before going home to help out with your father. I've your health to think about too. The last thing I need or want, is to have to find another nurse.'

'It's not as if I'm run off my feet at the surgery.' Rose glanced across at Lady Hilton who was studiously looking out the window. 'I just wanted to help. Anyway, there's at least three free afternoons a week where you don't have any patients. I know you keep them free for emergencies or unscheduled home visits, but so far they've been quiet and I've just been twiddling my thumbs. I could come here then.'

Jonathan's eyes followed hers. Despite the determined look and the upright posture, Lady Hilton needed help and they both knew it.

'I'll agree to it on one condition,' Jonathan said. 'You come here only on those free afternoons and on the other two we shuffle my schedule around so that there aren't patients booked in for when you're here. Jenny and I can cover the odd drop in or emergency between us. If that suits you, we have a deal.' He didn't need to say what they were both thinking. It was unlikely that the arrangement would be required beyond a few weeks at the most.

He smiled sadly at Rose and her heart skipped a beat. 'Thank you for offering. I've known Lord and Lady Hilton all my life. Anything that will make these last few weeks and days easier for them would mean a great deal to them…and to me.'

Jonathan told Lady Hilton what they had agreed, emphasising that they still needed to get Jonathan's schedule sorted out but that he didn't think it would be a problem. The relief in her eyes brought a lump to Rose's throat.

Jonathan turned down Lady Hilton's invitation to dinner. 'Next time, I promise. But it's getting late, and I really have to get Rose home. I'll phone you tomorrow morning and let you know what we've managed to sort out between us.'

The journey back in the helicopter was a more subdued affair. Rose found herself wondering about Jonathan. On the one hand, he seemed to like nothing better than to be partying along with his social set; on the other, as a doctor, he seemed to genuinely care about his patients. She had been guilty of making assumptions about him that appeared to be no more than figments of her imagination. In that regard she was no better than the press. She slid a glance in his direction. Why couldn't she have met someone like him before? Before her world had been turned upside down? And why did she have the sinking sensation that what she was feeling was a good deal more than she should for her boss?

CHAPTER FIVE

ON SATURDAY morning, she was sitting reading to her father when there was a knock at the door. Rose glanced out of the window, surprised to see a large four-by-four parked outside. Baffled, she answered the door to find Jonathan standing there with a broad smile on his face. He was dressed in faded jeans and a short-sleeved shirt. It was the first time she had seen him in anything apart from his suit and if anything he looked even more handsome. Certainly more approachable.

For once the sun was shining and although it was cool, there was a hint of summer in the air.

Open-mouthed, Rose stood back and let Jonathan in.

'Who is it, love?' Her mother came to stand behind her.

'It's Dr Cavendish, Mum.'

'Please call me Jonathan,' he said, holding out his hand and smiling charmingly at her mother.

'Why are you here?' Rose asked, suddenly conscious of the small house with its comfortable but worn furnishings. Then, aware of how rude she sounded, she apologised. 'I'm sorry, I'm just a little surprised to see you. I didn't think you even knew where I lived.'

Jonathan's smile grew wider. 'Your address was on your

file.' Then he frowned. 'I should have phoned, but I thought we had an arrangement?' In the cramped dimensions of the hall she could smell his aftershave.

'Arrangement?' Rose echoed.

'The tickets to the match. Remember? I promised I'd find a way to get your father there. If he'd still like to go, that is.'

Rose was bewildered. 'You've come to take my father? Don't you have a cricket match to go to?'

'There will be other matches,' he said dismissively, but Rose knew enough about cricket to know that despite his words he was giving up one of the most looked-forward-to events of the year. 'I'm planning to go to a party afterwards. Perhaps you'll come too?'

Rose shook her head, still confused. He had given up his day to do something for her father, a man he'd never met, and he wanted her to go to a party. Her heart skipped a beat. 'I couldn't. I've nothing remotely suitable to wear. Besides, I'm needed here.' It wasn't the whole truth. Her father was improving daily and required only minimal help now. But her at one of Jonathan's parties? Not on your life. What on earth would she have to say to his friends or them to her? The idea was ridiculous. Nevertheless, she had to admit to a small stab of regret. It had been ages since she'd been out. Besides, she had to admit that she was intensely curious about what sort of party it would be. Like everything else these days, it would be another new experience to add to her growing list.

Suddenly aware that they were still standing in the small hall, Rose remembered her manners.

'You'd better come in.'

She ushered him into the small sitting room. Her parents looked up, curious.

'Dad. This is Dr Cavendish. He's come to ask if you'd like to go to the football match this afternoon.'

Jonathan crossed the room and shook her father's hand warmly. 'I'm pleased to meet you, Mr Taylor. Your daughter tells me you're an Arsenal fan. Well, it so happens that I have tickets to the match today and I wondered if you'd like to come?'

'That's kind of you, son,' Rose's father said. His words were still slurred and Rose doubted that Jonathan would be able to understand what he was saying. 'But my leg's a problem. I don't think I could get up the stairs.' Although he was continuing to improve, pretty much managing to get himself washed and dressed, he had to lean heavily on a stick to walk. Rose doubted he'd be able to manage more than a few metres without a wheelchair.

'I have a plan for that,' Jonathan said. It seemed as if Rose had been wrong and that he could make out the words her father was trying to say. 'If I told you that I thought Rose and I can manage to get you there and to your seat without too much trouble, what would you say?'

Rose saw her father's eyes light up and her heart ached for him. She remembered how he had taken her to football matches when she'd been young, hoisting her onto his shoulders so that she could see better. They had never missed a home match until she'd left for university in Scotland.

'I don't know, lad. Maybe you should take my Rose and go on your own. You'd enjoy it better.'

'I'm not going to the match, Dad. Unless you go too. And I don't think Dr Cavendish plans on staying. He has something else on.'

'Did I say that?' Jonathan asked innocently. 'Can't imagine why. There's nothing I'd rather be doing, but I don't care to go on my own. So you and Rose would be doing me a favour by coming with me.'

'Go on, love,' Rose's mother prompted. 'You haven't been out of the house since…' She paused and Rose guessed she still found it difficult to admit even to herself. 'The stroke. A bit of fresh air will do you the world of good. And I could be doing with getting your father from under my feet for a few hours.'

Rose knew her mother didn't mean a word of it. Her parents still loved each other deeply. Her mother wanted to bring some joy back to her husband's life. Rose also knew her father wouldn't go without her.

'In that case, I say yes, I'd love to go.'

With Jonathan helping, it was difficult but manageable to get her father along with his wheelchair into the roomy back seat of the car Jonathan had brought instead of his sports car. When they arrived at the football stadium, Jonathan flashed something at the security guard and drove up to the front gate. With him on one side of her father and her on the other, they used the lift to reach the box where they were to be seated.

'Always wanted to see the footie from one of these fancy boxes,' Tommy said when they had seated him with a rug over his lap. 'Never could afford it.'

'We can go inside the lounge and have lunch first, if you like?' Jonathan suggested.

Tommy shook his head. 'You two go. I'm just as happy to stay here now I'm settled.'

'And I'd rather stay with you, Dad.' Rose turned to Jonathan. 'But please don't let us keep you from your lunch. We'll be fine here until the match starts.'

'Then I'll go and fetch us something to have here. I don't want to eat on my own. Any preferences?'

Several minutes later, Jonathan returned with a tray full of various goodies to eat. Rose noticed that he'd included several items that would be easy for her father to eat with his one good hand. Once more she was surprised and touched by his thoughtfulness. Her father was a proud man and wouldn't have touched anything that meant Rose had to help him in public.

As they waited for the match to begin, Jonathan and her father chatted about previous matches. It was the first time she had seen her father looked so animated since his stroke and she sent silent thanks to Jonathan. Doing this had surely been outside expected behaviour for an employer. She guessed it was to repay her for seeing to Lord Hilton. Whatever the reason, Rose knew she was in danger of falling for her boss. Her heart gave a sickening thud. Two more things she'd have to add to her list. Watching a football match from a box and falling in love for the first time.

Despite her father's team losing in the final seconds of the match, it was a good day and Rose was disappointed when it came to an end.

Jonathan drove them home, dissecting the game in excruciating detail with her father while Rose sat back in her seat, allowing their chat to wash over her. She was falling for a man with whom she had nothing in common. Why now? When, even if he could ever feel the same about her, she had no future to offer him? Perhaps it was because she didn't know what the future held that she believed herself in love? If what she was feeling *was* love. It was certainly lust. Infatuation. Every time he smiled her stomach somersaulted. Whenever he was in the room her heart would start pounding and she would feel short of breath.

If he touched her, even the slightest pressure of his hands as he passed her a mug of coffee or a set of notes, her knees would go all rubbery. But it was more than that, she knew, and her heart dropped to her boots. Regardless of his reputation as a womaniser, he was kind and gentle. Would anyone else have given up what he had just to take the ailing father of an employee to a football match? Rose doubted it.

Her mother was waiting for them when they arrived home. She too seemed better for having an afternoon off, although Rose knew that the sight of her father looking as he once had was worth more to her mother than any number of afternoons with her feet up.

Jonathan helped her father settle back into his chair. Rose could hardly look him in the eye in case he read her mind. It would be too mortifying for words if he guessed how she felt.

'I've asked Rose if she'd like to come to a party with me tonight,' Jonathan said suddenly. 'But she's turned me down.' He turned the full voltage of his charm on her mother, who was already putty in his hands.

'Rose?' Her mother turned to her. 'You didn't say no, did you?'

'I can't go, Mum. I'm needed here,' Rose said.

'Don't be silly. We can manage. Besides, you could do with some fun. You've been looking awfully peaky lately.' Rose could see the worry in her mother's searching look.

'And I don't like my staff to look peaky,' Jonathan added. 'I promise you, if you get there and you aren't enjoying yourself, I'll bring you straight home. Or we can miss the party. Do something else.'

Rose capitulated. The truth was, right now she could

think of nothing she wanted more than to have more time with Jonathan. Who knew how many opportunities she had left? If she only had a short time left, this was how she wanted to spend it.

'Okay, you're on,' she said. 'On one condition. Tonight you come with me and meet some of my friends.' She held her breath as she waited for his reply. Whatever he wanted from her, she had to know if it included wanting to spend time with her on her own territory. If he wasn't simply using her as an excuse to avoid whatever demons he had in his life, she needed to know that too.

'You're on.' Jonathan grinned. 'Lead me to it.'

Jonathan sat in the pub feeling, he had to admit, slightly awkward. Rose had been engulfed by a load of her friends and he hadn't seen her for at least ten minutes. Someone, he couldn't remember who, had stuck a pint of beer in his hand and instructed him to drink up. Why was he here? And more importantly, why was he so driven to find out more about Rose Taylor? There were any amount of women he could be dating, ninety nine per cent of them less prickly than her and none of whom would be insisting that he get up and sing. He groaned internally. Apparently getting up on stage was part of the evening entertainment. And Rose had made no attempt to hide her glee when she had told him that he'd be expected to stand up and do his bit. Still, he was damned if he was going to admit defeat. He just prayed that none of the paparazzi had followed him here. Thankfully, it was extremely unlikely. It would never cross their minds that he'd be found in a pub on the outskirts of London.

The pub was packed for a special Scottish themed night,

with people coming from all over London for it. The place was filled with laughter and the chinking of glasses.

Rose squeezed her way into the seat behind him. Instead of the usual tied-back hair she had loosened it until it fell about her shoulders in a sleek glossy wave. Her eyes sparkled and a small smile played on her lips. He had never seen her so animated.

Suddenly there was a call for silence and after a few minutes everyone quietened down. A man Rose had introduced earlier as Jack, an old friend, had climbed onto the make-shift stage and was speaking into a microphone.

"Most of you know Rose,' he said.

There was loud applause as everyone cheered and stamped their feet. Rose blanched slightly and muttered something under her breath. 'What some of you don't know is that Rose composes her own songs and plays the guitar as if she's making love to it.'

There were more wild cheers. Jonathan slid a glance at Rose. She played the guitar. This was the first he had heard of it. And wrote her own songs.

'I know she'll be happy to play us a tune—if we give her a loud cheer.'

There was more applause and stamping of feet. If anything, the uproar was even louder than before. Rose was shaking her head, her hair falling across her crimson-stained face. Then she got to her feet and amid more cheering made her way to the stage.

She took the microphone from Jack's hand. 'Sorry, everyone,' she said into the mike. 'I didn't bring my guitar with me tonight. So I'm afraid I can't play for you.' There was a sigh of disappointment then Jack turned round, holding a guitar which someone had passed to him.

'Sorry, darling,' he said. 'But we just so happen to have one here for you to play. Go on, you can't let everyone down.'

Reluctantly, Rose took the guitar from him. Someone pulled a chair across for her and she sat down, trying a few tentative chords. All the noise dropped away until there was complete silence.

'Okay, I'll play one song for you.' She held up a finger to emphasise her words. 'I'm going to play "*Fear A Bhata*". It's a Gaelic song my mother used to sing to me when I was a little girl. She sang it to me whenever she was missing Scotland, which was often. I'm playing it tonight for everyone who is far from home.'

In the silence Rose strummed a few chords then her husky voice wrapped itself around the packed room. Jonathan didn't need to be able to understand the words to know it was full of longing and loss. The sound of her voice did something to his heartstrings that he'd never experienced before. He was transported to a world where people longed for something they couldn't have. The Rose up there on the stage was a revelation to him. In the place of the shy, mousy Rose he had come to admire and respect was a beautiful woman who sang as if she knew all about heartache and loss. A woman with depths to her he had never guessed existed. A woman he found exciting yet restful. In that moment he knew that he was falling for Rose and the thought scared him witless.

When the final notes of Rose's song had faded away, there was complete silence followed by a burst of applause. There were cries of 'More' but Rose just shook her head and passed the guitar back before stepping off the make-shift stage.

Jonathan was finding it difficult to concentrate. For once he didn't know what to do. She slid back into the seat next to him, her cheeks flushed and her eyes bright.

'You didn't tell me you could sing like that!' Jonathan said.

Rose smiled briefly. 'It's not as if it's ever come up. It's just something I do for fun. When I'm in on my own and it's raining outside. Sometimes, when something touches me, I make up my own songs. I guess it's my way of relaxing.' She glanced at him and he could see the teasing look in her eyes. 'I've never sung in public before. I didn't think I could.' If he had found her interesting before, now he knew he wanted to know everything about this woman who was so unlike anyone he had ever met.

Then there was a sudden movement as chairs and tables were lifted and piled up at the sides. A group of three had taken to the stage. One was carrying an accordion, the other two fiddles.

Rose flashed him a grin. 'Can you dance?' she asked. 'It looks like you're getting away with singing tonight.'

Jonathan breathed a sigh of relief. 'Depends what kind of dancing you're talking about. I do a fairly mean waltz and not a bad foxtrot, but I'm getting the distinct impression that it's not the kind of dancing you're talking about, is it?'

'Nope.' Rose's grin grew wider. 'They do two types of dancing here. One is Scottish country dancing, the other line dancing. You must have learned Scottish country dance at your school in Scotland, surely?' Jonathan felt a wave of relief. They had been taught the formal Scottish dances with their intricate steps. He could do that all right. But, still, there was that suspicious little smile hovering on Rose's lips. It unnerved him.

He stood up and as the band struck up a tune and invited

everyone to take their places for an eight-some reel, he held out his hand to Rose. 'Shall we?' he asked.

But if he'd thought he was going to be dancing a dance that he had learned, he soon found out he was badly mistaken. Oh, the steps were the same, but the pace was quite different. It all happened at breakneck speed and in response to the fervour of the dancers, the band increased their tempo. Soon he was part of a dervish dance where everyone's feet were moving at the speed of light. As he whirled Rose around, her hair fanned out behind her. Then he was dancing with another partner who was forcing him to move ever faster. Not before time, the dance ended and Jonathan was able to get his breath back. But the respite was brief. Immediately the music struck up again. The Canadian barn dance was followed by the Boston two-step and the Highland Scottische. All carried out at break-neck speed. He just gave in to it and soon he found he was enjoying the exhilarating pace and being swept up by the rest of the dancers. For the last dance, the tempo slowed and the band asked everyone to take their partners for a St Bernard's waltz.

He pulled Rose into his arms, breathing in the scent of her as she placed her head on his shoulder. At first she was stiff in his arms, but as the music continued he felt her relax against him. It was strange how they seemed to fit together.

'So what do you think so far?' She raised her face and looked into his face with her amazing china-blue eyes. 'Not your cup of tea, I'm guessing?'

'Then it's clear you don't know me at all, Rose Taylor. How about we go to that party Jessamine mentioned for our next date?'

His words took even him by surprise. Just what was he

getting into here? He felt her pull away, but he wrapped her back in his arms.

'Our next date?' she said, her face flushing. 'But this isn't a date, is it? Just two friends out together.'

'Is that what you really think?' he said. 'Come on, Rose, pretending doesn't suit you. You and I both know that there's more to it than that. I want to get to know the real Rose Taylor and I suspect you're not immune to me either.'

She raised her face to look him directly in the eye. 'We both know that we can't have a relationship,' she said flatly.

'Why not?' he asked.

She looked back at him. 'You know why not,' she said steadily.

'I'm not sure I do.'

'I don't think mixing work and personal life is a good idea.'

'Why? Aren't we doing that now? I'm having a good time. Aren't you?'

'Yes but…' She trailed off, seemingly at a loss for words.

She was thinking she wasn't from his world and he wasn't from hers, Jonathan mused. Admittedly, they had different upbringings, different friends, different lives, but what the hell did it matter? Not to him. It did to her, though. Her expressive face couldn't hide her obvious disapproval of him and the frivolous lifestyle she believed he led. She seemed so sure they had nothing in common. But he had never felt this at ease in a woman's company. And he knew he had never wanted a woman the way he wanted her right now.

'Can't we just go out and have fun? As friends?' he asked, knowing damn well that he had no intention of just staying friends with her. 'Let's just see where this takes us? No promises on either side. Just two people who enjoy each other's company getting to know each other better.'

'I'm not very good at casual relationships, Jonathan,' she said. 'I know it's not very modern, but there you go, that's the way I am. I can do nothing about my background, but I won't change who I am just to suit you.'

'I'm not asking you to. I won't push you to sleep with me if that's what's worrying you.' He was unable to stop himself smiling at the thought of Rose naked in his arms. 'I promise I'll be a perfect gentleman. I'm guessing you could use a friend right now.'

'I do have friends,' Rose protested, waving her hand in the general direction of the room.

'But we can never have too many, can we? Come on, what do you say? Have a little fun. If you don't need friends, you do need something to take your mind off work.' He dropped his voice. 'And what's happening at home.'

If only he knew that what was happening at home wasn't the whole of it. And hadn't she told herself she would make the most of whatever time she had left? Take tonight, for example. Although Jack had tried to get her to sing in public before, she had always refused; the thought had scared her senseless. But then she had remembered her promise to herself and had forced herself to take the guitar. By closing her eyes she had been able to let herself pretend she was back in her room, alone, and once she had started singing she had lost herself in it. She had poured her heart-ache, the loss of her future into the music. And it had felt good. The applause had taken her by surprise; she had almost forgotten there were other people in the room.

When she'd opened her eyes, it had been to meet Jonathan's green eyes looking at her with what? Admiration? Surprise? Something was changing inside her, and she wasn't convinced it was just down to her illness. Somehow being with Jonathan made her feel as if she could do anything. The thought took her breath away. This wasn't supposed to happen. This wasn't part of her plan. But if she couldn't offer him a future, well, neither was he suggesting one. She held out her hand. He looked at her in surprise before enveloping it in his. His hand was cool in hers, his long fingers those of a surgeon. A thrill ran up her spine. More than anything else in the world, she wanted to know what it would feel like to be held in his arms. To have his mouth pressing down on hers. To lose herself in him—even if it was only for a short time.

'Okay.' She found herself smiling. 'I give in. I'll go with you to the party tomorrow.' She wagged a playful finger at him. 'But only because I've never been to a party on a yacht before.'

Jonathan grinned. 'If that's what it takes, I've plenty more types of parties to tempt you with.'

CHAPTER SIX

IT WAS bucketing down, Rose saw as she peered out from her bedroom window the next morning. So much for the start of summer. Her stomach was a mass of butterflies as she thought about the day to come. If she hadn't been so determined to follow through on the promise she had made to herself she would have been tempted to find an excuse not to go. Once again, she wondered if she was admitting the whole truth to herself. It wasn't just her vow to grab life with both hands while she could, it was that the life, just tantalisingly out of her reach, now held Jonathan. Who knew how long he'd be in her life? And she wanted to spend every minute she could with him. She was making memories that would have to last her a lifetime, however long that might be.

Pushing away the morbid thoughts, she considered her meagre wardrobe critically. The trouble was she didn't have the vaguest idea what one was supposed to wear to a party on a yacht. In the end she settled on her standby little black dress she always wore when she needed something more formal than her usual skirts and jeans. The best thing about it was that it was cut in a way that made her bony frame look sophisticatedly curvaceous instead of the sharp angles she was used to seeing.

By the time she had showered and dressed, the rain had stopped and the sun was shining. Maybe the day wouldn't be a complete washout after all.

Jonathan arrived to collect her, looking as sexy as hell in his faded jeans and short-sleeved shirt. He whistled in appreciation when he saw her and Rose was uncomfortably aware of the blush warming her cheeks. With a bit of luck he wouldn't notice.

The first surprise was that the yacht wasn't on the Thames. Jonathan had laughed when he'd noticed her bewilderment.

'I don't think many people keep their boats on the Thames. No, this one is moored off the coast of the Isle of Wight. They're sending the helicopter for us.'

Is that how everyone travelled in his circle? Rose thought a little grumpily. What was wrong with a car, although, come to think of it, getting to the Isle of Wight by road was, of course, impossible. Her head was beginning to ache. It had been a crazy idea to come. She was sure to be completely out of her depth.

Jonathan slid a glance in her direction. His face took on an uncharacteristically sombre expression.

'You're not having second thoughts, are you?' he asked.

It was on the tip of Rose's tongue to say, yes, she was and would he mind just dropping her off at the nearest station? But she bit the words back. She promised herself that she was going to try and be more adventurous and she was damned if she was going to bail out just because she was terrified she wouldn't fit in. After all, what was the worst that could happen? If everyone ignored her, she could…what? Swim back to London?

'I'll look after you, I promise,' Jonathan said. 'They're

really a good bunch of people. Some a bit wilder than others, but nothing too outrageous.'

Giving in to the inevitable, Rose made herself relax. At least, with Jonathan promising to stay close by, she wouldn't be left on her own.

The yacht was unlike anything Rose had ever seen before. For a start it was enormous, almost the length of a football pitch, and all gleaming white lines and stainless steel.

There were a number of people already there. Half of the guests were in bikinis or swimming costumes, the other half were dressed informally in shorts or jeans. Rose felt overdressed and uncomfortable. But there was no way, no way at all, she'd wear a swimming costume to a party, especially this early in the year.

Someone handed them a drink as soon as they stepped on board. Taking a sip, Rose grimaced and, looking around in case anyone was watching her, tipped her drink over the side of the boat. It was far too early to be drinking champagne.

Seconds later, to her dismay, Jonathan was swept up in a crowd and carried away. So much for his promise to watch out for her. To be fair, he wasn't to know just how cripplingly shy and out of her depth she felt right now. Rose leaned against the side of the boat, wondering how long she would have to stay before making her excuses. She knew she should introduce herself to one of the chatting groups, but she just couldn't make her hands let go of the rail.

'Hello.' A soft deep voice broke into her reverie. 'And who are you?'

Rose whirled around to find a blond-haired man with slightly unfocused eyes looking at her. Clearly he had been at the champagne.

'I'm Rose Taylor. Jonathan's nurse,' she said politely, proffering a hand.

'Pleased to meet you, Rose Taylor, Jonathan's nurse. I'm Henry. It's my sister's party.'

Rose craned her neck wondering which one of the guests was Henry's sister. It could have been any of the elegant women clustered on the deck. She could just make out the top of Jonathan's head in the centre of a group of attentive females. As if sensing her eyes on him, he turned and caught her eye and raised a questioning eyebrow. She shook her head slightly. Now someone was talking to her, she was no longer sticking out like a sore thumb.

Henry reached over and lifted Rose's glasses from her face. Her unease mounted as everything around her blurred. She reached for her glasses but Henry grinned and hid them behind his back. 'Hey, you're not bad looking when a person can see your face.' He swayed towards her, breathing the smell of stale alcohol on her face. 'Trust Jonathan to keep you as his little secret.'

Embarrassed and repulsed, Rose stepped back. But Henry stepped closer until she was almost pinned against the side of the boat. Over Henry's shoulder, she looked for Jonathan but all she could see were blurry shapes.

'Please give me my glasses back,' she said as steadily as she could. The last thing she wanted was to cause a scene in front of all these strangers.

Henry waved them in front of her. 'A little kiss in exchange?' he slurred.

Rose snatched the glasses from his hand. At least now she could see properly. Over Henry's shoulder, she caught Jonathan staring at them, frowning. Something in her face must have told him that she was extremely uncomfortable. Within moments he was by her side.

'Hey, Henry. Can I have my guest back?' Jonathan said smoothly. 'I think I should show her around.' He took Rose by the elbow and steered her away.

'Henry is best avoided, I'm afraid. He eats girls like you for breakfast.'

Suddenly furious Rose shook his arm off.

'And what makes you think I can't handle him? Just because I don't mix with the rich and famous every day of my life, it doesn't mean I don't know how to handle snakes like him. If he hadn't taken my glasses and I couldn't see, I wouldn't have needed you to…rescue me.' She almost spat the last words, her mortification at being the centre of attention causing her to direct her fury at Jonathan. She should never have come, no matter what promises she had made herself. Being mortified wasn't on her list of must dos!

Jonathan laughed. Immediately the anger drained from her.

'I should have known better. Of course you could handle Henry. One look from those diamond eyes is enough to cut anyone down to size.'

The world stood still. Jonathan reached over and gently lifted the glasses from her face. 'You do have amazing eyes, you know.'

Rose felt the strength go from her legs. He shouldn't be looking at her like that. It wasn't fair. He was making her feel as if she was just as beautiful as the rest of the women, and that was rubbish. Next to them, she was like a gawky schoolgirl. She snatched her glasses back from his hands. Thankfully everything swam back into focus. Why, oh, why did he have to smile like that?

Desperate for him not to see her blushing, she turned on her heel, almost falling over in the process. Once again, he reached out and grabbed her, steadying her against him. She could feel the heat of his body, smell his aftershave and it was doing all sorts of confusing things to her head. She looked up to find amused eyes looking into hers. Did he know the effect he was having on her? Of course he did. Someone like him would be used to it. She pushed against his chest and drew herself up to her full height. 'You were going to show me around?' she said stiffly, wishing desperately that she could think of something more amusing, more light-hearted to say.

The grin still very much in evidence, Jonathan indicated a flight of steps leading down into the boat with a nod of his head.

'Let's start inside.'

At the bottom of the steps was a sitting area filled with people, laughing and chatting. Jonathan steered her through the group, stopping only to say a brief hello and promising to come back later for a proper chat. But before they could get to the other side of the room, a girl with hair like a silver waterfall ran up to Jonathan and threw her arms around him.

'Darling, I've being looking for you everywhere.' Rose was conscious of curious eyes on her. But she was damned if she was going to let anyone else see how uncomfortable she was. She left Jonathan and wandered off by herself.

Off the main sitting area there were a number of bedrooms which, although small, were kitted out with the latest electronic equipment. Flat-screen TVs and state-of-the-art speakers. Each bedroom had a small but fully equipped bathroom.

She threaded her way back through the main sitting area. Jonathan had disappeared, so she went back up the stairs. The deck wrapped around the boat, and there was a jacuzzi at one end, what was it called? The prow? Several guests were in the jacuzzi, lapping up the sun. A couple of waiters and waitresses circled around, carrying trays of drinks and canapés. Rose helped herself to an orange juice and a tiny tart of something unrecognisable but delicious. Thankfully Henry was nowhere to be seen.

'Here you are,' Jonathan said, appearing at her elbow with the blonde. 'I've been looking all over for you. May I introduce Summer? Summer, this is Rose.'

Well, of course she'd be called Summer with hair like that. The blonde smiled at her, but there was a speculative look in her eyes that made Rose wonder.

'My goodness,' she said. 'Where did you buy your dress? Was it from some vintage market?'

Ouch. Was everyone at this damn party determined to make her feel small? In the past she might have mumbled something and walked away, but that had been before… Before she'd known there were more important things in life to worry about than rude, obnoxious people who had nothing better to do than make themselves feel superior at her expense.

'Yes, it was. How clever of you to know that,' Rose responded. 'I love wearing clothes that other people have loved wearing in the past. It makes me feel as if I know them a little.'

She took in Summer's outfit. The blonde was wearing tights that looked as if they'd been fashioned from the skin of a tiger and a gold lamé dress that just covered her bottom. Although she did look gorgeous, it wasn't the kind of outfit Rose could ever see herself wearing in a hundred years. It was far too trendy and far too short for a start. No, whatever they thought of her clothes, she preferred the simple black dress she was wearing. And if it was a few years out of date, she didn't give a hoot. In fact, she had just about as much as she could take of being given the once over and found wanting. She should have stuck with her original gut instinct and stayed well away. What would she and this crowd ever have in common?

But just as she was searching for the words to make her excuses, a dark-haired girl with an impish expression sidled up to Jonathan and tucked her arm in his.

'I've been admiring your dress ever since you arrived,' she said. 'I'm sure it's exactly like the one I saw last week on the catwalk in Milan. And I have to say, it looks better on you than it did on the model. Don't you think so, Summer?' The new arrival flashed Summer a look from green eyes.

'Rose, could I introduce Lady Ashley, my cousin? Ashley, this is Rose.'

Ashley held out a slim hand and grasped Rose's in a firm grip. 'I'm so very pleased to meet you. Johnny's being telling me all about you. Are you enjoying yourself?' She turned to Summer and said sweetly, 'Summer, I don't suppose you would mind very much grabbing one of the waiters? I'm famished.'

Summer glared at her before stalking off. Ashley winked at Rose. 'She's harmless really. She just has the hots for my dear cousin here. She can't resist having a go at the opposition.'

Opposition? Her? Was she out of her mind?

Out of the corner of her eye, Rose caught a glimpse of Jonathan elbowing his cousin in the ribs.

'And my dear cousin likes to exaggerate,' he drawled. 'I'm sure Summer has no interest in me whatsoever.'

Ashley raised one perfectly groomed eyebrow. 'Don't be naïve, sweetie. You know her type as well as I do. Just because her daddy earns millions, she thinks she should be marrying into aristocracy. And I'm afraid it's you she has her sights on.'

'I'm sure Rose isn't interested in whatever fantasies are filling your brain, Ash.' Although his voice was cool it was evident in the way he looked at his cousin that he held her in very real affection. 'Besides, I've made it perfectly clear that I'm not in the market for a wife. Not now. Maybe never.'

'Hey.' Ashley laid a hand on his arm. 'You mustn't talk like that. Just because Uncle Charles can't stay married for five minutes, it doesn't mean some people don't make a go of it.'

'I think that's enough on that subject for now.' Jonathan's tone was light, but there was a note of warning in his voice. 'So, Rose, have you seen enough? What do you say we get out of here?'

There was nothing that Rose wanted more. But she didn't want to drag Jonathan away from the party. Especially when they'd only been there for an hour.

Suddenly there was a cry of alarm from the other side of the boat. 'David! Help me, someone! Oh, God, I can't see him.'

Jonathan spun away, making for the other side of the boat where a crowd was forming. Rose followed close behind. Everyone was looking down at the water, muttering and pointing.

'David jumped in. I can't see him.' The girl's voice was frantic. 'I told him he'd had too much to drink to even think of going in the water, but he wouldn't listen. God, where is he?'

Jonathan was pulling off his shoes and top.

'Where did he go in?'

The distraught girl pointed. 'He dived in over the side. I think he hit his head. Please, Johnny, help him.'

Jonathan balanced himself on the side of the railings before diving into the water. Everyone waited in silence as he surfaced and looked around wildly. Then he dived again and again, each time coming up and shaking his head. Finally, just as some of the other men were preparing to join him in the water, he rose to the surface again. This time he was holding a body in his arms. Rose held her breath as willing hands hauled them back onto the deck. The man Jonathan had pulled from the sea didn't seem to be breathing. There were cries of distress and alarm. The girl who had called out dropped to her knees and cradled the head of the man in her lap.

'David,' she cried. 'Please wake up. You have to wake up.'

Rose pushed her gently aside. 'Let me have a look,' she said quietly. By this time a sopping-wet Jonathan had joined her on deck. She bent her head and breathed into the unconscious man's mouth. One twice, fifteen times. She watched to see if his chest would move, but it didn't. She looked up to find Jonathan's eyes on hers. She knew he was thinking the same thing she was. They would have to get the water out of his lungs before they could get him breathing again.

Together, they worked to pump the water from his lungs until, to their relief, David coughed, bringing up a large amount of water.

'Has someone called for an ambulance?' Jonathan asked.

'I have,' Ashley replied.

'Okay, I need a hand to get him into the little boat,' Jonathan said. 'Tell the ambulance to meet us at the jetty.'

David had regained consciousness, but looked confused and bewildered. His head was bleeding copiously. Jonathan examined the wound with gentle fingers. 'It's pretty superficial,' he said. 'Does anyone have anything we could use to stop the bleeding?'

Rose ripped a piece of fabric from her dress and used the material to staunch the wound. Oh, well, as Summer had pointed out, it *had* seen better days.

'What happened?' David moaned.

'You idiot,' his girlfriend cried out, before bending over and hugging him. 'You could have killed yourself. If it hadn't been for Jonathan and his friend, you'd be dead. Don't you ever do that to me again.'

Rose touched her on the shoulder. 'David's going to be fine, but we still need to get him to hospital. Inhaling sea water isn't the best thing for a person's lungs. Is there a medical kit on board? I'd like to put a proper bandage on his head.'

A medical kit appeared in Jonathan's hand. He quickly found a bandage and wrapped it around the piece of cloth from Rose's dress. It was crude, but it would do until the ambulance arrived.

Rose led David's distraught girlfriend to the side, while Jonathan and some of the other men lifted the small boat onto the deck and laid him inside. Then Jonathan looked at her, so she moved forward and stepped into the boat.

'As soon as we get this lowered, I'll join you,' Jonathan said.

Rose nodded and hiking her skirt up settled herself in

the boat beside the injured man. In the distance she could hear the wailing of an ambulance.

As soon as the dingy was back in the water, Jonathan let himself down the ladder and joined her. He started the outboard motor and headed the boat back towards land. Rose kept a close eye on David's vital signs, but it seemed as if he was going to be okay. Jonathan was still drenched to the skin but showed no sign of discomfort.

When they reached the shore, the ambulance crew took over. They asked a couple of questions and Jonathan brought them up to date. Soon the ambulance was speeding away with David on board.

'Well, that's one way of ending a party,' Jonathan said grimly, watching the ambulance disappear. 'I guess he's going to have a sore head in the morning. I don't suppose you want to go back?'

'Not on your life,' Rose said vehemently. Then she could have bitten her tongue. She softened her voice. 'Look, it was kind of you to ask me to the party, but all this…' she waved her hand in the general direction of the yacht '…is not really my cup of tea. I'm sure your friends are great but, well, to be honest with you, I think I'd rather be out for a walk and then curl up with a good book. I know it all sounds very boring, but it's what I like.' She smiled. 'An added bonus is that I don't spend too much of my time rescuing my friends after they've jumped into the water under the influence and bashed their heads.'

'Okay, then. Look, no one is expecting you back home for another few hours so why don't we spend the rest of the day together and you can give me another chance? We can do whatever you want to do.'

'Slum it, you mean?'

Jonathan looked offended. 'I wouldn't consider it slumming. For some crazy reason, Rose Taylor, everything you do interests me. I'd also like to show you my other side.' He grinned and Rose's heart flipped. She couldn't believe he was really interested in her. She so wasn't his type and that was okay, it wasn't as if there could ever be anything between them, even if she didn't have this awful thing in her head. And even if he was the most exciting, gorgeous man she had ever met. Anyway, when he realised she truly wasn't kidding about her life, she wouldn't see him for dust. The thought sent her heart crashing to her boots. However awful the day had been so far, she wasn't ready for it to come to an end.

'When do you have to be back?' he asked.

'I'm not expected back until later tonight. One of Mum's friends is coming around for a visit later, and she's offered to help Mum get Dad into bed.'

'I could do with a change of clothes. How would you like to see my country house?' Jonathan grinned at her.

Rose pulled a face. 'Of course you have two houses. Why didn't I think of that?'

'Er, two houses here, plus the family home. I'm afraid there are another couple abroad.' He held up his hands. 'Nothing to do with me. My father collects houses like other people collect hats.'

'What? And just passes them on to you?'

Jonathan looked offended again. 'He gave me the town house. I admit that. Simply to avoid inheritance tax. But the one I'm planning to take you to is all mine. I think you'll find it interesting. Come on, what do you say? In fact, I'd really like your opinion. Ashley tells me I should decorate, but that's not really my forte and I haven't a clue what to do.'

'Why don't you pay an interior designer to do it? Their taste is bound to be much more like yours.' But she couldn't help feeling curious. What kind of house did Jonathan like to call home?

'Okay, then,' she capitulated. 'Why not? But I'm warning you, I'll tell you truly what I think—no messing around. I have to be honest, your town house is not my cup of tea.' She had seen it once when she had brought over some urgent letters for Jonathan to sign. The opulent interior hadn't seemed to fit with the Jonathan she was getting to know.

Jonathan's grin grew wider. 'To tell you the truth, it's not mine either. That's what happened when I let an interior designer loose—that was my cousin's idea—not mine by the way. It's like living in a boutique. Or a hotel. I'm not going to risk that again.'

So a medical secretary, a nurse, now an interior designer. If she wasn't careful, she'd be taking on the role of house-keeper too.

Once they had flown back to London the drive took just under an hour. Jonathan drove fast, but he was a careful driver and Rose settled back and watched the countryside flash past. She still wasn't sure what she was doing or, more to the point, what Jonathan wanted from her.

Eventually he turned into a long sweeping driveway. Instead of following the driveway, Jonathan pulled up outside a small house close to the gates. It was a typical gatehouse of the type Rose had seen at the gates of every stately home she had ever visited—as a fee-paying visitor, that was.

'Here we are,' Jonathan said as he switched off the ignition. 'We can go up to the main house and say hello to Mary later. She's the cook.' His eyes softened. 'Actually, she's a damn sight more than a cook. She's lived in the house since before my mother died. She's been like a second mother to me.'

He opened the door to the gatehouse and stood aside for Rose to enter. There was a small hallway, not much bigger than the one in her parents' house. To the left was a sitting room. It was furnished simply with deep leather sofas and a couple of side tables. There was an open fireplace and in front of it a worn but beautiful rug. All along the side were bookshelves, and directly opposite where they were standing a window seat overlooked the garden. On the walls were more paintings like the ones in Jonathan's consulting rooms. The house was unexpected and a delight. Rose instantly fell in love with the room.

'There's another sitting room through here and a dining room and a kitchen. Upstairs there are three bedrooms.'

Whatever Rose had expected, it wasn't this. Somehow she'd imagined something full of boys' toys, not this cosy little house. It seemed she was constantly getting Jonathan wrong.

'It's perfect,' she said. 'I can't see why you want to redecorate.'

Jonathan looked baffled. 'That's what I keep telling people. But Ashley seems to think it needs to be brought up to date.'

'I wouldn't change a thing,' Rose said adamantly. 'But, of course, it's not my house.'

Jonathan smiled at her and her heart did the strange little somersault it always did whenever he looked at her that way.

'In that case, I'm going to leave it the way it is. I like it. I can put my feet up on the table and I can turn around without worrying I'm going to knock over some ornament or another.' He paused for a moment. 'It feels more like home than any place I've ever lived.'

While Jonathan disappeared to get changed, Rose walked across to the bookshelf. There were the usual classics as well as a number of thrillers. There was also a pile of medical journals on the floor. On the side table was a photograph of a woman and a man. They had their arms wrapped around each other as they picnicked on the lawn. Rose recognised the gatehouse in the background. She picked up the photograph for a better look. The woman was rather plain looking, except for her eyes which were an arresting shade of green. The man could have been a younger Jonathan.

'Your parents?' she asked Jonathan when he returned.

He took the photograph from her and Rose caught her breath at the look of sadness that washed over his face.

'Yes,' he said heavily. 'It was taken on their seventh wedding anniversary. Mother died shortly after that.' He placed the frame back on the table. It was the only photograph in the room. 'It didn't take long for Dad to remarry. Six months, I think it was. He recently divorced his third wife. I guess he's a man who can't stand his own company.'

The bitterness in his voice shook Rose.

'Don't you get on with him?'

Jonathan laughed harshly and turned away from her to look out of the window.

'No. I guess you could say we don't get on. He didn't want me to go in for medicine. He thought as the only son I should take over the family business. I don't think he's ever forgiven me for not doing what he wanted. And I can't forgive him for forgetting about my mother so soon. He could at least have waited a decent period before marrying again.'

'Maybe he wanted to provide some stability for you?

Perhaps he thought he was doing the right thing?' She walked across the room and touched him on the shoulder. 'Perhaps he's never been able to forget her and that's why he keeps marrying?'

Jonathan turned to face her. He ran a finger down her jaw. 'Ah, Rose. Trying to find the best in people all the time. When will you learn that there's not many people like you?'

'Hey, don't make me out to be some kind of saint. It makes me sound so boring.'

'One thing you're not is boring, Rose Taylor.' She held her breath as he tipped her face so he could see into her eyes. She was sure he was going to kiss her and her heart was pounding so hard she could almost hear the rush of blood in her ears. She closed her eyes, anticipating the feel of his lips on hers.

His mouth brushed hers in the lightest of kisses. She opened her eyes to find him looking down at her intently.

'Come on, let's take a walk up to the main house. We can see if there's any dinner going. If not, we'll go back to the village to find a pub. How does that sound?'

What just happened there? Rose thought, bewildered. Had she misread all his signals? It was perfectly possible. Once again she was reminded that she didn't know how men like Jonathan operated. All she did know was that she felt a thudding disappointment.

Jonathan read the confusion in Rose's eyes. She wasn't to know it had taken all his willpower to pull back from her. For the first time ever with a woman he wanted to take it slowly. She was becoming too important for him to rush things. He wanted to woo her gently—take his time, make everything perfect. She was too important to him to treat her as if she were simply another woman he took to his bed. He was beginning to suspect that he had found the missing part to him and the thought filled him with dismay. In his soul, he knew Rose wasn't someone who would love lightly. He owed it to her, and to himself, to be sure he wouldn't hurt her before he let things go any further. He bit back a groan. He had never thought about a future with any woman before, but it seemed finally he might have met the woman who could change his life. He was in deep trouble.

It was a substantial walk up to the house. As they turned a bend in the driveway the house came into view and Rose gasped. It was a beautiful large Georgian house, the facade grand but graceful. There were too many windows to count but Rose guessed that there had to be at least ten, possibly more, bedrooms.

'It's beautiful,' she whispered. 'Quite stunning.'

'I suppose it is,' Jonathan said thoughtfully. 'But to me it's just the house I was brought up in.'

They walked up a number of steps towards an ornate front door and stepped into the hall.

'Anyone at home?' Jonathan called out. 'It's Jonathan.'

His call was greeted with silence. 'Mrs Hammond, the housekeeper, is probably in her office. Let's have a look in the kitchen. Mary, our cook, is always in there. She's probably grabbing a snooze. Dad wanted to retire her years ago, but she won't have it. Says she'll go mad without anything to do. You'll like her. She still bakes every afternoon.' He sniffed the air appreciatively. 'In fact, I'm sure I can smell scones.'

He led her across the hall and down some stairs and along another passage with several doors leading off. 'In my grandparents' day this was the servants' quarters. At that time there were at least twenty people working in the house. Now it's just Mrs Hammond and Mary who live in. A couple of women come from the village every day to help with the cleaning. Most of the rooms are shut up. Dad only keeps the rooms he's using open, unless he has visitors. Then we draft in some more help.'

They followed the smell of baking to the end of the passage and turned left into the largest kitchen Rose had ever seen. There was an enormous old-fashioned range to one side and a huge scrubbed pine table in the centre. On top of the table was a pile of recently baked scones as well as a carrot cake. On the other side was a bowl of chopped vegetables. In the corner of the room was an armchair with a figure that, as he'd anticipated, was sleeping, snoring gently.

Jonathan tiptoed towards the sleeping figure and gently touched her on the arm. The old woman mumbled in her sleep before coming to. Faded grey eyes looked up in confusion, before the woman's face broke into a wide smile.

'Master Jonathan! How many times have I told you not to sneak up on me like that? You'll frighten me to death one of these days. I keep telling you, this old heart can't take surprises.'

'And I keep telling you that there's nothing wrong with your old heart,' Jonathan teased.

'Who is this?' Mary struggled to get up. Jonathan placed a helping hand under her elbow until the older woman had heaved herself to her feet.

'This is Rose. A friend.'

The faded grey eyes grew sharp. 'A friend, huh? You've

never brought a friend down here before. Does she know what she's letting herself in for? And what does Lord Cavendish have to say?'

'Who I'm friends with has nothing to do with my father, Mary.'

Rose stretched her hand out. 'I'm pleased to meet you, Mary. I don't think Lord Cavendish and I are very likely to meet. Jonathan and I aren't that kind of friends.' All the same, she couldn't help feel offended. Cheek.

'Hey, don't mind me, love.' She ruffled Jonathan's hair as if he were about ten years old. 'Jonathan here could do with a good woman. Someone with a bit of heart instead of the type he usually runs around with.' She sniffed disapprovingly.

'Shall I put the kettle on?' Rose offered, not knowing what else to say.

'No, away you go and wait in the drawing room. I'll bring up a tray shortly.'

'I'd rather stay down here, if we won't get in your way,' Rose said. 'It's such a cosy room.'

Mary sent another sharp look Rose's way. Then she seemed to make up her mind. Her mouth turned up in the faintest of smiles.

'I think you might have found a good 'un, Master Jonathan. None of those other women would think of stepping down here to say hello to an old woman. It would be beneath them.' Her eyes grew moist. 'Not like your mother, love. No airs and graces about her. She was never happier than when she was down here, sitting in that chair, chatting away to me, her dress and her hands covered in paint. She'd even roll up her sleeves and tackle a bit of baking when the mood took her. She just laughed when your dad told her it wasn't appropriate.' There was another loud sniff. 'This place has never been the same since she passed away. Bless her soul.' Now Rose knew who had painted the wonderful landscapes that hung on his walls at the surgery and his home. Jonathan's mother had been a wonderfully talented artist.

She sat back down in her chair while Rose put the kettle on the stove and found the tea things.

'You said hello to your father yet, son?' Mary asked Jonathan, while she watched what Rose was doing from the corner of her eye.

'Dad is here?' Jonathan said, sounding surprised. 'I thought he was in America on business.'

'He came back last night. Brought some woman with him. She's staying the weekend, so he tells me. She's already making all sorts of demands as if she owns the place. Get the rooms all opened up! Send to the village for more staff! She won't believe me when I tell her that we can manage perfectly well. She's already wrapped Mrs Hammond around her little finger by saying she needs more help. Well, that's your father for you. There's nothing like an old fool.'

A bell jangled furiously. Mary glanced to her left where a row of old-fashioned bells hung in a row. 'That's her. Probably looking for her afternoon tea in the sitting room.' Mary began to heave herself out of her chair. 'I suppose I'd better get a tray sorted for them.'

'You just stay where you are, Mary. They can wait a moment or two.' Jonathan squatted on his heels next to the old woman. 'Maybe they're right. More help would make life a lot easier for you. I thought you had people in from the village during the day? Where are they?'

'Oh, they're away home. They only do the cleaning. Said that's all they're paid for. And they're right. Mrs Hammond wants to get another cook, someone who's lighter on their feet. Someone who's younger and can manage to take trays up and down all day.' Mary folded her arms and her face took on a mutinous look. 'I'm not going anywhere. I've been here all my life and the only way anyone's going to get me out of here is in a wooden box.'

Although Rose's heart went out to the older woman, she had to hide a smile. She was getting the distinct impression that no one was able to make Mary do anything she didn't want to. This Mrs Hammond, whoever she was, sounded like a sergeant-major. And as for Lord Cavendish's friend, she sounded as if she'd be better off at the Ritz.

'Tell you what, why don't you and Jonathan have your tea and a chat? If you tell me how to fix the tray, I'll take it upstairs for you. I'll introduce myself while I'm at it. And while I'm away, you can tell Jonathan about those chest pains you've been having.'

'How did you know? I mean, what chest pains? There's nothing wrong with me.'

'Yes, there is,' Rose said gently. 'I saw the way you were rubbing your chest when you got up a few moments ago. And you seem a little short of breath. It's probably nothing, but worth getting checked out.' She pretended to look fierce. 'Especially if, as you say, you plan to stick around for a few years yet.'

'Now, Mary. Why didn't you tell me?' Jonathan said, frowning. 'You know I would have come to see you long before now if I'd thought you needed me.'

'Take no notice of Rose. She doesn't know what she's

talking about.' But something in their expressions must have told her that further protests would be a waste of time. 'Oh, well, then, if you have to have a look, go on. But don't you go saying anything to anyone, mind.'

While Jonathan returned to the cottage to fetch his stethoscope, Rose laid the tray under Mary's guidance. 'Just point me in the right direction. I'll be back as soon as I've handed this over.'

'It's the third door on the right at the stop of the stairs.' She paused and her mouth lifted in a smile. 'And if you could tell Lady Muck or whatever her name is that there has never been dandelion tea in my kitchen as long as I've been cook and there's no way it will ever be served here as long as I've breath in my body, I'd appreciate it.'

Rose carried the tray up the sweeping staircase until she got to the top. She smiled to herself. Now waitress was being added to her list of jobs.

She found the room she was looking for. The door was open, so she coughed and entered. A man got to his feet and instantly she recognised Jonathan's father from his photograph. He shared the same arrogant nose and wide mouth as well as thick brown hair with his son.

'Hello?' Lord Cavendish raised an eyebrow. 'You must be new. I don't think I've met you before.' His voice was welcoming, but more than that, to her chagrin, Rose was aware of his eyes sweeping across her body in the most disconcerting way.

'Just leave the tray over there.' The woman who had been looking out the window turned and waved at Rose with a dismissive hand. She was considerably younger than Lord Cavendish, closer to Rose's age, possibly a year or two older.

'I'm not new,' Rose said, placing the tray on a coffee table in front of the sofa. 'I'm here with Jonathan. He's having a look at Mary downstairs. She's not feeling too great, so I offered to bring the tray up for her.'

Lord Cavendish's eyes clouded with concern and something else—could it be surprise?

'Jonathan is here? To see Mary? Why didn't she say she was feeling unwell? I'll go and see her myself.' He hurried out of the room, leaving Rose alone with his guest.

'I'm Rose Taylor,' Rose introduced herself. Cool grey eyes swept over her and this time Rose could tell Lord Cavendish's guest was taking in her clothes, her haircut, assessing the cost and then wondering what on earth she was doing with the son of a lord.

'I work with Jonathan. I'm his nurse.' Now, why had she said that? It was none of this woman's business.

The grey eyes narrowed and she nodded to herself as if something had been cleared up.

'How do you do, Miss Taylor?' The voice was as cool as the eyes and Rose noticed she didn't bother to introduce herself. 'Did cook manage to rustle up some dandelion tea? She certainly had enough time.'

Hadn't this woman taken in a thing Rose had said? For the first time in her life she found herself detesting someone on sight.

'I'm afraid Mary isn't feeling well,' she said stiffly. 'Now, if you'll excuse me, I'll leave you to your tea.'

She found Jonathan and his father deep in conversation. Rose could sense the strained atmosphere between father and son.

'Mary needs to rest, Father. For at least a week, possibly longer.'

'And I've tried to tell her that on more than one occasion, but she won't listen to me.'

'When did you tell her? You've hardly been here over the last six months,' Jonathan said sharply. The two men noticed Rose and stopped their conversation abruptly.

'Father, can I introduce Rose Taylor? Rose, this is my father, Lord Cavendish.' Rose suppressed the inane desire to curtsy.

'I apologise for my lack of manners upstairs,' he said. 'I was anxious to check on Mary myself and to see my son. Who…' he shot a look in Jonathan's direction '…hasn't seen fit to visit for quite some time.'

'Now is not the time or place, Father,' Jonathan said warningly. It was the first time Rose had seen him look so grim. Something was clearly badly wrong between father and son.

'You are quite right, Jonathan. Now, if you'll both excuse me, I'd better find Mrs Hammond and see what can be done to find someone to fill in for Mary while she's resting.'

As soon as he had left, Rose turned to Jonathan. His normal open and cheerful expression was tight. 'How is she?'

'I think she has mild ischaemic heart disease. I want to arrange to have her admitted to hospital for proper tests, but she's not keen. But I've threatened to call an ambulance if she doesn't agree. Father's right. I should have called in here more often, especially when he's away.'

'Look, why don't you make some calls, and I'll go and check on Mary? Add my voice to yours if you think it would make a difference.'

'I'm sorry to have got you mixed up in this.' He grinned ruefully. 'So much for me trying to give you a relaxing day out away from work.'

He looked so regretful Rose's heart went out to him.

'I don't mind being mixed up in this, as you put it. Isn't that what friends are for? To help each other?'

Jonathan looked perplexed. 'Is it?' he said thoughtfully. 'I wouldn't know. I can't say I've ever had to rely on my friends before. They're always there when I need to let off steam and that's all I ever expected from them.' He smiled down at her. 'You're a good person, Rose Taylor. You know that, don't you?'

Ah, well, Rose thought dismally. It was good that Jonathan knew she was his friend—even if he didn't want her as his lover.

She found Mary right at the top of the house, several flights up. The older woman was sitting at the window, looking out at the garden. She folded her arms across her chest and glared at Rose.

'If you have come up here to try and persuade me to go into hospital, you're wasting your time. And you can tell Master Jonathan that from me.' She pursed her lips.

'You will probably only have to go in for a night, two at the most. Just while they do some tests. Then you can come back here, although I'm going to suggest that you move to a room that doesn't require quite as many stairs.'

'There's nowt wrong with this room. I've been in here since the day I started work thirty years ago and I see no reason to move now.' She blinked furiously, but she couldn't quite disguise the moisture in her eyes.

'What is it, Mary? What's truly worrying you? Come on, you can tell me.'

'If I leave here, I'll never come back. That woman down there with Lord Cavendish will persuade him to employ someone younger. I know she will. She's only been here a couple of days and already I can see that's she's imagining herself as the next Lady Cavendish.'

So that was what was worrying the old woman. Somehow Rose knew that Jonathan would never let that happen.

'This place is as much my home as anyone's. I don't have anywhere else to go. The only way I want to leave here is in a box.'

'How long have you been hiding your symptoms, Mary?'

'A month, maybe two. I thought it was indigestion at first. Then the pain started to get worse whenever I had to climb the stairs, so I knew it must be my heart.'

'Why didn't you call Jonathan? You must have known he'd be concerned enough to come and see you straight away.'

'Oh, he's got enough on his plate without me bothering him with my little problems. Anyway…' she leaned across and dropped her voice to a conspiratorial whisper. 'I can't make myself believe he's actually a doctor. Not the boy I've watched grow up. It doesn't seem right somehow.'

Rose pulled up a seat and sat down.

'You seem very fond of him,' she said.

'The poor mite was only little when his mother died. I'm probably the nearest, most constant person he had in his life as a child. Whenever he was home from school, he'd spend more time at the kitchen table with me than upstairs. When he wasn't running around outside, that was.'

'What about Lord Cavendish?'

'He was distraught when Jonathan's mother died. But his way of dealing with it was to throw himself into work. He couldn't see that Jonathan needed him more than ever. Then six months after Jonathan's mother died, Lord Cavendish returned from an overseas trip married to the second Lady Cavendish. That didn't last too long. He divorced the third wife a year or so ago, and now it looks as if he's preparing to marry again.'

'His fourth marriage?' Rose couldn't keep the shock from her voice. 'Surely that's a little excessive?'

'Ah, well. He always did have an eye for the women.' She moved her gaze back to the window and her eyes glistened. 'I don't think he's ever got over the first Lady Cavendish. Now, she was a real lady. Not in the sense of being from aristocracy, you understand, her own background was quite humble, but in terms of knowing how to treat people.' She pointed a gnarled finger to the floor. 'That woman will never compete in a hundred years.'

There was a tap at the door and Jonathan walked into the room. With a guilty start, Rose realised she had been gossiping.

'How's my favourite girl, then?' Jonathan said. 'Has Rose managed to talk you into going to the hospital?'

Before Mary had a chance to protest, Rose interrupted smoothly. 'I think Mary will agree to go to the hospital. She's just a wee bit worried that your father will replace her while she's away.'

It looked as if a thundercloud had descended on Jonathan's face. 'Whatever gave you that idea? I agree you could do with more help, but no one is thinking of replacing you. This house would fall down without you to look after it—and us. You've been here as long as I can remember. It's your home, Mary. Don't ever forget that.'

Mary looked relieved but then her mouth puckered. 'But it's not just to do with you, Master Jonathan, is it? At least, not for some time. Right now your father makes the decisions, and if he marries again, it'll be the new Lady Cavendish's wishes that take precedence.'

'My father might have his faults, Mary, Lord knows, but he'll never agree to replacing you.' His eyes narrowed. 'I had no idea he was planning to marry again.'

'Now, don't you go saying anything,' Mary protested. 'It's not official yet. At least, he's not said as much. It's just I heard his guest speaking on the phone. She was telling them not to make plans for the summer because she was planning a big party.'

Jonathan's lips thinned. 'You leave my father to me, Mary. Come on, I'm going to drive you to the hospital. They're expecting us. If you want to get a few things together, I'll let my father know what's happening.' He turned to Rose. 'I can't apologise enough, but there's only room in my car for Mary and I. If I ask my father to take you to the railway station, would you manage to find your own way home from there?'

'Of course. Really, it's no problem.' She smiled. 'It's far more important that Mary gets investigated, and the sooner the better.' She got to her feet. 'We'll leave you alone to pack your things, Mary. Take your time. There's no rush.'

Jonathan still looked livid when they left Mary. 'I need to go and find my father. It shouldn't take too long. Would you like to wait downstairs?'

'I think I'll take a stroll in the garden while I'm waiting. And if it's inconvenient for your father to take me to the station, perhaps you can call me a taxi?'

'He'll take you,' Jonathan responded grimly. 'One thing you can say about my father is that his manners are impeccable.'

The grounds of the hall were as lavish as the inside. Rose kept close to the house in case she was needed. To her right, a small rose-coloured archway invited her to explore. She dipped her head and entered a small hidden garden. She gasped with pleasure. Someone had taken the time to make this little spot less formal than the rest of the gardens. It was a mass of flowers and the smell of rosemary, lavender and mint drifted up her nostrils. Seeing a bench with views out to the open hills off to one side, Rose took a seat and closed her eyes.

Something was badly wrong between Jonathan and his father. She wondered if he'd have taken her to the house, or even to the gatehouse, if he'd known his father was at home. Somehow she felt sure he wouldn't have. How could someone not get on with their father? Especially when he was the only family member Jonathan had left. Rose couldn't remember ever having cross words with her parents.

She was beginning to realise that Jonathan was a much more complex man than she had ever imagined and she knew that every moment she spent with him she was falling deeper and deeper in love. The realisation was not a welcome one.

Voices drifted from the open window behind her. She recognised Jonathan's and his father's. Both men sounded heated.

'How can you think of marrying yet again?' Jonathan's voice was raised.

'What I choose to do with my life is none of your goddamn business. And speaking of marriage, when are you going to stop seducing every woman on the planet and get into a real relationship? You can't carry on the way you do for the rest of your life. At some point you're going to accept you have responsibilities.'

'That's rich, coming from you.'

Rose got to her feet. The last thing she wanted was to overhear the argument between father and son. She started to edge away from the window.

'What about that prissy little thing you brought with you? She looks like she has a sensible head. Why, for God's sake, can't you find someone like her to settle down with?'

Rose froze in mid-stride. This was so embarrassing. How dare Lord Cavendish refer to her as prissy? Even if she supposed there was an element of truth in the description. But she had to admit she was dying to know how Jonathan would respond.

'Rose? As the future Lady Cavendish?' Jonathan laughed harshly. 'Now you mention it, she'd be a lot more suitable than the last two *you* chose to marry. At least she has brains and a kind heart under that prissy exterior, as you call it. I can tell you she's worth a hundred of the women you married after Mother.'

Lord Cavendish dropped his voice and Rose could hear the sadness and regret in it. 'Why are we always arguing, son? You know I need your help. I'm not getting any younger and running my businesses as well as this estate is getting too much.'

'Are you all right? You've not being feeling ill, have you? When did you last have a check-up?' This time it was Jonathan's voice that was full of concern. Despite their earlier angry words, Rose could tell the two men cared about one another.

'I'm fine. I promise. I'd feel a lot better if I knew that you were settling down. You can't keep on living the way you do. God, man, your name is in the paper every other day. Always with a different woman. You need to get married—have children. I need to know before I die that there is going to be someone to carry on the family line.'

'You're a fine person to talk.' The anger was back in Jonathan's voice. 'Is that why you married Mother? Just to provide an heir for the future? My God, didn't you love her at all?'

'Love her? Of course I loved her. She was the best thing that ever happened to me.'

'Which is why you married again within six months of her death.'

Rose couldn't bear to hear any more. She tiptoed away until she could no longer hear the voices and waited by the front door of the house. She was tingling as she recalled the words Jonathan had used to describe her. Kind and clever. Well, she hoped she was. But she would have liked to hear herself described as beautiful and sexy as well, even if it was untrue. This way she felt like Jonathan's sister and that wasn't how she wanted him to see her at all. She wanted someone to find her exciting and interesting. She wanted *Jonathan* to find her exciting and interesting. If she didn't have a future, she wanted a here and now. And why not? Where had playing safe got her? She felt her blood heat her veins. Prissy. She'd give them prissy. She could be as exciting and interesting as the next woman and with a bit of help—possibly a lot of help—she could do sexy as well. It was as if she'd been sleeping up until the moment she'd realised her life could be snatched away at any time. Now she wanted to wake up and experience life before it was too late. And who better to show her that life than Jonathan Cavendish? After all, it wasn't as if she could break his heart.

CHAPTER SEVEN

'I CAN'T wait for it! Do you think there'll be loads of celebrities there?' Jenny was practically bouncing out of her chair with excitement. Jonathan had informed everyone that he was taking a table at the annual fundraising ball and they were all invited. It had been on the tip of Rose's tongue to refuse, but instead she had found herself agreeing. What harm could it do? And it was one more thing to add to her list. Besides, it was another opportunity to be with Jonathan outside work and although she knew she was storing up heartache for the future, she couldn't bring herself to deny herself a moment of him.

'I get the feeling there will be one or two.' Rose had to smile at Jenny's enthusiasm.

'We'll have to go shopping for something to wear,' Jenny said. 'And you'll have to go to the hairdresser.' She pulled out her mobile. 'You must go to mine. He's fantastic. He'll know exactly what to do with your hair.'

'What's wrong with my hair?' Rose protested. She eyed her colleague doubtfully, recalling the spiky hairdo she usually sported outside her job. If Jenny thought she was going to go punk, she had another think coming.

Jenny looked at Rose thoughtfully. 'I would die for hair

like yours. It's just a little old-fashioned, you know. It could do with an update. In fact, and I don't mean to be rude or anything, the whole of you could do with an update.' She wrinkled her nose. 'That cardigan you're so fond of wearing, for example. That has to go.'

'Hey, there's nothing wrong with it. It's warm and comfortable,' Rose protested.

'And makes it seem as if you're wearing a sack. Come on, Rose. You don't want to look like someone's maiden aunt. Not when all those glamorous people are going to be there.' She held up her hand, cutting Rose's protests off. 'You will not let the side down. I simply won't allow it.'

Dowdy? Someone's maiden aunt? Now she had two more derogatory adjectives to add to the steadily growing list. Up until recently nobody had ever complained about the way she looked. Or complimented her either, she had to admit. But she hadn't minded. Hadn't she always told herself that external appearances weren't important? But this was the new Rose, she reminded herself. The one who was determined to break out of her shell. Hadn't she promised herself to try different things? And if that included a new image, so be it.

By Saturday afternoon, Rose had been done to within an inch of her life. Jenny's hairdresser had cut her hair into a sharp modern style while keeping it long. He had parted it to one side and now it fell over one side of her face. If she had to keep blowing out little puffs of hair so she could see what she was doing—as Jenny had said, what did it matter if she looked chic and alluring? But the hair over her eyes wasn't the only thing obscuring her vision. Jenny had insisted that no way was she allowed to wear her glasses.

She had marched her to the optician and Rose was now trying contact lenses. She finally managed to get them in and blinked furiously as water streamed from her eyes. She'd give them until she had to apply her make-up and if they hadn't settled it was on with the glasses. The last thing she needed was to turn up looking like she had spent the day crying.

She and Jenny had been shopping for a dress and eventually, after what had seemed like hours of tramping around London, had settled on a silky, two-tone red number that shimmered as Rose walked.

'Wow! I had no idea you had a figure like that underneath those dreadful clothes you insist on wearing,' Jenny had said. 'I could diet for a year and still not have a body like that. Why on earth do you cover it up?'

'I'm too thin,' Rose had said. 'I hate the way my bones stick out all over the place. They used to call me pin legs when I was in school. Someone even accused me of being anorexic.' The memory brought painful feelings flooding back. At school she had been teased for being too thin and she had never lost that gawky, unattractive feeling. Now all the worries and anxieties about the way she looked seemed so petty and pointless. And Jenny was right. The dress did amazing things to her figure. The way it hung, the way it moved when she moved. For the first time in her life, Rose felt glamorous.

'And don't even think you're going to get out of buying new underwear,' Jenny had said. 'Are these mum pants or what?'

'There is nothing wrong with my underwear,' Rose protested. 'Okay, they might be serviceable rather than sexy, but who is going to see?'

'Seeing, as you put it, isn't really the point. At least not all of it. If you don't feel sexy under your clothes, how are you going to look sexy?'

Rose had to laugh. She let Jenny steer her to the lingerie department and allowed her to bully her into buying several lacy bras with matching panties. Rose dreaded to think what her credit-card bill was going to be like. But she had to admit she had plenty money in the bank and it was fun. It was the first time she could remember that she had spent so much money on herself. After all, she reminded herself with a stab, who knew if she would ever have the opportunity to dress up like this again? And right now saving her pennies for a rainy day seemed like an exercise in futility. One thing her illness had done was to free her from the small pointless worries of everyday life.

As she finished putting the finishing touches to her make-up, almost the way the girl at the cosmetics counter had shown her, she had to admit that now she was as far away from prissy as it was possible to be. She giggled. All she needed was a cigarette holder in one hand and a glass of champagne in the other, and she'd look like Mata Hari, even though she didn't smoke. And while the contacts had settled, she was sure the famous seductress hadn't blinked quite so often.

She sashayed down the stairs, revelling in the feel of the soft fabric of her dress against her skin.

Her father glanced up when she entered the sitting room and attempted a wolf whistle.

'Can this really be my little girl?' he said, his eyes glistening. 'So grown up and so beautiful?'

Over the last couple of weeks his condition had continued to improve. He was getting about fairly easily with one stick and his speech was less slurred. He was able to manage more of the activities of daily living by himself, even if it still took him twice as long as it used to. Being more independent had cheered him up enormously and Rose knew that soon her parents would be able to cope without her. It lifted some of the burden from her shoulders when she thought about what the future could bring— for them as well as her.

'Yes, Dad. I know it's hard to believe.' She whirled around. 'I find it hard to believe too.'

'I've never seen you so lit up,' her mother said quietly. 'Is it just the night out or is there another reason why you're glowing inside and out?' Rose had made sure her mother didn't see her torment and worry. Around her mother, she forced herself to think only about things that made her happy. Like Jonathan.

He had insisted on sending a car for her. She had tried to protest, saying she'd be quite happy to take the tube, but he had been adamant.

'You and the rest of the gang are my guests. There is no way I'm going to let you arrive on foot.' He had smiled down at her and her heart banged against her ribs. 'Just give in gracefully, kid. For once.'

But she hadn't expected to find him at her door. He looked jaw-droppingly handsome in his dinner suit and bow-tie. When he saw her, he looked taken aback. He bowed briefly from the waist. Then he whistled. 'You look absolutely stunning,' he said. 'Have you had your hair cut? It suits you.' Rose felt a wave of pleasure wash over her. Perhaps he was just being polite, but the look in his eyes told her he meant ever word.

'You don't look so bad yourself,' she quipped.

'I'll just wish your parents good evening,' Jonathan said, stepping inside the small hallway. He was so close she could smell the faint scent of his shampoo and the familiar spice of his aftershave. He touched her briefly on her shoulder and a shiver ran down her spine. 'There are going to be a few women there tonight with their noses severely out of joint. You do know that, don't you?' His breath was like a caress on her skin.

After a few brief words with her parents, he ushered Rose out to the waiting car.

Inside the stretch limousine was an over-excited Jenny, as well as Vicki and her husband. It was another new experience for Rose. There were seats along one side as well as a small bar. Jonathan reached into the bar and brought out a chilled bottle of champagne, which he popped with a flourish. When everyone had their glasses filled he toasted them. 'I hope you all have a great time tonight and remember it's all for a good cause.'

'I'm so glad you could manage,' Rose said to Vicki after she had introduced her husband, Russell. 'How are you feeling?'

'Much better. I don't know how long I'll last, but I couldn't miss it. It's my favourite night of the year. The one and only night I really get to let my hair down.'

Vicki, who had declined the champagne in favour of fresh orange juice, waved her glass at Jonathan. 'Are you going to be auctioned as usual tonight?'

'Not if I can help it,' Jonathan replied. 'I made a deal with the organisers this year. They've agreed I don't have to take part as long as I match the highest bid for one of the other guests.'

'Auctioned?' Jenny said, sounding puzzled. 'What do you mean?'

'Every year at this do they ask some of the eligible

bachelors to agree to auction a date. They have to parade up and down a catwalk while women bid for a date with them. It can get quite heated. At least, it did last year,' Vicki replied, grinning.

'What happened?'

Jonathan was frowning at Vicki, shaking his head from side to side. But she wasn't to be deterred.

'It almost caused a riot. The organiser made Jonathan remove his jacket and shirt. He was allowed to leave his bow-tie on. Not that that gave him much to hide behind.' Vicki chuckled. Jonathan was looking mortified.

Rose almost spluttered into her champagne. The image of a semi-naked Jonathan strolling down a catwalk was almost too much.

'Who won?' Jenny asked.

'That was the best part. It was one of the elderly matrons. You should have seen her excitement when she learned her bid was the highest.'

Everyone, even Jonathan, laughed. 'She actually bought the date for her daughter. I don't know who was more embarrassed, her or me. Still, we had a pleasant enough meal. But I will never do that again. No way. Uhuh.'

By this time they were pulling up outside the hotel where the dinner-dance was to be held. Although the hotel was famous, Rose had never been inside before.

As they climbed out of the car, they were swarmed by photographers.

'Look this way, Jonathan,' they called out. She pulled back inside the car. She hadn't expected this. There was no way she wanted to be photographed, even if it wasn't her they were after.

But she had reckoned without Jonathan. As the rest of

the group made their way into the hotel, he jumped back into the car and pulled the door closed.

'What's wrong?' he asked.

'I don't want to go out there,' Rose whispered. 'I hate having my photograph taken.'

'I don't much like it either,' Jonathan replied, 'but the best way to cope with it is to pose for a couple of photographs and then walk away.'

'I can't.' Rose shook her head.

'Yes, you can,' Jonathan said firmly. 'They are going to want a picture of the amazingly beautiful woman who has arrived with me.' He looked regretful. 'I'm an idiot. If I had thought for one minute that you'd hate the attention, I would have arrived separately. But it's too late now. The more you hide away, the more curious they're going to be. There's nothing else for it. We have to brave the lions in their den.' He grinned. 'Just follow my lead and it'll be over in a few minutes. Okay?'

Rose nodded and, head held high, stepped out of the car. Once again, there was an explosion of blinding flashes.

'Who is your lady friend, Jonathan? Is it serious? Are you settling down?'

Rose's heart sank as she realised that her climbing back into the car had only made matters worse. Now they thought she was someone.

'Hey, guys, give us a break.' Jonathan kept his tone even. 'Ms Taylor is just one of several guests I have with me this evening.'

'Does this mean your relationship with Jessamine Goldsmith is over?' another reporter asked.

'Ms Goldsmith and I are good friends and have never been anything more.'

'So there's no truth that she dumped you because you refused to name the day?'

'None at all. Now, if you'll excuse us,' Jonathan replied smoothly, 'I have guests waiting inside.'

'Could you tell us a bit about yourself, Ms Taylor?' Another reporter thrust his microphone into Rose's face and she almost stumbled. As quick as a flash, Jonathan reached out to steady her with one hand while with the other took hold of the microphone and pushed it away. 'Just carry on walking,' he said into her ear. 'I'll keep them busy.'

'It's okay,' Rose replied, lifting her head again. 'I can deal with this.' She took a deep breath and turned to the journalists with the biggest smile she could manage. 'I'm afraid there isn't much to tell. I work with Dr Cavendish. I'm his practice nurse. As he's told you, I'm one of a party of his staff. Now, I know that you are all interested in what this evening is in aid of. Perhaps you'd like me to bring you up to speed with the work of the charity?'

From the corner of her eye she saw the look of surprise on Jonathan's face, followed by a look of approval. She had made a point of looking the charity up on the Internet during a quiet spell at the clinic. She carried on, inching her way towards the hotel door as she briefly outlined the work of the charity, making sure that she kept smiling. Fortunately it seemed to work. As soon as another car pulled up at the kerb, the reporters turned away to catch the new arrival.

Inside, Jonathan was immediately surrounded by people. Rose left him to greet his friends and acquaintances, and spying Jenny and Victoria from the corner of her eye went over to their table. Jenny's eyes were alive with excitement.

'I've already spotted at least ten famous people,' she told Rose. 'Everywhere I look there is someone whose face I recognise. Isn't this brilliant? I can hardly believe I'm here.' She pointed across the room. 'I saw her film last week. Isn't she beautiful? Even more than she is in her films? And as for that dress, isn't it to die for?'

It was overwhelming. Rose felt drab and shy in the presence of so many well-known people, all of whom looked relaxed and confident. In the crowd she noticed Lady Hilton. Although she had a smile painted on her face, Rose could tell instantly, even from a distance, that she was worried. When she thought no one was looking her smile disappeared, to be replaced with lines of worry around her mouth and eyes. Forgetting her shyness, Rose made her way through the throng until she was by her side.

'Lady Hilton,' she murmured in her ear. 'Are you okay?'

'My dear girl, I didn't know you were coming. It's lovely to see you.' She raised her face for Rose to kiss. Although the older woman's voice was bright, she didn't fool Rose.

'How is Lord Hilton?' she asked quietly.

'Much the same as when you last saw him, my dear.'

As promised, Rose had been making regular trips to their estate to check up on Lord Hilton.

'He insisted I come tonight, even though I told him I'd rather stay with him. But he wouldn't hear of it. He said that the Hiltons had never missed this fundraiser in twenty years and we weren't going to start now.' Sophia smiled wanly. 'You know how much we both owe you, don't you, dear? Without your help we would never have been able to keep him at home. Jonathan's a lucky man. Goodall is with Giles tonight. I'll stay until the auction then I'll go home.' She glanced around the room. 'Where is Jonathan?

I'd like to speak to him.' Her voice regained some of its familiar strength.

It was kind of Sophia to think Jonathan was lucky to have her as a nurse. But Rose knew that the small help she had been able to give the couple had made a difference to the dark days they were facing. It had helped her too. There was a bitter-sweet poignancy in helping the couple through their last days together.

'Why don't you join us at our table?' Rose suggested. Then felt immediately embarrassed. Lady Hilton was bound to have friends to sit with. But, to her surprise, Sophia looked relieved.

'Thank you, my dear. I'd like that. It would save me having to answer questions about my Giles. Everyone means to be kind, but it gets a little difficult.'

'Come on, then.' Rose smiled. 'Let's get you seated and you can rest your feet. Vicki and her husband are at our table too. I'm sure she'd like to see you.'

Lady Hilton seemed glad to see Vicki. Jenny, on the other hand, was struck dumb for the first time Rose could remember. Rose suppressed a smile when Jenny attempted a small curtsy when she was introduced to Lady Hilton, and then, realising what she had done, blushed to the roots of her hair.

'Apparently the auction is going to start before dinner and continue all the way through,' Vicki told everyone at the table. 'There's a list of what's being auctioned under the menu.'

Rose picked up the bound, heavy pages of the auction items. There were cars and weeks on private islands, trips on personal Lear jets, diamonds, paintings and—she smiled—the date with one of London's eligible bachelors. That must be the event Jonathan had told them about. She wished there was something she could afford to bid on, but there was nothing she could afford. She would have to sit back and watch the fun.

'Are you bidding on anything, my dear? I think I'll make an offer on one of the paintings. I usually do and then slip it back into the auction the following year. We have far too many paintings as it is.'

'I'm afraid there is nothing here I can afford,' Rose admitted.

'Lady Hilton, Sophia, what an unexpected pleasure.' Jonathan's voice came from behind her. 'And to have you sit with us is a double honour.'

'I haven't taken your seat, have I?' Lady Hilton. 'If I have, I can easily return to my own table. I'm sure Rose would rather sit next to you than an old lady like me.' Her eyes slid to Rose and the sadness was replaced with a twinkle. 'Doesn't she look beautiful?'

'Yes, she does,' Jonathan replied quietly. 'Easily the most beautiful woman in the room.'

Rose felt a blush steal up her cheeks. But she knew better than to take his words seriously. No doubt it was the way he spoke to all women.

'Unfortunately, I won't be needing my seat for the next hour. Despite my best efforts, Lady Somerville has roped me into the bachelor date auction. She won't take no for an answer.'

Rose stifled a giggle. It was the first time she had seen him look ill at ease.

'Isn't that the thing you were telling us about in the car? The one you said you would never do again?' Jenny leant over, dragging her eyes away from the seemingly endless parade of actresses, models and pop stars.

Jonathan sighed heavily. 'I tried to tell her that I'd match the highest amount bid for any of the men in the auction, but she wouldn't hear of it. She says she needs me to make the numbers up, and I was the highest earner last year.'

'If I had the money, I'd bid for you,' Jenny said stoutly.

'Just remember it's all for a good cause,' Lady Hilton reminded Jonathan.

A woman was waving frantically from the other side of the room, trying to get his attention.

'Looks like I'm up. Wish me luck, everyone.' Then, with a last rueful grimace, Jonathan left them.

'You should bid for him,' Lady Hilton told Rose. 'He could do with a good woman. Someone to settle him down. I know his father worries about him.'

Rose was mortified. Jonathan and her? It was inconceivable. Lady Hilton should know that.

'I hardly think Jonathan and I are suited,' she said, keeping her voice mild.

'Why ever not? Don't you find him good looking and charming? He'll inherit a title when his father dies. Half the women in this room would jump at the chance to be the future Lady Cavendish.' She peered after Jonathan. 'What's wrong with him?'

'There's nothing wrong with him.' Rose wished the floor would open up and swallow her. 'It's just that I'm hardly suited to being the lady of the manor, am I?' And if that wasn't bad enough, she had no future to offer any man. But she wasn't going to talk about that.

'Rubbish, girl. If you think just because you're a commoner, and he belongs to aristocracy, think again. His mother, the current Lord Cavendish's first wife, was a commoner too. Things are changing. And for the better, I would say.' She looked thoughtful for a moment. 'I don't think his father ever got over the death of his first wife. She was the love of his life.'

'What happened to her?'

'She died when Jonathan was five. Pneumonia, would you believe? The poor mite was devastated. His father sent him away to boarding school just when Jonathan needed him most. I don't think Jonathan has ever forgiven him and I suspect he blames him for not noticing how unwell Clara was. How can a child understand that Cavendish sending him away was nothing to do with him? That his father just couldn't cope? The sight of him every day was just too much of a painful reminder. It was the way things were done. I'm not saying it was right. Then his father married again. Within six months. I think it was because he was lonely, but Jonathan never forgave him for that either.'

It explained the tension and anger between Jonathan and his father.

'Why didn't Lord Cavendish explain? Tell his son how he felt?'

Lady Hilton looked surprised. 'Men don't speak of these things, my dear. At least, not then. Oh, I know these days it's the done thing to talk about your feelings, endlessly. But that isn't the way Jonathan and his father were brought up.'

Rose felt a pang for the child Jonathan had been. How terrible to lose your mother and then to be sent away into a strange environment from the only home you had known. What would that do to a grieving child? At least she had always been surrounded by the love of her parents and had always known that they would do anything for her happiness.

There was no more time to talk as everyone was instructed to take their seats by a tall woman with short, platinum-blonde hair.

'That's Mrs Tenant, Rose.' Lady Hilton whispered. 'She used to be a model in the sixties. Her father was enormously wealthy. Perhaps even wealthier than Lord Cavendish. She married for love and she's been blissfully happy. She helps Lady Somerville run the auction. I have to say, between them, they've helped raise hundreds of thousands of pounds over the years.'

Mrs Tenant—Julia—welcomed everyone in a rich Yorkshire accent that was as far away from the plush London tones all around her as it was possible to be.

'We are going to start with the eligible bachelors' auction,' she said after she had spoken briefly about the charity. 'I know this is a favourite event for most of you. Now, we have five men, all single and all looking forward to their dates with the lucky women who win the auction. Don't be mean, anyone. Dig deep into those pockets.'

Everyone settled down, looking towards the runway that had been erected near the front of the room. A hush descended as Julia introduced the first 'bachelor'—a British tennis player who had been taking the country by storm over the last year. He swaggered onto the stage in a pair of tennis shorts and nothing else, looking, Rose thought, extremely self-conscious with a nervous grin on his face. There were a number of wolf whistles as he walked to the edge of the stage and flexed his forearm in a way that had become familiar to millions of tennis fans around the world.

'Who'll start the bidding? Come on, now, ladies, don't be shy. Who'll give me a hundred pounds?'

A sea of arms shot up. 'A hundred and fifty,' came a call

from the back. Rose swivelled around in her seat to find a young woman waving her arms in the air, a bundle of notes in each hand.

'Two hundred,' came another voice. Soon the bidding was up to four hundred and after Julia had promised that the player was throwing in a couple of prime seats for Wimbledon in June, the bidding rose to five hundred pounds before the triumphant girl who had started the bidding won her date.

Three others followed in quick succession. Rose felt sorry for the aristocrat with an unfortunate smile who only managed to raise two hundred pounds and she suspected his mother was behind that.

Jonathan was last to take the stage. He had, or someone had made him, remove his shirt. He strolled up the runway in his dinner trousers, bow-tie and jacket, his exposed chest smooth and muscular. If he felt self-conscious no one would have known from his confident grin. Rose felt a shiver run down her spine. He really was the sexiest man she had ever known.

The bidding started at three hundred pounds and quickly rose to five hundred.

'Come on, ladies. You can do better than that. Jonathan is one of London's most eligible bachelors. As far as I'm aware, there is no one in his life at the moment.'

The bidding rose by another hundred pounds. And even further. Suddenly, Lady Hilton's hand shot up. 'One thousand pounds,' she said firmly. Rose looked at the old lady in astonishment and was even more surprised when she received a saucy wink in response.

'One thousand pounds. Sold to Lady Hilton,' Julia said with a flourish. 'A new record.'

As she thanked everyone and the music faded away, Jenny and Vicki turned surprised faces towards Lady Hilton, who leaned closer to Rose and whispered in a conspiratorial voice, 'I bought him for you, dear.'

'Me?' Rose squeaked, thinking that Lady Hilton had lost her marbles. 'Whatever for?'

She leaned over and took Rose's hand in one of hers. 'Because I think you're right for each other, that's why. Even if he can't see it yet.'

Lady Hilton hadn't a clue how wrong she was. Rose was hardly the catch of the century. Even if she didn't have an uncertain future, unable to have children, bookish, what would anyone ever see in her? Let alone a man like Jonathan, who had dated some of the most beautiful and confident women in the world? Her heart stumbled. She'd enjoyed Jonathan's company over the last few weeks. More than enjoyed it, but soon it would be over. She'd be leaving, going back to her life in Edinburgh, whatever she decided to do about the operation. Her empty life, she thought miserably. She had been happy with it once, but that had been before Jonathan. Now she knew, however long she lived, her life would be lonely and grey without him.

Jonathan, who had replaced his shirt, slipped into the chair beside her. 'Thank God, that's over,' he said. 'I think I might just make my excuses for next year. But thank you, Sophia, for making the winning bid. Where would you like me to take you? Horseracing? To a polo match? I know you love both.'

Lady Hilton smiled wryly. 'As much as I'd like to go somewhere with you, Jonathan, I rather suspect that this will be my last outing for a while.' She turned her head to the side, but not before Rose saw a tear slip down her cheek. 'That's why I've passed my date on to Rose here. I know she's been working hard. Not least as she keeps popping in to see how we are, bless her. And I don't think polo or the racecourse is altogether what's needed. I need you to come up with something much more…' she hesitated. 'Appropriate for Rose.'

Rose was thoroughly embarrassed. Imagine Jonathan being tasked with taking her out as if she were a bag of shopping or a pet requiring to be walked. It was too much.

'There's no need at all to take me out,' she muttered into his ear. 'But perhaps we should pretend—as if it's ever going to happen—for Lady Hilton's sake?'

Jonathan grinned and Rose's heart pinged.

'I'm not one to back out of anything,' he said into her ear. She felt his warm breath on the nape of her neck and a delicious thrill ran down her spine. Goose-bumps prickled her arms, making her shiver. 'And I didn't have you down as a quitter either,' he continued. 'In the meantime…' he held out a hand '…shall we dance?'

Almost in a daze, Rose let him lead her to the dance floor. Thankfully she knew how to waltz. Memories of her father twirling her and her mother around their small sitting room to the music of Mozart and Strauss brought a lump to her throat. She had never dreamed she would be putting it into practice in such a setting.

Jonathan held her tightly. She could smell his after-shave and feel the hard muscles of his chest against her head. An image of his bare chest, tanned, defined muscles made her want to groan out loud. Who would have ever suspected he had a body like that? All that polo playing must help. She pushed the thought of heavily muscled thighs away before she became any more flustered.

She looked into his eyes. He looked back and her world tipped. Damn the man. Damn everything. Why did she have to go and fall for him? And why did she have to be facing an uncertain future? Why? Why? Why?

'You are the most beautiful woman in the room tonight and the most remarkable,' Jonathan whispered into her hair.

All at once, Rose had had enough. If Jonathan thought he could play games with her he had another think coming. No matter how she felt about him. *Particularly* because of how she felt about him.

She pulled away from him so she could see his face. 'What do you want from me, Jonathan?' she asked.

'What do you mean?' he asked as he whirled around the dance floor.

'I'm not the woman for you, believe me.'

He frowned. 'Don't you think I should be the judge of that? Believe me, Rose Taylor. You're exactly the woman for me.' He paused by a door leading outside and pulled her into the fresh evening air. The scent of climbing roses drifted up her nostrils, intoxicating her.

Jonathan's finger stroked her hair away from her face. 'I don't think you have any idea just how lovely you are.' He smiled. 'But it's not just the way you look, you're a very special woman, Rose. Don't you know that? I can't believe that no one has won your heart yet.' He frowned and a shadow passed across his face. 'Or has someone? Of course. What an idiot I've been. There's bound to be someone back in Edinburgh, waiting for you. God, do you love him? Would you dump him? Come out with me instead?' His smile was warm and tender. 'I promise you, you won't regret it.'

Rose's head was swirling. There was nothing she

wanted more right now than to tell him that there was no one else and, yes, she would go out with him. Every day for the rest of her life. However long that would be. But she couldn't. It wasn't fair to her or to him. All at once she knew he was falling in love with her and it made her heart soar, but she also knew she already cared too much to deny him the happy-ever-after ending he deserved.

'There's no future for us,' she said bleakly.

'So there is someone else.'

Rose hesitated. It would be easier to let him believe that. But she wasn't going to lie to him. Even if she couldn't tell him the truth.

'No, there isn't anyone.'

'In that case, I'm not going to take no for an answer. I owe you a date. And a date is what we're going to go on. Like it or not.' Although he smiled, Rose sensed the determination behind his words. And even though she knew she should avoid him, for his sake if not hers, she couldn't resist the temptation. Another memory. A few more moments with Jonathan to store away like a squirrel.

'Okay, then. If you insist, I'll go out with you. I guess it's not really a date anyway.' She tried to sound casual.

'Not really a date,' Jonathan muttered under his breath. 'If I insist? Well, I do insist. So that's sorted. This weekend. I'll let you know when and where later.'

Back at his flat, Jonathan prowled around restlessly. What was it about Rose that had got under his skin? Okay, so she was beautiful, but God knew he had dated beautiful women before. Even a supermodel. No, it wasn't that. It was her. That dogged air of determination mixed with an underlying vulnerability and genuineness that he had never come across before. She wasn't the least bit interested in his title or his wealth. She wasn't bowled over by him the way most women were. In fact, she gave the distinct impression she was unimpressed by him, almost disapproving.

That probably hit the nail on the head. She probably thought he didn't have a serious, committed bone in his body. And what was wrong with that? Wasn't it important to have fun in life? There would be plenty time for settling down in the future. A shiver of revulsion ran through him. The words 'settling down' and 'Jonathan Cavendish' didn't really go in the same sentence. Hell, he just had to look at his father and his serial marriages to know what a waste of time getting married was. He had a damn cheek to accuse him of a lack of commitment and responsibility. Look at the way he had treated his mother. She had hardly been cold before he had taken up with some one new. What kind of recommendation for married life was that?

But Rose was different. He suspected when she gave her heart, it would be for keeps. And the man she gave it to would have to be deserving. She was a challenge. That was it. That was the true reason he was attracted to her. Never before had he been turned down by a woman and it wasn't going to happen now. He would take her on the kind of date that she would like. Something that would convince her that he saw her for who she was and not just another woman. It was obvious that parties on yachts weren't for her. What did she say she liked? Being outdoors. Long walks, sitting in with a book when it was raining outside. Playing her guitar. What else? Picnicking.

He had gone about trying to impress her the wrong way. When they went for their date, he would show her he was sensitive and thoughtful and that he didn't need wild parties or crowds of people. He sat down on a chair by the window and looked out at the lights of London below. An idea was beginning to form in his head. He thought he knew exactly where to take her. Somewhere she would get to know the real Jonathan Cavendish.

CHAPTER EIGHT

JONATHAN collected Rose, as promised, on Saturday morning. He came in and spent a few minutes making small talk with her parents, accepting a cup of coffee from Rose's mother and engaging her father in a dissection of the latest football results.

'Just let me know when you fancy going to another match. I can always get tickets.' He paused. 'I don't suppose you're a cricket fan, are you? I've a couple of tickets for Lords next weekend.'

Rose suppressed a groan. If anything, her father preferred cricket to football. If the two of them started talking cricket, goodness knew when it would stop. She was delighted in her father's improvement. Managing at the football match had given him a lift. Every day he was more like the man he had been before the stroke and for that alone she could have kissed Jonathan.

'Now, you two. That's enough talk about cricket. Shouldn't you and Rose be getting on your way?' Rose's mother stepped in.

Jonathan rose to his feet. 'You know my flat actually overlooks Lords. Why don't you come to lunch the next time there's a match on? We get a great view from the drawing-room window.'

Rose's father slid a glance at his daughter. She knew he would love to go, but didn't want to agree without knowing how his daughter felt about it.

'It's up to you, Dad,' she said. But she gave him a small shake of her head. She really didn't want to be any more beholden to Jonathan than they already were. Despite her best intentions, they were being drawn increasingly into Jonathan's life, and she had to remember that no good could come of it.

'One day perhaps, son,' Rose's father answered.

'Any time, at all. Just let Rose know.' Jonathan jumped to his feet. 'I'll have your daughter back before it gets too late.'

She was back in a time warp. Get her home before it gets too late indeed. Who did he think she was? Cinderella?

'Don't wait up, Mum, Dad. It's just possible I'll go the pub and catch up with the gang when we get back.' Put that in your pipe and smoke it, she thought, pleased that she had made the point. She would decide when she came home. Not him.

'Where are we going?' Rose asked as they sped up the motorway, heading north. She hadn't known what to wear. He could be taking her anywhere, another party, lunch with some of his friends, anywhere. Not knowing, she had decided on a simple summer dress, hoping that it would see her through most eventualities. Her glasses were back in place as, try as she would, she still didn't quite have the hang of the contact lenses. But at least with her glasses she could see, and with her hair tied back in its usual plait, she felt collected and in control.

'You'll have to wait and see,' Jonathan said obliquely. 'I had the damnedest time trying to decide where to take you, but I hope I've got it right.'

'As long as I'm appropriately dressed, I don't care.'

'You would be appropriately dressed even if you wore a sack,' Jonathan replied.

Huh. More of his empty compliments. If she wore a sack, she would look like a bag lady. Who was he trying to kid? On the other hand, Jonathan would look perfectly at home where ever they went. Even in the faded jeans and open-necked, short-sleeved shirt he was wearing. A lock of hair flopped across his forehead and he kept brushing it away as he drove.

After an hour he turned off the motorway and onto a road bordered by fields which, in turn, gave way to a smattering of houses. A sign welcomed them to Cambridge.

'I don't know if this was the right place to take you,' he said. 'But I thought we could hire a punt and stop along the bank for a picnic. I used to do that regularly when I was a student here and I know just the place where we can tie up the boat.'

He looks nervous, Rose thought, her heart melting. She liked this more vulnerable side to him.

'Just as well it's not bucketing with rain, then.' She smiled to let him know she was teasing. 'Isn't this pretty close to where you live?'

'Yes. Cavendish House is just over half an hour to the west. And don't worry, if it had rained, I would have come up with another plan.'

'And the picnic? Did you make it yourself?'

He shook his head, looking sheepish. 'I had it delivered from Harrods.' Then they both laughed. 'Sorry, I guess old habits die hard. But, honestly, Rose, I don't think you would have found anything I made edible.'

He parked the car close to the river, near the town centre.

Rose was curious. She knew little about Cambridge other than that it was a famous university town and people punted on the river. 'Show me the college you went to,' she said. She really wanted to know more about him.

He looked perplexed. 'Are you sure you're interested? They all look pretty much the same really.'

'Not to me they don't. I'd love to see where Newton, Darwin and Wordsworth lived and worked. And all the others. Go on. Indulge me.'

He bowed from the waist. 'Your wish is my command. Come on, then. I went to Trinity. In fact, we can hire a punt from there. It's in the main street. Let's see if the porters remember me. They might even let me have a look at the room I was in.' He looked pleased, Rose thought. As if he wasn't used to anyone taking an interest.

He took her by the hand and led her down streets, past several modern buildings and ancient colleges. Rose kept swivelling her head to look at buildings, a round church, a medieval house, but Jonathan propelled her on.

'I want to show you the Bridge of Sighs first,' he said. He was like an excited schoolboy and Rose warmed to this new side of him. He was constantly challenging her pre-conceptions of him.

'It connects the older part of St John's College to the newer part.' He pulled her through heavy wooden gates, past the porter's lodge and into a courtyard. Rose stopped in her tracks. Elegant buildings with intricate stained-glass windows looked down from every side. Students scurried about chatting, books under their arms, oblivious to their surroundings.

'Wow,' she breathed. 'I think if I came here to study I'd never get any work done. I'd just want to sit and take in my surroundings.'

Jonathan looked at her strangely. 'I suppose it is magnificent,' he said. 'I guess I stopped seeing it after a while.' His mouth turned up at the corners in the way that always made her knees go weak. 'I love seeing it all through your eyes. It's like I never really saw it before.'

Rose's heart squeezed. Why did he keep saying those things? Making her believe he could love her?

'Come on,' he said. 'It gets better.' He led her through another archway that led onto a covered bridge. The stone bridge was intricately carved. Someone must have spent years working on it. Her father would love to see it, as only one artisan could really appreciate the work of another.

'I can see why it's called the Bridge of Sighs,' Rose said. 'It's so beautiful, you just want to sigh with pleasure when you see it.'

'It's named after the Bridge of Sighs in Venice,' Jonathan told her. 'People think it's a copy but, apart from the romanticism of the two bridges, all they have in common is that they are both covered.'

'Hey, don't spoil it for me. Imagine being able to do that.' Rose half smiled. 'I love that so I'll have one built just like it where I live.' She turned to Jonathan. 'That's the kind of world you live in,' she said softly. 'Where money and position makes anything possible.'

'You don't approve?'

'I don't approve or disapprove. I just can't imagine ever being in that position.' And that was the truth. Her world and Jonathan's were miles apart. They could have come from different planets for all they had in common.

'We're not so different, really, you and I, Rose.' Jonathan lifted his hand and tipped her chin until she was looking directly in his eyes.

Strange feelings were fizzing around inside Rose, making her breathless. What was he doing? Was he *trying* to make her fall in love with him? Didn't he know he had already succeeded? She pulled away, putting distance between them. If she stayed near him, she knew she wouldn't be able to stop herself from winding her arms around his neck.

'So where's the college you went to? What did you say it was called?'

'Trinity. We can get to it this way.' He took her hand again and led her towards a building covered in what looked like ivy, but which was what Jonathan told her was Virginia creeper. He pointed upwards. 'My last room was up there. It had a view of the river. Come and see the chapel.'

The chapel was breathtaking with its high arched ceilings and stained-glass windows. Pews lined either side, with a candle at each seat. Rose could imagine evening service, especially in the winter with the snow lying thickly outside and the music of the choir in the soft candlelight. She could appreciate the history in every stone, every worn flagstone and see, in her mind's eye, the centuries of scholars who had walked down the aisle before her.

'Seen enough?' Jonathan said quietly. He had been standing behind her, watching her closely.

She nodded. The more she knew about Jonathan the more she knew how much she wished things could have been different. The Jonathan she was learning about was someone she could imagine a future with. If she had one. The knowledge that soon she would be leaving, probably never to see him again, was tearing her up inside.

'If you want to look around some more, I'll just get the picnic from the car. When you've seen enough, wait for me down by the river. I'll only be a few minutes.'

Rose wandered around, torn up inside. In this chapel she could let herself hope that somehow everything would work out fine and that some kind of miracle would happen, freeing her from the threat of death hanging over her, giving her back her future. But she couldn't let herself think like that. Even if this thing inside her head never changed, even if she lived a long time, she still couldn't ever risk having children.

Pain lanced through her. She would have loved babies. Two, maybe three. Why did life have to be so unfair? She shook her head, angrily brushing away the tears that stung her eyes. There was no point in feeling sorry for herself. She had to stay positive. Back in Edinburgh she had a job she loved, many friends and her music. It was entirely possible that she would have many years in front of her to enjoy life. That would have to be enough. She would *make* it enough. Even if it was to be a life without children—or Jonathan.

By the time she made her way down to the river bank, she had managed to get her emotions back under control and when Jonathan appeared with the picnic basket, she laughed. Grief, how many did he think he was catering for? She couldn't help but look past him, half expecting a stream of his friends to be following close behind. But, no, it seemed as if it really was just the two of them.

'What on earth have you got in there? A kitchen sink? The kitchen?'

'I don't know, but it's damned heavy. They kept on asking me what I wanted and I didn't have a clue, so I said yes to everything. They did say there was wine, plates, a tablecloth. For all I know, they've stuck a set of tables and chairs in there while they were at it.'

'As long as the weight doesn't sink us.'

'Nope, we should be fine.' He lugged the basket down to the bank of the river. After a few words with the person hiring out the punts Jonathan jumped into one and set the basket down. He then helped Rose into the boat. She was delighted to find that her seat was padded and comfortable. She sat back, trailing her hand in the water as Jonathan balanced on the other end of the punt, using the long pole to push away from the side of the river.

Rose closed her eyes, letting the sun warm her face and allowing the gentle splash of water as Jonathan pushed them along to soothe her. They passed under overhanging trees of willows, their long branches reaching into the river. Rose was pleasantly surprised. This was exactly the kind of day out she loved. Jonathan had got it exactly right. It seemed she was always having to reassess her opinion of him. And the more she found out about him, the deeper she fell in love. Her heart contracted with the pain of it. How was she going to find the strength to leave him when the time came? She pushed the thought away, not wanting to spoil another moment of whatever time she had left with him.

'Aren't you going to serenade me?' she asked, looking at him through slitted eyes. 'Isn't that a necessary part of the deal?'

'You obviously haven't heard me sing, or you wouldn't be suggesting it.' He grinned back. 'But you can sing well enough for both of us.'

She shook her head sleepily. 'I can't sing without my guitar. Don't know why. Maybe it's because it gives me something to hide behind.'

As soon as the words were out, she could have bitten her tongue.

Jonathan looked at her curiously. 'Why would you want to hide? Do you truly not know how beautiful you are?'

Rose snorted. 'Nice try, Jonathan, but save the compliments for someone who believes them.'

'Has anyone ever told you that you are the most exasperating woman? Or that when someone gives you a compliment, a sincere compliment, you should accept it with good grace?'

'In which case, thank you, kind sir. And has anyone ever told you that you have a fine punting action?'

Jonathan laughed and passed a hand across his forehead. 'It's much warmer than I thought it would be. Would you mind if I took my shirt off?'

Ever the gentleman. All the men of Rose's acquaintance would have removed their shirts whenever they felt like it. But as Jonathan shrugged out of his, she bit down on her lip. Maybe she should have insisted he keep it on. Now she was going to have to keep her eyes averted from his chest lest he read some of the thoughts that were going through her head. She smiled. A man like Jonathan probably had a very good idea of was going through her mind.

'Would you like to try?' he asked. 'It's really very easy.'

'Sure,' Rose said.

'Okay, come over to where I am.'

Rose picked her way to the stern of the boat, where Jonathan was standing. As she came alongside him, the boat wobbled. In a flash Jonathan wrapped his arm around her waist to steady her. A tingling sensation started in her waist and was soon fizzing around her body. Just for a second she let herself breath in heady scent of his aftershave mixed with the masculine smell of his sweat. Then he released her gently.

'Stand with your legs slightly apart for balance. Then you push the pole all the way down until it touches the bottom. Push hard then pull it all the way up. No, that's not enough.' His hands were on hers, guiding them, and she could feel the heat of his body as he stood behind her. It was making her flustered. 'You have to pull the pole through your hands until you're almost gripping the bottom. And if you want to steer, you push the pole, when it's in the water, to the left or the right. Got it?'

It was much more difficult than Jonathan had made it look. The pole was heavy, unwieldy and Rose was glad Jonathan stayed where he was to help her. Nevertheless, she was determined to do it on her own, and after a little while she got into a rhythm.

'I can manage by myself from here on,' she told Jonathan. 'You sit down.'

'Er, are you sure? It can be hard work.'

She turned to look into his face. 'I can do this. Now, scoot. Go and relax.'

Okay, so their progress wasn't quite as smooth as it had been. The punt had a disconcerting habit of weaving from one side of the river bank to another, almost as if the damn thing had a life of its own, but at least she hadn't crashed it, and they were heading in the right general direction.

'The bridge we're passing under now is called the mathematical bridge,' Jonathan said. Rose allowed herself a quick glance up and away from what she was doing. The bridge was an odd-looking wooden affair, as if a child had taken giant wooden Meccano and stuck it all together. It didn't look very mathematical.

'Why do they call it that?'

'I'm not absolutely sure. Rumour has it that it was originally put together without nuts and bolts and a mathematician at one of the colleges wanted to know how it was done. So he pulled it apart. Only he couldn't get it to go back together without nuts and bolts.'

Rose peered at the bridge again, trying to see better. But with her attention distracted, she suddenly realised that she had forgotten to lift the pole from the water and it was now behind her. Panicking lest she drop the pole into the river, she held on for dear life. But all that happened was that she was pulled out of the punt and into the water.

She shrieked as she was submerged in water the colour of pea soup. Disoriented, she bobbed to the surface, gasping.

Jonathan had retrieved an oar from the bottom of the punt and was making his way back to her.

'You should have told me you fancied a swim,' he said, reaching an arm out to her. 'I would have found a better place.'

Rose was mortified and scowled when she saw the broad grin on his face.

She grabbed his hand and found herself unceremoniously hauled back into the punt where she lay gasping like a fish that had just been landed.

'Are you okay?' Jonathan had lost the smile and was looking concerned. But Rose could have sworn there was a hint of laughter in his words.

'Apart from the fact I feel like a prize idiot and that I'm soaked, yes, I'm fine. You could even say I've never been better.' She glared at him, but then despite herself she had to laugh. It hadn't been Jonathan's fault and from his point of view it must have been funny.

Jonathan retrieved the pole from the water.

'Shall we go back?'

'I'd rather get dried out first. I don't fancy having to walk through Cambridge town centre like this.'

'The place I was going to stop is just a little further.'

A few metres on and Rose was being helped out of the punt onto dry land. Jonathan heaved the picnic basket on shore and opened it. He pulled out a white linen tablecloth.

'Take this,' he said 'Remove your wet things and wrap this around you.' He pointed to some trees. 'There's a little hollow over there. You can't be seen unless someone actually stands over you. Your things will dry out in the sun.'

It was getting worse and worse. But Rose knew the sensible thing was to do as he suggested. The alternative, waiting for her clothes to dry while she was actually in them, wasn't really an option. She would freeze.

In the relative privacy of the hollow, she slipped out of her sundress. Leaving on her bra and pants, she wrapped the sheet around her toga style. Making sure the ends were firmly tucked in, she laid her dress on the grass to dry. At least she had taken her shoes off when she had first stepped on to the punt, otherwise they'd be ruined.

By the time she returned, Jonathan had emptied the picnic basket. He raised an eye at her unconventional outfit before opening a Thermos flask and pouring a cup of steaming-hot coffee.

'Here, this will warm you up.' Then he laughed. 'You look like a Greek goddess in that get-up.'

Rose squirmed with embarrassment under his gaze. Greek goddess, her foot. More like a drowned rat, she would have thought.

He handed her his shirt. 'Put this round your shoulders. It will help keep you warm.'

Rose shrugged into the shirt, which smelled faintly of

him. It came to just above her knees and realising it would cover the essentials she slithered out of the tablecloth. Now she felt almost normal again. She used the tablecloth to blot the worst of the river from her hair.

'So much for the tablecloth, I'm afraid.' She laid it next to her dress. The sun would dry it along with her clothes.

'You're still cold.' Jonathan reached out and took her feet in his hands. He began massaging them with the pads of his thumbs. Delicious ripples ran from her feet before pooling in her belly. She tried to pull her feet away, but Jonathan held them firmly. Giving up, she relaxed, propping herself on her elbows and closing her eyes, giving in to the interesting sensations his touch was provoking. The sun emerged from the clouds, warming her face. In the distance she could hear laughter as children played and the gentle sound of the breeze through the leaves of the tree. In all her dreams she would never have imagined this scenario. She and Jonathan, just the two of them, as if they were meant to be together, for ever. If she had known, she would have run and kept on running. Fate was cruel. To show her love now, to give her a glimpse of what might have been, was so unfair.

'That's better,' Jonathan said, releasing her feet. 'Now, what about something to eat?'

Rose wasn't sure whether she could eat anything. Her mouth was as dry as dust. She nodded, not trusting herself to speak. Jonathan unpacked the basket, laying out a bottle of wine, glasses, china plates and cutlery. Next came the food. There were tiny quiches, olives, crusty bread, cheese, cold meats. As Rose had suspected, there was enough to feed an army. Her mouth began to water. It had been a long time since breakfast.

Jonathan lifted an olive. 'You like?' he asked with a quirk of his lips. Rose nodded.

He held the olive to her lips. Her eyes looked into his and her breath stopped in her throat as her chest tightened. Involuntarily her lips parted and he popped the olive into her mouth. He watched as she chewed slowly, never taking his eyes off her. Rose's heart was beating like a pneumatic drill and she couldn't believe he didn't hear it. He trailed a finger across her lips, catching a slick of olive oil. Then slowly, ever so slowly, he leaned forward and placed his mouth gently on hers. Her head swam as she tasted him. The firm pressure of his mouth. His tongue flicking across hers. He groaned and pulled her into his arms where she rested between his long legs. His kisses grew more demanding. Rose gave in to the sensations coursing through her body, returning kiss for kiss. Letting her hands drift behind his head to pull him closer, revelling in the taste of him, the warmth of his skin, the solid strength of his muscles.

He trailed a hand across her neck, sending sparks of desire coursing through her. His hand slipped under the shirt she was wearing, searching, caressing her skin until she thought she would go mad with her need from him.

They lay down, stretching their bodies along each other, straining to meet along their whole length. She could feel the hardness of his desire for her against her hips and she shifted her body so that she fitted against him perfectly.

'I've never met anyone like you,' Jonathan said eventually. 'I can't believe I've lived almost thirty years without meeting you. I think I've been looking for you all my life.'

A cold breeze fluttered down Rose's spine. This wasn't supposed to happen. She wasn't supposed to fall in love with him, or him with her. It was meant to be harmless fun.

No broken hearts on either side. A few more days, then she'd be out of his life for good. The sun vanished behind a cloud. She shivered.

'You're cold,' Jonathan said. He reached out a hand and pulled her to her feet. 'Why don't we take the rest of this back to my place? I can light a fire, and we can eat the rest of the picnic in bed.' His eyes were glowing. There was no mistaking his intent. His green eyes were dark, almost pleading.

Rose knew she should run, but she also knew she couldn't. If all she had was this one night, then she had to have it. She could no more deny herself than fly to the moon.

Jonathan watched as Rose packed the food back into the basket. When he had seen her emerge from behind the tree, her damp hair in disarray, he had thought he had never seen anyone more beautiful, or more desirable. Then when she had slipped into his shirt, her long legs appearing to go for miles where his shirt skimmed her bottom, her nipples evident through the sheer fabric, she had sent his libido into overdrive. He much preferred this Rose even to the elegant woman of the fundraising dinner. Damn. He much preferred this woman to any of the sleek, polished women he had been out with over the years. What he had felt for them had been lust, pure and simple. What he felt for Rose was different. Desire, yes. So much it hit him like a punch to his solar plexus. But so much more. Tenderness. Joy in her company. Delight in seeing his world through her eyes. He reeled from the mixture of fear and excitement as he realised the truth. He loved Rose Taylor. He had been waiting for her all his life, and from now on nothing would ever be the same.

* * *

They were silent in the drive to his house. Rose kept sneaking little glances at Jonathan. The air between them sizzled with anticipation. Every time he caught her looking at him he would smile and her heart would flutter as if a hundred butterflies were trapped within her chest.

Inside his house, Jonathan closed the door and, taking her by the hand, led her to the bedroom. Kicking the bedroom door closed, he reached for her and pulled her into his arms.

'I've never wanted a woman the way I want you, Rose,' he said hoarsely.

Rose raised her face to his, knowing that whatever the next few days, weeks and months brought, she was exactly where she wanted to be for the rest of her life.

She wound her arms around his neck then his mouth was on hers and she gave herself up to him.

Much later they cuddled up in front of the fire, and finished off their picnic.

Rose leaned against his chest. His arms were wrapped around her as they watched the flickering flames.

'It won't be long before I go back,' she said quietly.

She sensed him take a deep intake of breath. 'You don't have to go. Stay with me.'

She twisted her head until she could see his face. 'I'm not talking just about tonight. I mean go back to Edinburgh. I have a life there. A home. Friends. Whatever this is, you and I know it can't last.'

'What do you mean? It can last as long as we both want it to.'

Sadness washed over her. Jonathan couldn't know that each moment could be their last. He couldn't know and, what was more, she was determined he would never know. She knew she could never hurt him like that. This thing in her brain could burst at any time. If it didn't kill her, it could leave her helpless and she would never be a burden on anyone. It scared her more than death.

'We're different, you and I,' she said softly. 'You have your life and I have mine. That's okay.'

Jonathan threw back his head and laughed. 'You think because I'm the son of a lord, because I'll inherit a title one day, that that means we can't be together. My God, Rose. This is the twenty-first century. Even princes marry who they want.'

'But we're not talking marriage, are we? We hardly know each other.' She shook her head, forcing a laugh. 'Let's not make more of this than it is.' She turned away so she couldn't see his eyes, knowing she was hurting him.

'I know you well enough to know you are everything I ever wanted. But I don't expect you to feel the same. That's why we need time. Time for me to convince you that I'm not beyond redemption.' He smiled wryly. 'Somehow I know my partying days are behind me.' He hugged her tighter. 'Don't give up on me, Rose. Not yet.'

His hands were on her body again. She wished he wouldn't do that. How was she expected to think clearly when her head was full of him? Her body burning at his touch, her need for him so strong? But this right now was all she could offer him. All she had. She turned around and sat facing him, wrapping her legs around his hips.

'Enough talking,' she said, before pulling his face towards hers.

The next days were the most bitter-sweet of Rose's life. She burned every memory of Jonathan into her head. During the day, they would steal kisses, small touches and share glances. Then at night, after she'd been home to check up on her father, he would collect her from her parents' house and drive her back to his town house. As soon as the door closed behind them, they would be in each other's arms, tearing at each other's clothes, often not even making it to the bedroom.

On the rare occasions they didn't see other she would sit in her room, strumming her guitar, composing lyrics to new songs in her head. It was the happiest time of her life—and the saddest. Sometimes her head would ache and she would be terrified it was a sign the aneurysm was going to burst. She spent hours on the internet going over the options, but if she was hoping to find an easy solution she was disappointed. As the doctors had pointed out, there were only two. She could have surgery. Or not. Whatever she decided, the outcome could be the same. Paralysis, possibly death.

Not much of a choice, then. Do nothing and continue to live as she had been. Making the most of every day. But it was a life without a future. A day-to-day existence. A life where she wouldn't marry, have children or, worst of all, Jonathan. And the other option? Have the operation, knowing the consequences, but also knowing it offered at least a chance for a future. One where she was free to love and be loved. Have children. Grow old.

Until she had met Jonathan, doing nothing had made sense. Now she wanted more.

She paced her little room, her throat tightening as she remembered happier times. Her father strong and healthy, the house filled with love and laughter, the future still a merciful blank.

One thing she knew for certain. She couldn't tell

Jonathan. He would insist on sticking by her whatever happened, and she couldn't allow that to happen. How soon would it be before his love changed to duty, regret, even loathing. Instinctively she knew he would never leave her.

Neither could she talk to him about it. He would want to help her make a decision. Then whatever she did, whatever the consequences, he would feel responsible. She loved him too much for that. No, only one person could decide what to do, and that was her.

Her aching heart told her the truth before her brain could accept it. She would have the operation. Place her fate in the hands of the gods. She would leave Jonathan behind, convince him somehow she didn't love him, then disappear from his life and have the operation. If it was a success, she would find him again and tell him the truth. And if it wasn't? At least she had set him free to live his life. She had a week left with him. And she would make the most of every minute.

'So I'll be back next week. On Monday, if that's okay with you?' Vicki propped a hip against the desk. 'I can't believe how much better I feel now that I've stopped being sick.' She dropped a hand to the curve of her belly and Rose felt a stab of longing that almost took her breath away. Now Vicki was coming back, she no longer had an excuse to put it off. Miss Fairweather had scheduled the operation for two weeks' time. Now that she had made the decision, she had told her parents. It had been one of the worst nights of her life. But she had found comfort at last as she had cried in her mother's arms.

Vicki glanced over at Jonathan's closed door. He was seeing a patient. 'He's going to miss you. I don't suppose you are free to cover my maternity leave?'

Rose smiled wryly. Vicki had no idea how much she hoped she would be able to be in a position to do that.

'I still have my job in Edinburgh. They're expecting me back. I don't think you can count on me covering you, although…' she reached out a hand '…I'll come back and see you when the baby is born.' Rose swallowed the lump in her throat. Please, God, let her be telling the truth.

'I'm going to miss you. Hard to imagine returning to the way it was here before you and Jenny.' Vicki indicated Jenny with a nod of her head. 'I think the patients actually prefer Jenny now they're used to her. She makes them laugh.'

'Just as well, then, because Jonathan's offered her a permanent job. Mrs Smythe Jones called into see Jonathan the other day. Apparently she's decided to emigrate to New Zealand to be with her sister.'

Vicki whistled under her breath. 'I didn't think she'd ever leave. This practice has been her life for nearly forty years. She was here when Jonathan's uncle started. She wouldn't retire last year even when Jonathan assured her that the pension the company would settle on her is almost as much as her salary. She said she'd be lonely at home. I guess if she's going to stay with her sister, lack of company won't be an issue.'

The two women turned to look across at Jenny who was patiently listening to the voice on the other end of the phone, offering periodic *oh, dear*s and *poor you*. They smiled at each other. 'I gather Jenny was out at lunch when Mrs Smythe Jones came for her chat. Somehow I can't imagine her letting Jonathan employ Jenny if she had seen the hairdo.'

Over the weeks Jenny's hair had reverted to the spiky look she loved. No one had said anything. Rose had only been glad that the piercings remained at home. Even if Jonathan and his patients accepted the hair, a nose ring was bound to be a step too far.

Rose would be leaving all this behind soon, maybe forever, and the thought was breaking her heart.

CHAPTER NINE

LATER on that day they received word that Lord Hilton had died in his sleep. Rose had become fond of the couple over the last few weeks and when Jonathan broke the news she was unsurprised at how sad she felt.

Jonathan pulled her into his arms and she rested her head there. It felt so good, so safe, and she wished she could stay there for ever. With him she could face anything, except what she feared most.

'How is Lady Hilton taking it?' Rose asked. 'Should I go to her?'

'She said to tell you that she is very grateful for everything you did for them. She has friends and family around right now, but she asks if you would come to the funeral. She says Giles wanted it.'

'Of course I'll go,' Rose said softly. She looked up at him. 'You'll be there?'

'I'm always going to be there, Rose Taylor,' Jonathan said firmly. 'Don't you know that by now?' The look of love in his eyes made her heart shatter. 'She's also asked if you could back to the house with the others after the funeral. She has something to tell you.'

Rose could hardly speak. Her throat was tight. He loved

her. She knew that without doubt, even if he hadn't said the words. Little did he know they could only have these last few days to do them for the rest of their lives. She had handed in her notice in Edinburgh, effective immediately, as the operation had been scheduled for the end of the next week. But she wouldn't tell Jonathan. For his sake, she would make him believe that she wasn't in love with him, that she wanted to go back to her life in Edinburgh. It would be hard to convince him, and the thought of hurting him was tearing her apart, but for his sake she had to make him believe her. If the operation was a success she would come back to him and tell him everything. If not? At least he would be free to live his life.

That evening Jonathan came down to her local again. They had been a couple of times and Jonathan was surprised how relaxing he found the pub and how welcoming Rose's friends were. Every time they had been there, Rose had taken her guitar and sung. Every day he fell deeper in love.

Tonight she took her guitar and perched on a chair on the stage. She caught his eye across the crowded room.

'I've a new song I'd like to sing tonight,' she said softly. 'It's something I composed recently. I hope you all like it. It's called, "All my tomorrows".'

Her voice was husky as she sang directly to him. The song was about love and loss, about making the most of every moment. The last line of the chorus was 'All my tomorrows are wrapped up in you today,' and as she sang the line her voice cracked a little. Something in the way she sang the song and in the way her eyes filled as the last notes died away scared him.

When she'd finished singing, she smiled a little shakily.

The room erupted as everyone clapped and cheered, but Jonathan sat stunned. If he hadn't known better, he would think she was saying goodbye.

Lord Hilton's funeral was held a couple of days later in the family church. Summer had arrived and the mourners gathered under a blazing sun. Rose tried not to think that soon a similar crowd might be gathered to say their last farewells to her. Instead, she resolutely pushed the thought away. She wasn't going to waste a moment of whatever time she had left thinking gloomy thoughts.

And Giles's funeral wasn't gloomy. It was a celebration of a remarkable man who, as it was pointed out, had stayed in love with his wife of fifty years right until the end.

Jonathan's father was there and after the burial he came up to Rose.

'It's good to see you again, my dear,' he said. 'Won't you ask Jonathan to bring you home for dinner so we can get to know each other better?'

Rose looked him directly in the eye. If anything happened to her, Jonathan would need his father. She didn't know if she could make things right between father and son, but she had to try.

'I don't know if I can persuade him,' she said softly. 'He seems to be very angry with you.' She took a deep breath and hurried on before she lost her nerve. 'He seems to think that you don't care about him. That perhaps you never did.'

Lord Cavendish looked aghast. Whether it was because Rose had the audacity to talk to him about what he almost certainly saw as a private matter, or whether it was because he didn't want to acknowledge the way his son felt, Rose couldn't be sure.

Suddenly his expression relaxed and he smiled grimly. 'I can see why my son is so besotted with you,' he said. 'But he can't think I don't care about him. My God, he is the most important thing in my life. Why would he think otherwise?'

'Maybe because you sent him away to boarding school after his mother died? I understand he's never lived at home since.'

Lord Cavendish pulled a hand through his still dark and thick hair that was so much like his son's. 'I sent him away because I thought it was for the best,' he said stiffly. 'I was away so much on business and without his mother…' He shrugged. 'There would be no one at home to look after him.'

Rose plunged on. Out of the corner of her eye, she could see Jonathan chatting to Lady Hilton.

'He was only a child,' she said. 'And you took him away from everything he knew and loved, just when he had suffered the most devastating loss. Didn't it occur to you that he'd need his father? At least for a while?'

Jonathan's father looked even more taken aback, if that was possible. He looked into the distance. 'I met Jonathan's mother when I was a young man at university. I loved her instantly. She was like a bright star in my otherwise lonely existence. A bit like I suspect you are to Jonathan. Like you, she didn't come from aristocracy and my parents didn't approve. It was different back then. Nobody cares these days. But it didn't matter what they thought. I couldn't imagine a future without her. I would have married her even if my family had thrown me on the street.' He smiled. 'Luckily it didn't come to that. We married and had a few short years together. She was a painter, you know. I under-stand from Lady Hilton that you compose songs? My Clara and you were very much alike. I was working all hours setting up my businesses while she painted. I guess it made her less lonely. Then Jonathan came along and I thought she would miss me less, so I spent even more time away from home.' His eyes were bleak. 'I missed her every second, but I thought we had years together.' His voice was hoarse as if tears weren't far away.

Unable to stop herself, Rose touched him gently on the arm, wanting to let him know she understood.

'Then when Jonathan was five, my darling Clara died. I thought I'd go mad with the pain of it. Every time I looked at Jonathan I saw his mother. I couldn't bear it. I had to throw myself into work. And I had to know they were being looked after. So, yes. I sent him away. I regret it now. I hardly know my son, and it's my fault.'

'But you married again. Several times, I gather.' Rose smiled to take the sting from her words.

'I wanted what I had with Clara, but it was no use. I never found it again.' He looked directly into her eyes.

'Have you ever been in love, Rose? I mean so in love that it feels that he's the missing part of your soul?'

Rose bit hard on her lip to stop the tears. She nodded.

'Then you'll know that no one else can ever measure up, no matter how they try. Your soul remains in two bits. A chunk of you is always missing, no matter how much you search.'

'But you still have part of her. In Jonathan,' Rose said, forcing the words past her frozen throat.

She followed his gaze until it rested on Jonathan. His eyes softened. 'I know I do. But I think I may have left it too late.'

'It's never too late.' Then, at the realisation of what she'd said, she added, 'At least, it's not for you two. Talk to him. I know it's difficult. But tell him what you told me, about Clara. I think you'll find he understands.'

Lord Cavendish gave her a long appraising look. He grinned and Rose's heart skipped a beat. In that instant she could see the man Jonathan would become as he aged. What she would give to be around to see it. 'I think I'm going to like having you around, Rose Taylor,' Lord Cavendish said slowly. 'Now, if you'll excuse me, I think I should go and talk to my son.'

Rose watched as Lord Cavendish walked over to his son. He placed a hand on Jonathan's shoulder and after a few words the two men walked off together.

Later, back in the Hiltons' home, Sophia asked Rose to come into her study for a few moments. Rose was baffled. The day was taking its toll on her and she didn't know how much she could hold it all together. But if Sophia Hilton could keep a brave face even if she was breaking up inside, so could she.

Lady Hilton opened a desk drawer and pulled out an envelope. She handed it to Rose.

'Giles wanted you to have this, my dear. In the short time we've known you, we've come to look on you as a daughter.'

Intrigued, Rose opened the envelope. Inside was a cheque, the sum of which made her gasp.

'What on earth…? You can't possibly mean to give this to me. It's far too generous and completely unnecessary.'

Sophia smiled. 'It's for your wedding. Giles and I both see the way things are with you and Jonathan. We don't have daughters of our own, and it gives us both…' She drew a shaky breath. ' I mean, the thought of you using it to get married gave us so much pleasure.'

'But I'm not getting married. J-Jonathan and I haven't even s-spoken of it,' Rose stuttered.

'But you will, my dear.'

Rose thrust the envelope back at Sophia. 'I'm sorry. I really can't take this. There isn't going to be a wedding, whatever you might think.' Her throat was clogging with tears and she could barely speak.

'Don't you believe he loves you? Is that what you think? Or do you think he won't marry you because you have some misguided idea about class? But, my dear, Jonathan's mother was the same and it didn't stop his father from marrying her. And back then people did make more of it.'

It was all too much. The funeral. The Hiltons' kindness. That a couple she barely knew had been thinking of her even while going through the most horrible and sad time. Knowing that her days with Jonathan were about to come to an end. She couldn't bear it.

'I'm sorry,' she managed. 'I really have to go.' And before she could disgrace herself by breaking down completely, she fled.

CHAPTER TEN

ON WHAT was to be their last night together, although of course Jonathan had no idea that it would be, Rose suggested they spend the night at his house near Cambridge. It was where they had first made love and the place she had been happiest in all her life.

If Jonathan suspected something, he gave no sign of it. In fact, he looked as if he was up to something. There was a hidden air of excitement about him that Rose had never seen before. Her heart was cracking with the unbearable realisation that this could be the last time she would ever be in his arms.

'We can pop into to see Mary first, if you don't mind. She's back at work after her time off and I want to check she's not doing too much.'

'Of course,' Rose agreed. The doctors at the hospital had diagnosed angina but with some changes to her diet and some additional gentle exercise they were hopeful she would live for many years yet.

They found Mary ensconced in her kitchen domain. The older lady had lost a little weight and was delighted to see them.

'Jonathan and Rose! Thank you for coming to see

me.' She sent Jonathan a mock severe look. 'Although how you smelled my baking all the way from London is anyone's guess.'

'Is Father here?' Jonathan asked Mary, after hugging her.

'He is. Thankfully without that woman. She seems to have been chucked. Thank God he saw sense before it was too late.' She dropped her voice. 'Why don't you go and see him? He's always talking about you, you know. Telling me how proud you make him and how very proud your mother would be.'

Jonathan smiled awkwardly.

'So he keeps telling me. This new father is taking a bit of getting used to,' he said. 'I wonder what brought about this change.' But the look he slid Rose told her he knew about their conversation, although until now, he hadn't mentioned it.

'Ah, my dear boy. It makes an old woman happy to know that you two have made up. He loves you, you know.'

Jonathan shuffled his feet uncomfortably. 'And I him, Mary. Now, any chance of us raiding your kitchen for some food? I'm going to steal Rose away for a private dinner in my cottage.'

His look sent bitter-sweet memories ricocheting around Rose's head. More than anything she didn't want to waste a single moment that they had left.

'Can't you stay for dinner? Your father would love to have the company.'

Jonathan looked at Rose for agreement and when she nodded her head he said, 'Okay. I suppose Rose and I will have plenty other times.'

Blast Lord Cavendish and blast her interference, Rose thought briefly. But wasn't this exactly what she'd engineered? Jonathan wasn't to know this was their last night.

Dinner seemed to go on for ever, although Lord Cavendish was surprisingly amusing company. It was good to see the two men, so alike, sharing jokes and later their memories of Clara. It seemed astonishing to Rose that Jonathan knew so little about his mother. Lord Cavendish included Rose in the conversation, making it obvious that his interest in her was genuine.

Finally, when it was almost ten o'clock, dinner was over and Jonathan made their excuses.

Once inside his house, he reached out for and brought his mouth down on hers as if he were drowning and she were a life raft. Although Rose wanted nothing more than to be naked beside him in his bed, there was another memory she needed to leave him with. A memory she hoped that when she was gone he would recall and know deep down that she had loved him and her leaving hadn't been her choice. She wanted to sing to him one last time, so that one day in the future he would understand why she had acted as she had.

She disentangled herself from his arms. 'I want you to sit there and not move,' she ordered.

Bemused, Jonathan wasn't having it. 'No way. Right now I want you too much to keep my hands off you.' And then he was kissing her again and Rose was lost. She gave herself up to him greedily, wanting to burn every part of him into her soul.

Later she lay in his arms and he looked at her through half-closed lids.

'I love you, Rose,' he said huskily. 'And I'll go to my grave loving you.'

Rose's heart sang. But she couldn't say the words he longed to hear. If she did, he would never stop looking for her.

She forced a laugh. 'Wow! That's a surprise. I had no idea you felt that way.' She slipped out of bed and started to get dressed, avoiding his eyes. If he saw her eyes, she knew her anguish would be plain to see.

She sensed his puzzlement.

'Is that all you have to say?' He leapt out of bed and came to stand behind her, wrapping her in his arms. 'Don't you get it? I love you and I want to spend the rest of my life with you. I want you to do me the honour of becoming my wife, Rose.'

Rose wriggled out of his grasp. 'But I don't want to marry you. I'm sorry, Jonathan, whatever we had, whatever this was…' She indicated the unmade bed with a sweep of her hand. 'For me it was just an interlude. Some fun. I'm going back to Edinburgh. My life is there.'

'Going back? You can't. What about us? Even if you don't love me now, I know you feel something.' He pulled his hand through his hair. 'I can't be wrong. Everything tells me I'm not wrong.'

She forced herself to continue dressing.

'I'm sorry, Jonathan, I could never marry someone like you. All you're really interested in is having a good time. When I marry…' Her voice cracked and she breathed deeply, knowing how much she was hurting him. 'It will be to someone who knows that there is more to life than having fun. Someone I can respect.'

'My God, Rose, I know I'm not the kind of man you would have wished for yourself. But I love you. I can change. No more parties, I promise. I didn't tell you but I've taken a part-time job at the local hospital. I'm going to complete my surgical training. It's what I always wanted to do.'

'What about your uncle's practice?'

'I'll employ someone else to keep it on. You've made me realise that I need more in my life. What I had before I met you was meaningless. Empty.'

'You shouldn't change your whole life around because of me,' Rose said sadly, 'especially when after tonight I'm no longer going to be in it.'

She turned and looked him directly in the eye. She knew the tears would come later. But she had to hurt him now, even if it broke her heart.

'I've had a good time, Jonathan. You showed me a different side to life and I'll always be grateful to you. But it's over. I'm going back to Edinburgh and there's nothing you can do, or say, that'll make me change my mind. I don't love you and I never will.'

Jonathan's green eyes turned cool.

'You've been stringing me along all this time, haven't you?' he said bitterly. 'None of this meant anything to you, did it?' He pulled his jeans over his hips. 'Well, I can't say I haven't deserved to be taken for a ride. God knows, I've hurt others. Now it seems it's my turn.' He laughed sourly. 'And the irony of it all is that I've spent all my life not believing that it was possible to love one person for the whole of my life. Until you showed me that that was exactly how my father felt about my mother. I guess at least I have you to thank for that.'

Rose recoiled from the look in his eyes. She longed to put her arms around him and tell him the truth. But she couldn't. If she touched him, she'd be undone.

He slipped his shirt on and picked up his car keys. 'I think I should take you home now.'

CHAPTER ELEVEN

ROSE lay on the hospital bed, feeling groggy. The premeds were taking the edge off her anxiety, but couldn't quite take it away. She wondered if these few minutes would be the last she would know.

'You can still change your mind,' her mother whispered. Behind the forced smile, Rose could see her terror.

Rose smiled faintly. She reached for her mother's hand. 'I've made up my mind, Mum. I'm going through with it.' Her head had been shaved where they were planning to operate. Knowing that they would do that, she had gone to the hairdresser yesterday and insisted they crop her hair. She hardly recognised herself. And not just because of the haircut. Her face was gaunt, her eyes haunted. She wondered what Jonathan would think of her new hairstyle. She closed her eyes. She could see him clearly, his smile, his eyes. She could almost taste his skin. She pushed the image away. She couldn't think of Jonathan. Not now. If she did she might not have the strength to go through with it; she might just persuade herself that whatever days she had left were better spent with him. But she knew she could never risk breaking his heart.

'Please let me call him.' It was as if her mother could

read her mind. She had begged Rose to let Jonathan know, but Rose had held steadfast. Instead, she had written the words to the song she had written for him, and asked her mother to give it to him should anything happen to her. Her father was at home, refusing to say what might be his last goodbyes to his only child. His doctor had advised him against coming to the hospital earlier, worried that the added strain would set him back.

'I'll be there when you wake up,' he had said before she left for the hospital. He had held her and kissed her hair, murmuring words that she remembered from her childhood.

'We've been through this, Mum, and you promised.' Rose squeezed her mother's hand. 'And if something happens to me, if I survive the operation but am brain damaged, remember you swore you won't tell him. I'd rather he remembered me how I was.'

'But…' her mother smiled weakly, '…you're going to be fine. Everything is going to be just fine.'

All too soon, they came to take her to Theatre. Rose could hardly bear the pain in her mother's eyes as they kissed for what could be the last time. Then she was in Theatre and the anaesthetist was asking her to count backwards from a hundred. Now she allowed herself to think of Jonathan. To bring his dear face into her mind, and as she drifted off, she imagined his lips on hers.

Jonathan was restless. Since Rose had left him, nothing could distract him from the thoughts and memories of her. He couldn't bring himself to attend any of the parties or lunches to which he still got invited. All he wanted was Rose. The only thing that kept him sane were his patients and his work. If it hadn't been for them he would have gone stark, staring mad. Several times, more often than he cared to count, he had considered jumping on a plane to Edinburgh to go searching for her. Maybe he could still persuade her to come back to him. He just couldn't believe she didn't love him, even a little bit.

Picking up his car keys, he made up his mind. He would call in on her parents. See how her father was doing. Maybe he could get an address out of them. At the very least, he could be where she lived. If he couldn't be with her, being where she was until recently would be the next best thing.

Half an hour later, he rang the doorbell. A taxi pulled up behind his car. After a long pause Rose's father came to the door. He was still leaning on his stick, but Jonathan was pleased to see he seemed to hardly need it. The droop to the side of his mouth had also improved. All in all he appeared to be making a good recovery. But it was the look in his eyes that shocked Jonathan. Never before had he seen him look so sad, or so frightened, not even when he had first met him.

'What is it?' Jonathan asked. 'Is something wrong?' His heart was pounding like a runaway train. Had something happened to Rose? Please, God, no.

Tommy shook his head despairingly. 'I'm sorry, Jonathan, I can't talk to you at the moment. My taxi's waiting for me.'

'Where's Rose's mother? Why isn't she here? Something's wrong. Is it Rose?' He blocked Tommy's path. He had to know.

'Please, Jonathan, I don't have time for this. I need to get to the hospital.'

'The hospital?' His alarm was growing stronger. There was no way that Rose's mother would let Tommy go by himself. There was something wrong. He knew it. It took every ounce of his strength not to shake the fragile man in front of him. Tommy looked at him steadily. 'She made us promise not to tell you. I think she was wrong, but I promised her.'

'Just tell me where she is.'

'I can't. I need to get to the hospital, but if you were to follow the taxi there, I couldn't stop you, could I?'

Jonathan read the message in his eyes. It was all he was going to get and it would have to do. But as he followed the painfully slow taxi through the thick London traffic, his mind was whirling with images he couldn't bear. His Rose. Dead or dying. Here in London. Why had she told them not to tell him? He didn't care. All he wanted was to know that she was all right. If he knew that, he could live the rest of his life without her. As long as he knew she was in it somewhere.

His fear almost threatened to crush him as the taxi pulled up outside the London Hospital for Neurological Sciences. Little clicks were going on inside his head. The sadness in her eyes. Her refusal to talk about the future. That song she had composed. What had the last line been? *All my tomorrows are wrapped up in you today*. What hadn't she been telling him?

Fear clutching his throat, he abandoned his car on a double yellow line—he couldn't care less if he never saw it again—and caught up with Tommy. He placed his hand under his elbow.

'She's here, isn't she?' he said flatly.

Tommy simply nodded. Something squeezed Jonathan's chest when he saw tears glisten in Tommy's eyes.

'Is she alive? Please, you have to tell me that.'

'I don't know,' Tommy said slowly. 'She's in Theatre,

having an operation for a brain aneurysm. It seems it's the same thing that caused my stroke. The doctors knew it was the hereditary kind, so they screened her for it.' His voice cracked.

'And they found something?' Jonathan could hardly breathe. It all made sense now. Terrible, heart-breaking sense.

'She's being operated on today. I'm here to sit with her mother and wait. We don't know if she'll survive the operation.'

'Survive?' he could hardly force the words past his clenched jaw. 'Of course she's going to survive.' But try as he may, he couldn't completely remove the fear from his voice. 'It's Rose we're talking about. And the woman I know is a fighter.'

When Rose opened her eyes she thought she was dreaming. Either that, or she had died and she was in heaven. But as soon as he spoke, she knew this was no dream and that she was very much alive.

'Hey, how're you feeling?' His eyes looked different somehow. Almost damp. As if he'd being crying. Which was ridiculous. Jonathan didn't cry.

'I'm alive?' The words were all she could manage. A vague memory of her parents' faces, their eyes bright with tears, swam into her head.

Jonathan slipped a hand under her shoulders and helped her take a sip of cold water. It tasted like nectar. She was alive and she could hardly believe it.

'The operation went well. Even better than the surgeon hoped. You are going to be fine. You have to take it easy for a while, but after that you can do whatever you want.'

She still couldn't quite believe what he was telling her.

She wriggled her toes. That was good. Then she stretched her fingers. Movement there too. She could move, she could speak, she could see and she could understand.

Her eyes were growing heavy. 'You found me,' she whispered, before she let herself give in to sleep.

He was still there when she opened them again. He was watching her, as if he couldn't bear to tear his eyes away from her.

'Hello, love.' Her mother's voice came from the other side of the bed. Beside her was her father. They were smiling and holding hands. Her mother stood and kissed her on the cheek. 'Welcome back to us.' She stood back and let Tommy come closer. Rose watched a fat tear slide down his cheek. Rose had never seen her father cry before and her heart ached for him.

'My child,' he said simply. 'My baby girl. You are going to have a long and happy life. Thank God.'

'We're going to leave you two alone for a few minutes,' her mother said. 'Jonathan refuses to go home until he's sure you're okay.'

She swivelled her head to look at him. His face was grey and he was unshaven. How long had he been here? Had she imagined seeing him earlier when she'd first come round?

'Don't try to speak,' he said. 'You've been sedated since the operation and you need time to rest.'

'How long?' she whispered.

'Two days. Two of the longest, hardest, scariest days of my life. How much worse for you and your parents to have lived with this for all these weeks.'

He touched her cheek with his finger. 'You need to sleep now. But when you wake up, I'll still be here. I'm never going to leave your side again.' He smiled sadly. 'No matter what you say. You're stuck with me.'

CHAPTER TWELVE

THE day was bright with promise. The sun shining just for them as Rose walked down the flower-edged path towards Jonathan. Her parents were sitting in the front row. Apart from a slight droop to the side of his mouth and a residual limp, her father had made an almost complete recovery. These days he was forever telling whoever would listen that his stroke had been the best thing that ever happened to him. After all, if it hadn't happened, Rose would never have discovered she had inherited the condition. He never finished the sentence, and he didn't need to. If her condition hadn't been discovered, if the aneurysm hadn't been removed, it was possible she might not be here. Not walking down the aisle to the man who in a few minutes would become her husband.

Instead of the traditional wedding march, a band was playing the song she had written for Jonathan. 'All my tomorrows are wrapped up in you today.' Rose's heart soared. She and Jonathan had many, many tomorrows in store for them. She still wasn't sure how she felt about being the future Lady Cavendish, but what did anything matter when she had Jonathan by her side? And he had promised it wouldn't change a thing—except perhaps end his party days. And that, he said, was no loss at all. He had everything he'd ever dreamed of. With the possible exception of four or five children. And they both agreed it would be fun making their babies.

She finished her walk up the aisle and as Jonathan looked at her, she caught her breath. She knew without a shadow of doubt that he loved her more than she'd ever thought it possible to be loved.

Holding her hand, his voice ringing out, he repeated the words from the Bible.

'"Do not urge me to leave you or turn back from following you; for where you go, I will go, and where you lodge, I will lodge. Your people shall be my people, and your God my God."' He touched her lips with his.

'Remember that, my darling. No matter what, you must never ever shut me out again. Do you promise me?' His voice was urgent, the pain of the days when he had thought he would lose her still evident in his voice.

Rose grinned at him. 'Are you kidding? You and I are stuck with each other. For better for worse, for richer, for poorer. In sickness and in health. And I for one am going nowhere. Not ever.' Happiness bubbled up inside her, filling her with a joy she had never known was possible. 'I'm here for all your tomorrows. I promise.'

THE HEART DOCTOR
AND THE BABY

BY
LYNNE MARSHALL

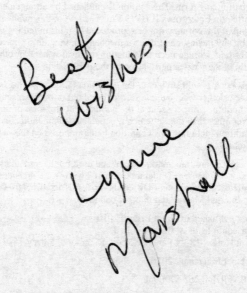

Best wishes,

Lynne Marshall

⬤ MILLS & BOON®

For my mother, Lura,
for teaching me unconditional and abiding love.

First published in Great Britain 2010
Harlequin Mills & Boon Limited,
Eton House, 18-24 Paradise Road, Richmond, Surrey TW9 1SR

© Janet Maarshalk 2010

ISBN: 978 0 263 87909 4

Harlequin Mills & Boon policy is to use papers that are natural, renewable and recyclable products and made from wood grown in sustainable forests. The logging and manufacturing process conform to the legal environmental regulations of the country of origin.

Printed and bound in Spain
by Litografia Rosés, S.A., Barcelona

Lynne Marshall has been a Registered Nurse in a large California hospital for twenty-five years. She has now taken the leap to writing full-time, but still volunteers at her local community hospital. After writing the book of her heart in 2000, she discovered the wonderful world of Medical™ Romance, where she feels the freedom to write the stories she loves. She is happily married, has two fantastic grown children, and a socially challenged rescue dog. Besides her passion for writing Medical™ Romance, she loves to travel and read. Thanks to the family dog, she takes long walks every day! To find out more about Lynne, please visit her website: www.lynnemarshallweb.com

Recent titles by the same author:

THE BOSS AND NURSE ALBRIGHT
TEMPORARY DOCTOR, SURPRISE FATHER
ASSIGNMENT: BABY

CHAPTER ONE

RENÉ MUNROE hadn't been this nervous since her first date at fifteen. Today, twenty years later, she worked like a madwoman to prepare a meal for her coworker, Jon Becker.

She used whole tomatoes and garlic cloves, fresh basil and, because she liked tangy instead of sweet, she added her signature dash of balsamic vinegar to the marinara sauce. Then she went the extra mile to make the pasta from scratch.

Tonight, if she handled things perfectly, could turn out to be an "extra mile" kind of night. The linguini looked delicious as she pulled the noodles through the gizmo, hoping all would turn out as planned. Add a salad of baby greens and fresh Italian bread from her favorite bakery, and she had a meal. A darn fine meal. A meal that might lead to a dream come true.

She brushed off her hands, grabbed the dishes and tableware and hipped her way through the swinging kitchen door to the dining room while trying to push nervous thoughts out of her mind. Could she pull this off? She distracted herself by setting the table.

Three years ago she'd found a classic Craftsman home in disrepair in the foothills of Santa Barbara. Since it was close enough to the medical clinic, she bought it for a good price and little by little began restoring it. The dining and living rooms were her favorite parts of the house. She'd knocked out one wall to bring an open, flowing feel to the area, but had maintained and refinished all of the built-in shelves and extra woodwork. This was a home she intended to live in for the rest of her life. A home she hoped to have a family in.

She believed in keeping design uncluttered, like her life, and the simple dining table and chairs with a matching buffet were the only furniture in this room. Sage-green walls brought peace to her roiling jitters, and were a perfect contrast to the abundant rich golden wood.

After tonight, if all went well, the last thing her life would be was simple.

She put bright red place mats on the table to contrast the subtle earthenware vase heavily laden with colorful dried flowers. She needed things to be just so tonight, and did a quick walk-through of the living room to make sure nothing was out of place.

A natural-rock fireplace served as the focal point, and even though she'd cheated with a gas log, the fire gave the living room that extra bit of coziness she wanted. Anything to help make easier the topic she was about to bring up with Jon.

One mad dash to the bathroom to touch up her makeup and run the comb through her hair, and she was ready… just as the doorbell rang. Perfect timing.

Jon stood on her porch with his typical serious expression and a bottle of wine in each hand. Along with his usual salt-and-pepper-brown closely cropped hair, he sported a new beard tracing a thin red-tinged line along his jaw, and wore a black fleece vest, long-sleeved gray shirt and jeans.

When she let him in, he smelled good, like sandalwood and some exotic spice, and it struck her that she'd never noticed his cologne before.

"Wow," he said. "You've really done a lot with the house. It looks great."

He'd helped her do a walk-through when she'd first considered buying it, and had given his nod of approval. After his divorce two years ago, she wasn't sure how to handle their mostly business relationship and, not wanting to send the wrong message, hadn't invited him back again. He'd struck her as a recluse since then, avoiding anything that smacked of social interaction. In fact, she'd been pleasantly surprised when he'd accepted without protest her invitation for dinner.

Had it really been that long since he'd been here? She thanked him and gestured for him to sit while she opened the wine, but instead he followed her into the kitchen.

"I thought I was the high-tech guy," he said, "but look at you, going all stainless steel."

"Yeah, I upgraded," she said with a laugh as she popped the cork out of the bottle, splashed some wine into the glasses and walked him back to the living room. Small talk had never been a problem with Jon, but they'd never ventured deeper than that, and definitely had never come close to what she needed to discuss with him tonight.

"We should probably let the wine breathe," she said, wishing she could catch her breath, too. The moment she'd seen Jon her heart started tapping out odd beats, and right this minute it felt as if someone was juggling in her stomach. What she was about to ask him was the craziest idea she'd ever had in her entire life.

"Dinner smells fantastic," he said.

"I hope you're hungry." She did her best to appear non-chalant, as if her future didn't depend on the outcome of tonight's meal. "Let's sit for a bit, and…uh, talk. I've got some cheese and crackers to go with the wine."

Long and lean, Jon settled into the hardy wood-and-earth-tone upholstered chair that went so well with the style of the house. Come to think of it, he looked as if he belonged there. She sat in its mate so they could both share the small table where she'd already laid out the appetizers. He tossed a couple of crackers topped with the nutty cheese-ball spread into his mouth before he sampled the wine.

When was the appropriate time to bring up the subject? Surely there wasn't any etiquette for when to broach the topic of artificial insemination amongst friends. She took a long swig of the wine and felt her mouth dry up. "I need some water—can I get you any?"

By now, with her uneasy behavior, he'd gotten that suspicious glint in his eyes, the one she'd often seen him give a patient fudging about their diet or medicine. She'd been way too skittish, and Jon could tell something was up.

"You seem really anxious." His eyes brightened. "Is it me?" He snapped his fingers. "It's the beard, isn't it?"

She swiped the air. "Gosh, no. Jon! The beard?" If she'd given it any thought at all, she'd admit the beard complemented his carved features, but beards were the last thing on her mind tonight. She took another sip of wine, then headed straight to the kitchen to gather her thoughts, soon emerging with ice water for both of them.

He waited with a thoughtful expression, brows faintly furrowed. "The beard was my daughters' idea." He scratched the triangular swatch beneath his lower lip, and straightened in his chair as if uncomfortable with the added masculinity.

"It's a nice addition. Really." Why did she need to say "really" if she'd meant it in the first place? Oh, if only her jitters would go away she might act like the normal person he knew from the clinic, instead of a nervous, stammering mental job.

He grew serious and shifted on the cushion, as if his curiosity had reached its apex. "There's a reason besides eating dinner that made you invite me tonight, isn't there?" His narrowed, probing stare made her spine straighten. "And I'm fairly sure it isn't to talk about my facial hair."

She needed another glass of wine and quick. "There *is* something I'd like to talk about, Jon." Oh, God, how was she going to do this? "But let's do it over dinner, okay?"

"Oh-kay." If he had an inquisitive look before, now he bore the expression of a sleuth about to solve the crime of the century.

She stood and he followed her to the table. She couldn't stand still and made a dash for the kitchen.

"Can I help with anything?" he asked through the door.

"Just sit. I'll be right back."

Thankful for the distraction, she swept through the kitchen, put the pasta on to boil, flung open the refrigerator for the salads and, gathering up the basket of bread before hitting the door, delivered the icy cold plates, dressing and bread all in one swoop.

The two of them became miserably bad at small talk as they ate, especially since she'd hinted at a much bigger topic. He glanced at her and her gaze flitted away, suddenly finding the bread of interest. She snuck another look at him; he chased a grape tomato around his plate. The mounting awkwardness made her grateful when the pasta timer went off and she rushed back into the kitchen to serve up the main course.

Jon tore the bread apart and dipped it into the sauce. "This is great, just great," he said after his first taste.

"I'm glad you like it." Normally she loved to watch a man enjoy his meal, but this time around all she could do was nod and smile, and try not to break out into welts over what she was about to bring up.

Deep breath. Swallow.

"So the thing is…Jon…I was, uh, wondering…" She nibbled on bread and twirled her fork around in the noodles, over and over again, no appetite whatsoever.

Jon leaned against the slated straight-back chair. She saw the wheels turning and the cogs meshing in his genius-level mind and knew she couldn't stall another second.

"You know you're driving me nuts, right?" he said, planting his fork into his pasta.

She closed her eyes and blurted. "What's your take on artificial insemination?"

His fork stopped midbite. He shut his mouth and dropped a look on her that said she'd potentially lost her mind, every last bit of it. "In general? Or for some specific reason?"

She swallowed what felt like a paper towel, a large and grainy paper towel. "Let's start with…in general."

"For someone who has fertility issues or no partner…" He began in his typical professorial manner, then narrowed one eye. "Is this pertaining to you?" he asked, an incredulous gaze on his face.

It was indeed pertaining to her and now was the time to get serious. No more skirting the issue. This tack was making her come off foolish and flaky, and on the topic of artificial insemination, she was anything but.

She'd done her homework, had read with interest about the local donor bank, no doubt supplied by multiple university students in need of extra cash. Wondered if she could go through with choosing an anonymous donor based on her list of specific requirements and qualities. Though it would serve her purpose, twenty-first century or not, how cold was that? Images of immature, beer-goggled university boys flashed through her mind, and a firm twist in her gut had kept her from logging into the Web site. Then she'd thought about her list of requirements and one particular face had popped into her mind.

She finished off the last few sips of wine and carefully placed the glass on the table. "I'm seriously considering it, Jon. I'm not getting any younger, and I don't see Mr. Right walking in my front door anytime in the near future." She grabbed his hand, didn't realize she'd done it until she felt his hard knuckles and lean fingers. She'd never touched him in this needful way before. "I want a baby, more than you can imagine."

"And you want my opinion about this because…?" It was his turn to guzzle the wine.

Her eyes couldn't stretch any wider. Since she'd finally opened up the topic, she decided to go all the way. "Traditionally, my wanting a baby would entail finding the right guy, getting married and settling down." She blurted her thoughts as her eyes roamed around and around the room. "Unless some miracle occurs in the near future, marriage and pregnancy isn't going to happen. But this is the twenty-first century, who says I have to be traditional?"

His suspicious look, along with the expression of terror, almost made her laugh as she went for the grand finale.

How *did* one go about asking a man for his DNA? She grimaced. Very carefully.

"And I brought the topic up with you, because in my opinion…you'd be the perfect donor."

He choked, bobbled his glass, which toppled over and spilled. They both jumped up to mop up the liquid.

"I'm sorry," he said.

"Oh, no, it was my fault for dropping a bomb on you."

He strode into the kitchen and reappeared with a towel, then when he'd absorbed the last of the wine with it, he produced a damp sponge to clean the wood. "I hope this doesn't stain."

"It's the least of my worries." She fought with several strands of hair that had fallen in her face during the fuss over the table.

He went still as the topic noticeably sunk in. "Wow. You're really serious about this."

She met his gaze and gave an assertive nod.

He scraped his jaw, and paced the dining room. "Wow."

"Will you at least think about it?"

"Wow." The bona fide genius, Jon Becker, had melted down to uttering a single-syllable echo.

She'd finally gathered her wits and was ready to talk business. "I've jotted down some thoughts about everything, and maybe you can give me your input—" oh, what an unfortunate choice of words "—about anything I may have overlooked?"

His dark eyes took on the wariness of a wild animal. He seemed to need to hold his jaw shut with his hand. After a few seconds considering her proposition, he dropped another look on her that made her take a breath. "You want me to be a father again at forty-two?"

She thought carefully how to best respond. "No, Jon. I want you to donate your sperm so I can be a mother at thirty-six."

He went perfectly still, stared at her as if he'd never seen her before. "You want a designer baby?"

Sudden calm enveloped her, and clarity of thought finally followed. "Let's sit down." She gestured toward the living room to the small sofa in front of the fireplace. He followed.

"I've already got my daughters, I don't want any more kids," he said. "And I'm planning a sabbatical once Lacy graduates and goes off to college. I've waited a long time to be free again."

"You won't have to be a part of the baby's life. I'm just asking you to be the sperm donor."

"Why not ask Phil? He's single. Young."

"He's also a playboy and irresponsible." She left out the part that she preferred Jon's nose to Phil's. "Jon, I've thought about everyone I know, and you are the top of the list. You're intelligent, healthy…you have an endearing personality—" How was she supposed to tell him the next part? She took a deep breath and spit it out. "And I think your DNA would work really well with mine."

"A superbaby?"

"A baby. Just a baby with a lot going for it. I'll take complete responsibility for the child. Nothing—I repeat, nothing—will be expected of you beyond your, uh—" her eyes fluttered and she suddenly needed to swallow "—donation." She tugged her earlobe and hoped she wasn't blushing, though her face definitely heated up. "All things considered, your job will be relatively easy."

Their eyes met and he seemed hesitant, as if he'd

mentally walked his way through exactly what his part would be, and was completely uncomfortable with her proposition.

"But we work together," he said. "How on earth am I supposed to not be involved?"

"I admit it could get tricky, but if you just put yourself in a clinical frame of mind, think of it as a scientific experiment between friends and colleagues, it could work."

He didn't look convinced.

She patted his hand, the same hand she'd never touched before tonight. "I just know we can handle this."

He didn't look nearly as sure as she professed to be, but she homed in to the subtle willingness to explore the possibilities with him, and seized her opportunity.

An hour or two or three later, after they'd discussed everything from health history to parental obligations or, in his case, lack thereof, to attorney input and whether or not to do home insemination versus clinical, intravaginal or intracervical insemination, the bizarre nature of their conversation seemed almost normal, as if two medical colleagues were discussing lab results.

"You feel like some dessert?" she asked.

He laughed, but admitted he did.

Amazingly, he ate every bite of the apple-and-berry torte she'd picked up at the bakery. Then, when it was time to leave, he hesitated. "I need time to think this over, René."

"Of course! I'm just grateful you haven't gone bolting out my door, peeling tire rubber trying to get away."

"I wouldn't run out on you." He squeezed her shoulder.

"I know that, Jon." She ducked her head against his chest, something else she'd never done with him before tonight, then quickly lifted it.

"I guess I'd better be going." It was almost midnight.

"When you make your decision, if it's yes, all you have to do is give me the nod and I'll have my attorney draw up a contract. If you do decide to help me with this, I won't hold you responsible in any way, Jon. You have my word. I promise."

He took a breath and got a goofy look on his face. "In that case, we could save all kinds of trouble and do this the old-fashioned way," he said with a devilish glint in his eyes.

An absurd laugh escaped her lips, and she socked his arm. Jon thought more like most men than she'd imagined. "You're such a joker." Though in the five years she'd known him, *joker* was never a word she'd use to describe him.

They'd had a conversation about creating a life without sex. He'd recited the statistics on success rates depending on his motility, and her fertility considering her age. They'd taken it to the scientific level, which made sense since they were both doctors, and he'd almost agreed to the plan. She wasn't about to throw one major potentially mind-blowing wrench into the mix, no matter what he suggested in jest. The old-fashioned way? No way. No how.

She bit her lip and stared at him. As their gazes fused, a new understanding bridged between them. Under the most unlikely circumstances, they'd taken their business relationship to a new level. Whether Jon decided to take her up on the deal or not, things between them would never be the same.

Jon could run a hundred miles and still not work out the crazy mix of emotions sluicing through him. He'd woken up early—hell, he'd never officially fallen asleep by true sleep study standards—and after tossing and turning he'd gotten up before sunrise and hit the Santa Barbara foothills. What little REM time he did manage had been cluttered with vivid dreams about babies and doctor babes, outlandish propositions and some interesting positions, too. At one point, René had straddled him. He liked that part of his dream, yet it had made him sit bolt upright, disoriented. And poof, the sexy vision had vanished.

A sudden steep hill forced him back into the moment, and he hit it with determination, refusing to slow his pace. Last night, in another transition from non-REM to early REM, he'd seen René as if looking through the wrong end of a telescope, motioning to him to follow her as she floated farther and farther away toward a baby. A tiny baby. In a test tube.

Crazy dreams matched by crazy thoughts.

His lungs burned with each stride, his leg muscles protested with aches and near cramps, but he refused to stop, refused to give in to the hill. That damn proposition. He had plans, for crying out loud! He was going to take a sabbatical and travel to the Far East. He'd study with Asian healers and cardiologists and learn their methods while imparting his knowledge. His daughters had reached the age where they'd be going out into the world, and he dreamed about doing the same. Finally!

It still seemed unreal that two years ago his wife, out of the blue, had asked for a divorce after seventeen years of marriage. It had sent him reeling in disbelief; even now the thought released a thousand icy needles in his chest. What had he done wrong? How had she fallen out of love with him? If he couldn't trust her to keep her word in marriage, what woman on this planet could he ever trust?

He'd withdrawn and lived the life of a recluse since then, even going so far as to take up long-distance running, anything to avoid other people. His medical practice and plans for a sabbatical had kept him going when he didn't think he could go on. That and his relationship with his daughters.

René had asked him to consider this "deed" a special gift to her, and that he wouldn't be involved beyond the initial donation. He could tell by the solidly sincere look in her eyes that she wanted a chance to have a baby, but would it be a passing whim?

And more importantly, based on his experience with his ex-wife, could he trust that giving his sperm would be the extent of his involvement with René?

That afternoon, the MidCoast Medical staff meeting dragged on. René stealthily tapped her foot under the table and listened to Jason recite the quarterly reports.

Her mind wandered, dying to know if Jon had made his decision yet, but doing her best not to make eye contact with him. She didn't want to pressure him.

"We've balanced our budget, which means we'll be able to buy that new lab equipment we've been wanting," Jason said, using a laser pen to highlight the slide behind him. "And if things keep up this way, in a few more months we won't have to send our patients to the local hospital for bronchoscopies. We can do them here."

"That would be fantastic," Phil Hansen said. "I've been waiting a long time for that."

The clinic, housed in a renovated Victorian mansion in downtown Santa Barbara, was thriving. The four-doctor practice had taken a risk and prevailed against the odds. They'd built a clientele from nothing and reached out to the community, and their hard work had finally paid off.

Jason gave his signature broad smile—the one he'd been

wearing ever since he'd fallen in love with and married Claire, the nurse practitioner. "Who'd have thought that five years ago when we conceived the idea to join forces and build our own clinic, we'd come this far?" he said, glancing toward his partners, then at his pregnant wife.

"Me," Jon raised his hand. "We did our homework, studied the demographics, discovered the perfect location and need for the clinic. We had your money, Jason," Jon added with a smirk, "and business expertise. We were bound to succeed."

He analyzed everything and, genius that he was, always did a fine job. René glanced fondly into his luminous brown eyes, which softened ever so slightly when their gazes met. She nodded and smiled. He smiled back—a masculine take on Mona Lisa. The kind of understated yet proud smile that made René react in her gut whether she wanted to or not.

Was he sending a subtle message? Had he made his decision?

Claire shifted in her chair, her brows knotted together and lips slightly pursed. René had seen that same look hundreds of times on the faces of her third trimester patients. Toward the end of the pregnancy, constantly searching for comfort, all they longed for was to get that baby out of there! René offered a smile of encouragement as she locked gazes with her newest friend in the medical group.

Claire attempted to smile back, then tossed a glance toward the ceiling as if searching for moral support. Though considered a high-risk pregnancy since Claire also had lupus, René had seen her patient through nothing but smooth sailing from the first day she'd examined her.

Claire was expecting her second child—Jason and

Claire's first together—and their newfound love was nothing short of a miracle. It gave René hope that anything was possible. Even for her.

As René listened to the rest of Jason's report, she stared at her lap, at the hands that had delivered countless babies…and the noticeably empty ring finger. Her thirty-sixth birthday was next month and this year, for the first time in her life, she'd become aware of distant keening. That ticking biological clock had never bothered her before, but now consumed her thoughts, drove her crazy with the desire to be a mother. Even to the point of making a fool of herself by asking Jon to be a sperm donor. Rather than cringe, she glanced longingly at Claire's very pregnant state.

Claire gasped.

René went on alert. "Are you all right?"

"Fine," Claire said, releasing the word with a cleansing breath. "Been having Braxton Hicks all day."

René quirked a brow. "All day? Why didn't you say something?"

Claire shrugged. "Second-kid syndrome?"

Since Claire wasn't due for another few weeks, she'd keep her eye on her as the meeting continued.

Phil shot up, forcing her to crane her neck toward the ceiling. His longish dark blond hair swept back from his face in a cavalier manner. Tanned and too handsome for his own good, he read his obligatory monthly OSHA report, and tortured them with rules running the gamut from what chemicals were acceptable to how to dispose of soiled dressings. She prayed the pulmonary faction of their group wouldn't tell them it was time for another disaster drill. And if he did, how soon could she schedule a vacation?

Claire let out another gasp, this time grabbing her back. René checked her watch. It had only been one minute since the last one.

CHAPTER TWO

JASON flew to his wife's side, the one she was holding with both hands. "Sweetheart, is there anything I can do?"

Claire diligently practiced her birthing breathing as René knelt in front of her. She put her palm on Claire's rigid stomach. The baby had dropped from yesterday's appointment and, from the feel of the rock-solid mound, was already engaged.

"I have an idea," René said. "Why don't we adjourn this meeting, and I'll take you to my office and examine you?"

"No argument from me," Claire said.

The confirmed bachelor of the group, Phil, had noticeably paled beneath his Santa Barbara tan. "I guess I'll take off, then," he said, looking relieved.

Jason gingerly assisted his wife to stand, and escorted her, like the deliciously doting soon-to-be father he was, to René's examination room in the clinic.

Jon stood perfectly still, obvious wheels turning in that wondrous mind of his. He glanced at René. "You need any help?"

"Don't know yet," she said, as she rushed out of the kitchen-turned-conference room. "Why don't you stick around just in case?"

Five minutes later, René placed Claire's feet in the stirrups on the table, gowned up and donned gloves, then started the examination. Holy smokes! Not only was she almost effaced and dilated, but her waters had broken.

"We're having a baby here," René called over her shoulder, which had Jason rushing into the room.

"That's what I was afraid of," Claire said, worry knitting her brows.

"Do we have time to get her to the hospital?" Jason asked, sounding breathless.

"Not at this stage." René gave Jason an assertive glance, then she saw Claire's questioning expression. "Don't worry, Claire. I'm here. I'll take care of you."

"Ask Mrs. Densmore if she can keep Gina tonight," Claire said to Jason.

He stood at Claire's side, eyes dilated and wider than René had ever seen them. "Everything's going to be fine," he said, squeezing his wife's fingers with one hand, fishing out his cell phone and speed-dialing their babysitter with the other.

From outside the door, she heard Jon's voice. "How can I help?"

"Get a case of the absorbent towels, and warm some baby bath blankets, then start an IV for me," she said.

A familiar-sounding scream tore from Claire's chest. "Jason, get our morphine supply and an antiemetic. It might help Claire take the edge off before she goes into transition." René waited for the contraction to diminish, then positioned the fetoscope to get an initial heart rate. She delivered babies at the local hospital, not in their clinic, and electronic fetal monitoring wasn't available here.

"Oh, and call for standby ambulance transportation," she added. After the birth, both mother and child would need to be admitted to the local hospital for observation. René bent her head and concentrated on timing the strong and steady beats. *One hundred and thirty beats a minute. Good.*

René stared into Claire's stressed-out green eyes, sending her calming thoughts. Only thirty seconds later another contraction mounted, and perspiration formed around Claire's honey-colored hairline. René continued listening for abnormal deceleration of the baby's heart rate with the contraction, and was relieved to find a normal variation. Only a ten-beat dip.

Jason lurched back into the room with the IV supplies, and when his hands proved too shaky to stick his own wife, Jon stepped in and started the IV as Jason titrated a tiny amount of morphine into the line to help ease Claire's pain in between the contractions. She didn't want Claire too relaxed when it came time to push; the baby could come out floppy instead of vigorously crying.

The labor went on for another hour and a half, when René felt the rigid beginnings of a massive contraction. Now fully effaced and dilated, Claire had moved into transition.

"Push," René said.

Though Claire seemed exhausted, she gave her all. This time the head fully crowned. When the next contraction rode in on the tail end of the first, René continued her encouragement. "Use the contraction, Claire," René said. "Push!"

Jon hovered at René's side. "I'll get a basin for the afterbirth," he said. "Are you going to need to do an episiotomy?"

"Don't think so, but get a small surgical kit for me just in case." She intended to do her part to slow down the passage of the head to avoid any tissue tear.

Jon dashed out of the room as if he were the expectant father, and when he returned, René put him to work tracking the baby's heart rate through the fetoscope so she could concentrate on the birth. Not only was he fascinated with the listening device—typical of him—he was most likely figuring out a way to make a better one.

All was well, but the contractions came so quickly and hard that Claire didn't have time to relax in between. Wringing with sweat, she looked exhausted, ready to give up. Along came another contraction.

"Bear down, Claire! Push! Push!" René urged, as she cupped the baby's head in her hands and moved it downward as Claire pushed with everything she had. Her legs trembled and she let fly words René hadn't heard since the last Lakers basketball game she'd attended.

She slipped the umbilical cord free of the baby's face, and assisted as first the head, then one shoulder and then the other, slipped out. No sooner had the mouth cleared the birth canal, than the baby cried.

Obviously relieved after delivering the hardest part— the head—Claire wept.

René glanced up long enough to see tears fill Jason's eyes. "Oh, my God," he said. The room went blurry for her, too, but she couldn't dwell on the swell of emotion taking over; she had a baby to finish delivering.

The baby slipped out, and René skillfully caught him, as she'd done so many times over her career, but this one felt more special than all the rest. It was her partner and friend's baby. This infant sent her dreaming of birthing her own baby, of daring to hope she'd get the chance.

"It's a beautiful boy," she said, wiping the baby's mouth and face with the warm and soft blanket that her new assistant, Jon, had handed her. He gave her another. After a quick check of the perfect little body, she wrapped the baby up as if the most precious thing in the world, and Jon produced a syringe bulb to suction the baby's mouth and nose. He'd thought of everything. Had he thought of his answer yet?

The baby continued to make a healthy wail, music to her mother-longing ears. René laid the newborn on Claire's stomach, and pressed to feel for another contraction, then prepared for the afterbirth. Jon held the large stainless-steel basin in readiness.

Jason hovered over Claire and the baby, as they laughed and cried together. René was too busy to hear everything they said, but knew *love* had been mentioned several times. And the name Jason James Rogers, Junior.

She glanced at Jon and saw the familiar look of wonder that new life always evoked. He met her gaze and held it, adding a smile. Could he read her thoughts, her desires? His short-cropped salt-and-pepper-brown hair had always made his eyes look intense, but she'd never seen that fiery excitement there before. Did he understand how she felt? How every cell in her body cried out for the chance to be a mother?

New life. Nothing compared with the wonder. *Especially if the newborn belongs to you.* Jon glanced back at the happy family, and she prayed they might perform a silent miracle on her behalf.

Jason kissed Claire's forehead, as a distant siren rent the air. René could practically palpate their bonding. There was something about a baby that changed everything, that turned lovers into a family, and sealed a bond outsiders could never fathom. She'd seen it countless times, but this time it plunged straight into her heart.

Her chest clenched and ached for what she longed for, for the answer she depended on to provide the portal to her dreams. She couldn't look at him again for fear she'd beg him to say yes.

"You want to do the honors?" She'd double clamped the umbilical cord and held it with gauze, handing Jason sterile scissors from the suturing pack. For a general practitioner, he looked apprehensive. She gave him an encouraging wink. When he'd finished, she applied the plastic clip on the baby's end of the cord and smiled at the squirming newborn—healthy and strong, though small and a good three weeks premature by her calculations. Babies were nothing short of a miracle; she'd been convinced of that since her first delivery.

There went that clutch in her chest again, the one that made it hard to breathe. She couldn't look at Jon, but felt his gaze on her.

"Congratulations, man," Jon said to Jason. Memories of his wife giving birth flashed before his eyes. Nothing had awed him more, or given him greater satisfaction, than seeing his daughters brought into the world.

He didn't have to look at René to know what she was going through; she'd thoroughly explained her deep hunger for motherhood to him last night. How must it feel to deliver babies for everyone else, and at the end of the day still be alone?

Jason grinned so hard his eyes almost disappeared. Claire patted his hand and welcomed the baby to her chest with the other. From the corner of his eye, Jon watched René's reverent gaze as a pang twisted in his gut. He couldn't take it. Couldn't take the feeling or the implication a simple answer of yes would bring, so he bent to gather the soiled towels and stuff them into the exam room hamper.

The air was too thick with yearning and he'd never been

the kind of guy to make dreams come true, just ask his wife. He needed to change the mood. "Do we get paid overtime for this?"

Not usually one to make light, his joke made everyone blurt a relieved laugh. Combined with Claire and Jason's euphoria, joy filled the room from every angle, and against his better judgment, the feel-good rush fueled a growing desire to grant his coworker her biggest wish. He couldn't let it influence him. His decision would be made the same way he made all of his medical determinations, based on logic and common sense. Nothing less.

René looked at him, the makeshift assistant, while the lovebirds and new baby continued bonding. Her expression had changed, as if she understood how much pressure she'd put on him, and how unfairly the perfect timing of this birth had played in her favor. A warm smile appeared on her face, as if the sun had cracked through thunder-clouds. How could he not smile back?

"You're not bad for a novice," she said.

So she'd opted to keep it light, too. Relief crawled over him, as if a welcoming blanket. Birth or no birth, he wasn't ready to make his life-altering decision, though her can-didness went far to nudge him along.

He flashed a capable look, one that conveyed *I can handle just about anything.* "You're not the only one who's full of surprises, René."

"You want to hold him?" Claire had already dressed her contented-looking baby in blue by early the next morning.

René grinned. "I'd love to." She'd popped in last night and found Claire sleeping, the baby swaddled and content in the bedside bassinet, and Jason lightly snoring in the lounger, so she tiptoed outside and read the pediatrician's report instead. When the nurses assured her that Claire's fundus was firming right up and there were no signs of excessive bleeding or fever, she'd gone home rather than wake up the new mother and father.

This morning, Jason was already down in the business office settling up, and they'd be heading home to introduce the baby to his big sister, Gina, as soon as René performed her discharge examination.

The six-pound boy squirmed when she took him and tucked him into the hook of her arm. The feel of him sent her reeling. He smelled fresh, like baby lotion and new life, and the clutching in her chest nearly took her breath away. She detected eye movement beneath tightly closed lids with no hint of lashes, and wondered what babies dreamed about. She gently pressed her lips to his head, and inhaled the wonders of his being pure as the first light. The longing in her soul for a baby swelled to near-unbearable proportions. His fine light brown hair resembled a balding man's with a noticeably high forehead. On him it was adorable. Her eyes crinkled as the smile creased her lips.

His tiny hands latched on to her fingers, barely covering the tips. The flood of feelings converged—tingling, prickling, burning—until her eyes brimmed.

Her mouth filled with water, and she swallowed. "He's so beautiful," she whispered, discovering that Claire's eyes shimmered with tears, too.

"I know," Claire said. "Babies are miracles, aren't they?"

Overwhelmed by the moment, wishing for a miracle of her own, her breath got swept away and all René could do was nod.

* * *

Jon wolfed down three bagels loaded with peanut butter and downed a pint of orange juice straight out of the carton when he arrived at work. He hadn't slept for a second night, and the usual runner's high had eluded him somewhere around mile eight that morning. He scrubbed his face and strode down the hall.

René was just about to knock on a patient exam room.

"Got a minute?" he said.

She started at his voice and snatched back her hand. "Oh!"

He headed for her office, stopped at the door, tilted his head and arched his eyes to guide her inside.

René's breathing dropped out of sync, coming in gulps. She followed Jon toward her office as tiny invisible wings showered over her head to toe. Oh, God, what would he say?

She stopped one step short of entering the room, swallowed the sock in her throat and gathered her composure. She pasted a smile on her face in hopes of covering her gnawing apprehension, and proceeded inside, then prayed for courage to accept whatever Jon might tell her.

Would she have to go back to plan A, and the donor clinic? God, she hoped not.

"So, I've been thinking," Jon said, the second she stepped over the threshold. "A lot." He engaged her eyes and held her motionless.

"And?" she whispered, closing the door.

"I'm bowled over by this, René. I'd be lying if I didn't say that. I don't understand why you insisted on asking me when Phil is single and available." He held up a hand to stop her before she could begin with the plethora of reasons all over again. She'd recited A to Z quite thoroughly, twice, the night before last. "But I believe your sincerity in wanting this—" he glanced toward the door as if to make sure no one was within hearing range, and though it was closed, he lowered his voice anyway "—baby. I saw it in your eyes last night. This isn't some freaked-out biological-clock whim. This is the real deal."

She nodded her head vehemently.

"I trust you'll stick to your word about my small role in it."

"To the T, Jon. I promise." Oh, heavens, she didn't want to anticipate too much, but it sounded as if he might take her up on the plan. She could only hope and pray. And hold her breath.

"It feels really callous on my part knowing how I plan to take a sabbatical and all, and I care about you as a coworker, and, well, I don't want things to change professionally." He scrubbed his jaw, and the now-familiar facial hair. "This could really ruin our working together."

"I wouldn't want that, either, Jon." Oh, hell, in his swinging pendulum of emotions he'd convinced her from one second to the next to give up on him. Did she really want to sacrifice their professional friendship because of her desire for a baby? Could she blame him for wanting nothing to do with her outrageous plan?

"I'd want to think we could talk things through whenever we needed," he said. "That though I'd be nothing more than a clinical donor as far as the baby goes, I'd like to be your friend. And as a friend and donor I should be able to share in your happiness, like everyone else here in the clinic."

She nodded at his reasonable request, afraid to get too hopeful in case he pulled the rug out from under her dream. "I'd want that, too. I don't want to lose what we have, Jon. Never."

He stepped closer. "What *do* we have, you and me?"

He studied her eyes, making her feel under a microscope. Those winged creatures returned, dropping anxious nectar over the surface of her skin. She took a slow, intentional, quivery breath.

"We have five years of hard work and wonderful achievements to share," she said. "We've laughed, celebrated, mourned and prevailed together over every setback in our clinic." She took a step closer to reach out for his hand. "No matter what happens, if you say yes, you will always be a special friend, Jon." His long fingers laced through hers, still feeling foreign, though warm, regardless of how many times she'd clutched his hand lately.

"No one can know a thing," he cautioned. "If it comes out, I'll leave the clinic."

The importance of anonymity worried her. As with any risk, there was a cost. Was she willing to accept the guilt of changing Jon's future if someone found out? Was she willing to let him pay the price? Confidence leaked out of her pores, leaving her insecure and wobbly. Maybe plan A was the only way to go, but Jon gently stroked her thumb with his, and a silent soothing message transmitted between them.

"I promise," she whispered. A sharp pang in her gut, over the thought of ruining whatever relationship they had, forced her to face the gravity of their possible pact. This was it. Right here, right now. Her dream, their deal, was about to become a reality. The air grew cool and seemed to rush over the surface of her skin, setting off goose bumps.

His molasses-brown gaze swept over her face, as if searching for honesty. Could he look deep enough to see the longings of her heart? She'd meant what she'd said with all of her being.

"After you're pregnant, I want superfriend status." A tiny tug at one corner of his mouth almost turned into a smile.

"You'll do it?" She grabbed his other hand and squeezed both, reeling with hope. The surge pushed her up onto her toes, ready to jump up and down, or kiss his cheek, based on his final decision.

"Yes," he said. "I'll do it."

At the beautiful sound of his reply, she did both.

CHAPTER THREE

THE reward for getting the exquisitely lovely René Munroe to smile was one large dimple and a satisfying hint of an overbite. Jon had once read a study on facial esthetics and found that, in general, men preferred a slight overbite. Come to think of it, seeing her grin like that, he did, too. She'd squealed, jumped up and kissed his cheek when he'd agreed to go through with her plan. She'd kissed him so hard he felt the imprint of her lips half the afternoon. He'd never seen her so animated, and it surprised him, made him wonder how much more there was to know about her.

Since his divorce, after work, he liked his alone time. Preferred it. He'd already done his run for the day and wasn't sure how else to work off this new itchy feeling. And oddly enough, the last thing he felt like being right this minute was alone. Sure he had a day filled with patients ahead of him, but what about after that? He wouldn't get his girls until the weekend.

"You want to go for a coffee after work?" he blurted. The thought of going home to his "man cave"—as his daughters facetiously referred to it—after such a momentous agreement, had little appeal. "We should probably get to know each other a little more."

"That sounds perfect," she said.

Perfect. She used the word frequently, and when it came to describing her it suited…well…it suited her perfectly.

"I'll see you later, then," he said, heading for the door with a new spring in his jogging shoes.

At the end of the workday, they locked the clinic and hiked the two blocks over to State Street, and caught the electric trolley heading north to an alfresco coffeehouse. They'd committed to coffee, not dinner. It was a start. Even though it was late January, the temperature was sixty-five degrees, and the outdoor restaurants all had outdoor heating lamps for their patrons' comfort. If he inhaled deep enough, he could smell the crisp, tangy sea.

"Do you ever get tired of delivering babies?" he asked, as they rode.

"No. It's wonderful, isn't it?"

Jon nodded and thought back to the birth of both of his daughters. Amanda had been born at a midwife center eighteen years back, and Lacy, at home, under water, eighteen months later. His ex-wife had wanted it that way. He'd felt as if he'd run a marathon after each labor and delivery, but had never been more ecstatic in his life. Watching Jason and Claire last night had brought back long-forgotten memories.

Somehow lecturing patients about their tickers didn't quite measure up, though of course he understood the importance of the heart sustaining life. It just couldn't quite compare with the theatrical bang of a delivery.

"I never thought I'd see Jason happy again," she said.

Hmm? Oh, he'd taken a tangential thought trip, and quickly focused back in. "I guess there's hope for all of us, then," Jon said, deciding, on a scale of one to ten, he probably sat around six on the happy meter—not ecstatic, not miserable, just making due, especially since his divorce.

He'd forgotten what this type of elation felt like, being more used to the endorphin variety from his long and hard runner workouts. Emotional highs were…well…unusual these days. Definitely nice, but different.

He glanced at René smiling with cheeks blushed from her hard work and the brisk evening air. Her amber eyes hinted at green, probably because of the teal-colored sweater she wore. *As a pool reflects the sky, light eyes reflect surrounding colors*. Where had he recently read that, and why had he lost his train of thought again?

"You've sure made me a happy camper," she said, with a perky glance out the window, which made her earrings sway.

Never having been in the business of granting wishes before, he enjoyed the swell of pride and rode along with it.

He noticed René always wore extralong earrings, and right now the colorful beads and loops almost reached her shoulders, and for some odd reason it fascinated him the way they swayed with the movement of her head. Mesmerizing. But that was neither here nor there; he was on a mission to get to know René better, not notice her earrings or how they swayed with her long, thick hair. There had to be some relevant question he could think of to ask.

For the life of him, he couldn't figure out why a woman such as René wasn't happily married. She should be having a baby with her doting husband instead of soliciting his services.

His services? The thought tickled the corner of his mouth into a near smile and he looked straight ahead so she wouldn't notice. He'd really agreed to do this crazy thing. For René. Two years ago, when Cherie had kicked him to the curve without so much as a hint of being discontent, who would have ever thought about agreeing to such a ridiculous idea? That smile kept edging up his face, and he kept staring out the front window to hide it.

When they reached their stop, they hopped off the trolley, walked half a block and ordered their brews at the shop, then sat outside to enjoy the clear evening sky. In the distance, he could see the lights flicker on Stearns Wharf and wished he could hear the waves crashing against the pilings.

Beneath her shrouded gaze, René sat quietly, as if waiting for him to break the ice, to bring up the next step in their plan—admittedly, the trickiest, as far as he was concerned.

Not ready to go there yet, Jon took a drink of espresso and winced at the bitterness. "Since we don't know much about each other, I'll start. My girls are both in high school. Amanda's going to graduate this June, and Lacy next year. Amanda has applied to every Ivy League school she could think of since she's got it in her head that, if she wants to go to Harvard Law, she's got to do her undergraduate studies at an equally prestigious school."

Everyone in the medical clinic was well aware of his divorce two years earlier, how hard it had hit. But no one could possibly know, since he'd worked extrahard at hiding it, how devastated he'd been. How he never saw himself ever loving again, beyond his daughters. They'd seen the happy family guy turn into his current recluse status, and he'd complained bitterly to anyone who would listen about how Cherie had practically cleaned him out financially. But he'd always stopped short of the point of how he didn't think he could go on, and how he never ever wanted to commit to another relationship because of it.

On a more practical note, he didn't need to bore René with the difficulty of supporting his family at the level to which they'd become accustomed, while living on his own and saving for both daughters' college funds.

Still, having taken the business risk with his colleagues and opened the clinic, he'd refused to bail for a higher-paying job when Cherie demanded the outrageous monthly alimony. The clinic was all about autonomy, which mattered a lot to him. It was all he had left. That same autonomy was what fueled his sabbatical dreams.

René sipped her tea concoction as coils of steam circled her face. He could smell the peppermint all the way across the table. She lifted intriguingly shaped brows, brows he'd never really noticed before now.

"And Lacy?" she asked. "What are her plans?"

Jon barked a laugh. "She's thinking more in line with Oahu U." He made the "hang loose" hand gesture associated with the laidback Hawaiian Islands. "My girls couldn't be more different if they tried." He shook his head, knowing both daughters had genius IQs. Sometimes he wondered if his genes were a blessing or a curse.

"As long as they're happy, right?" she said.

He nodded wholeheartedly. Ah, to be young and free to start over again, but happiness was such a subjective state of being. At forty-two he was the picture of health, which should make him happy, yet sometimes he felt unnecessarily weighted down by responsibility. At times like that, his sabbatical plans helped keep him going.

Since divorcing and moving out, he'd occupied eight hundred square feet of high-tech loft where he practiced urban minimalism. His daughters were the ones to name it the "man cave." As long as he had his books and stereo equipment, and visitation rights with his girls, he'd make do—even if he couldn't satisfactorily explain the temporary feel of his current living situation.

She watched him closely, forcing him to say something. Anything. "And I suppose this deal we're making will make you happy?" he said.

With warm eyes hinting at wisdom well beyond her thirty-plus years, René studied him as if on the verge of telling her deepest secret. That near-perfect smile stretched across her face. "You have no idea."

The moments yawned on with the two of them cautiously watching each other. She told him how her parents had retired and moved to Nevada. How she was an only child. How all of her best friends were married and how she always felt like the odd woman out whenever they got together. He asked where the men in her life had all gone. Her relaxed expression became peppered with annoyance.

He knew the war chant—men, the callous heartbreakers! He could repeat the same, only changing the gender. Yet he wanted her to open up, to tell him something personal, so he bit his tongue. If they were going to make a baby together, he felt he had the right to know more about her.

"Ten years ago, I'd thought I'd found my soul mate, but instead, he dumped me, crushing my heart beneath his feet as he walked out the door." She glanced at him. Could she tell he knew exactly how she felt? "Sorry for sounding overdramatic, but that's how it felt. Since then, I've had a series of less-than-satisfying relationships, and I'm pessimistic when it comes to the topic of permanent love."

Jon had been married so long, and hadn't pursued much in the way of romantic relationships since his divorce out of commitment fears, but he'd heard enough women around the clinic moan about the same thing. Love and permanence didn't seem to fit. He figured the world of dating wasn't such a great place to be these days, but for the life of him and his old-school ways, he couldn't figure out what kind of guy would let a woman like René get away.

Watching René sip her tea, Jon figured the ticking of her biological clock influenced her every thought. Sure, lots of women were waiting until their early forties to have their first babies, but she'd have to risk the time to find the right guy, get married and get pregnant when it was a well-known fact that fertility declined with each year after thirty. She'd made it very clear she wasn't willing to take the chance. He'd computed that if she waited much longer, she'd be in her late fifties with teenagers, and that thought, having two teenagers himself, gave him pause. It was all luck anyway, and if he knew one thing about René, it was that she wasn't a gambler. If she was going to respond to her brewing and strengthening desire for motherhood, she'd have to act…well, soon.

"Have you really given up on finding the right guy?" He lifted his brows, prodding, then when she didn't immediately answer, he switched to a more challenging look.

Her gaze danced away. "Not completely."

Since she wasn't about to open up, he let slip a sudden thought. "Someone like you could make the right guy very happy, but after you have a baby—" *my baby;* the quick thought took him by surprise and not unpleasantly "—it may be more difficult to find him."

"Who?" she asked.

"Him. The right guy."

"Having a baby on my own may not seem like the perfect solution, but it's what I want. I don't need a man to validate me. And if the consequences are being a single mother, I'll deal with them like a big girl."

For the third time in as many days she placed her hand on top of his. Her warmth enveloped his and on reflex he responded and twined his fingers through hers. This hand-holding business was starting to feel normal. His eyes latched on to her almost-caramel gaze and held it, unwavering.

She squeezed his hand. "You're giving me the most important gift I've ever wanted. How will I ever be able to thank you?"

He thought long and hard about the right response. He thought about the greatest gift in his life—his daughters—and though his answer might come off as being lame, he meant it. "You can thank me by being a good mother."

René had pulled the lucky straw when it came to choosing offices. Hers was in the front of the American version of the Queen Anne Victorian house. The three-story, cream-colored structure proudly bore the official Santa Barbara historical site emblem. Her corner office was nestled in the polygonal-shaped tower, which came complete with ceiling-to-floor bay windows. She'd covered them in sheer white lace, and loved how the sun danced in patterns across the walls in the afternoons.

She'd splurged on a Chinese-inspired walnut desk with cabriole legs, and one huge Oriental rug over the wood floor. The office seemed more befitting of a princess than a middle-class girl from Tustin, California.

Her parents had cashed in early on her brains, and scholarships flowed throughout her high school and college years. She'd never relied on anything but hard work and innovative thinking to get her through, though many attributed her success to her looks rather than sweat and elbow grease. It didn't seem worth the effort to hold a grudge for their uncharitable assumptions.

She'd tried her best to be the perfect daughter, the perfect student, the perfect girlfriend—that one had never paid off—and the perfect medical practice partner and doctor. The last required long hours and dedication to the clinic, and left little room for a normal social life. Now, thanks to Jon's decision, she could skip over all of the preliminaries and have her shot at motherhood.

His one request? To be a good mother. He hadn't said perfect mother, no, just a *good* one. A good-enough mother. And that's what she'd try with all of her heart to be.

A rap at her door, followed by her nurse escorting her next patient into the office for a consultation, forced her out of the all-consuming thoughts.

After greetings, René engaged the tension-filled eyes of her last patient of the day. The woman sat across from her desk wringing her hands. Her husband sat waiting beside her, straight as a giraffe, eyes more like a hawk.

"I'll get right to it," René said and smiled, fingering a printout report. "I received your endometrial biopsy results this morning, and they were benign." She smiled again, and noticed that relief hadn't washed away the couple's furrowed brows and apprehensive eyes. "That means it was negative. You're clean. No more cancer."

The middle-aged patient and her husband shared a sigh, smiled and hugged. The scene made René wish all her medical "news" could be as good.

After they stood and shook hands, and René had instructed the patient to stop by Gaby's desk and make a follow-up appointment, she folded her arms and paced the room. She was at her prime, in excellent physical condition, and good health should never be taken for granted. Now was the perfect time…for…

Her eyes drifted to the one wall reserved for every baby she'd ever delivered. The ever-growing collage of pictures—big and small, ornate and plain—called out to her. She scanned the gallery and thought again about becoming a mother. Chills tickled her neck.

She sat at her desk, stared at the detailed crown molding along the ceiling and tapped a light rhythm with her pen. More exciting thoughts about parenthood whispered through her mind. Her dream really could come true. She could barely wait.

With her restless gaze wandering the expanse of the office, she nibbled a fingernail, while her crossed leg pumped a breakneck beat. On the opposite wall was a framed photograph of the four MidCoast Medical partners the day the clinic had opened. She meandered over and took the picture in her hands. They all smiled. She was flanked by Jon on one side and Philip on the other, and next to Jon stood Jason, the owner of the building. The day was one of the happiest of her life. She remembered hugging each of them, and sharing a bottle of champagne. She thought about the hope they all had, and the desire to serve the local Santa Barbara community, back before Jason's wife and daughter had died and Jon was still happily married.

She'd expected to marry, too, but life had surprised them all. Only Philip, the happy bachelor, seemed to make it through the past five years unscathed.

Well, it was her chance now. The sperm bank had called to tell her Jon had made an appointment for today— Valentine's Day! He had skipped part of his morning clinic for an appointment, and she'd quietly chuckled over the reason—to donate his sperm, designated for her. But when it hit her between the eyes that her dream was about to come true, the gesture touched her so deeply she'd flat-out cried. Now she grinned and shook her head. Jon was right about two things: he was full of surprises, and no matter what happened after this, their relationship would never be the same.

Who knows how long she stared at the photograph. Jon's image made her smile. His lanky frame, angular features, friendly demeanor and over-the-top intelligence gave her confidence she'd chosen the right man, and right now, she owed him another gigantic thank-you. And maybe another home-cooked meal?

Jon stared down Antonin Grosso. The stocky man sat across from his desk with arms folded, and a stubborn glint in his eyes.

"Your thallium treadmill showed an abnormality suggestive of arterial blockage."

The man scrubbed his face with a beefy hand. "Please, doctor, I'm a butcher—speak the English!"

Jon grimaced. True, layman's terms were his downfall. "You may have a blocked artery in your heart. I can't stress enough the need for an angiogram. Oh, uh, that's a study that will tell me if any of your heart arteries *are* blocked." He fished through his patient education pamphlets and found the right one, then handed it to him.

"I no need this test. I feel fine."

"Feeling fine and being fine are two different things, Mr. Grosso." Jon ran his hand over his stiff spiky hair and re-considered the explanation in butcher's vernacular. "Take your prime beef. It may look fine, but until the U.S. government checks it out and approves it, you won't know if it's diseased or not." He stared at the man while the analogy computed. "You look good. You feel good. But your heart isn't so good. This study says so. We may need to unplug the arteries so your heart gets more blood and feels better."

Something clicked. The man's expression brightened. "You mean like that plumbing guy? My pipes need cleaning?"

Jon snapped his fingers and pointed at Mr. Grosso. "Exactly! Your pipes may need cleaning out. We need to schedule an appointment for a special test to decide if they do."

"I don't know. That sounds dangerous. I need to talk to my wife first."

"Okay. Talk to your wife, but make it soon. I'll talk to her, too, if you'd like. Bottom line—you need this test, Mr. Grosso."

"Okay, okay, but I feel fine." He rose to leave, and Jon stood, too.

"It's Friday. I want to hear from you by next Wednesday." Jon waved the EKG and treadmill results around to impress the patient that he had solid proof he needed the angiogram. "You have to get this done ASAP."

The man glanced over his shoulder, then hung his head when he grabbed the doorknob. "We'll see," he mumbled.

Jon sat on the edge of his solid oak behemoth of a desk and shook his head. Before he had the chance to mutter a single curse, something grabbed his attention, and two young ladies rushed him.

"Dad!"

"Hi, Daddy!"

Amanda and Lacy threw their arms around him and

hung tight. Every frustrated physician-oriented thought he'd been thinking flew out of his head. His teenage daughters had a way of doing that for him.

"Hey!" he said, smiling. "You guys are early."

"Mom had a hot date," Lacy said, with a strong hint of sarcasm.

Ack. Cherie hadn't even tried to hide her multiple trysts from the girls since the divorce. Hell, she'd started extramarital dating before they'd even finalized the divorce. The thought still boiled his blood.

While deep in a group hug, he noticed René walk up to his door. Her intent expression changed to comprehension when she spied the girls. Since his office was in the back of the building, and the copying machines and bathrooms were in the middle, he knew she only came to this part of the clinic if she needed to talk to him.

She shook her head and flipped her hand in a wave, mouthed "thank you" and started to walk away. The sparkle in her eyes, since he'd agreed to be her sperm donor, had made everyone in the clinic take note. He'd heard his nurses comment to each other. "What's up with Dr. Munroe?" "I wonder if she's in love!"

His daughters turned their heads toward the door and caught sight of René just as she turned to leave. "I just wanted to wish you a happy Valentine's Day, Jon," she said, expertly covering for herself.

"Hey, same to you."

He grinned at the thought of having put that gleam in her flashing eyes. Briefly, he wondered what would have transpired if his daughters hadn't arrived early. Would she give him another squeeze of the hand and kiss on the cheek, a gorgeously grateful smile, and eyes so filled with joy his heart would palpitate? He felt guilty how simple his part of the agreement was, but if she wanted to make this huge deal out of it, it was fine with him. As long as no one found out. As long as it wouldn't change his life or routine, or plans for China.

"Who was that?" Lacy asked.

"You know, Dr. Munroe. She's one of the partners," he said. He continued the group hug with the girls, and smiled.

"She's really pretty," Amanda said.

"Why don't you ask her out?" Lacy added.

"A date?" He made an incredulous laugh. "Who needs that when I've already got my favorite girls?"

Even if it would cost him a dinner out and involve some sort of shoes or clothes shopping, he wouldn't trade his bi-weekly visitation weekends with his daughters for anything in the world. Especially on the most interesting Valentine's Day he'd had in a long time.

CHAPTER FOUR

MONDAY morning, René had to teach the last "What to Expect When Expecting" class since Claire had delivered prematurely. Ten women in various stages of pregnancy sat rapt with attention at the day's topic: Epidural or Natural Birth. René already knew what her personal preference would be. Natural birth.

One woman was unfamiliar to René, and since only MidCoast Medical patients, in particular her OB/Gyn patients could participate, she questioned her.

"Oh, I'm Gretchen, Stephanie Ingram's doula. She was called into court today."

The lawyer was involved in a high-profile murder case, and René had often lamented about the horrible timing of it with her pregnancy.

Hmm, a doula. Stephanie had hired an assistant to provide nonmedical support during the pregnancy and delivery. Claire had recommended her. The doula would perform nonmedical duties—anything from back rubs to aromatherapy, to errands, or anything else the future mom might need. The doula's goal was to organize and support the mother through the entire process. *Sounds like some-*

thing I may require in the near future, if all goes well. It was never too soon to plan ahead.

"May I have your business card?" René asked.

Gretchen Lingstrom—freckled, redheaded, tattooed and eyebrow pierced—beamed as she handed her the card.

After the class had ended, René searched out Jon. She wanted to bring him up to date on the chat with her lawyer. Both of his exam rooms were closed, which meant he was seeing a patient.

She peeked around the corner of his door. He sat, head down, scribbling away with his left hand. For an out-of-this-stratosphere smart guy, he definitely had an artistic side. One thing she remembered was that he kept a journal, and it was something she'd always admired about him. He'd admitted it to her at the first clinic Christmas party after his divorce, where he'd had a bit too much to drink. He'd clearly been hurting at the time, and said it helped him relieve stress and work through his divorce. She'd never realized how hard his divorce had been on him until the other night, when they'd set out to get to know each other after agreeing to make a baby together. She wondered if he was writing about how backward their process was.

René smiled and tapped on the door. Her stomach went quivery and her heart bumped up its rhythm, and she didn't understand why.

"Hey," he said, a welcoming gleam in his eyes.

"Hey. I just wanted to bring you up-to-date. I got word the…uh…specimen made the grade. We're all set to go as soon as I—" she glanced down the hall and back, then whispered "—ovulate."

Surprisingly, his cheeks rouged up as he gave her a lightbulb broad smile and a thumbs-up sign.

* * *

That afternoon, Mrs. Grosso stood somber faced before Jon, with Antonin doing his best to hide behind her four-foot-eleven frame. "He no want the test. It's too much. Too dangerous."

"Mrs. Grosso, are you aware that your husband could die from a heart attack if he doesn't take care of his arteries?"

She glanced over her shoulder; Antonin made such a minute head shake only his eyes seemed to move. She let go a long string of emphatic Italian words, obviously berating him for denying that fact prior to now.

"No. No. No," Antonin said. He couldn't be swayed.

Worry etched her brow as she shrugged. "What I'm going to do?"

Jon looked into his patient's eyes. "If I make an appointment for an ultrasound of the heart, where they just bounce sound waves off your chest, will you go?"

"No cutting? No needles?" the man said.

Jon shook his head. "If you see for yourself there is a blockage, will you promise to have the test—the real test—to save your life?"

The missus poured out more Italian, this time using her hands and arms for accentuation. Antonin's grumpy face took on a more thoughtful expression.

"You'll already be in the hospital and we can handle things from there. What do you say?" Jon said.

The man stared at the floor and mumbled, "Oh-kay."

Jon clapped his hands. "That's the spirit." He hopped behind his desk and punched in a phone number. "Let's see how soon I can arrange the ultrasound." *For the walking time bomb.*

He got put on hold, used his index finger to play with the silly little patch of hair under his lower lip. The patch his girls had insisted he grow. They said it would make him look sexy. He almost laughed out loud. Did a man want to look sexy at forty-two? A really odd thought occurred to him. If René had handpicked him to be her donor, was there anything about him she found sexy besides his DNA?

He squashed the thought immediately. The last thing he wanted was to foul up his plans for freedom with any kind of commitment.

As he waited on hold, and the Grossos spoke in excitable Italian, hands and gestures flying, his mind drifted to the vision of René at his door that morning. She wore a little white sweater over her earth-tone patterned sheath dress. The half-sleeved sweater with a shiny bead-and-stud design up the front had been the perfect accessory. He'd noticed that about her. She was good with details.

And he liked that. Liked that he knew she'd always do a job thoroughly, down to the miniscule touches. He thought about the dinner she'd made the night she'd asked him to be her sperm donor—she cooked that way, too. Whenever they had potlucks at work from now on, he'd twist her arm to cook. There was something in the way she combined herbs and spices that made her dishes exceptional. If she weren't such a fantastic doctor, he might suggest she'd missed her calling, but if she'd become a chef, he'd never have met her.

An uncomfortable feeling spun in his stomach. These were useless thoughts, fanciful thoughts, that a man with plans for a sabbatical shouldn't bother to have. As he continued to wait to speak to a hospital operator, he thumbed through his journal, past the part detailing life's recent surprising turn, and back to his list of cities in China that he planned to visit after he attended the world cardiac conference in Beijing—2011; the year of the rabbit.

In light of the new circumstances, for some dumb reason, the year of the rabbit struck him funny.

The following Saturday morning, René rode her bicycle on a different route, along the Cabrillo Boulevard bike path. The early morning air was crisp and the sun bright. She squinted, despite wearing sunglasses. Up ahead on the palm-tree-lined path, a tall, fit figure ran at a near sprinter's pace. From the crowd of joggers, she'd recognize him anywhere.

She'd never seen Jon jogging, and definitely had never seen him shirtless before. It shook her a little. His musculature surprised her, too. Intrigued her. Long waisted, like a swimmer, his shoulders were broad and his upper arms were surprisingly buff. Jon? His stomach was flat and obviously no stranger to crunches. Another surprise. Long solid legs finished off his six-foot frame, and carried him at a rapid clip along the shore.

He concentrated on his run, and didn't see or recognize her when she pedaled toward him. Maybe it was the bike helmet? Vanity prompted her to take it off and fluff out her hair before she called his name.

"Jon!" She waved.

His pace stuttered, he turned and followed the sound.

"Jon! Hi!"

He waved and ran off the path, circling back toward her. "What's up?"

"Just enjoying the sunny morning."

"Yeah, it's beautiful today, isn't it."

As they chitchatted, she worked hard at concentrating on his face so he wouldn't think she was checking him out.

His gaze passed over her shorts-clad legs once or twice. What was that about?

A large group of cyclists advanced, so she cut things short.

"I just wanted to thank you again for…you know."

"Ah," he said, suddenly finding his running shoes fascinating. "That."

They exchanged a secret-handshake kind of look, something that was quickly becoming routine.

"Yeah. That. You know how grateful I am."

"Yep."

"Okay. Well, I'll see you Monday," she said.

He nodded and waved. She noticed the well-formed muscle ripple up his arm and shoulder, and couldn't stop herself from waiting until he'd run off before putting her cycle helmet back on. Once she'd set off, she couldn't resist a glance over her shoulder for the back view. She swerved and had to put her foot down to keep from falling. But it was worth it! A straight spine with triangular muscles fanning across his back, flexed with the natural swing of his arms. His torso angled down to trim hips and a backside barely covered by his shorts. Never in a million years would she have imagined him to look this hot. She'd come to a dead stop and soon realized several more cyclists were headed her way, so she pushed off and continued in the opposite direction.

She'd been up all night thinking about Jon. Not in a sexual way. No. But in a new and different light—a beam of potential. Seeing him like this mixed her up, especially now, when things were moving ahead as planned.

She had nothing but respect for Jon Becker. They'd been through a lot together launching the medical practice. She remembered how flattered she'd been when Jason and

Jon had approached her about joining them on the venture. She'd only been board certified in OB/Gyn for a year and yet they'd invited her to take a chance on a new direction for her career, one where she had more say and control. She remembered blinking two or three times and saying yes! And she hadn't looked back or regretted it since.

She'd almost broached the subject foremost on her mind with Jon last Friday afternoon, just to tell him thanks for what seemed like the hundredth time in the past few weeks, but he'd been waylaid by his girls. She'd caught them in a cuddle with the oldest, Amanda, sporting a sleek dark-brown bob, kissing his cheek, and the honey-haired Lacy, with wild shoulder-length curls, snuggling his chest. He never looked happier than when he was with them. A prerequisite for what they'd planned was that it couldn't affect his relationship with his girls in any way. They'd never know, and she'd do anything to keep it that way.

René pedaled beyond the beach volleyball courts toward the pond. Her mind wandered back to Jon as the hodge-podge of her thoughts practically made her eyes cross. They'd worked closely together for five years. Not only was he a person she admired and trusted, he was a genius, and ethically minded—a great combination for father material. She had nothing but respect for him and cared about him as a friend. To admit he was a damn fine specimen of a man on top of everything else was far too confusing.

No way would she allow herself to examine that freshly discovered secret. Even though he'd looked fantastic in those jogging shorts, there was no place for emotion in this plan.

She circled the pond and headed toward home. She'd been tracking her menstrual cycle for the past few months, and if all went well, she'd be ovulating next week. Deep in thought, she glanced up and nearly screamed. A four-seat bicycle surrey almost ran her off the road. She veered from the path and onto the grass, and stopped just before rolling over the curb and into the street, heavy with fast-moving traffic. Once she regained her breath she got right back on the bike and pedaled faster.

If she got herself killed, she wouldn't be able to get inseminated!

The following week, Jon's morning cardiac clinic had been brutal. One complication after another—a surprise diagnosis or three, word of a cardiac arrest of one of his oldest patients and then he'd had to break the news to Katerina and Antonin Grosso that, after having the echocardiogram, Antonin definitely needed a triple bypass graft, *molto presto*.

Just before noon, as Jon discussed the pros and cons of blood pressure medicine with his newest cardiac patient, his intercom buzzed.

It was René. "I've got the contract. Can you meet me at Stearns Wharf for lunch today?"

"Sure," he said, pleased about the prospect of seeing her away from work again.

She gave him the time and hung up.

He'd managed to compartmentalize the whole artificial insemination agreement since the day she'd dropped the überbaby bomb. But the call shook him out of his complacency, his heart *lub-dubbed* more per minute than usual and he held the receiver with a suddenly moist palm. There was no way he could convince himself his part in their deal was insignificant when a new life might be created as a result.

He scratched his forehead, and remembered he had a

patient sitting across from him. "Yes. Well, let's discuss beta blockers versus calcium channel blockers."

The patient's expression drew a blank. "Sorry," Jon said, then stated a brand name for each drug classification he'd mentioned and noticed an ember of understanding in his patient's previous dull gaze. Together, they chose the best medicine suited for his condition and lifestyle, and when at the end of the appointment they shook hands, the patient thanked Jon profusely.

The morning seemed to drag on, while Jon had second, third and even fourth thoughts about actually going through with the contract. He remembered the bright spark of hope in René's eyes when he'd agreed, and relived the unbridled excitement when she'd hurled herself into his arms, hugged the wind out of him, then kissed his cheek so hard he swore he felt her lips there the rest of the day.

He smiled. He could make René's dream come true. How often in life did a man get that kind of opportunity with no strings attached? He thought about his daughters and how much he loved them. How parental love surpassed romantic love, at least it had in his marriage. While marital love might weaken and fade away, the love of a child grew stronger every day. The joy those girls had brought to his life went beyond measure, and René deserved her chance to experience the same.

He removed his doctor's coat, replacing it with a light-weight bomber-style jacket for the crisp February day, and set off on foot to meet René at the wharf after her morning surgi-clinic at the local outpatient center.

As he approached their agreed-upon restaurant, the crunching and creaking of the wooden planks from behind made him turn. He spotted her car. She'd been lucky enough to find a parking place on the often-overcrowded wharf. A nervous zing buzzed through his system, and he quickly ignored it. He was a man of his word—he'd made a promise; he couldn't back out now. After all, he'd already given the specimen!

The cornflower-blue sky went on forever, an occasional cloud scudding past. The sun glare ricocheted off the ocean, making it hard to see anything beyond her silhouette as she got out of the car. She walked closer, and the beam on her face matched the shimmering waves. The sun kissed her chestnut hair, highlighting a touch of red he hadn't noticed before. She tucked her arm through the crook of his elbow like an ambassador of goodwill.

"Lunch is on me," she said, as the wharf's resident pelican swooped overhead and landed on the nearby railing.

Over a bucket of all-you-can-peel shrimp, she produced a manila envelope and withdrew its contents. "I've pored over this document, every single line, and I think you'll be pleased with what my lawyer drew up."

He wiped his hands on a napkin and maintained her steady gaze and ceremoniously accepted the contract, then fished his reading glasses out from his shirt pocket.

"Once I've got your signature, they'll release your specimen to me."

By the time the main course of halibut and mahimahi got served, he'd signed it.

"That's that, then," he said, glancing up, noticing the glassy tears threatening to spill over her thick lashes. Oh, no. He could never take it when a woman cried. It always made him feel so helpless and baffled and downright uncomfortable. His girls had mastered the art of tearful manipulation, but René's tears were genuine. He'd do anything to stop them, but what?

Though he thought better of it, he did what he'd do with Amanda, scooted closer and gave René a hug. She clutched him so hard, he wasn't sure whether to pry himself free or just enjoy it.

"Thank you," she repeated over and over.

"I've got to admit I'm very curious how this puppy's gonna turn out."

"Me, too!" More tears appeared—tasteful tears, not the blubbering kind, just gracious, womanly drops down her cheeks. On her, it was beautiful and he had the urge to kiss each one away, but that would be him in a movie, not the real guy sitting here next to her, the guy who worked with her every day, so he stopped the urge immediately. Still wanting nothing more than to stop her crying, he took the joker route.

He covered his mouth with the back of his hand, and mumbled an aside. "Okay, I've done my part. Now it's your turn."

She sputtered a laugh and tossed him a thankful look, one that seemed to wrap him up and warm him all over again. The gaze let him know he was the most special person in her life at the moment. He liked how it felt, wondered if she sensed the ever-deepening place she'd found in his life, too. It confused the hell out of him. The moment couldn't go on forever, and they did have a delicious-smelling lunch before them, and, well, he scooted his chair back as the special feeling settled quietly in his chest.

A week later, after the most recent blood test showed a surge in René's luteinizing hormone, indicative of ovulation, she canceled her morning appointments and rushed to her OB doctor's office. She lay on a cold examination table with her feet in stirrups.

She glanced at the ceiling with a new perspective on the patient's side of the experience. The room was cold and the thin sheet offered little comfort on top of the oversize patient gown. Her personal gynecologist smiled at her from between René's legs.

"Ready?" she said.

René nodded, her throat growing tight with anticipation.

She and Jon had agreed not to discuss the mechanics of their situation. He'd done his part when the time suited him, and now she'd do hers. She still laughed to herself about how he'd made his deposit on Valentine's Day. Could she consider it romantic?

"Here it is," her doctor said, raising a thin catheter connected to a syringe with the sperm inside. "Future baby, right here, if we're lucky."

The doctor chattered as René felt cold hands and necessary invasive instruments get placed, and finally the deposited sperm around her cervix.

"I'm going to put a sponge cap over your cervix. Leave it in place for eight hours." Her doctor friend patted her hip. "Good luck. Now lay here for thirty minutes. My nurse will let you know when you can get up."

If there was a chant to will one sperm and her egg to meet, she'd chant it. Failure was not an option. She pulled her feet out of the stirrups, moved farther up the exam table and relaxed.

Maybe daydreaming about a perfect ending would enhance the process. In her case the perfect ending was a pregnancy.

She let her mind wander and, instead of a chubby baby face appearing, a different scene played out before her, shocking her slightly. She'd told Jon that Mr. Right wasn't going to walk through her door anytime soon, yet the vision of him standing on her porch the night she'd hit him up with her artificial insemination plans gave her pause. In a once removed and cockeyed sort of way, he *was* Mr. Right.

She couldn't help but wonder if in another situation, if she wasn't pushing so hard for a baby *right now* and if he wasn't counting down the days to his freedom, that maybe things could have been different between them. In all their years of working together, they'd never once looked at each other in an interested way. And it was useless to speculate about things that would never be. She didn't have the luxury of time anyway, and this day was what it was—a day to hold her breath, keep a positive attitude and hope for the best.

And if optimism could affect her state of mind and the cells in her body and, most importantly, her uterus, she figured she had the best chance ever to get pregnant.

CHAPTER FIVE

JON hadn't been intentionally avoiding René for the past month, but he'd figured he'd done his part in their deal, and there was no point in making her uncomfortable just because he was curious. Beyond curious. Besides, he didn't want to get involved.

Since he'd donated and signed her contract, he'd stayed out of her way and figured things would play themselves out however they were meant to be. It surprised him to acknowledge—as a scientist first and foremost—he could be so fatalistic. Since agreeing to take part in René's plan, he'd started realizing all kinds of new things about himself. Such as, he really, really hoped this pregnancy would take.

What was up with that?

Jon welcomed his next patient into the exam room as if a special guest. "Mr. Grosso, how are you doing?"

"Not so great." The man gingerly rubbed his chest.

Mrs. Grosso beetled her brows. "He still tender."

"Yeah, tender." He massaged circles around his sternum.

"That was a big operation, and right about now your skin nerve endings are coming back to life in the area where they opened your chest."

"It feels strange. I can't explain."

"But you're not having chest pain, right?"

"No. No chest pain. Just sore now."

"That's progress. Take off your shirt and let's have a look."

After performing a thorough examination, Jon invited Antonin to get dressed and meet him in his office. He exited the room and strode toward his door. On the way, he noticed René with a bright smile, standing at the mouth of the hall. He slowed his step. She gave him a subtle thumbs-up.

What? He did a double take to make sure he hadn't imagined it. He tilted his head as if for reassurance that she had indeed given the high sign. She nodded rapidly, continuing to smile so wide she could star in a commercial for toothpaste.

He went to his office and picked up the phone, punching in her com line number. After the second ring she picked up.

"Are you saying you're pregnant?" *It took on the first try?*

"Yes!" Her excitement burst through the receiver.

A moment lapsed, as a swell of something bathed him. Joy? Pride? Nah, that would be absurd, but, hey, *it took on the first try!* "I think this calls for celebration," he said.

"Definitely." She sounded breathless.

"I've got a bottle of nonalcoholic sparkling cider the girls didn't drink on New Year's. How about tonight at eight. My house."

"See you there." She hung up.

"Congratulations," Mrs. Grosso said, while assisting her husband into his office.

"For what?"

"You wife. She pregnant?"

"Oh. No. Just a friend of mine."

Mrs. Grosso still knew how to look coy. "Your girlfriend?"

"Just a friend."

He shuffled the stack of lab reports on his desk and waited for the couple to settle in. It might prove harder than he originally thought to keep a secret about the fact that he had something to do with René's pregnancy.

René tapped on Jon's steel door five minutes early. It sounded like a vault opening, and he must have been waiting just on the other side, it opened so quickly.

"Hey," he said, eyes bright. His black tailored shirt, with sleeves rolled to his forearms, hugged his trim, long torso. The jeans fit just right, too. She'd noticed he'd shaved off his beard earlier in the week and missed it, but evening stubble darkened his face. The image set off a burst of excitement on an already-overloaded day. She chalked it up to fatigue mixed with euphoria.

"Hey," she replied as she entered his loft. The perfectly square main room was decorated with clean urban minimalism, and surprisingly unusual artwork balanced out the sparse furniture. Dare she say sensual artwork, with warm and inviting shapes and colors? She scanned the room, and noticed an alcove separated by a Japanese paper screen that was most likely his bedroom. A closed door next to it she pegged as the bathroom. The mantel sans fireplace came complete with a large mirror and—she had to look twice—larger than life-size angel-wing artifacts? Jon?

"My daughters tease me about that one, too," he said as a smile slid across his face. "Found them in Venice. Couldn't resist. The shipping fee was astounding."

A laugh tickled up from deep inside. She imagined Jon in Italy making plans to ship his art home, using sign language and pointing to the wings. Then another peculiar thought popped into her mind about him and Cherie dividing up their property during the divorce, and Jon insisting he keep those serene angel wings. What kind of man would want to look at angel wings every day? She smiled at him, a man who'd already proved himself as an angel. It felt good to be here, to share the news she'd been bursting to tell the world all day.

She followed him toward the spotless new kitchen wedged into the far corner of the completely undivided room. Her eyes bugged out at the conference-size black-enameled dining table, and how he'd taken over half of it with his computer equipment.

"Do you entertain a lot?" This was certainly a side she'd never seen of Jon.

"Me? Are you kidding? Nah, I just like how it fits here, and the girls really spread out with their books and laptops and all. It works for us."

"It's impressive how much thought you put into the girls when you moved here."

"As you'll soon find out, kids become the biggest part of your life. Even bigger than medicine. It's great."

He retrieved the alcohol-free sparkling cider from the ice bucket and popped the cork faster than she could blink. "Let's toast to our success."

"Yes, of course! That's what I came here to do, to celebrate."

That devilish sparkle she sometimes noticed appeared in his eyes. "I have to know one thing," he said. "Was it as good for you as it was for me?"

She sputtered a laugh and delivered a firm sock to his deltoid. Feeling a bit like a schoolgirl again, she rolled her eyes at his tasteless and very macho joke. "Ugh."

"Sorry. Couldn't resist." He lifted his glass. "Here's to

our success. May the baby be healthy and pretty as her mother if it's a girl, and if it's a boy outrageously masculine like his fah…sperm donor."

She almost spit out the cider. "Who are you, and what have you done with Jon Becker?" She loved seeing this playful side of him, hadn't seen it nearly enough during their five-year acquaintance.

"I've got to admit, I'm really jazzed about this successful kid experiment of ours." He reached out and patted her waist.

The gesture sent an electrical jolt through her stomach. She couldn't look into his bright gaze so she glanced over his shoulder, down the wall, directly into his bedroom. Wrong move. More minimalism smacked her between the eyes. That and an inviting king-size bed neatly made with a warm brown duvet on display by recessed lighting. A prurient image popped into her mind. She blamed it on hormones and quickly glanced away, then sipped more cider to avoid his stare.

"You have no idea how ecstatic I am," she said.

He took her by the arm and guided her back to the living room section of the loft.

She sat on the chrome-and-cushioned navy-blue couch, placed her cider flute on the glass-and-brushed-nickel coffee table and admired a small peacock sculpture next to three oversize art books—another fanciful surprise about Jon. The contrast with the "man" furniture was a breath of fresh air.

"So tell me," he said. "I'm all ears."

She felt coy and girlish as her cheeks grew warm. "Well, you did your part."

He nodded. "That I did. And, might I add, magnificently." There was that teasing, full-of-himself glance again.

She fought the smile tickling the corners of her mouth. "And I did mine."

"Yes, I see how this story is shaping up. Intriguing." He lifted one brow.

"And three weeks later, I missed my period. We did a blood test this morning and sure enough it took!"

"Fantastic. What a team, huh?" he said, looking beyond pleased.

Maybe it was the new rush of hormones, or extreme gratitude, but before she could stop, she'd thrown herself into his arms.

Jon wanted to keep the evening all about René and the pregnancy, but here she was smashed against him, and he knee-jerked a response. He enfolded her and held her close, doing his best to deny the most basic of all reactions between a man and woman. He couldn't let this happen. There was no point.

After all his years in chemistry lab, he knew it took at least two ingredients to react. Him and her. In his case, at this particular moment, *combust* was the word that came to mind.

Did she have a clue what she did to him each time—twice now but who was counting—she'd flung herself into his arms? It was the dumbest thing he could do to let his guard down, yet he savored the delicate feel of her spine and shoulders, inhaled the shampoo-fresh scent of her hair. He'd missed this part of a relationship.

Casting his misgivings aside, he stopped holding himself back and kissed her head, soon finding the smooth skin of her cheek. Memories of closeness and pleasure flashed in his brain. He hadn't felt her tense or pull back, so he kissed her earlobe. It was warmer than his lips.

She adjusted her head and her mouth was right there for the taking. Any man in his right mind would kiss her, but a gentleman, a colleague and friend, a man who dreaded commitment and dreamed of China and a year away, should ignore that plump lower lip and its upper, perfectly fitted mate.

He ignored the warning, exhaled and dipped his head. Just a taste, that would satisfy this curiosity he'd harbored for the past month. How did it feel to kiss René Munroe?

Moist and warm, and open, her lips pressed against his, so soft, so inviting. He meant to restrain himself, but the lure of her lips made him quickly forget. He covered her mouth and flicked his tongue over the smooth surface, felt the tip of her tongue and explored it. She tasted like sweet cider, but so much better. He drew back and kissed her from another angle, finding the same sweet invitation. Again and again they joined mouths, deepened, flicked and swirled tongues. His body, with a mind of its own, shifted toward her in a desperate attempt to make as much contact as possible. One arm held her close, as the other grazed her butter-soft skin.

One long crimson polished finger touched his chin and slid down his throat, dipping below his collar. Hell, at this point she could pinch him and that would turn him on, too, but that finger and the sensual trip down his neck made him groan. He weaved his hands through her hair and deepened the kiss, then followed the curve of her arms and hips, moved inward and cupped her full and pliant breasts.

Wrong move. Her head snapped free from the kiss. She closed her eyes, though he'd seen the bright blaze within them before she did, and pulled away from him.

"Oh, my God. What have we done?" she whispered.

He ignored the stirring in his gut, and acted as surprised as she did. He needed to do something, to lighten the mood, to distract them from the trail they'd foolishly embarked on. "Hold on. Hold on. We can pretend this never happened." *Like hell he could.* "Blast that sparkling cider. It does it to me every time."

His clumsy attempt at humor helped them both save face, but he needed to say more. This attraction wasn't in the contract, but damn he'd wished they'd taken time to explore other avenues for her to get pregnant. Like the tried-and-true natural way, the way they could easily fall into bed if his better senses didn't keep cropping up. He knew where that would lead—to something he could never give.

He'd already let her down. He dropped his head and glanced first at his feet, then at her. "I'm sorry if I took advantage of the opportunity."

She screwed up her face. "Jon, I threw myself at you."

"But that was out of happiness, and I went right into sexual mode…"

"Stop."

His gaze flew to hers. She offered a measured look. "I think now we're both aware of something we hadn't bargained on. At least, I hadn't," she said, pushing the thick hair he'd mussed out of her face.

He nodded. "I've got to tell you, it's pretty damn strong on this side of the couch." He crossed his foot over his knee, knowing he couldn't possibly hide the full body reaction she'd caused.

"You didn't sign a contract for a girlfriend and a baby."

"You've got a point there. We can't ignore that you're going to have a baby."

"Taking a risk to explore this—" her hand swam back and forth, gesturing to him and her several times "—this *thing* between us is too risky. Unfortunately, our timing is off."

"Story of my life." He went for humor again, a sorry

attempt to lighten the heightening confusion and his droop-
ing spirits.

Her caramel gaze drifted demurely to her lap and her
hands. "You don't want anyone to know you're the father."

"Right."

"And you're planning that sabbatical."

"Right again. And you wanted a baby without any
strings attached. And the last thing I ever want again is
commitment. Any commitment."

"Right. So we've got to go back to how it was
before—" she glanced at him and quickly at the floor
"—before we realized…"

"That we turn each other on." He finished the sentence
for her, used the words he wanted her to hear, not her
beat-around-the-bush, let's-make-this-all-go-away-nicely
explanation.

She sighed. "Yes."

At least she'd admitted it. He'd have to settle for that
crumb when the whole cake sat right before him, fresh
baked and ready to… Okay that was another poor analogy,
but damn it, it was exactly how he felt. He'd take her in a
New York minute, ravish her, have her naked and on his
bed before she realized what a great lover he was, and
before he could stop himself from making a huge mistake.
His ironic laugh tossed him quickly out of the fantasy. He
scrubbed his face. "Yeah, okay, well, what do we do now?"

She stood, looking solemn and at least half as perplexed
as he felt. "We stick with the plan. We're colleagues. We
work together. And you've done an incredibly wonderful
favor for me."

Jon heard the resolve in her voice, but her body language
wasn't nearly as certain. He watched her fidget with her

hair and look everywhere but into his eyes, then came to the only logical conclusion—anything between them was impossible, out of the question, not going to happen.

So that was how it would be.

CHAPTER SIX

THE next morning, Jon steered clear of the clinic lounge. He wasn't ready to see René again after last night. One kiss had led right to insomnia, tossing and pulling sheets, adjusting and readjusting the pillow and cursing like a horny college kid.

He thumbed through his latest journal, waiting for his nurse to put his next patient in the exam room. He never wanted to go through the turmoil of a relationship again. Cherie's surprise departure had left him emotionally drained, and with nothing left to give. Maybe that's why he'd signed on to a sure thing—make baby, stay out of the picture. Hmm, write that down. Exclamation point!

So why the hell had he kissed René?

True, if life made sense it wouldn't be nearly as interesting, but the crazy logic of needing to stay aloof and disengaged from a woman who was carrying a child he'd helped make nearly made his head explode. He wasn't able to say "carrying *his* child." No. The connotations that went along with that would surely do him in. And besides, he'd been absolved of the duty, and rightfully so, what with his future plans. He had to keep the proper frame of mind about the situation. He'd signed on to the project, and…it had been a success. *On the first shot*. He couldn't help puffing out his chest as a macho, top-of-the-world feeling rustled through him.

Stop it. He couldn't allow the prideful thoughts to mix him up any more than he already was. It was a favor. They had a contract. She wanted a baby of her own, and he had plans for a year's sabbatical. Theirs was a business relationship, nothing more. Write that down!

Turned out the fallout was a bitch, though, and he had the filled journals to prove it.

René had made her hospital rounds before her scheduled surgery that morning. It was almost 1:30 p.m. before she made it in to the MidCoast Medical clinic for her afternoon appointments, and she was grateful for the busy and distracting morning. The last thing she could handle was seeing Jon.

She parked in the back and entered through the porch, a continuation from the wraparound porch at the front of the clinic. Several terra-cotta flowerpots burst with color and lined the picket railing. She inhaled the winter scent of pine tree and reached for the chilly glass doorknob.

The redone hardwood floors throughout the hallway sparkled with care. Jason had spared no cost when it came time to refurbishing this grand old house, and she never grew tired of admiring it.

"Ah, you're just in time for lunch," Jon said, looking chagrined, as she pushed through the door in the kitchen.

How had this happened? Normally he was already seeing his afternoon panel of patients by this time. So much for avoiding him.

"What are you doing here?"

"Morning clinic ran late when I had to admit one of my patients into the hospital for an EPS study." He spoke in between popping potato chips into his mouth. "Young kid. Basketball player. Passed out at a game. Got zapped with an AED."

"Wow. That's not good."

"Good news is he survived, and after we figure out what sets off his arrhythmia, we'll know how to treat it and keep him alive."

She nodded. Even now, desperately trying to stay out of his way, she was glad to see him. He looked sharp in a mint-green button-up shirt and tie with some sort of hieroglyphics on it, no doubt spelling out the meaning of life or something equally as important. His trousers fit him impeccably, and she couldn't help but have a quickie flashback to the day she'd seen him stripped down and jogging. And the way he kissed.

This line of thinking had to stop.

René plopped into a chair and put her feet up on another. She'd stayed awake half the night thinking about the irony of asking a man to help her get pregnant, then, after the fact, realizing she was attracted to him. She'd live with her decision, though. Had to.

"What held you up?" he said.

"I was in surgery all morning. My tubal ligation clinic. Two of the women were younger than me and they've already met their personal baby quotas, and wanted to make sure they didn't have any more." She glanced over her shoulder to make sure no one else was around. "And here I am just starting out. Ironic, huh?"

She fiddled with the single braid she always wore on surgery days and happened to pass glances with Jon. He nodded. She'd made the mistake of pondering her circumstances in front of him. He was bound to comment.

"You smell like chocolate," he said, ignoring the irony and throwing her a curve. "What's got you stressed?"

Like he didn't know. And from the looks of the dark circles under his eyes, he didn't get such a great night's sleep, either.

"What do chocolate and stress have to do with each other?" She'd play dumb.

"I've seen you go for that chocolate stash in your purse when you're under pressure."

She blurted a laugh. "Guilty as charged, but this time it was more out of necessity. My blood sugar took a dive after being in the O.R. all morning, and I forgot to bring any lunch."

"Here," he said. "Have half of my sandwich." He pushed a portion of a sub sandwich loaded with deli meats and vegetables under her nose. "You need to eat, now that you're…"

"Jon, you don't have to look out for me." Though the sandwich did smell delicious and her taste buds had already gone on standby.

"Someone's got to do it." He flashed a smart-ass smile, the kind that made his eyes crinkle at the corners. "Take it. It's loaded with those dill pickle slices you love."

How could she refuse?

Ravenous, she took a huge bite, then said muffled thanks while dabbing at some mustard at the corner of her mouth.

He watched her with a quiet inward expression. "I like watching you enjoy your food." He smiled again.

Then as if he'd only meant to think it and not say it out loud, his gaze darted away.

"We're not going there, remember?" she said.

"Yup." He finished the last of his half of the sandwich and rose to leave.

A bittersweet pang made it hard to swallow. He was the smartest guy in the room—any room—and he always acted the humble and perfectly mannered doctor. Even now.

Her decision had already blurred the lines of their working together, and they both felt completely awkward about it. Unfortunately, that was the way they'd have to handle their business association—all manners and etiquette.

No matter how unsatisfying that approach would be.

Two weeks later, word of René's pregnancy had obviously gotten out when one afternoon Jon witnessed every female in the clinic circling her, fawning and gushing with well wishes. "Oh, congratulations!" "I'm so excited for you." "When's the big day?" What he didn't hear was, "Who is the father?" And for that, he thought, ducking his head and making a U-turn, he was grateful.

René proudly stood in the center, beaming, as Jon knew pregnant women often do. His ex-wife seemed to walk on air when she'd first gotten pregnant—that is, until morning sickness kicked in. René held her head high, chin up with pride. She wore a white peasant blouse with a paisley patterned knee-length skirt, and looked so damned pretty he could hardly contain himself. Her exotic almond-shaped eyes sparkled with happiness, and when she glanced at him just before he made his turn, their gazes met and merged for the briefest of moments. He read her gratitude, nodded, and though wanting to make a beeline for his office, he went against his will so as not to come off suspicious acting.

"What's going on?" he asked, hoping his high school thespian days might still serve him well.

"Dr. Munroe is expecting!" Gaby was the first to respond.

"What's she expecting?" He'd go for the lame-and-loving-it facade.

His nurse and two others groaned over his sorry joke. René was the only one gracious enough to smile. If he'd been at arm's length, she probably would have cuffed him.

He drew closer as a rally of mixed emotions made him stiffen. "When's the due date?" He'd been so busy kissing her the night she'd come to his loft to celebrate, he'd forgotten to ask the most basic questions.

"November," she said softly.

"Hey, that's a great month—that's my daughter Lacy's birthday month, and she's a great kid." Why the sudden onslaught of nerves? Could he overexplain more if he tried? How ironic that this baby would be born in the same month as one of his other children. Other children? Only children. He had no claim on this one. The contract said so.

"From what you've told me, I can only hope my baby will have half the verve of Lacy," she said with a smile, and a subtle knowing look.

Out of the blue, he wanted to hold René, to stroke her hair and run his thumb over her lips. To kiss her, deeper than he had the night they'd almost crossed the line. Did it show on his face?

The nurses had gone quiet. The fact he and René were staring at each other as if everything else on earth had disappeared may have had something to do with it. He knew he had to do something, knew this invisible thread joining them had to be severed. He schooled his expression and finished the last steps to reach her, awkwardly patted her back, and when she reached for a hug, he made sure there was at least a foot worth of air between them. This was the kind of hug coworkers gave each other; he'd seen it countless times, but it bothered him to fake it with René.

"Hey, congratulations. I'm really happy for you. Really."

He knew of all the phony business he'd just pulled off, this was the one true statement. He definitely was happy for her, just didn't know where *he* fit into the picture. Actually, he did know where he fit as far as pictures went, and that would be *out of it*. Completely. Which suited him just fine.

"Thank you," she said, patting his back.

"Hey, it was nothing," he said. *Oops!* He'd taken her superficial thanks and applied it to their personal business.

His nurse, Lois, stared at him with a screwed-up face. "You are such a dork. You didn't have anything to do with the doctor's baby!" she snorted.

Oh, if she only knew…

Grateful Lois had saved his slipup, he cleared his throat and made a self-effacing smile, striving for the absent-minded professor effect. "You know what I mean." His eyes never left René's, and now her cheeks were tinted peach, which was very becoming with her light olive-toned skin. She nodded her understanding, and he turned and headed back for his office, feeling moisture under his arms, and a grimace on his face.

If this was the way things were going to be at the clinic now that the pregnancy was out in the open, he wasn't sure he'd survive.

The next week, Jon arrived at work later than usual. The early April morning had been bright and clear after a string of rainy days, and he'd made up for it with a long, solid run. After ten miles, showered and feeling like a new man, he strode through the clinic toward his office when he overheard the distinct sounds of someone heaving. The sound came from the forgotten, sequestered bathroom in the far corner of the ground floor. He paused and verified that someone was definitely losing their breakfast, and rather than risk also getting queasy merely from the sound effects, he pushed on.

A few minutes later, René emerged from the tiny bathroom. She tried to slink by Jon's office, but failed.

"You okay?" he called out, brows raised, eyes dark with concern.

She self-consciously ran the back side of her hand across her mouth, and stopped at his door. "That hormone surge really messes up the system."

"Tell me about it. I used to puke right along with Cherie."

He could always manage to get a smile out of her, even after she'd thrown up for fifteen minutes straight. "I'm interviewing doulas today."

"What's that?"

"They're people who take care of the pregnant woman. They offer physical and moral support. Sort of like a preggers woman's girl Friday."

"I see," he said, wearing an expression that gave the distinct impression he hadn't a clue what she was talking about.

"Since I'm going through this alone—" she purposely avoided his pointed stare "—I thought I'd hire one earlier than necessary for the extra help."

"Sounds wise."

She couldn't read the look in his eyes, but speculated there might be a twinge of regret. Was he sorry he'd donated the sperm? She hoped not. "This is the first time in my life I've felt complete." She glanced at Jon. *Well, almost complete.*

He'd paused behind his desk, and she suspected the significance of what she'd just said had sunk in. "I'm really glad to know that," he said, an earnest expression on his face.

They spent more time than necessary gazing at each other, searching each other's eyes, which got awkward. She needed to make her feet move, to start her day, before the next wave of nausea swept through.

"I better get back to my clinic," she said, looking down the hall.

"René?"

"Hmm?"

"If there's ever anything you need, don't hesitate to get in touch. Remember, I've got superfriend status now."

The damn hormones stretched her emotions as if rubber bands, and Jon's simple offer made the room blur. "Thanks," she said, as she made a swift getaway. She couldn't let him see her cry; he might think she wasn't happy, and she was. "I really am happy about being pregnant."

"Good. And for the record, I never thought you weren't."

She was; she was happy. It was the alone part that kept stumbling her up.

She rushed into her office and closed the door. What was the matter with her? She'd been going back and forth between throwing up and crying for two weeks now. She knew pregnancy wouldn't be easy, but being an obstetrician, somehow she thought it might feel more clinical for her. She couldn't have been more wrong. Being pregnant ran the gamut from elation to hysteria, exhilaration to total exhaustion, confidence to near panic over the thought of raising a child. Alone. There was that word again.

She collapsed into her desk chair, resting her head on the back. Tears leaked from the corners of her eyes. She swiped them away, refusing to slip into another crying spell. Here she was carrying a baby, two beings sharing one body, her body, yet she'd never felt more alone in her life.

Week sixteen of the pregnancy, mid-June

Gretchen Lingstrom, Stephanie Ingram's doula, was her choice after several interviews, and Gretchen had already given her homework. René lay on her bed reading at midnight, refusing to rest on her clinical laurels. Determined to experience the pregnancy as a future mother and not a doctor, she dutifully perused the pages of *The Natural Way to a Successful Pregnancy and Delivery.* Gretchen's special mix of essential oils brewed on the bedside table, and though she would have preferred human company, the scent offered her a degree of comfort.

It had been a long day, and she was tired. At least she wasn't throwing up anymore now that she'd made it through the first trimester. She stretched out on her bed; the pillows looked so inviting. With hands behind her head, she allowed her mind to drift to fanciful thoughts about decorating the second bedroom as a nursery. What colors would she use? What style of crib? Would she keep a bassinet in her bedroom? And for how long?

Something odd happened. A vague flutter south of her navel stole one hundred percent of her attention. As if a large butterfly were trapped beneath her abdomen, she felt the first movement of life in her uterus. Her hand flew to her stomach. "Quickening," she reverently whispered the medical term for what she'd just felt.

She held perfectly still so she could savor the magical flapping motion to memorize it forever. Normally a woman didn't feel the first signs of life until eighteen to twenty weeks, but she'd noticed her obstetric training had made her profoundly aware of her body and each stage of the pregnancy, and this was no exception.

She'd had the ultrasounds, knew she was pregnant. Felt it in her tender and growing breasts; saw it in the insidious change in size of her waist, hips and stomach. But nothing could compare to this feeling, this affirmation of life. Warmth bubbled up and over her skin from a depth of emotion she'd never imagined. Riveted in the sensations, she couldn't move. Her eyes prickled and leaked with joy. She grinned and lay still, taking it all in for several more seconds.

René wanted to share the special moment with someone. Her parents were in Nevada, and it was too late to call them. Likewise, any of her girlfriends who had young families themselves would already be asleep. Though Gretchen had told her she could call day or night, the only person she really wanted to talk to right now surprised her. Jon.

He'd kept his distance over the past month, and she'd missed him. But hadn't he been the one to insist on superfriend status?

She reached for the phone and punched in the numbers. On the second ring a husky voice answered.

"Did I wake you?" she asked, knowing full well she probably had.

"No! I was reading and must have dozed off," Jon said, and she was grateful he knew who she was without asking.

She liked how he sounded and imagined him on his navy-blue sofa, cardiology journal opened on his chest, hands folded over it, feet crossed at the ankles on the coffee table, goosenecked lamp positioned just so over his shoulder.

"Is everything okay?" he asked.

"I'm fine. Beyond fine. I just felt the baby move for the first time."

"You did?"

She heard the genuine interest in his voice. "I did." She smiled so wide her lips felt as if they might split. "Just now. It was the strangest sensation. I loved it."

"Wait until that little one gets bigger and starts kicking—you won't be nearly as amused." A smoky laugh rumbled from his chest. She liked it.

"We'll see."

"We will?"

"Figure of speech," she said. He'd signed a contract releasing him of any duty to the child. She knew it. He knew it. So why had she called him?

"I've missed you," he said, honey-warm tones in his voice.

She held her breath, hoped he wouldn't notice how eager she was to answer. "I've missed you, too."

"What are we going to do about it?"

Wishing she could say anything but what she knew she had to, she cleared her throat. "Nothing, Jon. We made our deal, now we have to stick to it."

"Ah, our pact with the devil," he said.

What could she say?

After a brief silence, rather than hang up on her, he changed the subject, brought up how he'd overheard his nurses discussing who the father of the baby might be, and as she vocalized her protest, they conversed like old friends hooking back up after a vacation. They quickly moved on to other topics, and skirted the reality of their situation—that she carried his child and he was going to China—and managed to talk on and on.

And on…

René squinted and peeked from under her lid. The bedroom light was still on, glaring in her face. She glanced at the clock; it was two in the morning. She clutched at the phone on her chest and moved it back to her ear. Instead of the *beep-beep-beep* of the disengaged line she'd expected, she heard soft, deep breathing through the receiver. She hadn't fallen asleep on the phone since junior high school. And sweet Jon hadn't hung up, either.

After a murmured snore, Jon swallowed. She smiled with a distinct picture in her mind of a guy with tousled hair and a sexy shadow beard. What would it be like to wake up next to him?

"Jon? Jon? Wake up."

"Huh?"

He yawned and obviously stretched. Did he have a clue where he was and who he was still on the phone with?

"Good night, Jon."

"Love you," he said, midyawn before he clicked off.

What? Her hand flew to her mouth. Did she just hear what she thought she'd heard? A chill snaked its way down her spine with the possibility he might actually love her.

Nah. Couldn't be. It was the middle of the night; surely she'd imagined it.

Still, René hung up and relived those two haunting words over and over again, and each time tingles tiptoed over her skin. Until she couldn't bear to indulge in the fantasy anymore, she put on her scientific hat, then rationalized away every possibility: She hadn't heard him correctly; he'd thought he was talking to one of his daughters; he was dreaming; he'd been sleep talking; the poor man was out of it and confused on top of that. At two in the morning any explanation would do, except the one that whispered he'd meant it, the explanation that stirred her hoarded hope and made her tremble inside.

A little part of her, a part she'd buried and kept throwing more dirt on, wanted to believe he'd meant what he'd said. Hoped with all her might he had. Okay, there, she'd admitted it. She weaved fingers through her hair and stared at the ceiling—she wished things could be different with Jon. This time a cold chill settled in her chest and dug an icy trail to her heart. This had never been part of the plan. Now, besides dealing with her pregnancy, she had to wrestle with the reality that she wanted something more with Jon.

The next morning, when she saw him at work, he nodded and acted as if nothing, absolutely nothing, had changed between them. All right, so he had been more than half-asleep, and didn't recall or have a clue of how he'd ended their phone conversation.

Case closed.

She'd be a big girl and get over it. Though the instantaneous flicker of hope that maybe he'd meant exactly what he'd said, gave her pause. It sent her off to her office wishing she hadn't rushed into this contract with Jon, knowing if she had to choose over again, she'd go right back to Jon Becker to be the father of her child. But for the second chance, she'd make sure her proposition involved the old-fashioned way.

There was no way Jon would be able to continue to work here and remain uninvolved in René's pregnancy. How in hell had he managed to skim over that incredibly important detail when he'd made his decision to be the sperm donor?

Superfriend status, my eye.

He scrubbed his face and leaned against his office door. He had to think of a way around the consequences.

In the meantime, he must avoid René whether he wanted to or not. He'd sneak in the back of the clinic in the morning, eat lunch in his office and sneak out the back door at the end of the day. He'd survived worse, like divorce after seventeen years of marriage when he'd never even suspected his wife was unhappy. He was the last thing in the world René needed, and staying out of her life should be a walk in the park, comparatively.

There was a tapping on his door, and he glanced briefly at his watch. Not quite time for his last patient appointment, but this could be a chance to finish the afternoon clinic early for a change.

He opened the door and found René standing on the other side. She'd pulled her hair back today and wore large silver hoop earrings. If she were any other female colleague, he wouldn't have even noticed. But with her, he had—immediately after noticing the depth of her eyes and the few golden flecks sprinkled judiciously in her irises.

"Can you do a cardiac consultation for me?" she asked, all business.

"What have you got?"

René handed him a heart test strip and he saw several premature ventricular contractions—PVCs—scattered across the six-second, twelve-lead EKG.

"Where is she?"

"In my office," she said, already starting down the hall.

René ran the patient's medical history by him as he followed her to the examination room. "She's eight months pregnant with her fourth child. She's undernourished, her blood pressure is mildly elevated and she states it's always like that. And when I listened to her heart, I thought I heard a third beat in diastole."

A distant picture gathered in his mind, a unique condition that affected one in ten to fifteen thousand deliveries. The patient history had the markings of high-risk pregnancy all over it, one that should have been followed from early gestation, maybe even counseled against long before conception. Why hadn't René consulted him before now?

"By what you're telling me, she could be in peripartal cardiomyopathy. I won't know for sure with the physical exam, but I may need to admit her to hospital to get to the bottom of this. Did she have problems with her other deliveries?"

René slowed as they approached the examination room and glanced toward the floor. "I've never seen her before today. The history is sketchy at best. I don't think her kids are living with her," she said quietly. "When I asked why she waited this long before getting prenatal care, she just shrugged. I was shocked when she told me she was eight months pregnant. I thought she was around five months."

She bore a concerned expression that, the more he learned about the patient, rubbed off on him.

"Is she homeless? How did she get an appointment with you?"

"I do several pro bono appointments a month, and she said someone told her about me. Honestly? I think she may be involved in sexual services, and most likely lives on the street or in cheap flop motels."

"Not the best circumstances to be pregnant in. If it turns out she does have what I'm suspecting, she'll have to be admitted to the hospital, and we can get social services involved, for both her and the baby's sake," Jon said.

"I had my nurse draw a complete blood panel, and I got

samples for STD tests when I examined her." René
knocked on the door.

"What about a drug screen?" he asked.

"I thought of that, too." She swung the door open.

Jon glanced at the thirty-something woman, thin as a
slip though pregnant, who sat on the examination table.

"This is Chloe Vickers," René said, "and she is eight
months pregnant. Today was our first appointment, and I'm
concerned about her blood pressure and her heart." She spoke
to the patient, as if making sure she understood why the
male doctor was in the room. "Dr. Becker is a cardiologist."

The woman's cautious gaze darted between them, her
pasty skin almost opaque.

Jon produced his top-of-the-line stethoscope, warmed it
with the palm of his hand and placed the bell close to the
sternum in the birdlike rib cage. He listened intently, first
on the right side at the second rib interspace, then he moved
the bell to the left. He worked down to the third rib interspace, then to the lower sternal border. He repositioned
Chloe on her left side and listened again, then had her sit up
and lean forward and he listened to her heart once more from
this angle. There was indeed a proto-diastolic gallop present.

Twenty minutes later, after a thorough physical examination of her heart, and additional gathering of medical
history, Jon called the local hospital from René's office to
arrange for more tests and patient admission. He glanced
across the baby collage as he waited for the house on-call
doctor to pick up, and worried about the outcome for this
mother-to-be.

"I've got a patient for you. Chloe Vickers. She's a thirty-
four-year-old female, multiparity, currently at thirty-two
weeks' gestation with abnormal EKG and elevated BP. I

suspect peripartal cardiomyopathy. I want her on bed rest and sodium restriction for starters. Labs are pending. And if the echocardiogram confirms my predicted diagnosis, we'll need to arrange for cesarean section ASAP."

He glanced at René, who hadn't left his side since she'd brought him in for the consultation. Other than the faint tension lines between her brows, she was the exact opposite of Chloe Vickers. She was fit and the picture of health; her color was creamy light olive with pink cheeks, and there was a spark of life in her deep honey-colored eyes. He tore his gaze away, while hoping René had lots of extra energy today, because Jon suspected she may be doing a last-minute surgical delivery before the day was over.

With the added risk that Chloe might take off if given half a chance, Jon personally arranged for her to be driven to the hospital, met her there and walked her to the office of admissions.

So much for sneaking out of the clinic early today.

The next morning Jon cruised by René's office on his way to discuss his schedule with the receptionist, Gaby. The door was closed. A young woman with bright red hair, a stained-glass-patterned tattoo covering one arm and a brow ring, sat just outside, flipping through a magazine.

Immediately forgetting Gaby, he pushed on to knock on René's door to see how she was doing, and the woman jumped to her feet.

"Sorry, but it's Dr. Munroe's quiet time," she said.

"Pardon?" He must have heard wrong. Since when had René employed a bodyguard?

"She's resting. She had a long night of surgery, and needs extra time with her feet elevated to make up for it."

"And you are?"

"Gretchen. I'm her doula." She extended her hand at the end of her highly decorated arm.

Oh, right, René had told him about hiring a woman as her pregnancy advocate. He shook her hand and made a U-turn. He'd wait until later to quiz René about their patient and how the C-section had gone, and besides, he really did need to talk to Gaby about his schedule.

At noontime, René didn't come into the lunchroom, and even though he'd promised to avoid her as much as possible, he went looking for her. He'd been too busy all morning to call her office, and after seeing the size of Chloe's heart on X-ray, he became really curious about the health of the infant.

With cardiomyopathy of this magnitude in their latest patient, it made sense that the dusky lavender-rose color of her lips had nothing to do with lipstick and everything to do with low oxygen.

He forked several bites of spaghetti and meat sauce before his curiosity got the best of him. He shoved his food aside. Rounding the corner to René's office, determined to get some face time, he came to an abrupt halt. Tattoo lady stood behind René's chair, massaging something into her temples.

"Take several deep breaths," she said, and René did as she was told. "That should help your headache."

This was wrong. Totally wrong. If she needed someone to give her a head and neck massage he could fill that bill. Hell, he could be a lot more creative than smelly cream and deep breaths. He'd distract her with a leisurely afternoon in his bed, working her into a frenzy and satisfying her every need.

Damn, he had to quit thinking this way, because he wasn't doing himself any favors. He'd had to fight off his imagination daily since he'd kissed her, and his resolve was growing weak. He cleared his throat, and Gretchen snapped her head toward him.

René glanced up bearing a sheepish look, and peachy-pink cheeks, the color of the afterglow he'd guarantee her if she'd only jump into his fantasy—a fantasy he shouldn't be having in the first place, remember!

"Hi," she said.

"Hey. It smells like—" he sniffed the sweet aroma "—peppermint?"

"And eucalyptus," Gretchen added. "Perfect for tension headaches—that's what pregnant women suffer from when they don't get enough sleep."

"Ah." He honestly couldn't think of a proper response.

"Gretchen, thanks so much, but I'd like to talk to Jon if you don't mind."

The full-bodied and freckled, where she wasn't tattooed, woman gathered her huge bag of goodies and prepared to leave the room. "Don't forget to take your prenatal vitamins. Here." She set a plastic container in front of René. "This is your lunch. It's perfectly balanced for you and the baby's dietary needs."

He understood women had different perspectives than men on many levels, but had their clinic nurse practitioner, Claire, really recommended this woman to René? And René had hired her? Which part of the equation was he missing?

He folded his arms, leaned against the door and waited for the woman to leave. René slanted him a look filled to the brim with apologies and embarrassment. Once the woman had cleared the door, he took the seat across from René's desk.

"I had no idea she would go this far," she whispered.

He glanced over his shoulder. "She's definitely into her job. I guess that's a good thing."

She shrugged. "She's nice enough. Very caring."

"She could use a hint about knowing when to stop playing bodyguard, though."

René let go a soft laugh. Up close he could easily see the fatigue, and a touch of purple smudged under her eyes.

"How'd the surgery go?"

She sighed. "Rough. It was really rough. Chloe had an incredibly high tolerance for anesthesia, which threatened her baby. I had to work fast, and the poor thing was so tiny due to IUGR. She barely weighed three pounds—at eight months' gestation! Can you believe it?"

"Yikes. It's not surprising about intrauterine growth retardation, because Chloe's heart is a mess, and hasn't been delivering enough oxygen to the fetus. Chances are she'll suffer progressive deterioration of her heart, but there's a slight chance it could go back to normal size. By six months from now we should know if the disease has reversed or not."

"If we can keep track of her," René said, unconsciously rubbing her tiny baby bump.

If he didn't know better, he'd never suspect she was even pregnant, but he'd known the results, and she'd called him at the first sign of life. He'd been flattered that she wanted to share the news with him, then had the audacity to fall asleep on the phone. Yeah, Mr. Exciting—wasn't that what Cherie had always called him?

"As for the baby, well, that's another story," he said.

"Do you suspect brain damage?"

"It's very possible."

"At least her baby's in the NICU and social services will make sure she's taken care of properly," René said.

"Good."

"Let's hope the little one's a fighter."

Jon thought about the baby inside René, hoping it was a real fighter, too. He also thought about Gretchen and her bag of surprises, and suspected that from now on, René would share all things on the pregnancy front with her. So much for superfriend status. A pang of envy made him stand. He had no right to expect anything more.

"I guess you'd better eat your lunch," he said, slipping out of the room. "And whatever you do, don't forget those vitamins."

He left her quietly laughing. It was the least he could do. Feeling as irritable as a duck in the desert, he thought how things would only get worse as her pregnancy progressed. He wanted to be involved, yet the price he had to pay was too great. And it wasn't fair to René to insinuate himself into her life, only to leave.

"I think I know who the father is," Lois whispered to Gaby near the front desk.

"I'll tell you who I think it is, then you can tell me who you think it is. Maybe we think it's the same person." Gaby's gaze lifted in time to see Jon pass. She quickly guarded her look and pretended to do some work. Lois flashed a glance over her shoulder, displaying similar surprise.

Maybe it was better to leave sooner than later.

He knew three or four doctors in practices who'd expressed an interest in him joining them, but had been too content to ever give it a second thought before. Maybe now was the time to start a job search; that is, if they would also be okay with him going on sabbatical.

CHAPTER SEVEN

Eighteen weeks' gestation, late June

RENÉ lay on the paper-lined exam table as her doctor performed an ultrasound. The ethereal outline of the baby seemed to emerge from what looked like a triangular-shaped dust storm. A perfect profile of an alien child came into view, complete with huge head and torso, tiny hands, feet and turned-up nose. Could anything possibly be wrong with her baby?

She was thirty-six, and she recommended amniocenteses to her patients beginning at age thirty-four to rule out genetic disorders and chromosome abnormalities. In her opinion, this study needed to be done.

Once her doctor established the placement of the baby in her uterus and marked it, her nurse swabbed René's belly with topical disinfectant, then placed a paper sterile field with a whole in the middle over the X marks the spot. Under constant ultrasound guidance to avoid injuring the fetus or placenta, a long needle was inserted into her abdomen. The pinch of entry through the skin was bearable thanks to topical anesthetic, but then came an odd pressure as the needle pierced her uterus and entered the fluid-filled sac surrounding her baby. She wouldn't describe it as painful, but the process of withdrawing the fluid gave an odd pulling sensation as the syringe sucked thirty ml. into its barrel, and that definitely got her attention. Could the minor procedure cause a problem? She knew there was a small risk for miscarriage by having this done, but in her opinion, the greater gamble was not being prepared for a handicapped baby.

Gretchen was quick to be at her side, and René was grateful not to be alone through the procedure. But holding Gretchen's hand left her wanting, and oddly enough she had a brief fantasy about Jon. Why couldn't she get beyond him? In her thoughts, he sat beside her with narrowed eyes watching her every move, as if monitoring her well-being. The fanciful vision of Jon worrying about her gave an added sense of security to the procedure, even if only made-up.

Within a few minutes, everything was over and she was dressed.

"You know the routine," René's OB doctor said. "We'll send the specimen to the special lab where they'll analyze the cells and study the chromosomes. Report any bleeding immediately."

Now all she had to do was wait two long and nerve-racking weeks for the results.

"By the way, do you want to know the sex of the baby?"

René had quickly looked away from this ultrasound, as she had with all the others to avoid seeing anything that might expose the sex. Many of her patients wanted to know the gender in advance, but not her.

"No, thanks," she said, opting for the gift of surprise at the birth.

* * *

"What are you going to give Dr. Munroe for the baby shower?" Jon overheard his nurse, Lois, ask Christina, the medical aide, the next day.

"I was hoping to go in with someone so we can get her something really nice."

Jon craned his neck to better hear the conversation.

"Oh, I'd like to do that. Let's decide what we should buy at lunch," Lois said.

"Sounds good. Um, who do you think the father is?"

"There's no telling. A woman like Dr. Munroe could have any man she wanted."

"You think she arranged to get pregnant? She never mentions a boyfriend, and she's getting on in age," Christina said.

"You mean, like a sperm donor, or a wham-bam-thank-you-ma'am?"

Jon had heard enough. He pushed back his chair and strode to the office door. "Ladies? Don't you have work to do?" He thought about making a snide remark about how it wasn't any of their business who the father of René's baby was. He tried to figure out how he might react if he wasn't personally involved. As it was, he felt paranoid, and thought it might seem too obvious if he said what was on his mind, so he gritted his teeth and forced a smile.

"Oh, sorry, Dr. Becker," Lois said. "I'll get your next patient in the room ASAP."

He rubbed his jaw. He hadn't thought about an office baby shower. Now he'd have to come up with a gift for René that wasn't too personal. Something well-built…and functional…like him. Right. That was the last thing she needed. Or wanted.

He smiled, deciding to give René the same thing he'd

given Jason and Claire for their son, a top-of-the-line stroller. On a whim, he made up his mind to purchase one with a special and extra feature, and he knew exactly where to buy it, too.

Saturday morning, René indulged herself in a shopping spree. She'd seen her hospitalized patients that morning and told Gretchen, who was beginning to overstep boundaries and get on her nerves, that she preferred to do this alone.

The woman had proved to be a bit overbearing with her ideas and suggestions, and René didn't want a comprehensive rundown of every nursery item that caught her fancy. She just wanted to shop for her baby…in peace.

The Babies, Babies, Babies! store was nestled in an upscale, Mediterranean-styled corner mall on Coast Village Road in nearby Montecito. She stepped into the display room and almost gasped at the assortment. How in the world would she be able to choose which crib, dresser and changing table she wanted with a gazillion sets? Every color, style, size—simple to ornate, over-the-top to understated to trendy—were on hand for the choosing.

She wandered toward the cribs: natural wood, cherry wood, dark wood and white; French country, modern and Scandinavian styled. There were cribs that could break down to become head- and footboards for future toddler beds, cribs big enough to take up the entire second bedroom in her home and cribs for twins and triplets. Everything seemed to have double functions, and for these prices she could see why.

Her head spun at the overabundance of merchandise with too many choices, and wished she'd invited a friend along to help her decide. She glanced across the store at the checkout desk and needed to grab the nearest crib rail for support. Should she hide? Why?

There stood Jon, Saturday casual in jeans and a snug bright green polo shirt he hadn't bothered to tuck in. He produced a card and handed it to the lady.

Funny how the sight of him made her feel a bit giddy these days, especially since he'd been making himself scarce at work. At first she thought it was the hormones messing with her body, but she'd noticed a consistent tingle shower each time she'd seen him since their kiss. Man, he was a good kisser.

She had no right to think about him in that way—there was no purpose in it—yet occasionally her mind would drift to that night at his loft.

He turned just when she'd been remembering their kiss, and must have seen her with quite an expression on her face. His gaze gravitated to her lips, then, as if he'd been caught red-handed in some nefarious deed, he blushed. Full out, all the way to the shells of his ears, he reddened, and it became him.

With piqued interest, she forged her way over to the counter.

He took a few steps toward her, closing the wide gap between them. "What are you doing here?" he asked.

She glanced at her stomach, beneath the blue plaid pin-tuck tunic top. "Shouldn't I be asking that question?"

"A guy doesn't have the right to come here? How sexist, Dr. Munroe."

She laughed. "Fine, you're right. What'd you buy me?"

He pulled in his chin. "You're awfully presumptuous, aren't you?"

"Okay, play dumb. I'll find out eventually. In fact…"

She approached the counter, noticed his Saturday-morning didn't-bother-to-shave stubble and felt that tingle buzz all over again. She faced the salesclerk. "May I ask what this gentleman purchased?"

The clerk's eyes widened as her gaze darted toward Jon. He placed his index finger over his lips, and the woman nodded. She gave René a sympathetic smile. "I think since he paid for it, I have to keep my lips sealed. Sorry."

René tossed Jon a glance loaded with attitude. "Okay, I get it. So since you're here, want to help me pick out a crib?"

An hour later, after Jon had proved what fantastic taste he had, she made her purchase and arranged for home delivery the next week. He'd found a well-made yet not overbearing crib that matched the natural woodwork in her Craftsman home. The fact he'd thought about it surprised her, and she'd thanked him profusely for helping her make the decision.

"I'm good at painting, too, in case you're wondering," he said. "Looks like you've got a week to whip that room into shape before the furniture arrives."

"Are you offering?"

"We could negotiate, but only if you'll feed me."

Could they manage to be in a room, alone together, and not make lust-filled fools out of themselves again? She wasn't sure it was worth the risk.

He must have read her mind when he dipped his head and lowered his voice. "I'll be good, I promise."

From where she stood, she could take his statement two different ways, and the first to pop into her mind made her cheeks heat up.

"I'm sure you will," she said, smoothing her hand over her hair. She stared at her feet until the warmth receded, then headed for the exit with Jon hot on her heels.

Just before she'd made it out the door, over in the corner, she spotted a bassinet. A perfect bassinet. White wicker complete with hood. She stopped abruptly, and Jon ran into her.

"Oh, sorry," he said, his chest pushed against her back, hands on her shoulders. "Didn't see your brake lights."

She glanced behind; his chin was eye level. He may not have shaved but he'd definitely showered, and she was close enough to smell his faint cologne, a heady spice scent with a touch of lime. The tingles cascaded from head to shoulders to arms, making her grateful she'd worn long sleeves and he couldn't see her goose bumps. He'd also managed to erase her mind.

"Is this what you were looking at?" He approached the bassinet, a quizzical lift of his brows.

"Yes," she said, finding her voice again. "Isn't it perfect?"

He locked into her gaze. "Perfect," he repeated, though she had the distinct impression he wasn't commenting about the bed. Needing to change the direction of her mind, she focused on the bassinet.

"Oh, my gosh, look. It converts into a rocker." She laughed. "Does everything here have a double function?"

He smiled and mindlessly set the bassinet to rocking.

"I can just imagine the baby in it," she said, slowly lifting her eyes to his. The subtle expression in his velvet brown stare made her hold her breath.

"The baby will arrive before you know it," he said.

A contract worth of unspoken words traveled between them. As long as he was in her life, she'd be reminded of his connection to the child. A signature on paper couldn't rub out the truth—they'd made a baby together. This child would be theirs, though she'd vowed to never include Jon in the upbringing. She'd wanted it that way and he'd demanded it, as he'd be gone in another year.

Yet she longed for his input, like today, when he'd helped her choose the furniture. It had taken what had previously seemed overwhelming, and made it easy, and fun. And under Jon's tutelage, she was sure to enjoy painting her first room. Too bad he'd consented to not have anything to do with this baby, because if today was any indication, they'd be great together.

She'd crave his wisdom on so many topics over the next several years, yet she'd have to walk the fine line of colleague, coworker and friend. She'd always second-guess her decisions and wonder if Jon would handle things differently, if he'd approve of hers. He didn't want any more children. He'd made it clear—he was happy with his daughters and, at forty-two, he looked forward to a different kind of freedom when they went away to college. He had plans to study medicine in China. He'd laid it all out for her the night she'd asked him to be the sperm donor. How clear could it be?

Yes, yes, yes, she'd said, brushing each point away. She'd been so focused on what she'd wanted that she'd overlooked the bigger picture, the one where she and the baby stood in the center, looking on the outside at Jon. The gap that felt empty without him.

The last thing he needed was to start all over again; she knew it as sure as the baby in her womb. And she'd asked enough of him already. She took one more glance into his deep, distancing eyes, and forced her gaze away.

"Yes, my baby will be here before I know it."

Okay, she'd finally read him loud and clear. The bassinet was for her baby. *Her. Baby.*

* * *

Jon walked his patient to the small lab located across from René's office, as an excuse to drop off the paint chips. She'd talked about yellow, or peach, or powder blue— something light and airy—the morning they'd chosen the baby furniture. He'd stopped her before she could name any more colors.

Last night he'd dropped by the paint store and found some samples he thought she'd like, and wanted to show them to her this morning. There was Gretchen, fussing with flowers and candles in René's office.

"She's with a patient," she said, in answer to his quiz-zical, narrowed stare.

"I'll come back later, then," he said.

He almost asked, *Don't you have a job?* but realized this *was* her job, but surely she must have other clients, too. About to pocket the samples, they apparently had caught her attention.

She approached and reached out her hand. "Are those for René?"

So they were on a first-name basis now. He nodded, annoyed that it bothered him what Gretchen called René.

"May I see them? Color in a nursery is very important. Hmm. That's a no. Oh, this? I don't think so. Maybe this one. I'll run them by René later. We're planning to paint the room this week."

Had René changed their plans? They hadn't set up a firm date, but he'd thought tomorrow night would be good. He hoped, once she'd seen the paint chips, and made her choice, he could pick up the paint on his way home from work tonight and get started on the job ASAP.

Under the circumstances, he couldn't very well tell Gretchen his first choice was the pale yellow. Or that it reminded him of Lacy's nursery, and how it had always felt so happy in that room. Yellow was universal for boys or girls, and he wanted to think that the baby would have a bright and cheerful room to grow in. Gretchen was the last person he'd want to know any of that. As far as he was concerned, it was none of her business.

When he got back to his office, confused over the change of plans—plans René had apparently forgotten to share with him—and annoyed as hell that he felt like a blighted boyfriend, he picked up the intercom and dialed her number.

"Hello?"

It was Gretchen. So he hung up.

Twenty weeks' gestation, early July

How many patients would Jon have to tell today they were walking time bombs? First came the forty-year-old guy with an extra hundred pounds on his frame and a lousy family cardiac history, then the sixty-year-old woman who thought she'd had a pinched nerve for weeks until his office EKG showed she'd already suffered a small myocardial infarction, not to mention the thirty-four-year-old woman with a lipid profile so out of whack she was well on her way to becoming human margarine.

What really got to him—the icing on the morning's pitiful patient cake—was telling a twenty-year-old college student that his heart had deteriorated to the point of him needing to be put on a heart transplant list. Days like this came far and few between, but when they did, they zapped him. Mentally. Emotionally. Physically.

He used to gravitate upstairs to Jason's office to shoot the breeze when work got to him, or he'd spend his lunch hour running off the stress, or having a beer with Phil after work, but today, since he hadn't seen much of her lately, and because he missed her, Jon decided to pay René a visit.

He peeked around the waiting room corner to see if Viking guard Gretchen was anywhere nearby. She was nowhere in sight, so he hightailed it over to René's office.

For a woman who'd previously kept an open-door policy, too often lately he'd found René's door closed. Today was no exception.

"She got her amniocentesis results today," René's nurse, Amy, said, her brows pinched with worry. "She's been in there ever since."

An adrenaline alarm shot through Jon's center. Was the news bad? There was a one to four hundred chance of birth defects with a thirty-six-year-old mother. He knew the stats, but had tried to ignore them for René's sake. Had he made a blunder beyond forgiveness?

A whirlwind of doubts and fears took him by surprise, and he knocked on the door with an unsteady hand. "It's Jon."

"Come in," she said, her voice sounding muffled.

Jon opened the door and found René crying.

CHAPTER EIGHT

"COME in." René squinted out the latest batch of tears, then quickly dabbed beneath her eyes with the tissue before Jon entered her office. She avoided his gaze, first having to push away the stupid fantasy that had confused and set her off crying. *Jon confessed his deep and abiding love for her, then begged her to marry him. She said yes.* A pregnant lady could daydream, couldn't she?

She couldn't fool him; the pained twist of his brows and rush toward her desk proved it.

"Is everything okay?" he asked, hand on her shoulder, squatting beside her chair. *Sure, if daydreams could come true.*

She turned toward him, admiring the empathy spilling from his dark eyes. "I'm fine, just emotional as all get-out these days. Everything sets me off."

"The baby's fine?"

She nodded and smiled. "The amnio is normal, and with all the new movement I'm feeling I'm thinking up a nickname. What do you think about Tumblelina?"

"Is it a girl?" he said, an excited hitch to his voice.

"I opted not to find out. Maybe I'll just go with Tumbler for now."

"Okay. The baby's fine, but you don't seem fine," he said, gazing deeper into her eyes. "What else is going on?"

She sighed. "I fired Gretchen this morning."

Jon blinked, lowered his brows and tilted his head. "So these are tears of joy?" he said with a smirk.

She lightly cuffed his shoulder. "She wasn't that bad."

"Trust me, she was," he said, standing, then sitting on the edge of her desk.

That got another laugh out of her, and she'd forgotten how good it felt, until it occurred to her that the last time she'd laughed had been with Jon. "She was overenthusiastic, maybe a little nearsighted on the boundary thing and, bottom line, I just couldn't see myself going through something as special as childbirth with her."

"So it's a good thing. You should be smiling, not crying." There went his hand on her shoulder again, long fingers lightly massaging away her concerns.

She fought the urge to lean into his touch. "I was supposed to start the classes on labor training in two weeks. I skipped the first several since I know all that stuff, now I'll be conspicuously starting the class late, and without a coach. It's going to be weird. That's all."

Jon hopped to standing, paced around the room. He stopped, hands on hips, and stared at his top-of-the-line running shoes, then clicked his tongue three times, a habit she related to his style of thinking. He turned his head and gave a measured gaze, then tapped his chest and shrugged. "Here's your coach."

"Jon. I can't let you do that." Was it indecision she saw in his eyes?

"I've gone through it twice, and I'm a damn good

coach. If you don't believe me, ask Cherie, if she'll talk to you about me."

With Jon on her side, insisting he could replace her doula, her downtrodden mood shifted to something more lighthearted. Though the gesture was beyond sweet, she couldn't let him go through with it. "Jon, the last thing you want to do is get involved in my birthing classes."

"You're telling me what I think? Trust me, René, you have no idea what I think."

"But…"

"I think I just volunteered to be your answer. Let's have dinner after work tonight and talk more about it." He glanced at his watch. "I've got another patient waiting. I'll pick you up on the way out later."

Before she could protest, and admittedly it came slow because she couldn't think of one reason to, he had his hand on the doorknob. "Let's eat at that Mediterranean alfresco on Cabrillo," he said as he slipped outside.

She glanced back at the amniocentesis results and smiled. The baby was healthy, she'd gotten rid of her nagging doula, and Jon had just insisted he wouldn't let her go through the birth alone. It wasn't exactly like her fantasy, but it had come a lot closer than she'd dared to hope.

Jon closed the door and fought the pang of sadness. René had looked so pitiful. He'd never seen her like that before. Pitiful shouldn't be in the dictionary that described René. Independent. Yes. Competent. Of course. Vulnerable? Never! Perfect. Definitely. That always came to mind when thoughts of the lovely Dr. Munroe breezed through him. It tore at him to see her so unguarded, made him need to do

something about it. He couldn't bear to leave her alone in
that condition.

A cold wave hit when he reached his office and started
to realize the ramifications his volunteering would have.
Not only had he volunteered, he'd insisted to be her birth
coach. Was he out of his mind? Not really. Turns out René's
happiness meant more than any fallout he'd have to deal
with, like caring for her when he knew damn well he had
no business getting close. He had nothing to offer her long
term; maybe this interim gesture would make the inevitable
loss less painful.

He shook his head, feeling another secret pact coming
on, and barely able to handle the first, he wasn't sure if he
was ready for another.

He shuffled through the top drawer of his desk. Where
was that journal when he needed it?

Three hours later, at seven o'clock, pleasantly full and definitely tired, René invited Jon in for a quickie peek at the
baby furniture.

They'd had effortless and enjoyable conversation all
through their Greek-with-an-American-twist dinner. He'd
reassured her about his birth-coaching abilities, and altered
her attitude about jumping in late with a group of people
who'd already bonded. Now she anticipated a great experience with Jon at her side, and it felt good.

She offered him peppermint tea and oatmeal chocolate-
chip cookies for dessert back at her house, and he'd said
yes before she could finish the sentence.

They had tea, dessert and more casual conversation
carefully centered on MidCoast Medical Clinic. After one
final agreement about his being her Bradley birth coach—

another secret they agreed to keep from everyone they worked with—he followed her down the hall.

Because she wasn't completely sold on the color choice, tiny butterflies flitted through her stomach at the thought of sharing the baby's room with Jon. Would it pass his approval? To overcompensate, she swung open the door with great flair and switched on the light. "Ta-dah!"

Dead silence, uncomfortably long.

"Purple?" Jon said, an incredulous look on his face as they stood in the nursery.

"Heather. It's called heather, and Gretchen said it's a soothing color for babies." The remnants of her confidence dissolved.

"Maybe girl babies. What if it's a boy?"

"She assured me it's a unisex color."

"Not. So not." He must have spent the weekend with Lacy, and one of her favorite teen phrases had rubbed off on him, because he never said things like that. He shook his head and took a ministroll around the room. "You didn't mention purple when you ran down your list of colors to me."

René kept her smile to herself. Okay, so maybe his reaction wasn't so much about hating the color as it was about being disappointed she'd ignored his suggestions and painted the room with her ex-doula?

"What about bright?" he said. "Simple? Not overpowering? Yellow. Like we talked about."

She'd been on the fence about the final results of Gretchen's shade brainchild. Now that Jon had pointed out the dreadful mistake, she couldn't deny it another second. Suddenly overcome with anxiety about choosing the wrong color and messing up her baby before his or her life began, she ran her hands through her hair. "I hate it. I hate the room this color."

Jon's expression changed from disappointment to concern. "Come here." He pulled her into his arms. "On the bright side, the furniture looks great! And you don't have to leave the walls this way. I'll repaint them for you."

Why did it feel so inviting and comfortable in his arms? She could stay here for hours and hours breathing in his clean, musky scent, enjoying the solid wall of his chest, if he'd let her. "You will?"

He nodded. "Of course it'll take a coat or two of primer first, which will increase my original price from one to two home-cooked meals."

Without giving it a thought, she kissed his cheek. "You're on. Thank you. Oh, thank you."

He went still for a millisecond, then, as if erecting a protective barrier, he held her at arm's length and gave her a playful glance. "Throw in the birth-coach thing, and I'm seeing a whole lot of free meals coming my way."

His smile nearly melted her, but she was stuck two feet away at the end of his firm grasp, definitely out of kissing range, and obviously the way he wanted it.

Note taken, Dr. Becker.

Jon would have liked to stop the clock, savor how René felt in his arms, inhale the rich aroma of her hair and skin, but he knew better. It had been so long since he'd held her like that, and he missed it. Man, he'd missed it. Now, he literally kept her at arm's length, to keep from making another huge mistake.

He'd made a month's worth of plans with René, something else he should have known better than to do. He was playing with fire by pushing his way into her life, knew the cost would be a bitch, but right now, seeing her eyes sparkle and warm to his touch, knowing she was carrying his baby, even if once removed, he threw all good sense out the nursery door.

"So tomorrow after work we'll pick out some paint, and I'll get started. And what day do we start the class?"

"A week from Wednesday," she said.

"Next Wednesday it is, then." He glanced at his watch as an excuse to keep from making a total fool of himself. He couldn't let her see how happy he was about these plans. He had to save face, pretend all he really wanted to do was help her. He was such a liar. "I'd better be going. Let you get your baby sleep."

He knew he shouldn't get excited about spending so much time with her, knew it would hurt both of them down the line. He needed to tell her about the few nibbles on his job search, needed to be up-front about that. She deserved to know he'd started researching airfare to China, and had been in touch with a cardiologist from one of the Beijing universities.

He'd signed on as a sperm donor, but felt the need to make the kid's journey into the world an easier one, even if only by way of support for the mother. All of this was temporary, just until the baby was born.

Even with this logical line of thought, he made a snap decision to ignore all the warnings and live in the moment. He pulled her close, kissed the smooth skin of her forehead and, while he was in the neighborhood, inhaled the sweet shampoo scent that he liked so much in her hair. Before he could sink deeper into trouble, he released her, hightailed it down the hall and let himself out.

Twenty-two weeks' gestation, late July

"Dinner's ready," René called from the doorway.

Jon had moved all the baby furniture to the center of the nursery and carefully covered it with old sheets. He'd placed a huge dropcloth over the hardwood floor and had the paint splatters to prove its worth.

"Be right there," he said.

She'd spent an hour chopping, sautéing and baking their dinner, even mashed some potatoes since she remembered how he'd raved about them once at their clinic potluck.

It seemed strange having a man puttering around in the house while she cooked. It felt good, too good. She couldn't allow herself to get used to it; she'd made her plans and, due to her circumstances, they didn't include a man, just a baby.

She'd laid out the table; he appeared at the dining room door drying his hands with a paper towel, and with a yellow primer smudge on his cheek. "Two walls down, two to go. Mmm. Something smells fantastic."

The tone of his voice, the content expression on his face and the familiar compliment soothed like magical fingers over her concerns. The scene reminded her of cozy times when she was a child and her father came home from work, always appreciative of her mother's dinner efforts.

What would it be like? she mused as she busied herself with a hand towel.

On his best behavior, he pulled out her chair, then sat across from her. She wouldn't be able to dodge his intense stare, and worried he might read her thoughts as he seemed to have a knack for that. It took her a moment or two to empty her mind, relax and enjoy the meal she'd prepared.

As always, he ate with great pleasure. He chewed, smiled and occasionally winked when his mouth was full. Their conversation consisted of discussing pertinent items of business from the clinic before drifting to the more personal.

"Turns out both Amanda and Lacy are going to the Santa Barbara Summer Soiree."

"Really?"

"Amanda's boyfriend's best friend couldn't find a date. Don't tell Lacy I told you that—I'm not sure she even knows. The guy's a nerd like I was in high school, and Amanda pawned her sister off on him. I've been sworn to secrecy, but figure my secret is safe with you." He gave a self-deprecating glance, followed by a smile. "I suspect Lacy couldn't care less who her date is as long as she gets to buy a new dress."

René laughed softly, enjoying his confused fatherly expression. Maybe it was his voice, deep in tone and always a pleasure to listen to, or the rich food, but the baby kicked her in the ribs. She gasped.

"You okay?" he asked.

"Fine. Sometimes when I eat, the baby gets very active. Usually it's because of a glucose rush, but maybe my stomach makes too much noise?"

He laughed, and shoveled more food into his mouth, and she marveled over the simple pleasure and how she enjoyed having a man, this man, around. Somehow, she wanted to get inside his head and figure him out. "How does it feel having a daughter about to graduate and set off for the east coast?"

"Weird. Really weird. I'm taking it one day at a time, and this weekend I've got to go dress shopping with both of them."

"Isn't Cherie going to handle that?"

"She's taking a weekend cruise with her latest boy-friend." If he was supposed to look sad, he didn't—irritated, yes. "Besides, if I'm paying for these dresses, I want to have some input in what they look like, you know?"

"That's only fair." She smiled at what his taste might be. "Things might get intense if you suggest a turtleneck and the girls insist on showing some cleavage."

He nodded, then got quiet and stared at his plate. "I can't figure out where the time went. I still remember bouncing them, one on each knee, and coloring with them." He glanced at her and smiled, crinkling the corners of his eyes. "They used to beg me to color with them, and I thought I'd hate it, but you know what? I loved getting down on the floor with them beside me, getting to smell their hair, and see their sweet faces so close while they concentrated. Amanda always smelled like apple juice, and Lacy used to lick her lips over and over in deep concentration while she scribbled her crayon all over the paper. I worried she'd chap her lips. Silly, huh?" He glanced beyond her shoulder at somewhere very distant from the dining table.

Her throat throbbed. "Not silly at all," she said, as the all-too-frequent tears gathered, clouding her vision. Jon moved toward her, placed his hand on her cheek and thumbed away the overspill.

"In case you're wondering what kind of mother you'll make, I'm here to tell you you'll be fantastic."

She tried to look at him, but was too embarrassed about her leakage and quickly glanced back at her plate. She'd done nothing but cry around him lately, and it had to stop. He removed his hand, and she was sorry, missed the feel of his nearness and warm fingers.

"You're a natural, René. Trust me on that. You'll do fine."

She'd made her bed, now she had to lie in it. What had seemed like the perfect solution for her situation had brought a flood of surprises. She loved sharing a meal with Jon, loved having him around, but he wasn't a part of her life. He couldn't be. He saw his daughters growing and leaving home, and she would never ask him to give up his newfound freedom or travel plans to start all over again as a father. His bitter divorce hadn't helped his attitude toward trusting women, either. What would he think if she changed the rules midgame? Wasn't that exactly what his wife had done? No. She couldn't disrupt his life any more than Cherie already had.

He'd given her a wonderful gift, and she couldn't abuse his trust.

"Can I ask you a favor?" he said.

Surprised out of her thoughts, she nodded. "Of course."

"Will you come with me on Saturday to help the girls pick out their dresses? You know, as my backup in case they do go for that cleavage look."

"I'd love to."

The room grew thick with longing, and he must have sensed it.

"I'd better get started if I'm going to slap on the rest of the primer tonight. I'll lay down the daisy yellow tomorrow night, if you're going to be around."

"I'll give you a key in case I get called in for a delivery. One of my patients is very close to her due date."

He glanced at her stomach, then into her eyes. "Pregnancy becomes you."

"Thank you," she said softly, thinking that the smudge of paint on his cheek became him, too. Lately, his appeal had grown to such proportions that it would be hard to think of anything she wouldn't find endearing about him.

Amanda watched with interest as René smoothed the pale apricot silk skirt, and adjusted the finely beaded spaghetti straps of her dress.

Jon sat unnoticed in the lone chair in the changing room, as each daughter took turns modeling their choices. He'd nixed several of the racier cuts and flashy styles, but this classic look suited Amanda perfectly.

As preplanned with René, he lifted his brows twice in approval.

"Some strappy silver shoes and long dangly earrings, maybe a matching pendant, as long as it doesn't compete with the beads on the bodice, and you've got yourself a look," René said, as if a fashion guru.

Amanda's shoulders relaxed and she twirled one last time for Jon.

"I like it. How much is it," he said.

René furrowed her brow. "You said money was no object."

"Yeah," Lacy chimed in, drifting closer to René in solidarity, knowing full well how much he'd already laid out for her dress.

He'd talked Lacy out of a cross between gothic and chic with the excuse that black was not a summer color. She'd settled on a sea-blue halter dress with a plunging back instead of front. René had promised to do her hair and loan her the perfect necklace and earrings. Now, it was Amanda's turn.

"Okay," he said. "We'll take it."

Amanda flashed him a sweetly pleased glance and he smiled at her. "You look beautiful. Both of you. I can't believe my little girls have grown up."

"Aw, Dad, can we skip the sob story just this once?" Lacy said.

He laughed, and noticed a look of admiration on René's face. She blinked when she caught on he was watching her.

"Let's get you out of this dress, Amanda, before he changes his mind!" She scooted his oldest daughter back into the changing room as Lacy snuggled on his lap.

"Dad, I really like René. I wish you could find someone like her."

"I'm not looking for anyone, kitten, you know that."

"So you say. Still, I worry about you being all alone, especially when I move to Hawaii."

"Worry all you want, but I'm counting down the days until I'll be a free man again."

Lacy giggled and lightly cuffed his chest. "Not. So not."

Okay, she knew him through and through, and though he professed to want to be a free man again, the thought of his daughters being on opposite ends of the States nearly made him break into a sweat. He'd deal with it when needed. Not today. Not when he'd just seen two of the prettiest young ladies in Santa Barbara buy their favorite dresses.

"It's so exciting how René's going to have a baby on her own."

"Don't go getting any ideas, young lady."

"Of course not! I've got plans."

Amanda and René stepped out of the dressing room, Amanda draping the dress over her arm. "We're ready."

Lacy sprung from Jon's lap and grabbed the hanger with her gown and, as she passed René, stopped. "If you ever need it, I'd love to babysit for you."

"That would be great, Lacy. I'll definitely take you up on that offer."

"If I weren't going away to school, I'd offer, too," Amanda parroted the sentiment.

His girls never offered to do anything they didn't want to. René, with little effort, had managed to make a big impression on them. But what was surprising about that?

Twenty-six weeks' gestation, late August

Normally, August was a hot, dry month, and the third week of the partner-coached birth class was right on the money temperature wise. The sight of René answering the door in a long brown-with-white-batik-pattern sundress, a motif that looked suspiciously like a Rorschach test, had Jon reading sexual images into the design before she could even say hello. He kept his primal reaction to himself, and purposely locked eyes with her to help him do it.

This more voluptuous version of René, including protruding stomach, was a sexy sight to behold. It charged the positive and negative energy between them, heating to a simmer his new and constant companion whenever he was around her—lust.

He'd taken notice of the change at work more times than he'd care to count, batted the wicked thoughts out of his head and did his best to think nonsexual thoughts about her. Most days he'd lost the battle. And this extracurricular activity with his "coworker," the woman he'd insisted to help with delivery since he felt responsible for her in a twisted pact-with-the-devil sort of way, proved to be his undoing.

Damn. This coaching business was far harder than he ever imagined. It required getting up close and personal. He'd gritted his teeth through the first two classes, being forced to be near René, yet keep his boundaries. Each week seemed to get worse, drove him to his limits, which seemed far closer than he ever imagined.

Some guys took cold showers; Jon jogged. Lately, he'd jogged so much to keep his mind off of her that he'd lost a few pounds.

Tonight, she'd worn her hair up in a ponytail and the sight of a few loose strands of hair on her delicate neck nearly made him salivate.

It didn't help a bit when the older female instructor kept referring to him as the husband of Dr. Munroe. René had piped in with "birth coach" on the first night, but it didn't seem to register and after the second class they just let it slide. He'd slant her a sideways glance and roll his eyes and pretend it was such a pain to be mislabeled, then she'd smile and blush, and the misunderstanding was all worth it.

He wished he knew what she was thinking. Was she as sorry as he that they'd taken the greatest invention on earth—sex—and turned it into a science project between friends? That they'd scrolled over the best part and had gone right to the big finale, missing all the fun?

Oh, wait. Those would be *his* thoughts.

The instructor was droning on, and he needed to pay attention, if he was going to be any help at all to René.

He understood the "sleep imitation" stage and "sleep-breathing" technique necessary in early labor. In class, he'd helped René practice, helped her focus inside, and he liked how it gave him an excuse to study her up close. In the medical clinic, he used to sneak peeks at her once in a while when they worked closely together, but had never let himself indulge in her beauty for long. She was totally out of his league.

He liked how her bottom lip curled ever so slightly, and

that hint of a cleft on her chin. He'd admired her single dimple for years, but she always concentrated in class, and rarely smiled.

Tonight, her breathing was barely noticeable, and the instructor had the partners sit behind and place their hands on their diaphragms. This required taking her between his thighs and snuggling with her, a position of torture complete with heavenly scents and a serious desire to nuzzle his nose in her hair. His fingers splayed ever so slightly as she practiced sleep-imitation breathing. Okay, it was a cheap shot, but he enjoyed the view of her cleavage from the over-the-shoulder angle, and wondered if she sensed his pulse speed up.

Tonight, the instructor had sent them home with a specific assignment, but he didn't know how to carry it out, unless…

For friends who'd never had to search for conversation, the ride home was painfully quiet. He worried René had picked up on his ramped-up sexual attraction to her, didn't want to make her uncomfortable by it. But my God, even if she wore bottles for glasses, she couldn't miss it.

"How am I supposed to observe you sleeping?" he said, when they reached her front porch.

She laughed softly. "Maybe I can video tape myself?" She opened the door. "You want to come in for some herbal iced tea?"

Why stop the torture here? He wouldn't pass up the opportunity to spend more time with her, even though he thought herbal iced tea was a vile waste of perfectly good water. "Yeah, please. I'm parched from all that practice."

A second bubble-smooth laugh rolled from her tongue; it landed on him and set off yet another reaction. The innocent sound started on his skin, raising the hair, then reached inside and tightened his muscles, the exact opposite of what they'd learned to do in class tonight. But stiffening up was his only defense to keep from mauling her. He was at the edge of his restraint, dangling on the end of the rope, wondering how long he could possibly hold on. Why in the world had he gotten himself involved? Oh, yeah, he'd offered, because he couldn't stand to see her unhappy. Sap. Hopelessly aroused sap.

She looked beautiful. He wanted to touch her, the same way he got to in class tonight when the instructor had them lightly massage each body area that needed to relax for the "letting go" exercise. He swallowed the dry knot in his throat, and instead of touching, he followed her into the kitchen and leaned against the door frame, safely across the room.

She moved fluidly about the kitchen in that damn sexy sundress. It swayed and folded around her hips, and before he knew it, he'd lost control of his tongue.

"You know what my favorite part of the class was?"

She tossed him an inquisitive over-the-shoulder glance as she got down two tall glasses.

"The letting-go exercise," he said, not caring that his voice had slipped into husky mode.

There'd been a lot of slipping and sliding into a new direction over the past three weeks with René. He'd seen her skin prickle at his touch, heard her soft breaths of relaxation and had the pleasure of sitting close like a real life-partner for two straight hours each week. He hadn't set out to let this intimate shift happen, but it had, and he didn't have a clue how to deal with it. It went against every natural instinct he'd ever had. Don't get involved with business associates. Don't ruin a perfectly good friendship. Never sign contracts and agree to donate sperm!

He'd spent almost a month of Wednesdays with her being called her husband, and knowing she carried a part of him inside her. As wrong as he knew it was, the term had started to feel right.

They'd practiced the birthing techniques to help her relax, which involved constant yet gentle touching. Her soft skin beneath his fingertips had felt like nirvana and nearly had been too much to bear. He couldn't shut off the quiet roar of desire building and cresting even now, and for the first time he dropped the shield, and didn't bother to stop himself.

As she poured tea into the glasses, he moved toward her and, from behind, placed his hands lightly on her arms. Halfheartedly, he quelled the urge to nuzzle her neck with his mouth. His lips hovered licking distance away and he inhaled the same faint scent of strawberry-mango skin cream as he had in class.

"The reason it was my favorite part was because I got to put my hands on you." His voice, heavy with the last threads of restraint, almost cracked when he whispered over her ear. He slid his hands over her baby mound and wondered at the warmth and roundness.

She didn't tense as he worried she might with his wildly overstepping his bounds; rather, she let her head rest on his shoulder and sighed. It felt so damn good to hold her again, to feel her respond to him so naturally. He'd savor this moment, as it might be the only one they shared if she drew the line, stopped him from making a huge mistake.

"The instructor did say you should practice before bed." His gravelly whisper stumbled over the *B* word. He could tell from the angle of her jaw that she smiled.

"I'm not sure all that practice would help me relax," she said quietly.

He was about to spin her around, when she moved voluntarily toward his body. Her arms wrapped around his back, and she nuzzled her cheek against his chest. He loved the feel of the baby pressed safely between them, the feel of her arms drawing him in.

They stood like that for several seconds, getting used to each other in this brand-new way, gently rocking back and forth, caressing, enjoying the feel of each other. They were this odd couple, family-to-be, a choice they'd made based on her wish.

And their future?

He stroked the thick layers of her hair, she lifted her chin and he claimed her mouth with a breath of a kiss. Tender. Gentle. Warm.

She subtly opened her mouth, and he pressed against the silky moisture of her lips, as the last threads of his self-restraint snapped.

CHAPTER NINE

RIGHT there in her kitchen René was swept up by Jon—and she let him. She loved it when he dug his fingers into her hair and kissed her, crazy with passion. He took charge of her; his hands wandered her arms and across her back as if he'd been waiting for this moment for months. There were no awkward fumbles or insecurity in his demanding kisses; no, his mouth was skilled yet the kisses sincere and she believed each one. She skimmed the muscles of his chest and shoulders with her fingertips, soon wrapping her hands around his neck, drawing him closer and indulging in his taste.

She peeled her lips away only long enough to catch her breath, then quickly dove back in for more of the heady wine that was Jon.

His hands moved to her hips and he pulled her closer, as close as the baby would allow. His palms slipped up her sides, tracing her frame, then gently over her sensitive breasts. He cupped her and, surprised, she moaned contentedly. Under his touch, chills and tingles weaved together on her skin in wheels of pleasure.

This was no ordinary kiss. It was loaded with desire and a pinch of frustration, as if he couldn't get enough of her.

To find herself five months pregnant and the object of his arousal turned her on. She longed for more, as her hand slipped under his shirt and hit pay dirt with the warm, smooth skin of his back. She'd seen him with his shirt off, remembered ever since how slim and toned he was. The feel of him was so much better than the mental picture she'd held on to since that day by the beach.

"This is a terrible idea," he said in ragged spurts, his tongue probing and exploring.

"I know," she breathed over his mouth, kissing him back.

"You're pregnant," he said.

She laughed through the kiss. "Really? Wow."

Amusement rumbled through his chest, and he kissed her harder while holding her hips flush with his. If they were naked, he'd be nearly inside her, and the thought made her even moister with anticipation.

She'd routinely counseled her patients on sex during pregnancy. Knew it was safe at this stage, that with all the extra hormones, the experience could even be heightened. Under the confident hands of Jon, she had no doubt how good things would be.

A quick run of her hand over the bulge in his jeans sent her obvious message. Yes. She wanted him. No doubt at all. Couldn't think of anything she'd want more right this minute than Jon inside her.

Jon knew it was a bad idea, beyond bad, out of the question. Yet here he stood at the foot of René's bed, slipping the straps from her breathtaking sundress over her shoulders, being rewarded with the sight of her full breasts, and pregnancy-darkened nipples. The silky feel of her skin was his final undoing. He needed the rest of the dress removed. Now.

"You're beautiful. My God. So beautiful," he said, sighing over her lips, then delivering a light, quick kiss.

She dipped her head and glanced up at him, as if shy about his seeing her protruding belly. He wanted to reassure her that he didn't care, but the vision of the dress sliding down and over her hips left him speechless. He hoped the look in his eyes told the entire story.

He ripped off his shirt and unzipped his jeans faster than a strike of lightning, then stepped up to her and pulled her almost completely naked body next to his. It felt like heaven with his skin flush to hers, and the warmth they built between them belly to belly. He stroked and caressed her velvetiness, as their deep kisses imitated the motion they'd soon share on her bed.

It was going to happen. There was no turning back. For an instant a slight hesitation registered in René's eyes as they maneuvered toward and reclined on her bed, and she slipped the final garment off and over her feet.

"I guess I should be on top," she said softly, like a shy girl, putting his concerns to rest.

He wanted to growl his answer, but refrained while he disposed of his briefs in a flash. "Only if you want to," he said, desperately hoping she wouldn't change her mind. She didn't. Her enlarged pupils mesmerized him, inviting him closer, and he obeyed.

"This has been a long time coming. Let's take it slow," he whispered, with a grainy voice, gently moving a lock of hair behind her ear. He kissed her there and smelled the mix of perfume and woman scent, and grew firmer.

They faced each other. He savored every inch of her, the vision tattooed in his brain. Interlocking his fingers with hers, he waited, giving her one last chance to change her mind. She rolled away and turned down the light in answer.

He spooned up behind her, reaping the warmth of her hips and bottom pressed against his erection. When he lifted and smoothed her soft breasts, the warm tips tightened and puckered and he rolled her back toward him so he could kiss them. She responded to every touch, even when he explored her round stomach with its taught skin.

The baby moved and René's eyes brightened with surprise. "The Tumbler," she said.

He smiled with reverence, deferring to the active baby they'd created, waited until it stopped its antics, then immediately kissed her again, needing to have her on top of him, needing to be inside her.

They rolled together, she straddled his hips and the thought about taking his time vanished. He found her heat and pressed at her entrance, then with her help slid inside, soon overtaken by her warmth and moisture, the heavenly feel and fit of her. How could he possibly last with her wrapping him so tight?

"I guess we don't need to worry about birth control," he said, trying to distract from the intensity of sensation sizzling through him with each lift and drop of her hips.

The picture of her on top of him—hands anchored to his shoulders, head dropped back, a sublime expression on her face, pregnancy-enlarged breasts, round, darkened nipples, faint veins tracking her pale skin, and baby mound hovering above his waist as she lifted and dropped against his thrusts—would be forever etched in his mind. Never would he forget this moment.

They fit as if they belonged together, as if for years this day had been scheduled and impatiently waited to happen.

She was the most beautiful sight he'd seen in years, and she drove him to the brink with each roll of her hips. Tension strained in his groin, as he grew firmer and throbbed inside her.

By the expression on her face, he knew he was taking her along with him on this urgent trek for release. He let her take control, set the pace, adding to his pleasure. Guiding her hips, he restrained himself as she lifted and lowered and he thrust into her deepening heat.

Several minutes later all restraint vanished. They found a wild pace, driven by heat and sensation and sweat. The room went dark as he anchored her hips and increased the force. She clamped down over him in climax and her rhythmic massage brought him to release. The intensity nearly catapulted him off the bed.

He wrapped her tight in his arms and they rocked along as the last few spasms rode themselves out. Her damp cheek stuck to his wet chest until he lifted her chin and kissed her. She moaned her approval, then snuggled against his shoulder again, spent.

If he lifted her arm and let go, it would drop like a rag doll, like the instructor had told them to practice for homework.

It turned out his technique for the relaxation "letting go" method had worked far better than anything Dr. Bradley could have ever dreamed up.

René awoke to Jon's kiss on her forehead.

"Goodbye. I need to get a run in before work." He was dressed and leaning over the bed.

She'd slept soundly entangled with his body, sounder than she had in weeks.

She rose up on her elbows and wiped her sleep-heavy

eyes, attempting to get a handle on the moment. "So soon? What about breakfast? Maybe I could make something." The last thing she wanted was for Jon to make love and run away.

He sat on the bedside and smiled at her, though his eyes didn't participate. It unsettled her, as if a warning of her massive mistake.

"That sounds great," he said, "but you know me and running. I've got to do it." He patted her sheet-covered hip and gave an intimate lover's glance. "Thanks for everything." As if he hadn't gotten the point across last night that she totally turned him on, he soul-kissed her. Then left.

That was it?

Last night the same kind of kiss had sent her reeling with desire. Now, it felt more like a slap in the face. The reminder of his lips all over her body was more than she could process compared to this cheap replica send-off kiss.

He'd made love to her a second time during the night, and she was tired, but if he'd invited her to do it again this morning, she would have...until two seconds ago.

A wave of confusion sent her back onto the pillow. If she could sleep a while longer, tune everything out, when she woke up maybe things would make more sense than they did right now.

She rolled onto her stomach and covered her head, fighting off a cringe. What had she done? She broke into a slick, icy sweat.

She'd taken a huge risk with him last night. She'd given him everything she had in order to show her feelings. Now, he'd literally run away. How stupid of her to lose control. To open up to him. Whether she'd planned it or not, baby step by baby step he'd become a part of her life. And now they'd crossed a forbidden line.

Pain jumbled with heartache and confusion, muddling her thoughts even more. Mindlessly, she rubbed her stomach.

Why did this feel like a repeat of her last breakup? She scraped her teeth over her bottom lip. Was Jon capable of being so heartless? She couldn't allow the insecure thoughts or negativity while she was pregnant. The baby needed peace to grow, not stress, and pursuing a relationship with Jon would only bring pain. She'd do anything to guard against a repeat performance.

She flung the pillow across the room and sat at the bedside. No way would she let him see how she'd fallen for him. If he had a clue how she felt, she'd never be able to face him again. And she'd never know if anything further with their relationship was only out of pity. She swallowed the fist-size knot in her throat. After all the promises she'd made about their business deal, the guarantee she'd given him, he'd think she'd tricked him into becoming more than a donor. A boyfriend? A lover? A father?

A cold rock sat on her chest, heavy and aching. She couldn't ignore the pain. She'd made a huge mistake. She closed her eyes tight and rubbed her temples. Breathe. Breathe. The weight of her blunder made it hard to inhale.

A few moments later, having solved nothing, she glanced at the clock. Reality replaced the scrambled thoughts. She had to make hospital rounds on her inpatients before she started her morning clinic. The big mistake would have to be revisited some other time. Right now, she was ever so grateful for the distraction of her job.

"Wrong, wrong, wrong," Jon chanted as he jogged the toughest hill he could find. He'd been thinking with his body, not his brain, when he'd made love to René, and had made the biggest blunder in his life. The problem was he'd spent too much time with her, eaten too many of her meals. He'd let the lines blur between business and pleasure. Okay, that was an understatement, but where the hell was his IQ when he'd needed it? Showing off in his pants, that's where.

How could he make such a mistake?

He'd told her from the start he didn't want to get involved with the baby, that he'd raised his family and didn't need another, that he had plans for a year's sabbatical, and he looked forward to his freedom, but here he was fresh out of her bed and reeling with confusion. The more time he spent with her, he couldn't stay emotionally aloof, and last night, the distance he'd swore he'd keep had disappeared.

Damn it all. The last thing he'd bargained on was developing feelings for René Munroe. She'd painted such a simple picture that night she'd convinced him to share his DNA. He'd bought it, hook, line and sinker.

He wanted to kick something, mostly himself, he was so angry. He punched the air, as if training for a prize fight as he pounded up the steep hill. His lungs burned and were on the verge of bursting for air.

He'd tell her it was one big mistake. Surely she knew it, too. They'd gotten too close in class and later got carried away, and he forgot his promise. He'd beg, grovel if he had to, in order to get her to understand. He had a bad track record where relationships were concerned, and a nasty divorce to prove it. He never wanted to hurt her. Never. But this couldn't be—this thing between them. It was never supposed to happen in the first place. And now, it had to end.

She'd understand. She was a superbright woman, and her goal was to have a baby, not inherit a lover along with it.

He'd talk to her, apologize with all of his heart, tell her he'd fulfilled his duty, then step into the shadows for the rest of her pregnancy. She needed peace during the next few months, not turmoil, and all he'd done was mess everything up.

His thighs gave out; he plunked down on the nearest patch of grass and hung his head between his knees. He spit out the sour taste in his mouth, then rinsed with the bottled water he wore on his waistband. He held the cool bottle against his throbbing forehead.

How could he be a father and in China for a year at the same time?

She'd understand. He was sure of it.

Thanks to a superbusy clinic, Jon snuck through Thursday morning under the radar and, coward that he'd turned into, was grateful. But he couldn't avoid what must be said. He couldn't let René think he was avoiding her. He'd already messed things up enough. At noon, he took a deep breath and knocked on her office door.

Her eyes softened when she first saw him, before an obvious shift to cool and guarded. "Come in," she said, in a measured tone.

He scratched his cheek. "Uh, about last night," he said, after closing the door. She waved him off in a glib manner, and the sting surprised him. "I've really complicated things, haven't I?"

She went still, narrowed her eyes. "Single-handedly? I think I was in that bed, too."

He let go his breath. "The thing is—"

"Jon." She rose and walked up to him, close enough to feel her breath as she whispered. "The contract is in place. We can step back and think things through, if you'd like."

"Yes," he said a bit too quickly. "Yes, I think that's a good idea."

He thought he saw something flicker in her eyes. Hurt? Disappointment? Before he could explain more she gestured toward her desk. "Now if you don't mind, I've got a stack of paperwork I've got to get done so my patients can get continuity of care when I'm off on maternity leave."

That was it? She'd dismissed him?

"I'm really sorry," he said, "if I've messed things up."

"Not a problem," she said, her usual warmth replaced with a prickly facade. "Really."

Their incredible night of love had been sliced down to a mere "oops" moment. No problem, she'd said. Except it was a problem, a monumental problem. Jon Becker didn't get involved with or make love to a woman unless he cared about her.

He stood there for a few seconds as her tone shifted from tolerant to get lost, and he knew he'd fouled up even more than he'd imagined.

As Jon left her office a confused ball of tension, he glanced at his watch. If he hurried, he'd have time for another run during lunch.

Friday was René's office baby shower. He'd thought about skipping the party and delivering his gift in person at her house over the upcoming weekend, as another excuse to talk to her privately. He needed to straighten things out between them. But it would be so obvious if he didn't come to the party today. Everyone else would be there.

The medical clinic closed two hours early every other Friday and today was deemed the perfect day to have her baby shower. Claire was in charge and had gone all out, decorating and planning the menu and baking the cake. Jason looked on with pride as she fussed over the finishing touches.

Jason's gaze stumbled on Jon. He gave that knowing man-to-man look. "It's payback time," he said.

"Huh?" Jon's IQ had virtually disappeared since falling for René.

"You know, René hosted the baby shower for Claire, now its payback time."

"Ah." Jon nodded, and swallowed against the permanent dry lump in his throat. "I guess I'd better go get my gift," he said, and disappeared to his office.

An hour and a half later, Jon stood at the outskirts of the ring of office employees who cooed and fawned over René, who was queen for the day.

He'd almost had to sit down and catch his breath when she'd removed her doctor's coat and revealed another, even sexier, sundress beneath. The halter-top cut enhanced her shape, and the bright patchwork pattern of orange, dark pink, gold and brown brought out her olive coloring and made her hair look auburn. To say she was stunning would be an understatement. She blew his mind with beauty, and he was almost certain she'd dressed this way to taunt and get back at him. By the rapid-fire beat of his pulse, she'd achieved her goal with little effort.

He ate his raspberry-filled white cake and did his best to act nonchalant when she chose his huge box to unwrap. Claire gave him a knowing glance, since he'd given her and Jason the same gift. Yeah, it was uncreative but functional, and the medical clinic partners had grown to expect no less of him.

But he'd gone one step further with René. She read his bland card without expression, then swept her thick-lashed eyes over him and thanked him with an undecipherable nod. Her smile was reserved, her beauty riveting.

She tore off the wrapping paper and gasped. "Jon, this is fantastic! Thank you."

From a safe distance across the room, and with a schooled expression, he said, "You're welcome."

He'd given her an all-terrain stroller. René was almost positive there was a message buried somewhere in there, but she'd been known to read into things, and often the results had been disastrous. All-terrain meant the stroller was built for all surfaces, all speeds. The hills and valleys of Santa Barbara could be explored either walking or *running*. He knew she wasn't a jogger, yet here was this special stroller.

She flashed on Jon running behind the stroller, pushing their baby along on his daily run, then stopped cold. She could become addicted to thoughts like those, and after Jon had done everything but run out her door yesterday morning, she couldn't allow one more fanciful thought about Jon Becker to sneak into her mind. It wasn't in the contract.

He'd made it beyond clear that they'd made a mistake and it would never happen again. But he did deserve a personal thank-you. He'd given her a great gift—actually, two great gifts. She patted her pregnant belly. The least she could do was be gracious.

She waited until most of the staff had left. Jason and Claire were packing all of her gifts into the back of their new van and wouldn't let her help, so she took the opportunity to slip down the hall to Jon's office.

He'd nearly broken her heart by taking off so fast the other morning. They'd crossed over the line and blurred the set-in-stone verbiage of her carefully drawn contract when they'd made love. She hadn't been thinking straight since.

He'd been attentive and considerate, an incredible lover, the kind of man that sent a woman dreaming about the future, and a lifetime together. There was no doubt in her mind he'd been as turned on as she'd been, but had it changed his feelings about her, too?

He'd said it had been a mistake, every last bit of it, that they should both know it, and it had cut down to the bone. He'd said as much again yesterday in her office. She'd tried to cover for the heartache, but even now, even after losing sleep hashing and rehashing the status of their relationship, she wasn't so sure he'd meant it. Maybe her foolish and fanciful thoughts had made her blind, but her feelings had changed toward him. She'd fallen in love. It was the last thing she'd planned on happening, but it had. The thought made her knees wobble. How could she keep him from catching on?

On the other hand, how could he change his mind about her if he didn't have a clue how she felt? Around and around she went, not knowing what she'd say when she actually saw him, though knowing full well it was best to keep her change of heart close to her chest.

After all, she needed to protect herself and the baby.

He wasn't at his desk, so she decided to leave him a note of thanks. She found a pen and paper, then noticed his screen saver—a picture of proud papa between two gorgeously dressed young ladies. Those tasteful yet flirty soiree dresses she'd helped pick out must have made him burst with pride when he'd seen his daughters in them.

I'm really looking forward to my freedom, she remembered him often saying.

Regardless of how many hidden messages she imagined in his gift, she couldn't ask him to start all over again as a father. It wasn't in their original deal, no matter how much she wanted him to change his mind. And she couldn't exactly will him into loving her.

A travel brochure on China held a prominent position on his desktop. Oh, God, could she ask him to give up that trip, too?

Her gaze drifted to a letter next to the brochure with a well-known university letterhead logo at the top. *We look forward to meeting you at the job interview on...*

She stared in shock at the first sentence. He really didn't want to be involved with her, not if he was planning to leave the clinic. She'd been such a fool to allow such fanciful thoughts. After the sperm donation, she should never have let him near her again.

Someone cleared his voice. It was Jon, standing in his office doorway. She couldn't let him know how foolish she'd been to fall for him, how completely out of touch she'd gotten with the original plan. She couldn't let him see her heart shatter. She reached somewhere deep inside and found her composure.

"Oh, hi," she said. "I was going to leave you a thank-you note." Could he hear the quaver in her voice?

"I was helping Jason get squared away with all the loot. You really made out today." Did he need to sound so casual?

"I did, didn't I." It was her turn to clear the fullness in her throat. A stealth pang of emptiness struck so hard she could barely breathe, but she couldn't let him know. He must never know her real feelings. "I wanted to tell you how fantastic that all-terrain stroller is. Tumbler and I will get lots of use out of it."

He closed the door and took a few steps toward her, a tentative expression on his face. "I don't want you to get the wrong impression." He searched the corners of the room as if to find the best words, and she got the distinct impression he wanted to let her down easy. Damn him.

His hesitation and avoidance of tackling their problem head-on infuriated her. *Come out with it. Tell me you don't want anything to do with me. Tell me you don't care about me. Don't let me stand here loving you, when you can't return it.* Heat burned the tips of her ears and the room dimmed. Humiliated, all she wanted to do was save face.

"You think you took advantage of me?" She didn't care if his nurses might be around and could hear through his door. Gossip had been running rampant over who the father of her baby was. "I was as much responsible for what happened between us as you were, so don't give yourself so much credit," she said, sounding harsher than she'd meant, but her emotions had taken over. Before she could break down in front of him and let slip that she'd fallen in love, she charged past him and out of the room.

She'd been stupid enough to think he might have feelings for her. He sure could have fooled her by the way they'd made love, but he'd already been planning to change jobs, and hadn't even bothered to mention it during their casual chatter between the bedsheets.

Nothing made sense. Her love. His aloofness. Their lovemaking. His withdrawal ever since. None of it. But right now, the part that hurt the most was that he let her leave his office without so much as a touch.

The next Wednesday night he showed up at her door when she was on her way out. "What are you doing here?" She faltered over the sudden pop of adrenaline circulating through her. To make matters worse, Tumbler jabbed her ribs with an elbow or heel.

"It's Wednesday, the final birthing class, right?" Jon said.

Damn, why did he have to make everything so difficult? She wanted more than anything for things to go back to the way they'd been, but it was impossible. Not with the feelings she'd been carrying around for him since they'd made love. Her initial anger had cooled off a bit, but the disappointment had cut deep and still festered.

"I relieve you of duty," she said, with a huff and a single shoulder shrug. It took everything in her power to act and sound blasé. Her lower lip quivered, so she caught it between her teeth.

"Nonsense. I said I'd be your coach, and I have every intention of fulfilling my promise."

She ignored the hurt expression on his face, focused on the cold phrase, needing desperately to hang on to her anger.

"I'm an independent, modern-day woman. I don't need you. I'll have a nurse help me when I deliver."

"You know as well as I do those L&D nurses have four other patients assigned to them, and you'll wind up going through lots of contractions alone. I'll help you." He made a solid point, but she brushed it off with another shrug. "This is nuts," he said, sounding exasperated and scraping fingers through his hair.

With the last of her resolve she used her strident voice. "Maybe, but it's what I've decided."

"I'm not going to let you give birth—" he stalled for a second; did he stop short of saying *to our baby?* "—alone."

Her mother used to chide her impulses with an old saying, "Be careful what you wish for." Well, she'd gotten exactly what she'd wished for, a baby of her own, and she was ecstatic about it, but the rest of the grief, the falling in love with the sperm-donor part, she could never have imagined. Check another one off for Mom.

Jon frustrated her so much—being everything she could dream of in a partner, yet refusing to commit—she could scream.

"You're driving me crazy, you know that?" she said. "You want to be involved, then you don't want to be involved, then—"

"Ditto on the driving me crazy bit," he said, grabbing her elbow as if saying the conversation was over. "Now let's go."

"No!" She shrugged free. "And besides, tonight is that stupid last-class party. I'm not going," she said.

"Then why are you holding a tray of canapés?"

She shoved two of them into her mouth. "Becauth I'm pwegnant and alwayth hungwy, thath why!" She slammed the door in his face.

CHAPTER TEN

Thirty-four weeks' gestation, early October

RENÉ sat at her desk. She hadn't bothered to turn on the light. Early afternoon autumn shadows dappled her office walls, causing a bleak effect. Normally she loved the lacy silhouettes dancing like fairies around the room, but today they only emphasized an expanding pit of loneliness. Something vital had gone missing from her life. Jon.

She wished she could say things had gone back to normal after she slammed the door in Jon's face seven weeks ago, but the word *normal* no longer applied.

With chin cupped in palm, elbow anchored on the desk, her eyes darted around the room, deep in thought. As always these days, her other hand rested on her bulging stomach.

She was a soon-to-be single mother, who'd thought for sure she knew what she was doing when she'd succumbed to the lure of wanting a baby on her own. She didn't regret it. Not that part. No, being a parent promised to fulfill her life in ways she couldn't begin to fathom.

The nursery was completely ready with each tiny item of clothing, blankets, sleepers and T-shirts laundered and neatly folded and in their place. Jon had done a wonderful job of painting, the bright yellow walls were far more agreeable than that god-awful purple Gretchen had talked her into. Really, what had she been thinking?

René could ask herself that—what in the world had she been thinking?—about a lot of things. And one major thing in particular—the decision to ask a friend and coworker to be the sperm donor. Jon had been partially right when he'd accused her of wanting a designer baby, but truth was she'd love this kid no matter how things turned out. Smart, average, fat, thin, pretty, plain—none of that mattered. The love she felt inside for this child transpired every superficial characteristic life could throw at her.

In retrospect, yes, she should have stayed with a sperm-donor clinic, but knowing a part of Jon would always be in her life brought her a minute amount of selfish comfort. And she longed for more of it.

She never could have believed how much support he would be. And how empty she'd feel without him. When she'd made her original plans she'd only known Jon as a smart man, one she admired, the kind of man who would have good DNA. Along the way, she'd learned how wonderful he was, how witty, capable, warm and caring he could be. How he appealed to her on so many different levels, and yes, that he was a fantastic lover, too.

But they'd signed a contract; he'd fulfilled his role, and had big plans for his future. She was stuck in love and in limbo.

She hadn't planned on falling in love with him. She'd only planned on having a baby.

Jon had obviously taken her message about staying out of her life to heart and had left her alone since the day of her last birthing class. He'd also taken a couple weeks' vacation in early September to get Amanda situated back east at the university, and, she feared, to interview for that job offer she'd seen on his desk.

When they occasionally ran into each other in the clinic, they were civil but distant, and the loss of his friendship had left a gaping hole in her core. She missed him so much. So far she hadn't found a way to forget him. How could she, carrying his child, feeling it move and grow inside her, knowing it carried his genes and dying to find out what the baby would look like?

René toed off her bronze-colored flats and let go a sigh of relief. She drew circles in the air with her toes, then elevated her feet on the adjacent chair.

When she thought about names, she wanted Jon's input. What was his grandmother's or mother's name? Did he have a favorite guy name? Did he like traditional or modern-sounding names? She stopped herself. The baby belonged to her and her alone. She had a contract stating as much, and he'd agreed to it. So why did it matter what his view on names was? And why couldn't she get that through her hormonally infused head when she'd found out from Claire that his middle name was Evan! She hoped her baby was a girl so she could name her after her mother, Yvonne. But if it were a boy…

After next week, she'd be on maternity leave and wouldn't have to deal with running into him or hearing his voice across the clinic, or noticing how fantastic he looked in his suits with the quirky added touch of sneakers. Or re-membering how his hands felt on her body when they'd made love, and making love was exactly what it was, no one could convince her otherwise. They hadn't merely had sex to relieve some feral itch. No. They'd swept each other into the living, feeling truth of the matter; they'd opened up and held nothing back. She knew she'd touched his soul, could feel it when Jon had been inside her and his pearly black eyes delved into hers, and his expression had taken her breath away. He couldn't disguise that "deep into you" stare, and she'd felt it to her trembling core.

Her watch alarm went off. She checked, then silenced, it. Quiet time was over whether she was ready or not. Back on with the shoes. Another sigh and push off from her desk to help her stand. She took inventory of her office with faint silver strands of light fighting off the lengthening afternoon, and losing. The tone paralleled her mood; she shook her head.

She hadn't meant to highjack Jon's plans. He deserved his freedom, his trip to China; he'd talked about it from the beginning. He'd lived up to his part of the bargain, and she needed to step aside to let him live the rest of his life.

Instead of sighing, she let out a quick breath through her nose and chided herself. *You made the rules, kiddo.* So why was she so lonely and so damn mad at him?

In the meantime, she had more patients to see, and her feet ached from carrying all the extra weight around even though she wore natural-fitting shoes for support. She'd started to waddle, and had hit the always-searching-for-comfort-but-never-finding-it stage. When she looked at herself, all she saw was her belly, and lots of it. How could she possibly grow any bigger?

She blew out a breath and her hair lifted from her forehead. September was almost over, and October traditionally was a hot month in Santa Barbara. Since she was hot all the time now, at this size, how would she get through the coming month?

About to open her next patient chart, her intercom line buzzed.

"Dr. Munroe, it's Gaby. Is it okay if I add on one of your patients this afternoon?"

"I think I can squeeze someone in. Who is it?"

"Lisa Lightner—she's on the phone now," Gaby said.

Lisa was due to deliver her first baby in three weeks, and she'd had a smooth pregnancy up to now. They'd often exchanged pregnant anecdotes with each other, and had developed a special bond because of it.

"What's wrong?"

"She didn't really say, just that she doesn't feel right."

A flashing yellow light blinked in the back of René's mind. Lisa wasn't a complainer or a hypochondriac; if she thought something wasn't right, René knew she should look into it.

"Tell her to come right in, and let Amy know."

Forty-five minutes later, a very pregnant Lisa sat on the exam table making René feel small in comparison.

"What brings you in today, Lisa?"

"I feel like I can't catch my breath." She punctuated her words with shallow gasps.

With her uterus pressing on her diaphragm, René knew it was a common complaint, yet she took her pulse, which was rapid, and listened to her lungs and breath sounds, which were also fast, though her lungs sounded perfectly normal. Her blood pressure was mildly hypotensive, but within her normal range.

"Any chest pain?"

"I wouldn't call it chest pain. I just don't feel right."

"We'll get an EKG to rule anything out. Have you had any unusual leg pain or injury recently?"

Lisa shook her head. From her history, René knew Lisa had never had coagulation problems, but pregnancy could sometimes pull some pretty hairy cats out of the bag.

To be on the safe and thorough side, René examined her patient's lower extremities, and though no varicose veins were present, she did locate one tender area on the back of Lisa's calf beneath a small bruise. "I'm going to order a D-dimer blood test, and if it's positive, we'll do an ultrasound of your leg to rule out deep vein thrombophlebitis."

"What's that got to do with being out of breath?"

René didn't want to scare Lisa, but if she did have DVT, a pulmonary embolism could be the cause of her shortness of breath. There was no way she'd tell her that; though rare, pulmonary embolism was the leading cause of maternal mortality during pregnancy and up to six weeks postpartum.

"It's just a precaution, Lisa. I need to rule out all the possibilities before I make my diagnosis. Your lungs sound normal, no crackles or wheezing, so that's good. Let me have my nurse check your oxygen saturation and do that EKG before you go to the lab. We'll figure this out before you leave today, I promise."

Making a diagnosis of pulmonary embolism in a pregnant woman was a tricky task due to the tests required and concerns about fetal radiation exposure.

"I'd like you to stick around while we wait for your STAT lab results."

Lisa nodded, and René waddled off to see her next patient, but her mind stayed on Lisa. She wanted to discuss the case with Phil, the pulmonary doctor in their practice. After she'd seen the other patient, she called Phil's office, but he wasn't there.

When she inquired where he was, her nurse, Amy, told her it was his morning to do bronchoscopies at the hospital. She knew that. Her memory seemed to have shrunk in direct proportion with the growth of her abdomen. René lifted her phone receiver to call Jason, the family practice guy in the group, then remembered that after Jon had come back from vacation, Jason and Claire had left on theirs.

That left Jon, the person she'd dodged for the past month. The person she was trying her hardest to forget and get over. Patient well-being trumped her personal concerns, so she walked to the back of the mansion-turned-clinic to find him in his office.

He was on his way out, focusing on a report and heading for his closest exam room. "Oh," he said, when he noticed her, his pupils briefly widening, then going back to normal.

"Can I run something by you?" she said, itchy with discomfort and confusion at being so close to him.

"Of course."

She gave him the thumbnail sketch on Lisa. She refused to look into his dark stare and, instead, she noticed the intricate geometrical interlocking pattern on his forest-green tie.

Before she could finish with Lisa's history, Amy rushed up. "It's positive. The D-dimer is positive."

René thanked her. "Have you done the EKG? Oh, and put her on oxygen before you call for medical transportation to the hospital. She needs to go to the E.R. for an ultrasound of her leg and further testing."

"You might want to get a normal saline IV going, too," Jon said.

She and Jon stood in the hall and discussed the tricky situation of diagnostic testing for PE in a pregnant woman. They agreed the best test would be a ventilation perfusion lung scan, and if that proved indeterminate yet the clinical suspicion remained, pulmonary angiography would be a necessary evil. She hated to put both mother and baby at risk, but knew something much worse could happen if they didn't treat a blood clot lodged in the lung. She worried about ordering a test for a pregnant patient that would involve radiation, even though in low quantities, but Jon pointed out the V/Q scan had the least radiation of any other diagnostic tests for PE.

Being able to discuss the medical possibilities with Jon was reassuring and she was grateful to have him here. She'd missed his knowledgeable input, but more importantly, his friendship. Maybe it was time to let him know exactly how she felt. Maybe after all this—

Before she could say a word, the interdepartment alarm went off. "STAT patient assist in first-floor waiting room."

René's pulse spiked to where she could feel it in her temples. A sinking feeling had her praying it wasn't her pregnant patient. She and Jon rushed to the front of the clinic to find Lisa collapsed on the floor with a huddle of people around her.

Jon directed Amy to take over crowd control while he rushed for the crash cart. René went down on her knees beside the patient and felt for her pulse. Lisa was semiconscious, and fighting for air.

"Get some oxygen over here, and call an ambulance. Gaby, call her husband and tell him to meet her at the E.R. Cough for me, Lisa," she said, hoping the exertion might help break up any potential lung clot blocking her breathing. Lisa did as she was told, but with little effort. Once the oxygen mask was in place, René asked her to cough again, and she coughed a little harder.

"I'm afraid I'll wet my pants," Lisa said.

Relief showered over René, and she grinned. If a patient was worried about wetting themselves, they couldn't be too far gone. "You're going to be okay, Lisa. Hang in. We're going to get you to the hospital." Hopefully it was a small clot that would resolve easily with treatment.

Jon and Amy lifted Lisa onto a gurney and they rolled her into the first-floor procedure room.

Jon inserted an IV, and René calibrated the patient weight and started the appropriate amount of heparin via piggyback into the IV. Because the drug didn't cross the placenta, it was the safest anticoagulant to use during pregnancy.

Jon stood by the crash cart with the Ambu bag in readiness, as Amy set up the heart monitor and pulse ox. The patient's vital signs were challenged but stable. And most importantly, her oxygen saturation was within normal limits.

The strain and fear evident in Lisa's eyes tore at René's heart. How would she feel in the same situation? Scared to death! She held Lisa's hands tight and leaned over her. "We're going to get you through this."

"What about my baby?"

"Little Sara's going to be fine. It's you we need to focus on right now." Unlike René, Lisa had insisted on knowing the sex of her baby.

When the ambulance siren ripped through the air, René let go a relieved sigh. "The E.R. will do any tests necessary to rule out pulmonary embolism, and they'll treat you with anticoagulants. We caught it early thanks to your suspicions about something being wrong."

Fifteen minutes later, with the patient in stable but guarded condition and on her way to emergency, René called in her report to the local E.R., only then noticing how shaky her hands were. When she'd finished, she called Lisa's husband on his cell phone to bring him up-to-date. Lisa's support system was in order. Her husband would soon be at her side. This was a luxury she didn't have, by choice, at least in the beginning. Now she wondered how big of a mistake her original and seemingly well-thought-out plans had been. The baby kicked in protest, and she gasped.

Jon rushed to her side. "Everything okay?"

She nodded. "Just a little shook up from all the excitement." Completely aware of his hands on her shoulders, she'd missed him, missed his company and friendship, and wished with all her heart things could be different.

"Let me bring you a cup of tea from the kitchen." In a flash the warmth from his touch disappeared.

"Thank you," she said, enjoying the brief respite in their strained relationship. "I'll meet you there."

She made one last quick phone call, took a deep breath and gathered her shaken wits, then followed him down the hall.

They sat together in the kitchen and sipped the peace-offering tea, and for a fleeting moment René pretended life was as it had been before she'd asked him to help with her pregnancy plan.

"There's something I want to tell you before you hear it anywhere else," he said, shifting in his chair, giving a wary glance.

She held her teacup with both hands, within sipping distance, swept her gaze from the pale honey-colored liquid to the tentative set of his eyes and the deepening crease between them.

"I've decided to take a job with another practice, and I'll be gone before you come back from maternity leave."

Afraid she'd drop the cup, she set it on the table before it could spill. Her throat tensed and her stomach cramped. She carefully schooled her expression, working to shut down the sudden anxiety as it nipped at her composure.

How should she respond? *I'm sorry I've chased you away. I'm sorry I used you, if that's what you think. Please know I never thought of it that way.* But as she stared at a lone crumb on the table, all that came out of her mouth was, "I'll miss you, Jon."

She'd sacrificed their friendship and would have to pay the price. Their contract relieved him of any obligation to their child; he'd only agreed reluctantly to signing it in the first place, and with one major stipulation—that no one would know he was the father.

Rumors and suspicions were flying around the office like unwanted flies. It was only a matter of time before someone put it together. Maybe he should get out before her misguided plan could cast an unbecoming shadow over his spotless reputation.

How could she be disappointed? She'd set every single stipulation in place. Why should she feel abandoned? He'd never once promised to stick around. She swallowed the surprising words throbbing in her throat—*What about me? Do you care at all?*

"I'll miss you, too," he said.

They sat in strained silence, her unspoken words tensing the air.

A muscle worked in his jaw, as if he had something more to say, but thought better of it. He stood. "Guess I'd better get back to work."

She blinked. That was it? How could she suddenly be so angry at him? She had no right. He wasn't a mind reader. He didn't know how she felt about him. But damn it, she was angry. Furious.

She wanted to hate him for being so casual about up-ending her life. Why did he have to keep coming around?

Why had she let him? Hell, even his daughters liked her. Why couldn't she win him over?

Thanks to Jon she would have a baby of her own. Though she wished with all of her might that things could be different, under no circumstances would she let him back. The pain of losing him once had been enough for a lifetime.

Her mother's famous saying whispered through her mind again—*be careful what you wish for*—and the hair on her arms stood on end.

Two weeks later, on a bright fall morning, Jon walked with Phil Hanson from the clinic parking area. Phil had a smile on his face, and Jon figured that meant he'd had a great date the night before.

"How do you do it, my friend," Jon asked.

"Do what?"

"Survive out there in that sea of women." Jon had felt nothing but icicles whenever he and René were in the same vicinity at the clinic since he'd told her he was changing jobs. He wanted things to be the way they were before, but took responsibility for messing them up. If he could take back that moment of weakness when he signed her contract, rationally believing he could handle it, he would. Yet the crazy contract was what had brought them together like never before. Would he trade their intimacy for the status quo?

He hated the confusion.

"Ah, waxing poetic this morning, I see," Phil said, with a Jack Nicholson smile and sunglasses to match.

If he'd been released in a sea of women, he'd surely be dead, because he could barely survive the effects of one special person. René. She'd talked him into her motherhood plan, and he'd taken things one step too far. Now he'd been relegated to mere office associate, and the whole thing stunk to high heaven.

"Nah, just licking my wounds," Jon said.

Phil's smile took on a whole new dimension, as if they were old military buddies and had been in battle together. "You think I never have to do that? Come on, a man works without a net and he's bound to get hurt."

"What do you mean?"

"Us guys jump into dating with our zippers opened and forget about the consequences. We forget about the Pandora's box of complications that goes along with sex. Once the ladies find out we're really as shallow as they suspected, they dump us. What do we do? We dust ourselves off and jump right back in with someone else. It's a wild ride." He patted Jon on the back, and forked toward his office next to René's. "But it's exciting and well worth the adventure."

Jon stood watching him, wondering if that counted as a heart-to-heart talk between guys. And more importantly, had he learned anything?

Yeah, he'd learned that René deserved someone more exciting than him. Wasn't that what Cherie had opted for after seventeen years?

He glanced in the direction of René's office, but her door was closed. She hadn't arrived at work yet.

He thought about her every single day and hated the fact that he'd fallen for her. She hadn't bargained for that, didn't deserve the extra frustration, and though it had been the toughest thing he'd ever done, he'd stayed out of her way the past couple of weeks like she'd wanted when she'd slammed the door in his face.

They'd signed a contract and he'd honor it.

Damn straight he would.

By midmorning, Jon couldn't help but notice René still wasn't at work. He checked his calendar to see if he'd miscalculated the beginning of her maternity leave. Nope. Not due off for another two weeks.

He strolled out to Gaby, who talked excitedly to René's nurse, Amy. "Did you hear the news?"

"What's up?" he said.

"Dr. Munroe is in labor!"

CHAPTER ELEVEN

JON raced into the maternity ward, straight to the secretary's desk. He leaned over the counter, catching his breath. After he'd told Gaby to cancel all his appointments for the day, he'd broken a speed limit or two on the drive over. Though he worked closely with this hospital, Labor and Delivery wasn't a regular stop on his rounds.

Fortunately the ward clerk recognized him from when he'd followed up with Chloe Vickers's heart condition.

"I'm looking for René Munroe," he said, breathless and practically vibrating with excitement.

"Hi, Dr. Becker. She's in labor so she's not having visitors."

How should he put this, direct and to the point? "I'm not a visitor, I'm her birth coach."

That got the clerk's attention. From above her computer monitor, her eyes sprung open and she gave him a disbelieving stare, complete with eyebrows nearly meeting hairline. "You're her coach?"

He nodded, putting on an air of authority, while straightening the knot of his tie and catching his breath. "Where is she?"

The clerk pointed him to the room number, and he

rushed around the corner. The labor room was surprisingly homey with hardwood floors, an overstuffed chair next to the hospital bed disguised by a bright quilt comforter and soothing pastoral prints framed and hanging on the walls. But she wasn't there. He stepped outside and glanced up in time to see her walking toward him. She pushed an IV pole along the carpeted hall, and was draped in nondescript hospital gowns, one on backward acting like a robe to cover her hind end.

Surprise stopped her midstep when she saw him. "What are you doing here?"

"Reporting for duty. I'm your birth coach."

"No, you're not. I dismissed you, remember?"

He'd play along, but having let her down enough lately, he had no intention of leaving. He pulled on his ear. "It was so obvious that you didn't mean it."

She tossed a glare at the ceiling. "Did so."

He decided to try the tried-and-true distraction method. "Who's helping you?"

"I'm doing fine by myself."

"When did you go into labor?" he said, joining her step for step.

"Last night."

"Why didn't you call me?"

She broke the pace. "Because you're not my coach anymore." Irritation oozed over each word. He knew how edgy labor could make a woman, and chose to ignore it.

"How far dilated are you?"

"None of your business." She resumed the pace.

He took off his jacket, flung it over his shoulder and loosened the knot of his tie. "I'm not leaving."

"Nurse?" she said, to a passing L&D employee in bright

pink scrubs and with a blond ponytail halfway down her back. "I don't want him here."

She turned out to be a student nurse, who had no idea how to handle the situation. "I'll get the charge nurse," she said, looking at a loss and extremely anxious.

Ha, Jon thought, he knew one of the L&D charge nurses. He'd taken care of her father's heart attack last year. If he was lucky it would be her and he'd convince her to let him stay regardless of what René said. In the meantime, he followed her down the corridor.

"Don't make a scene, René. I want to help you."

"Not going to happen." She turned to walk in the other direction.

"Come on, let's go back to your room," he said, reaching for her arm.

She pulled away from his grasp. Grumpy from labor or not, her reaction surprised the hell out of him. He might need to take another approach.

"I'm supposed to keep walking to help speed things along." She shot past him in a new direction.

He strode up behind her. "Then I'll walk with you."

She stopped again, and he almost ran into her. "I want you to leave."

The charge nurse approached. Unfortunately, it wasn't the one he knew. This called for drastic action, and he'd do whatever it took. He flung his arm around René's shoulder. "Come on, honey pie, let's keep walking." He'd play the patient partner to her testy labor lady.

She responded with an alien death glare.

"Is this man bothering you, Dr. Munroe?"

"I don't want him here."

"I'm the birth coach," he said, fighting to keep his hand

on her shoulder even as she pinched his fingers. "Her doula. I see the labor has really made her cranky." He smiled and sidestepped when she tried to kick his foot. Fortunately she was only wearing the hospital-issued no-skid sock slippers.

The no-nonsense charge nurse glanced back and forth between them, appraising the situation.

"If you don't believe me, check her paperwork," he said. "My name's Jon Becker, Dr. Jon Becker, and it should be there." They'd filled out the forms together in the first Bradley birthing class. "And while you're at it—" he decided to go for broke in case he got thrown out of the hospital in the next few minutes, and because he wanted to make sure René didn't get dehydrated in his absence "—can you bring her a cup of ice chips?"

René gasped and grabbed her side, standing like a statue as the obvious contraction mounted.

Jon seized the opportunity to take over. "Okay, let me get a wheelchair and I'll take you back to the room." He saw one halfway down the hall and charged toward it. "Don't worry, I'm here and I'll take care of you," he said, rolling it back. "I'll even make the pillows just how you like them."

He had the wheelchair behind her knees before René could say "ouch" and Jon assisted her to sit, then rolled her to the room.

"Don't forget the sleep breathing. Think like an animal, go inward." He used calming low tones to help her stay focused, the way he'd been taught.

The charge nurse must have gone to check the paperwork, because they were alone again, and Jon helped René get into the awaiting bed. She let him.

He whispered encouraging words and rubbed her arm while helping her lay on her side. He put a pillow behind her back, two under her head and one between her knees the way they'd practiced in class, and again, she didn't protest.

He lightly stroked her hair and massaged her neck. Every lesson they'd learned together came back to him, plus a few he'd remembered from the birth of his daughters. He'd be useful to her. He owed her no less.

When her breathing returned to normal, she glanced over her shoulder and whispered a surprising, "Thanks."

"You're not kicking me out?" He smiled tenderly at her, wanting more than anything for her to understand he'd be there if she needed him, as long as she let him.

She shook her head, eyes half-mast. A second later her earnest gaze went directly for his pupils. "The baby's almost four weeks premature. I had a bloody show yesterday after work, then I realized I'd been having irregular contractions most of the afternoon. It's too early—I'm scared."

"Hey, you're in great hands." He reached for her fingers and offered a reassuring squeeze. "This hospital is top-notch. The baby will get all the help she needs."

"She?" she said, with a toss of her thick lashes. "You know something I don't?"

"Actually, with my two-girl track record, just call it a hunch."

The L&D nurse stepped back into the room, ice chips in one hand, monitor wires in the other. She went to work setting up the external device, then did a cervical check. Out of courtesy, Jon looked away while she did.

"You're six centimeters dilated and fifty percent effaced. Looks like we're getting somewhere."

A combination apprehensive and excited smile creased

René's lips. Her raised eyebrows cried out for reassurance. He wasn't used to seeing her look insecure, but the pyramid of lines on her forehead and the constant lip licking told him she was. She glanced toward him and he made an encouraging nod.

"Piece of cake, huh?" he said.

"That's easy for you to say." She huffed.

He ducked when she tried to swat him with one of the pillows.

"Things might get ugly," she warned with a flinty look.

"I can take it," he said, giving in to the need to smooth her hair. "Hey, I've got my mp3 player—you want to listen to some music?"

"Sure." She nodded, a whole new attitude to his being there, which buoyed his spirit.

She sat up and he put the ear buds in place, and let her choose whatever she wanted to listen to from his personal list.

She settled back into the pile of pillows. He spoon-fed her a couple of ice chips, treating her like Cleopatra.

"Just do me a favor," she said, around a mouthful of ice.

"Sure, anything."

"Don't ever call me 'honey pie' again."

A laugh tumbled out of his mouth as she gave her warning. He took note. A gaze passed between them, communicating a book's worth of regulations, and maybe forgiveness. For now they'd put all the confusion about where they stood with each other aside and work as a team for one goal, the birth of the baby they'd made together.

Four hours later, during a lull between contractions, René twirled her hair around her index finger. "Tell me something silly about you," she said.

"Me, silly? Man, that's a tough one." After some

thought, and under the time constraint of wanting to say something before the next big one came along, he remembered a long-buried factoid. "I used to, probably still do, know all the words to 'Bohemian Rhapsody.'"

She bleated a laugh. "You're kidding. Okay. Tell me."

He'd do anything to smooth the furrow between her brows and ease this ordeal she was going through, and figured what the hell. After a moment of digging through his memory, he recited every single word to the old Queen song.

Her laughter trickled out, and he savored this sound compared to her last contraction and the injured animal echoing in his memory. Thankfully, the nurse had started titrating a mild sedative into her IV to help her relax between contractions, and the result was noticeable.

"Your turn," Jon said, taking advantage of her new and relaxed state.

She looked all innocent, as if the game had changed.

"Come on, I told you mine, now you tell me yours," he chided.

"Okay." She sighed and glanced at the ceiling, a light blush coloring her cheeks. "I used to know all the dance steps to *Thriller.*"

"Ha!" He could just imagine René dancing like a zombie, and it cracked him up. "Someday I'm going to make you show me."

The sentence had slipped out with little thought. The consequences sent them spiraling into the reality of their relationship. There would be no someday. Their eyes fused and communicated questions and answers and regrets, though no word was spoken.

"Sure," she said.

After several more seconds of strained silence she shook

her head, then grabbed her belly with both hands. "Oh, oh, oh. Tumbler wants out."

"Come on now, breathe." He jumped back to duty, soothing her, helping her find a tolerable position, waiting for the contraction to pass.

The L&D nurse checked in, did another cervical exam and monitored the baby. The fetal heartbeat had become a mesmerizing rhythm and a reassuring sound in between the contractions. Their little Tumbler was working hard, too, and Jon wouldn't forget that.

"Maybe you should take a break," the nurse said to Jon. "Go eat something. You don't want to run out of steam when the real show starts."

He thought he'd been watching the real show for more than four hours. He'd been holding René's hand, and neither of them seemed to realize how natural it was. She let go and prodded him with a direct look, then a wink. "Go on. Take a break. I'll be fine."

He didn't want to leave her, but the nurse had made a good point. "I'm not hungry, but maybe a quick visit to the men's room and a bottle of water will do me some good."

"Go, go," she said, acting as if she didn't need him.

Once alone, Jon dealt with his torn feelings. It felt so right to be with her, yet he had a job transfer arranged for the end of the month. And China? What about China? Was he here out of a sense of duty or because he cared for her? When he saw their baby, how would he react?

He splashed cold water on his face and washed his hands, avoiding the answers, soon rushing back to her side.

Back within five minutes, she was noticeably glad to see him. He resumed his position at her bedside, touching, massaging, and repositioning her—anything she wanted to make her relax between contractions as the afternoon dragged on into the evening.

Two hours later, drenched in sweat, writhing in midcontraction, René rolled onto her side. Jon rubbed her lower back until he thought his arm would fall off. She clutched his other hand so tight, he'd lost feeling in his fingers.

"You can do this, René. Don't quit."

"I can't. I'm dead."

"Come on, honey. Don't give up."

After the contraction eased up, she got a peculiar expression on her face; a laugh vibrated and rolled out of her chest, taking him by surprise.

"What's so funny?" he asked.

"I'm an OB doc. You'd think I'd know how horrible labor is. Truth is, the nurses take care of my patients, and I just show up for the grand finale."

"Humbling, eh?"

She gave a self-deprecating glance, then slid into the next contraction with a *"Yeow!"*

After another quick check, the nurse made the call. "Okay, it's time to deliver this baby." She pushed a button on the wall. Then over her shoulder and through the com line, she called the charge nurse. "Page Dr. Stevens. We're ready for a baby to get born."

René looked at Jon with a see-what-I'm-saying lift of her brows.

He grinned. "Are you ready?"

"I changed my mind. Can I check out now?"

He laughed. "I know you can do this, honey, and if I can help in any way I will."

An amused look crossed her face. "I think you already did." It only lasted a second before a grimace appeared, followed by the horrific painful expression only a woman in transition can make.

The doctor arrived and did a quick vaginal examination, determining the position and station of the fetal head. Jon winced.

"Bear down," the doctor said, as the next tsunami contraction rolled through.

Jon was there by her side, holding her hands, prompting her just like the doctor and delivery nurse were. "Push. Push, honey. Come on, baby, you can do it."

His eyes latched on to hers and he could have sworn her look of terror changed to trust. She put her chin to chest, and let go a guttural animal sound and pushed so hard he was afraid she'd have a brain aneurysm.

"We're almost there," the doctor said.

She went limp after the contraction eased off, as if too exhausted to move or breathe. He held her against his chest, wiped her sweat-wrung brow, kissed her head and cuddled her. She felt more precious to him than anything on earth. "You're doing great. You're almost there," he whispered in her ear.

Soon the now-familiar fetal monitor started its earthquake detection and her moan seemed to originate from her toes.

"This is it," the doctor said. "Bear down."

Exhausted, Jon tensed and didn't make a peep when her grip and nails drew blood on his palms. "Push, René. Come on, baby, push. You can do it. We're almost there." His voice was hoarse with fatigue, and he could only imagine how wrung out René must feel.

But she grunted and growled, and pushed and pushed like the trooper she was, and he admired the hell out of her for it. Loved her.

Soon a mewing sound came from the foot of the bed. From Jon's angle a slick and hairless object popped out and slipped into the doctor's awaiting hands.

René cried out in sudden relief. In awe, Jon bit his lip and held his breath. Shivers of joy coursed through him. His blurry gaze melded with her watery amber eyes. He wanted to yell, *We did it!* but couldn't form the words. They smiled, clutching each other's hands, passing volumes of thoughts and feelings between them. How could a single word express the wonder, the elation?

The nurse burst their moment by handing the baby to René, and he became the center of their existence. The reason they'd come together in the first place. The final note of a beautiful symphony.

The tiny body jerked and spasmed and imitated a griping kitten. He and René laughed together with utter joy. Joy that Jon hadn't felt since his daughters had been born.

"It's a boy," the doctor declared.

Chills ran the course of Jon's body as he looked at the baby. A son!

Overwhelmed, he needed to find somewhere to sit down as the blood receded from his head and down to his toes.

"Uh-oh, husband down," the doctor said.

"Lean against the wall and slide down," the nurse directed, busy with the newborn.

Jon found the nearest wall and fought the darkness over-taking his vision. He skid his back down the wall all the way to the floor, then put his head between his knees and snagged a couple of deep breaths. "Sorry, René," he mumbled, as if this had been the only way he'd let her down. A beat later, everything else faded away.

A boy. Their baby was a boy. A small, but healthy boy.

Willing himself not to go completely out, he glanced up in time to see René cuddle new life to her chest. "Oh, God, he's gorgeous," she said, with a grainy, exhausted voice.

Jon closed his eyes. Yes. Yes. They'd done great work, the two of them. Feeling a bit stronger, he took his time standing, and when he was sure he was back to normal, he approached the bed.

"Don't touch him," the nurse said. "Your hands were on the floor."

He pocketed his hands and leaned over René to have a look at the baby. She gazed up at him, eyes glistening, and with a joyous smile stretching her lips. "Thank you," she said, serene and angelic. "I've got my baby."

He wanted to say, *No, thank* you! *Thank you for reminding me what living is, for pulling me out of my cave and forcing me to interact with life and to feel again.* But his thoughts were flying too fast, and he couldn't form a single syllable. Instead, he leaned over and kissed the delicate crease on her brow, savored her warm skin beneath his lips, and when he'd recovered his voice he whispered, "My pleasure. Truly."

Their eyes connected again. Something solid and everlasting passed between them, the sense of family he remembered so well from the birth of both of his daughters. A bond that could never be altered bridged between them, an impermeable connection in the form of a fragile baby joined them heart to heart, whether he wanted it or not.

A sting of panic shot through Jon's center, jolting him back to reality. This wasn't part of the contract. She wanted a baby, not him. He was nothing more than a conduit to her dreams. He had to remember his place, steer clear of the dangerous lure the thought of having a son had brought.

There was no place in René's plan for him.

And he had a life…with plans. He already knew he couldn't work side by side with her, and be uninvolved. Now, with the birth of their son—correction, *her* son—the only thing left was for him to move away. Far away. It was best for all three of them.

From the beginning, she'd made it clear she wanted this baby all to herself. Hadn't she tried to banish him from the delivery room? He'd bulldozed his way in. This cocka-mamy baby-plan stunt wasn't how families got formed. Any fleeting thoughts about being a part of their lives were a sham. And no matter what, no matter how much his instinct contradicted his future plans, he was going to China.

He glanced at mother and baby, a near-perfect picture of bliss; still, he ached to be a part of it. Taking to heart the nurse's advice—*don't touch him, don't dare touch him*—he backed away.

As they cleaned up both mother and baby, Jon stood dazed, an outside observer. Finally, the nurse announced she was rolling René back to the ward.

Reeling with confusion, Jon hung back. If she loved him, maybe things could be different, but she'd never hinted at anything close to that, and he'd never had the guts to tell her…

Someone was speaking to him.

"Sorry. What?" he said.

"Spell your last name for the birth certificate." The ward clerk was finishing up the paperwork.

That damn contract waved like the Great Wall of China between them.

"Oh. You've got it wrong," he said. "I'm not the father." How could he ever face himself again after this bold-faced lie? "I'm just the birth coach."

* * *

René overhead Jon's faltering voice, heard it crack when he said he wasn't the father, and the euphoria slipped from her grasp. She held her baby close, the precious life she was responsible for, as the point drove hard into her heart—it would just be the two of them. She tried with what little strength she had left not to let the devastating ache in her chest subtract from the most incredible moment of her life. She had a baby. With tears prickling her eyes, she swallowed hard against her reality.

She kissed her son's perfect little head and whispered, "It's just you and me, kid."

CHAPTER TWELVE

Two weeks later

RENÉ finished diapering Evan, and patted his thigh, then pretended to eat his toes. The baby squirmed and stretched, then yawned, obviously bored with her adoration. She grinned and made the final snap on his terry sleeper before swaddling him. Filled to the gills with her breast milk, he was ready for his nap.

She'd seen the dreamy look in the eyes of new mothers, but never, ever could she fathom the depth of emotion and love having a baby could evoke, until now. She mindlessly hummed and savored the intensity of her feelings for Evan. This was how life was meant to be, filled with love and purpose.

She cuddled her boy, sniffed his baby scent and kissed his ever-fattening cheeks, then put him in the bassinet.

A few moments later, she stood in the living room that had been half overtaken by It's a Boy balloons, congratulatory plant baskets and flower arrangements. She looked out the front window at the avocado tree in her yard, while Evan took his second nap of the day.

She should be ecstatic about her small but mighty boy,

and no doubt about it she was, but sometimes ladies got a little blue after giving birth and, unfortunately, she'd become one of them. She loathed the constant whispering sadness that subtly eroded her newfound happiness.

As if fresh out of rehab, she only allowed herself to think about Jon once or twice a day.

Jon had stayed by her side throughout the entire labor. Even after she'd acted horribly and banished him, he'd hung around to coach her through the ordeal. She didn't know how she would have made it through without him. Then, when it was over, he'd disappeared.

After they'd cleaned up the baby and announced he'd weighed five pounds, fifteen ounces, and she'd been rolled off to her room, Jon had never shown his face. And since she and Evan had been home, he hadn't called or come by.

His neglect stabbed at her and hurt worse than labor.

And the lingering heartache looped over and over in her brain. *You've got it wrong. I'm not the father,* he'd told the nurse. She'd heard correctly.

He'd given her free rein over the child, just like their contract agreed he would. She'd gotten her wish…and couldn't be more miserable if she tried.

Staring out at the tree, she shook her head, fed up with the blues trailing her everywhere she went. She'd been proactive her entire life, yet now she sat passively back like a hurt and sulking teenager.

Well, she'd had enough of this nonsense. Even if Jon wasn't going to be a part of their lives, he should at least come to see the baby now that his birth-misshapen head had rounded, his umbilical cord had dried and fallen off and his scrawny body had started to fill out. Evan was so beautiful. If Jon saw how the boy looked like him, even at this early stage, how his eyes were dark and intense just like his, maybe he'd think twice about taking that other job or going to China.

If she told him how she really felt, not the part about being livid with him for staying away, but the depth of her love for him that she knew beyond doubt wasn't merely because of gratitude, maybe he'd reconsider.

She'd given him two weeks to mull things over, to come to his senses and accept they were meant to be together. Still, he hadn't come. She didn't want to lose Jon; the thought loomed overhead, sending shivers through her like a cloud of ice. The breath left her lungs too quickly as she worried she may already have lost him.

He needed to know she loved him.

She remembered his smiling face and encouraging comments when she wanted to give up during labor, and how his hands seemed to find the perfect spot to massage when the baby's head pressed on her spine. He'd seen her at her worst. God, did she really say some of those horrible things? After so many hours in labor she must have looked more like a horror movie star than human. And she'd never, ever, admitted to anyone that she knew all the steps to *Thriller!*

She covered her face in her hand and couldn't help but smile along with the grimace. The man knew everything about her. Except that she loved him.

Another anxious pang sent her striding across the room, chewing at her lip.

René didn't know what she would have done without Claire, who'd come by every day since Evan was born. The look of shock on her face when René finally opened up and told Claire who the sperm donor was had been priceless. If she weren't so miserable, she might laugh. Just yesterday, Claire warned that Jon and Jason were actively looking for his replacement at MidCoast Medical, as if she knew more was at stake than just a change in job. René had shuttered her reaction and changed the subject back to the baby rather than let on how the news had quaked through her.

But the news tore at her already-punctured heart, and after Claire had left, she'd cried. She'd sobbed until her ribs ached and her eyes were swollen, and the baby's nursery monitor forced her to put her attention somewhere else. Thank goodness for Evan, for holding her together, for giving her something to live for.

She settled on the couch and stared at her lap and the hands with a noticeably empty ring finger. She'd never even tried to tell Jon her real feelings, and as smart as he was, he wasn't a mind reader.

René made a ragged sigh. She'd had enough wallowing in self-pity. Like the story went, if she wanted change, she have to make it. Standing, she walked to the kitchen, to the wireless phone charging in its cradle, as electrical currents strong enough to light the moon coursed through her. With a trembling hand, she punched in his number. If she didn't at least try, she'd never forgive herself.

It was late enough Saturday morning to know he'd be finished with his run. And, by God, she'd talk to him today, no matter how hard or scary, and find out why he hadn't been by to see their baby.

Or her.

There was no excuse for it, unless he was a coward, and how could she possibly love a coward?

Her shoulders slumped from their militant tension. She was so full of nonsense. The only thing that mattered was the truth. How could he change his mind about leaving if she didn't tell him how she truly felt?

She was in love with him. He deserved to know.

Jon's hand cramped as he finished another page in his journal. How did a man explain to his son why he wouldn't be a part of his life? It seemed he'd been writing everything he wanted the boy to know in life for two straight weeks.

Notes to my son.

Was it even fair to use the word *my* in referring to Evan? He only knew the boy's name, after his middle name, from the women at work. Claire and the other nurses couldn't stop talking about René's new baby. They gossiped openly about who the father might be, suspecting she'd used a donor. Claire had started looking at him different, but maybe he was being paranoid about that.

At the clinic, he'd clenched his jaw so tight so often it had started crackling when he ate. But who was eating? He'd lost his appetite, had turned into an insomniac and had been listless for two weeks.

How many times had he started out the door to go see René and the baby? As many times as he'd turned back.

The phone rang and his pulse sped up when he saw René's name in the caller ID box. As rough as it had been, twisting and ripping at his conscience, he'd kept his word. The baby was hers and hers alone. She needn't worry about that.

"René," he said, disguising the uncertainty. "I was just thinking about you."

"You were?" She sounded surprised, and it sent another pang of guilt through his chest. "I need to talk to you. Will you come to see us?"

Could he handle being near René and seeing Evan? If

he saw everything he'd be leaving behind, would he be able to hold it together in front of her? By now she'd heard his hesitation, and he needed to say something.

"Yes. When?"

"Now. Please."

He'd been hiding behind a contract, but now that he'd heard her voice again, he knew something much deeper had been the real reason he'd been avoiding her and their baby. He was torn between his longing for freedom and allowing himself to love her…and start a family all over again. Some misguided loyalty to his daughters still held him back.

Funny how a man can convince himself he's a great guy, a fantastic father, live a decent life, be a fine doctor who cares about his patients, give to all the right charities, yet still be a coward—a coward who longs for freedom, whatever the hell that is, but who would never find happiness even if he stumbled through freedom's door. Not under these circumstances. Not since knowing René.

If he could make it through this visit and hold his ground, he'd be free to go back to the life he'd planned. Regardless of how empty it would be.

Jon arrived at René's house with armor firmly in place. He couldn't let her mesmerizing eyes lure him into changing his plans. He'd earned his freedom, damn it, and their contract spelled everything out. At least he hadn't let her down in that regard. If she expected more, well, that was her mistake. Not his.

One glance at her standing in the doorway with her hair full and resting on her shoulders, wearing oatmeal-colored pants and an olive-green tank top, and he forgot his house-of-straw plan.

* * *

René's heart had been bouncing around her rib cage since she'd called Jon, almost making her dizzy. Seeing him walk across her driveway toward her house sent a thousand flapping wings through her chest. She clutched the door frame for support, praying she'd recover before he came inside.

She couldn't help but stare at him. He wore his usual Saturday morning warm-up suit and running shoes, and he looked pale, maybe a little thinner than she'd remembered. He delved into her eyes with a questioning stare.

How should she begin?

She'd take the perfect hostess route, then work her way around to the heart of the matter—her *heart* and whether or not she *mattered* at all to him.

She forced a smile and held open the door for Jon. As if strangers, she wasn't sure how to greet him. A kiss on the cheek? A friendly hug? A mere handshake?

He saved her from making the decision by saying hello and giving her a quick, lackluster squeeze on the arm when he entered her house. The kernel of hope she'd sheltered and groomed in his absence withered a bit.

"You look good," he said, far too casually, his eyes betraying him.

"Thank you."

His gaze wandered around the room, as if looking for evidence of her son.

"Wow, I guess I should have sent a plant like everyone else," he said, looking a bit chagrined.

It tortured her for him to act like such a stranger.

"Evan's sleeping. Would you like to see him?"

He avoided her eyes, but nodded yes. If he didn't react to her son, she'd know for sure that he didn't care a damn about either of them.

"Of course," he said.

He followed her quietly down the hall to the scene of their crime, her bedroom, where she'd set up the bassinet. When she opened the door and he could see the boy's head, he inhaled. A smile stretched across his lips and he leaned over the white wicker, the bassinet he'd helped her pick out and set up for her, to study the baby up close.

"Wow," he whispered.

After several seconds that seemed more like an eternity for someone holding her breath, he glanced at her.

"He's beautiful, René." The tender eyes she'd grown used to had returned.

Chills skimmed her skin. Their baby was living proof they should be together, but unless she told him how she felt, he would stick to the rule of contract.

"He looks like you. Don't you think?" she said.

He narrowed his eyes and pulled in his chin, then with a tilted head took another look at his son. She watched his forehead smooth, and his eyes soften. Slowly, like the sun peeking over the horizon, his smile returned.

He nodded. "He does, but I have a better hairline."

A laugh bubbled up her chest, the first in two weeks. The baby squirmed, and Jon put a finger over his lips.

They tiptoed out of her bedroom. Once safely back in the living room she sat on the sofa since her knees felt like noodles. The thought of baring her soul made her hands tremble.

He sat across from her, studying her every move. How would she get this out without collapsing? This might be her only chance to tell him, and she wasn't about to waste it.

"I think you should know I haven't been completely honest with you," she said.

He sat beside her with hands on his knees, eyes alert.

"Jon." Her voice quavered and she closed her eyes. "I love you."

He took a deep breath. "René." If he had anything else to say, it had stalled. His fingers found her hand and stroked it. "René."

This wasn't the response she'd hoped for, far from the bear hugs he was so good at giving, but she wouldn't give up. "I think I started loving you the day you said you'd be my birth coach, and when we made love, I knew for sure."

"But you never even hinted at it."

"I'd asked enough of you, and we had a contract."

"And I talked nonstop about leaving for China."

"And China," she repeated.

She sensed panic in his voice. Maybe it was a mistake, but at least now she knew for sure that he didn't feel the same way about her. That he was counting the moments before he could escape. She'd never have to guess again.

She pressed her lips together, to fight off the threatening tears. "Don't worry." She glanced at his restless eyes. "The contract stands. I just thought, that is, I hoped, that maybe…"

He shot up. "Love and commitment weren't part of the deal. Remember?"

"I wrote the rules. Yes. I remember." Her ribs clutched so hard she could hardly breathe. She didn't dare try to stand. He knelt in front of her and grasped her shoulders, his dark eyes piercing through her.

"René, honey, I can't do this. I can't start over. It's not that I don't care for you. I do. You have no idea. But I never would have consented to your deal if I thought it would turn out like this."

She hung her head, unable to bear looking at his reddening face and pleading eyes. She'd known the truth and insisted on trying to change it; how foolish of her to think three little words could make everything different. "Do you think I wanted this?"

He shook his head. "It took us both by surprise."

"I know," she mumbled.

Dead silence sucked the life out of the room.

"I've got to think things over," he said, grazing fingers over his hair. He skimmed her cheek with a kiss, gave her a lightning-quick hug, then dashed out her door.

A moment later she realized he hadn't even bothered to get in his car, but had taken off on foot.

Panic tore into Jon. The pavement burned through his running shoes. When he'd taken up long-distance running after his messy divorce, little did he know how handy it would come in.

So that's what he'd turned into, a man who ran from a woman who loved him and the inevitable commitment. An SOB who didn't plan to stick around for his son. Could a paltry journal make up for a missing father?

He scraped fingers over his head and increased the speed. He needed to burn, to sear, the guilt puncturing his resolve. Lacy would graduate next June. He'd leave for China the next week…except he still hadn't officially signed up for the trip and the deadline was quickly approaching.

Each tangy sea breath stung through his chest as he reached the shore. High tide. The waves lapped the sand in dependable rhythm, their fluorescent froth lingering as if to remind him what he'd left behind. A part of himself.

Come on, this wasn't in the plan. A beautiful woman asked him to donate some sperm and he'd agreed. How the hell shallow was he?

He glanced ahead. What were these people doing on the bike and jogging path? Couldn't they read the signs? A young couple pushed a stroller and moved to the side when he said, "On your left," as he passed. They smiled and waved at him, as if they were oblivious and happy.

Across the park lawn another couple, older compared to the first, pushed a double-wide stroller with twins, and the father shouldered a third child in some sort of backpack seat contraption. Why were they smiling?

The dark-haired woman's face morphed into René's. Ice invaded his chest and sent a chill down his spine. She'd be alone. Would she be smiling?

He thought of the devastated expression he'd left on her face just before he ran out her door.

He'd fallen in love with her, too. Damn it! He'd explained away every symptom over the past few months, and had convinced himself that the developing feelings were nothing more than midlife growing pains. A forty-two-year-old man gets propositioned—in an unconventional manner—by a gorgeous younger woman, and the giddy feelings that ensued were nothing more than flattery. That was the story he chose to stick to.

The easy conversations, the great meals, the stolen glances and secret thoughts had been figments of his imagination. His heightened sense of honor and duty to René were what any man in his situation would have done. The birth coaching? That was a bit overboard, but still, any other man in his place would have offered to do the same, wouldn't they? Did that equate love?

The constant thoughts about René had been another story. He'd conceded that he liked having her attention, her adulation, even if it had been a snow job to get what she wanted.

But that line of thinking never rang true about René, and he'd never allowed himself time to think things through in that regard. Besides, he knew firsthand she wasn't like that. And now, she'd told him she loved him.

Surely her profession of love was the product of postpartum blues and wonky hormones. When she came to her senses, she'd thank him for running off, leaving her to her original plan of single motherhood.

What was with the strollers today? He made a quick sidestep to avoid another one, an all-terrain stroller exactly like the one he'd given René. Just because it was a sunny October afternoon, did every family in Santa Barbara have to brandish their kids?

He made a U-turn and headed back on the grassy patch bordering the sidewalk. If he saw one more baby he'd yell.

I love you. René's words repeated in his brain. She'd bared her soul and what did he do? He ran away. Literally.

He let roll a string of curses blue enough to make a soldier blush, and prodded the running pace.

She'd looked so vulnerable sitting on her couch. Her eyes shone with emotion when she'd said she loved him, and instead of returning the sentiments, he'd tried to talk her out of it. He'd used the pitiful excuse of his sabbatical, his new job, his daughters and his divorce, then dropped her on her head and left.

He didn't deserve René.

She'd be better off without him. How could a woman like René—giving, fun, compassionate, tender, smart, sexy as all hell—consider him to be a person to love?

He tripped on a crack, flung forward and shoulder rolled back to his feet, as if he'd been kicked in the backside. He stood still while gathering his composure and looked around suspiciously. What the hell was that about?

As he started to run again, Evan's innocent face appeared in his thoughts. He ran faster. How will he fare without a father in his life? A boulder of guilt landed in his stomach, rolling toward his toes, but it didn't slow his pace. How could he run away from them? What kind of man was he?

He saw yet another happy family out for a stroll. This time the young mother looked like Lacy. Hadn't she begged to babysit for René, then elbowed him, and with a knowing look and lift of her brow communicated how cool she thought René was? *I wish you could find someone like her.* Well, damn it, he had! Could his daughters accept a stepmother and half brother?

His ex-wife had pounded the point home that he wasn't good enough to spend a lifetime with. That's what René would want, a lifetime; what if he let her down, too? No, she'd be far better off without him.

Everyone would be better off if he stayed alone, yet he ran so fast he expected to spontaneously combust.

Who was he kidding?

He didn't want to be alone any more than he thought René wanted to be a single mother. And after two years it was more than time to kick Cherie and her negative comments to the curb. He was better than that. He deserved more. He deserved René. And Evan.

Here was this fantastic woman, the mother of his child, telling him she loved him, and he had a shot at a sweet kind of happiness he'd forgotten existed. He'd been so busy being a recluse, he'd put the possibility out of his mind. Thanks to his miserable divorce, he'd buried his feelings so deeply, he didn't even recognize the signs as they appeared one by one until he'd fallen in love with René.

Hell, he'd been in love with her for months. He just hadn't recognized it for what it was. It had happened in that moment when he couldn't let her go through the birthing classes alone. The moment he'd volunteered, he'd been hers. The same moment she'd said she'd fallen in love with him.

The contract stood in their way, and out of insecurity over his failed marriage, he'd let it. Used it, even.

Turns out, René loved him, too. That is, if she hadn't burned his picture in effigy since he ran out of her house— he glanced at his watch—a half hour ago. As if possible, he quickened his stride and thought his lungs might burst, but he deserved the pain. He'd hurt the woman he loved and he needed to get back to her before she changed her mind about him.

He needed to undo the hurt he'd caused. A jab of side-stitch pain felt like payback. He deserved several more, yet he smiled.

He loved her. Hell, yeah. He loved her, and couldn't wait to get to know his son!

The palm trees blurred past. His breath came in rhythmical spurts. Heading back to René's he'd never run with such purpose in his entire life.

René had come undone. She'd melted into a puddle of tears and cried until she thought she'd heave. It was all her fault. She'd been the one to come up with this idea of having a kid with no strings attached, but she hadn't bargained on Jon becoming everything she'd always wished for.

He'd been there for her: dependable, strong, funny at the most unpredictable moments, tender at others. He was a father through and through. The love for his daughters shimmered from his eyes whenever he spoke about them, which was often. It pained her to realize Evan would never know such love from his father. Could she make up for it? Would she be enough?

She'd tried to compose herself, washed her face, checked on her son who was still sleeping, fortunately, and made herself a cup of peppermint-and-chamomile tea. She needed something to help settle her stomach and calm her nerves before she next nursed Evan. It was so much harder to let down her milk when she was nervous or uptight.

Oddly, her crying jag had left her feeling a modicum of relief. If only it were permanent. Since sobbing, she'd attained a state of repose that felt a bit like levitating over hot coals, and she waited to fall into the fire as she sipped her tea.

Movement by the avocado tree caught her eye. It was Jon racing toward her porch. Her stomach took flight. She jumped up as he hammered on her door. She opened it and he blew in like the north wind, strong, brisk and with a biting scent.

Jon dug his fingers into her hair and angled her face toward his, then planted a firm kiss on her mouth. Just as quickly he broke free.

"Forgive me. Please forgive me," he huffed.

He kissed her again, this time clutching her flush to his body. "I was such a jerk. No. I was a complete ass. How could I be so awful to you?" He nuzzled her neck and kissed her beneath her jaw. "Please don't hate me." Another kiss, this one on her brow. "I love you. God, I love you."

"Jon," she said, barely a sound.

"Tell me you forgive me. Please." He grazed her ear with another kiss, then whispered, "Please."

She hesitated. *You love me?* Could she forget the heartbreak he'd put her through for the past two weeks, and the devastation he'd left in his wake when he'd run off after she'd told him she loved him? Had she heard him right? He loved her?

If he thought he could break into her house, kiss her up and make everything all better, just like that, he had another think coming.

But she couldn't deny how her heart nearly burst when she saw him run back to her. Relief greater than anything she'd ever known had coursed through her veins at the mere sight of him. Her lips found his neck and tasted the salt from his sheen. Why had she kissed him if she hated him? If she couldn't forgive him?

He'd come back to her, knowing full well that she loved him, professing his love in return. What more proof did she need?

"I forgive you," she said, barely audible.

"You do? Fantastic."

He hugged her as if she might disappear if he let go.

"I want the world to know who Evan's father is," he said, waltzing her around the room. She was incapable of resisting. "I want to be there for him when he takes his first step, reads his first book, throws his first baseball, when he kisses his first girl. I want to see it all, watch him grow, hear his voice change, send him off to college and then…maybe you'll come with me to China?"

She laughed at his audacity.

"You do forgive me, don't you?"

His intense brown eyes blasted into hers; she could

hardly stand to look at them. They made her knees get wobbly and her mind fog up. She was angry as blazes at him, remember? Forgiveness was one thing, but what about trust?

He cupped her arms and held her in place. "I want to love you every day for the rest of my life. I want you to be the first face I see in the morning and the body I hold to fall asleep."

"Jon." It sounded more like a plea.

"I love you, René, and I know you love me, too." He pulled back and smiled at her. "You already told me, remember?"

She cuffed his arm. "And you ran off."

"I promise never to run off again."

"What about that new job?"

"Leave the MidCoast Clinic? Never."

Could she believe him? He *had* come through on all of his other promises to her. You bet she could.

The nursery monitor crackled with mewing and grunts. Evan was waking up. She took Jon's hand and led him down the hall. Together they watched their boy stretch and curl until he found his voice and made a heartfelt cry.

She reached for him. Jon stopped her.

"Let me," he said.

When he held their son with noticeable confidence, René let free the breath she'd been holding. This wasn't a dream. This was Jon being the father she'd wished for.

Jon rocked Evan in the crook of his arm, and smiled at her. This time, she was the one to offer a kiss along with her heart, and he eagerly accepted both.

Her mother's saying repeated in her mind yet again— *be careful what you wish for.*

How true. René had wished for a baby of her own, but

it turned out she hadn't wished big enough. Things hadn't turned out as she'd planned—they'd ended up even better.

Her yearning for a family had been short by one person—a father. The desire had been so buried she hadn't even known it. Now, with Jon at her side holding her son, *their* son, a grander and more perfect wish had finally been granted.

EPILOGUE

One month later

"HURRY, Jon, or we'll be late," René said, slipping on her second earring.

Jon kissed Evan one last time before handing him over to Lacy. She grinned and cuddled her half brother as if her own.

"Don't worry about a thing," she said. "I've got both of your cell numbers, Claire is just a few blocks away and I'm getting really good at taking care of my brother." She kissed the boy. "Wait until Amanda finds out. She'll be so jealous."

It would be their first night out together since the baby had been born and he'd moved in. Just the two of them having dinner in a special seaside restaurant without a single interruption. Heaven.

His daughter gave him a kiss on the cheek followed by a knowing look. He planned to propose to René tonight and Lacy couldn't disguise her suspicions. They'd marry in the summer, when Amanda had a break from her studies and could attend.

He'd start his sabbatical this summer, too, but China was the last thing on his mind. Nope. He'd decided to take the year off, anyway—to be a house husband while René continued her practice. He thought of it as a grand adventure, something only a guy full of surprises might do, an adventure he wouldn't miss for the world. And René practically jumped with glee when he'd told her his astounding plan.

He stood grinning like an idiot at his daughter and son.

René's long slender fingers circled his wrist. "Are you ready?" she asked.

"You bet I am." He glanced at her empty ring finger, then patted the small box in his jacket pocket. That finger wouldn't be empty much longer.

Do you dream of being a romance writer?

Mills & Boon are looking for fresh writing talent in our biggest ever search!

And this time...our readers have a say in who wins!

For information on how to enter or get involved go to

www.romanceisnotdead.com

 **MEDICAL™**

Secrets. Lies. Time to come clean...

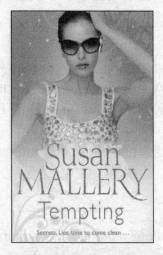

Dani Buchanan is horrified when her father turns out to be a presidential candidate. And then the tabloids find out...

Katherine Canfield is unable to bear children. Dani's a reminder of what Senator Canfield could have had – and Katherine's jealous.

Adopted Canfield son Alex is tempted by Dani. With the scandal of the century brewing, can he pursue a relationship that could tear his family apart?

Available 3rd September 2010

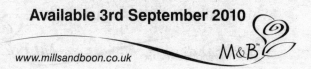

M&B